Nicole Alexander is a fourth-generation grazier. She has a Master of Letters in creative writing and her novels, poetry, travel and genealogy articles have been published in Australia, Germany, America and Singapore.

She is the author of seven previous novels: *The Bark Cutters*, *A Changing Land*, *Absolution Creek*, *Sunset Ridge*, *The Great Plains*, *Wild Lands* and *River Run*.

Also by Nicole Alexander

The Bark Cutters
A Changing Land
Absolution Creek
Sunset Ridge
The Great Plains
Wild Lands
River Run

Divertissements: Love, War, Society – Selected Poems

An Uncommon Woman

NICOLE ALEXANDER

BANTAM

SYDNEY AUCKLAND TORONTO NEW YORK LONDON

A Bantam book
Published by Penguin Random House Australia Pty Ltd
Level 3, 100 Pacific Highway, North Sydney NSW 2060
penguin.com.au

Penguin
Random House
Australia

First published by Bantam in 2017
This edition published in 2018

Addresses for the Penguin Random House group of companies can be found at
global.penguinrandomhouse.com/offices.

A catalogue record for this
book is available from the
National Library of Australia

NATIONAL
LIBRARY
OF AUSTRALIA

ISBN 978 0 85798 949 9

Cover photograph © Roux Hamilton/Arcangel
Cover design by Blacksheep
Internal design and typesetting by Midland Typesetters, Australia
Printed in Australia by Griffin Press, an accredited ISO AS/NZS 14001:2004
Environmental Management System printer

Penguin Random House Australia uses papers that are natural, renewable
and recyclable products and made from wood grown in sustainable forests.
The logging and manufacturing processes are expected to conform to the
environmental regulations of the country of origin.

For my father

Ian Alexander

20/10/1931–2/4/2017

Baker's Run

Western Queensland

200 miles west of Brisbane

September 1929

≪ Chapter One ≫

The land was thick with aged trees and prickly pear. The smaller succulents grew in dense clumps, fleshy and spine covered, while others stretched skyward, tangling with their brethren ten feet into the air so that the way ahead resembled an ancient forest. Overhead snatches of blue sky teased the riders as they picked their way through a section of countryside made unusable by the prickly invaders. The noxious plant covered the ground in varying sizes with scant dirt in between and Edwina Baker, accompanied by her brother, Aiden, was somewhat surprised to find birds still present, as if the very presence of the spikey monstrosities should surely compel them to fly elsewhere.

This part of their property suffered from one of the worst infestations, with the pear having made a good two-thirds of their land useless for any form of agriculture. Edwina didn't normally ride out here. Just the sight of so much of the weed made her mad with frustration. They had cut, burnt, hoed and applied chemical to the invasion for as long as Edwina could remember. It was an ongoing battle to eradicate the dreaded plants and she hated to think of the money and effort that had been expended on the task. The plant was virulent and drought tolerant. Its seeds were carried by birds, especially crows who loved the fleshy cactus. Their father said for many years that the bush carried an albatross about its neck until something could be done about the species. By 1920, millions of hectares of land across Queensland and New South Wales had been infested. Now useless, enormous areas were abandoned by their owners.

But there was hope and they carried that hope in a saddlebag.

The horses were careful with the path they chose and Edwina slowed her mare a little more, wary of being stuck by one of the taller plants with their needle-like spines or small hair-like prickles. Today she was optimistic that things would improve. That the pear would be destroyed and the land reclaimed. 'Here,' she announced. Aiden ignored her, riding on to the patch selected to be tested.

They dismounted in a cramped clearing bordered by the pear. From a saddlebag Aiden retrieved a gauze-covered wooden box, which he placed on the ground, prising the top free with a pocket-knife. 'Here we go,' he breathed. Inside were numerous eggs pasted within small paper quills together with a quantity of pins.

'Do you think it will work?' Aiden asked as Edwina read the enclosed instructions.

'Father said there have been excellent results in other places,' answered Edwina. 'The scientists are very encouraged. But we need more than just one dead plant in ten. That wouldn't even make a dent.'

Edwina fastened a pin to one of the paper quills, and Aiden watched as she attached the paper with its enclosed cactoblastis eggs to a fleshy, oval green-coloured pad.

'They're borers apparently, eat right into the stem,' she announced.

Brother and sister set about fastening more of the quills. When the box was half empty they packed it away to be used in another location.

4

'You should go home now, E,' suggested Aiden. 'I know you wanted to help with the pear but this isn't the place for you. Not when I'm seeing the men.'

'And what am I meant to do? Sit in the house and sew?' she replied, as they remounted and continued walking their horses through the scrub.

Aiden burst out laughing. 'We both know that's one thing you can't do.'

Edwina flipped him with a battered felt hat.

'You know these men aren't used to seeing women,' he continued, 'even one like you.' Aiden took in her trousers, shirt and waistcoat.

Edwina moaned. 'Yes, you're right of course. I should have dressed for the occasion.'

'I'm serious. They're on the road for months on end. Living in camps. Working in the bush. All I'm saying is keep quiet when we get there and let me do the talking. Father told me to check on the ringbarkers while he is in town on business. By myself. He said nothing about you being allowed to come.'

Edwina gave a huff. 'It's not like I haven't been out here before. Anyway, by yourself, did you say? Right, and that's why Davidson is following us at fifty paces.'

Aiden swivelled in the saddle and frowned. Sure enough their aboriginal stockman and sometime overseer was waiting quietly at a distance. 'How long has he been there?'

'I noticed him earlier,' replied Edwina flippantly. 'There's no point looking so annoyed, Aiden. You know Father's rules. No-one goes riding alone in the bush if you're going further than four mile from the house.' Ahead the prickly pear thinned. Edwina clucked her tongue and her mare, Heidi-Hoe, trotted past her brother.

Aiden patted the compass in the pouch at his waist and then the waterbag hanging from the saddle. 'I'm never without it or this,' he called after her.

'Surely by now you don't still need a compass.' Edwina spurred the horse on, cantering away from her brother. Aiden was quick to pursue and they raced through the scrub, jumping fallen limbs and boughs and skirting trees. When next they slowed, brother and sister checked to see if the aboriginal still followed. Sure enough Davidson was there, one hundred yards behind them, waiting beneath the shade of a brigalow tree, both he and his horse motionless as if they'd been spirited from one place to the next.

'You won't lose him,' commented Aiden.

'I wasn't trying to.'

'He can track anything, you know.'

Not, Edwina thought, that they'd ever had proof of the old man's ability. He'd appeared out of nowhere a good decade ago. Walking in from the scrub and staying as if he'd been on the farm all his life. Their father assumed the man had been thrown off a mission for not being a full-blood, and took to wandering the bush before searching for work. It was possible. The man, named Davidson by their father, had become indispensable to the running of the property although no-one had ever heard him utter a word of English or any other language.

The spring scents heavy in the air were gradually replaced by the stench of burning. Edwina rubbed at her eyes. The smoke was strong on the morning breeze. It always seemed as if half the district was burning off a good part of every year. The continual clearing of the land, of scrub and prickly pear and trees was, she knew, a necessary task if people were to make a success of their properties. Particularly where the pear invaded, rendering the land useless for the grazing of stock or planting of crops. But all Edwina saw from this continual task of trying to tame the earth was more work. Work that stretched out endlessly from dawn to dusk. Except at the times when their father went to the town of Wywanna for business, presenting the all-too-rare opportunity of not keeping to the set of tasks allocated on a weekly basis.

Behind them Davidson kept a discreet distance.

'Father is more worried about accidents or injury than one of us getting lost,' Edwina pointed out. Their father, the recipient of a nasty fall some years ago when the horse he'd been riding shied at a snake, placed his salvation in Davidson's hands. If the aboriginal had not been with him that day, he may never have been found.

Ahead, glimpses of creamy-beige could be seen through the trees. They rode in that direction, ducking under low branches as patches of sunlight stippled the tawny shades of the bush. Rabbits scuttled from underfoot and the red tinge of a fox dashed across their path as they reached one of the bore drains that spread across their land like an artery. It petered out into the distance as the thick brush slowly thinned to be replaced by more open country. It was a new world out here. Their father's land improvements were evident. Belts of dead trees stretched forlornly away to their left like skeletal spines while across the bore drain, timber recently girdled by axes waited to die.

The ringbarkers' camp came into view abruptly. It was a rough collection of battered tents pitched in an area practically devoid of trees. There was a smell of something rotting; the only sign of life a couple of smouldering cooking fires. Beyond that the sluggish water of the drain meandered into a distant haze.

'It's a bit . . .' Edwina couldn't think of the right word to describe the scene before them.

'I told you you shouldn't have come,' replied Aiden.

An untidy line of washing partially rested in the dirt from where it was strung from sagging twine. Through the clothes a straggly looking dog appeared. More rib than animal, it barked at their arrival. From a tree hung an assortment of hessian bags, safe from ants and the dog.

'Tea, treacle, flour, a bit of salted mutton. They don't need much,' commented Aiden, following her gaze. 'Father said these blokes cook anything apparently – rabbits, goanna, kangaroo.'

Edwina nodded. 'I've never tried goanna.'

'This from the girl who when we were kids used to help me skin mice and pin their hides out to dry in the sun.'

'That was different. We were playing mousies and I needed skins to trade as well,' countered Edwina, although she couldn't imagine doing such a thing now.

'Be damned if a man should put up with that.' The voice came from further along the bore drain. Men appeared from behind a stand of trees.

Edwina, beginning to urge her horse forwards, was stopped by Aiden's hand on her arm.

'Stay where you are, I'll see what the commotion is about.' Aiden rode off, leaving Edwina alone. Heidi-Hoe nickered restlessly as the starving dog circled, baring its teeth. She scanned the area. Davidson wasn't to be seen. With a flick of the reins she trailed her brother.

A broad-shouldered man, with braces stretched sideways by the size of his stomach, was dangling a bag in the air. He stood two feet taller than the man opposite and was enjoying his opponent's attempts to reef the bag from his grip. The smaller man was doing his best to jump into the air, much to the delight of the onlookers, who cheered him on with every attempt.

'You can do it, Panny,' they yelled. 'C'mon, try harder!'

'Give 'em back,' Panny complained.

The spectators, an assortment of men who appeared never to have seen the inside of a barber's shop, watched on with amusement.

'Laugh if you want,' Panny yelled, 'but they're your tatties too!'

As Aiden walked his horse towards the group, the teaser lowered the bag and the men fell back, muttering.

'Well it's the young cove himself, the boss's son.' The speaker thrust the sack into the smaller man's hands. 'Just having a bit of fun.'

'Morning, Mr Sears,' replied Aiden, addressing the contractor in charge of the gathered men.

Drawing level with her brother, Edwina felt the eyes of every man upon her. In response she sat up straighter in the saddle as one by one the men took stock of her appearance, before briefly tipping their hats. Some of the workers were reminded of the gentlemanly habit with a swift elbow in the sides. A couple smirked, two or three looked away. They shoved hands in pockets and mumbled.

'Tatties.' Panny clutched the bag. 'He took our tatties.'

'Well, you know what these Irish are like,' Mr Sears said to Aiden, ignoring the complaint. 'Anyway, it was just a bit of fun. I didn't mean nothing by it. The men were grumbling 'cause Will Kew took off yesterday. So I thought I'd take their minds off him.'

'Will Kew?' Edwina repeated to her brother, aware of the men's focus on her.

'He was the cook,' answered Aiden.

Edwina didn't recall the man. They all looked the same to her, dressed in their raggedy work clothes.

'Elected cook,' Panny clarified. 'Not that he was able, miss. I mean, how's a boy supposed to cook a meal when he barely knows what food is? Comes from a soldier settler's block over the border.'

'So you need someone to take his place?' asked Aiden.

'I'm sure Mr Sears has things under control,' said Edwina, her reply greeted with a scowl from her brother.

'Took off he did, miss, to join the circus.' Passing the sack of potatoes to one of the ringbarkers, Panny produced a folded newspaper from a coat pocket and presented it to Aiden. 'If Will thought he had it bad on that starvation block of his pa's, wait till he tries to find another job here. Said he didn't like killing things. Killing things. Like a person has the right to pick and choose.'

Aiden read the section headlined in bold print, *Colby's Circus and Menagerie*, before passing it to Edwina.

'The Colby Brothers are coming Saturday,' explained Panny. 'Now I don't know what day it is, but as Will's gone, they must be coming soon. Didn't wait for his pay or nothing.' His tone was one of disbelief. 'He's owed five pound.'

'Oh, that is a problem,' said Aiden.

'And how's the ringbarking coming along, Mr Sears?' Edwina handed the newspaper back to the Irishman. Difficulties with staff were not their concern. That was Mr Sears' domain.

'One thing this lot can do is kill trees. You tell your father that I checked them ones we did last year, miss.' He gestured to the wasted shapes spotting the landscape. 'Dead as a doorknob. They're ready to be cut and the stumps dug out.' He wiped at his nose with the back of his hand. 'We'd be pleased to handle the job for you. You ask your father if a Chinese gang could work as quick as us or for the money, miss. And tell him I'll be wanting to talk business when he's able. I've been good to him I have. Real good.'

Edwina always thought of trees as such wise old plants. To destroy them just didn't seem right, especially in such large numbers. Thinning she could understand, but this – she glanced at their surrounds – this was different.

'Not your cup of tea, eh, miss?' queried Mr Sears, studying her.

Edwina chose her words carefully. 'It's a pity to see so many killed.'

The contractor laughed, his large stomach rippling. 'You and that young Will Kew are a fine pair.' He turned to Aiden. 'I've not seen your father for a good couple of days,' he said. 'You might ask him about that matter he and I discussed, Aiden. Put in a word for me?'

Aiden responded slowly. 'I've not much say when it comes to my father, but I'll mention it to him.'

Davidson reappeared, sitting patiently on his horse a few yards away. At the sight of the aboriginal the ringbarkers picked up their axes and wordlessly went back to work.

'You best be off,' Sears told them. 'I don't need no trouble with Davidson, the white-eyed crow. He keeps the blacks away from us and in return we keep our heads down.'

Edwina kept pace with her brother as they retraced their path back through the camp. 'What was he talking about? There are no blacks out here.'

'Some of the men reckon they've seen them. Glimpses, mind; probably their imaginations. There're no blacks left here. The government's rounded most of them up, well, apart from those working on properties.'

Behind them Davidson's attention remained on the ringbarkers as they peeled off into the scrub. He was always watching everyone, all of the time. It unnerved some, although Edwina had grown used to his ways. An old man who'd once worked on the property told her that a crow could tell the difference between a good human and a bad, that they were able to communicate the same and were equally happy solitary or foraging within a group. Davidson was the loner kind, their white-eyed crow.

'I told you that I would do the talking, Edwina,' said Aiden. 'It's just not right you interfering like that.'

'I'm sorry, Aiden, but Mr Sears is in charge. Father always says that our role is to simply make sure the work is progressing, listen to their grievances and –'

'*My* role,' corrected Aiden crossly.

They could have easily begun arguing; instead, Edwina held her tongue.

'Anyway,' said Aiden as they walked their horses towards the camp, 'they're a rough lot. Next time you better stay at home.'

'Rough or not it doesn't make any difference as long as they do the work,' replied Edwina, ignoring her brother's comment. 'Though I can see why some landowners are replacing their ringbarking teams with Chinese contractors. I've heard that they're cheaper, keep orderly camps and are quite subdued in comparison.'

11

'I'd rather have men we know. Mr Sears wants to buy a block of land on the outskirts of Wywanna. Have a permanent base in the district,' answered Aiden.

'And he wants Father's help,' finished Edwina. They walked through the camp. One of the tents was torn badly, a gaping flap poorly stitched together. A copper sat overturned in the dirt and flies buzzed around an indistinguishable mass.

Edwina always hated it when they were developing land dense with timber. She had to remind herself that if the rains came at the right time, by next year the skeletal earth behind them would be flush with new vegetation and far more productive. If only that plant life were natural grasses and not more wheat. She would make a point of speaking to her father again about her idea. Clearing was a necessary evil out here. It was how you made country. But the way you used that land was even more important when it came to making a decent living.

The thwack of axes biting into wood grew in volume, echoing through the timber and scrub. Behind them the starved dog followed them to the camp's edge and watched them leave.

❧ Chapter Two ❧

Hamilton Baker leant against the windowsill of the permanent rooms he kept in the dusty town of Wywanna, watching as Gloria Zane began to undress. It was late Tuesday afternoon, far too early for such amusements, but availability and necessity combined to quell his fastidious attitude to the proper use of one's time. Not that the time of day ever bothered Gloria. She was one for the moment. A seizer of life in the truest form. Today his lover wore an embroidered pink silk kimono-style gown and she dropped it dramatically on the large four-poster bed, revealing a matching chemise. The sight quite stymied all thoughts of the two children he'd left behind on the property. Davidson could be relied upon to keep an eye on them.

'Well?' asked his lover.

Hamilton was more than pleased to see Gloria's breasts freed from the restrictions of current fashion. 'Better,' he replied. Flat chests and drop-waisted styles did nothing for him, but Gloria was all for keeping up with the young.

The woman was well built, of more than pleasing proportions. If one didn't look at the pudgy hips of middle age or the dimpled thighs she could well have passed for a younger woman. Hamilton observed the way Gloria settled in the velvet chair like a cat, her bottom padding its way into the soft cushion. Not that he wanted a younger woman. Younger women were hard work. They wanted things, expected things, and some complained like screeching cats when they didn't get their own way. He'd had any number of those types in Sydney, years ago, where bordello women fancied themselves to have airs and graces. Gloria on the other hand was savvy to the ways of the world, specifically men. And apart from a sharp mind and athleticism, she needed nothing from him. Gloria Zane was rich.

Gloria's moneyed taste was evident in her decorating skill, although Hamilton rather suspected that the two rooms he occupied, bedroom and adjoining sitting room, were most definitely not the environs a respected country matron would inhabit. The windows were hung with pelmeted curtains of gold damask, the velvet chairs the palest of pinks, greens and yellows with the walls painted in a rather striking burgundy. Hamilton couldn't actually say that he found Gloria's taste to his liking, nor had his description of a relaxing environment been met, yet if one wanted to be stimulated, in every sense, this was the place. 'So, my dear, what news from your broker?'

Gloria crossed her legs and, extending a manicured hand, prettily lifted the hem of her chemise so that the tops of her flesh-coloured stockings were visible. 'It's all margins, margins, margins. Borrow more to invest. George tells me that half of America reads the financials. Cab driver or barber, everyone's an investor these days.'

'So we grow wealthier by the minute,' confirmed Hamilton, although his thoughts were fixed on his lover's creamy thigh.

'The market remains buoyant. However, the Americans are facing some stiff competition from my English countrymen at the moment in terms of foreign investment. Good for us, I say. London was always the centre of the financial markets before that pulsing Wall Street artery sucked the power away from us.' Gloria lit a cigarette before taking a sip of champagne from a saucer-shaped glass, her blood-ox lipstick rimming the crystal. 'I'm quite interested in investing in the motor manufacturing industry, Austin and Morris in particular.'

'Automobiles. Everyone wants one of those new-fangled contraptions.' Hamilton tugged repeatedly at his nose. Automobiles put his boot factories out of business. Why people couldn't just keep walking or riding he had no idea. He hated automobiles. And he hated spring. It was that time of the year when everything blossomed, while at sixty years of age he was rather inclined to shut down. There was altogether too much heat and dust out here. How he'd managed to endure the bucolic lifestyle of drudge-brown Queensland continued to confound him.

'Come now, Hamilton, you are not quite as old-fashioned as you would have me believe.' Resting the cigarette in an ashtray, Gloria walked across the thick pile of the rug to the elaborate dressing table with its collection of bottles, compacts and cut-crystal flagons. Pulling delicately at the chemise, she leant forward, powdering her chest with a large pink fluffy puff, studying her handiwork in the gilt-edged mirror.

The angle afforded Hamilton a generous view of Gloria's not insubstantial cleavage and a fine spectacle of her upper thighs. He'd always been a man predisposed to the wondrous curves of a plump woman's arse, a feature that had attracted him to his wife. Now he knew better. Sense and attentiveness should always come first in a woman, physical attributes a close second. Very close.

'You're distracting me,' he complained.

Gloria smoothed her short, waved hair, slid matching gold snake bracelets onto her upper arms and pouted.

'I detest those things,' he explained.

15

'Well, you don't have to wear them, my dear,' came her reply before she resumed her position in the velvet chair. Her cigarette now a trail of cinders, she lit another.

'You're obsessed with those things. I blame what-cha-ma-call-him who discovered that Tut fellow.'

'It was Howard Carter, darling, the second cousin of my second cousin twice removed. Practically family, when you think about it. And the world's obsessed with all things Egyptian, not just me.' She exhaled a long lungful of smoke.

Hamilton sipped his champagne gloomily. It never failed to amaze him how women could be gratified by the silliest of things, fashion and fads. Thank heavens Gloria's similarities with the majority of the female race were not all encompassing.

'Considering the falling farm prices it makes it difficult to remain enthusiastic about Australian agriculture. The good news, however, is that people are drinking more.' She lifted her glass in salute.

'So the rum business is good?' Hamilton topped up their champagne saucers.

'Excellent,' Gloria confirmed. 'I've quite shied away from buying up soldier settler blocks from the government. You know, some of that country is beyond marginal. And the labour involved for those families . . .' She gave a huff of annoyance.

'A bit of outdoor exercise never hurt anyone.' It certainly wasn't harming his children. 'You forget, a life in the countryside was recommended by doctors for the healing of injuries sustained in the war. It's a fine social experiment.'

'Poppycock,' answered Gloria, 'absolute poppycock.' She drew ferociously on the cigarette so that the tip glowed red. 'Sending people out to the bush with no experience. Why, I've heard of families living in tents made of hessian bags.'

'Plenty of timber to be had in these parts,' replied Hamilton.

'Compassionate soul, aren't you?' Gloria stubbed out the cigarette.

Hamilton envisaged his lover standing on a soap box in London's Hyde Park.

'And you, Hammy, how is that money-lending business of yours doing?' Gloria spilt champagne with an animated wave of her hand and dabbed at the silk chemise.

Hamilton stared at the prominent nipple through the now sheer material. 'The district's been feeling the strains of the economy for a few years now. The smaller borrowers are all clamouring for an extension on their loans.' Hamilton took a gulp of the champagne and, keeping his gaze fastened on the burnt pink areola disappearing behind the drying silk, removed his jacket and hung it in the wardrobe. 'I've stopped extending credit until things improve.' Unbuttoning his vest, Hamilton lay his pocket watch on the dresser. 'It's the pastoralists that have the money.' He tugged at the knot in his necktie, loosening it. 'Invariably they come to me for privacy, and with their asset base I'm assured of repayment.'

'I do love a man skilful in negotiations.' Gloria held out her glass, her lips curling in satisfaction as the bubbles rose to the surface. 'Why don't you close up shop for a while?' She stifled a yawn. 'We could take a cruise. Head to Europe, England. It's been three years since I returned to Devon and the family seat. We could visit the distillery in Scotland.'

Hamilton didn't bother answering. In the street below a team of horses dragging a heavily laden wool wagon turned slowly into the wide thoroughfare. Pedestrians, riders on horseback, sulkies and automobiles quickly made way for the twenty-foot-long dray and its team of twenty-four horses. The ship of the outback swayed and creaked. The bales, tightly secured by rope, were stacked three high. There must have been nearly five ton of wool on board.

'And what has captured your attention?' queried Gloria.

The heady smells of lanolin, horseflesh and saddle grease reached his nostrils as a woman raced from a nearby shop to gather up a runaway child. Hamilton scanned the bales, noting the station name stencilled on each pack. Wangallon. That was one family who didn't need his services, the Gordons of Wangallon Station. The driver, who was heading the team on horseback with the well-trained lead horses steering the load, kept up a steady pace. Behind them they deposited a trail of manure and the scent of money. 'Wangallon wool,' he offered by way of explanation. Turning his back on the impressive sight, Hamilton focused his thoughts on one of the main reasons he enjoyed visiting town.

'It's that time of year,' answered Gloria, unfastening the suspenders clipped to the top of her stockings.

That was Gloria; she was never one to be impressed by money. The truly wealthy never were. Undoing his cufflinks, Hamilton sat them on the dresser along with the now furled necktie.

'Frankly I see Australia as a country of empty spaces which will never be filled. But if you're so enthusiastic about dirt, does that mean you're finally going to expand?' Gloria made a show of lifting each leg onto the bed and pointing her toes carefully, rolling the silk stockings to her ankles before removing them with a theatrical flourish.

'No. Not after the battle I've endured with that blasted pear. I have Aiden and Edwina putting out insect eggs today.'

Stepping out of her chemise, Gloria stood quite naked except for knickers and suspender belt.

The saliva gathered in his mouth as Hamilton took in the sight of her full, dangling breasts. He gave the smallest of nods, waiting for the remnants of her silk and lace attire to be disposed of. As if reading his mind, Gloria undid the suspender belt, dropping the flimsy garment to the floor, and stepped out of her knickers. The fuzzy darkness of her reminded Hamilton of one of his favourite Ziegfeld Girl collector cards.

'And when am I going to have the honour of visiting your stronghold, Hamilton, and making the acquaintance of your children?'

I've decided it's time. This cloak-and-dagger relationship is not to my liking.'

Hamilton slipped striped braces from his shoulders. 'You know my dilemma.'

Gloria allowed her fingers to drift languidly across her breasts. 'How is your matchmaking on your daughter's behalf proceeding?'

Hamilton hoped for an advantageous marriage but, as yet, not one respected family had stepped forward to lay claim to Edwina. Unbuttoning his shirt, Hamilton draped it across a chair. His relationship with the divorced Gloria was, he guessed, not helping Edwina's chances. A fact his lover had alluded to before. It was a conundrum Hamilton couldn't breach. 'Edwina needs a husband's firm hand. She is stubborn and opinionated, like her mother.' And like her mother, his daughter was beginning to display the same mood swings and outspokenness that characterised Caroline's later life.

'I know you worry about her, but young people have changed, my dear. They have far more wants and needs than we ever did at their age. Blame the war, blame the austerity since then. Everyone is trying to find their place in a new world.'

'I've purposely kept Edwina away from your so-called new world for her own protection. Anyway, when she is married,' he concluded, 'we will be married.' This was not the first time they'd discussed matrimony, not that his lover seemed taken with the idea.

'If you don't bring her to town and show her off she'll never marry. And you did say she turned twenty this year.' Gloria drained the champagne and crossed the room. Expertly unfastening his trousers, she proceeded to manipulate his manhood with a touch that inevitably made him believe that his lover had undergone some training in the arts. 'I would so adore you to grow a moustache,' she breathed. 'I do love hair on a man. You and your freshly shaved skin, you look like a boy at times, my dear. A very naughty boy.' She squeezed a little more.

'Yes.' The word was a mumble as he plied her breasts.

'We've been fornicating with relish for years.'

Hamilton moaned. 'Three months a year.'

'I'm not looking for a gold band, my darling. I would simply like to be treated a little more respectably. In public.'

His hands drifted to her waist. 'Aha.'

'The world has changed. Why, the young ones are out dancing and drinking until all hours and I have it on good authority that they pet quite freely with those they are not married to.'

The blood was draining from Hamilton's head.

'We are wealthy, lovers, each without partners. I don't even have the encumbrance of a child. We can do what we please. Society be damned.'

That, however, was the problem. In a world where the success of a business and the right connections went hand in hand, acceptance in the right circles was imperative. Besides, Hamilton couldn't picture Gloria visiting the farm. Although he'd intentionally maintained a modest homestead for the benefit of his children, keeping the extent of his fortune a secret from them, he doubted Gloria would be impressed by his self-imposed austerity. The woman wasn't fickle but still, one never knew with the fairer sex.

'You are overwrought,' breathed Gloria into his neck. 'Relax, my darling. Relax.'

'I purchased the tickets you wanted,' murmured Hamilton, cupping her buttocks. Gloria was invariably appeased with a gift of appreciation.

She gave a little gasp. 'For the circus?'

'Yes.' That was Gloria. A woman in love with life itself, with the simplest of pleasures that he invariably held in disregard. Flowers, a keepsake left on her pillow, a piece of cheap silk purchased from the Emporium. Or tickets to the bloody circus. Closing his ears to his lover's excitement, Hamilton pushed Gloria backwards onto the bed, stepping out of his trousers.

'I love it when you're in one of your moods,' she replied, opening her legs with a girlish giggle. 'Peek-a-boo!'

God, to be young again, thought Hamilton. He would roll Gloria over, take her from behind, tug her hair as he rode her until this woman that he had somehow fallen for cried out in ecstasy. Hamilton collapsed onto her almost desperately, feeling the soft pillows of her breasts, the length of her limbs, the liquid warmth of her centre. Come on, old man, he chastised himself. Hamilton thought of the Ziegfeld Girl as their lips touched and, with a grim smile, he clutched at the sheets and rode the woman beneath him home.

⋘ Chapter Three ⋙

Edwina and Aiden observed the automobile warily from across the boundary fence as it weaved between the deeply furrowed trunks of the towering brigalows. The vehicle moved slowly along the dirt road, carefully detouring left and right as if the gleaming metallic object was aware of the foreign environment it travelled through. Within the open machine sat the driver, his face concealed by goggles and a low cap. Accompanying the man was one other passenger, a female judging from the multi-coloured scarf billowing in the wind. The woman resembled a parakeet, Edwina thought admiringly, barely noticing the wallaby they'd been tracking as it bounded away low and fast into a wall of wicker-like bush.

'He's gone.' Aiden reluctantly drew his attention away from the automobile and gave a huff of annoyance, replacing the rifle in its holster.

'Do you think they saw us?' asked Edwina.

'We're on our farm, they're on theirs,' he countered. 'Did you see that automobile? A Model T Ford. I'm sure of it. What on earth is an automobile doing out here?'

'It's probably just as well you didn't shoot with *them* on the other side,' Edwina cautioned, secretly pleased for the escaping wallaby.

'Maybe I should have,' came Aiden's reply.

The vehicle vanished behind the pendulous green leaves of flowering wilgas and low scrub.

'You'd think the Ridgeways would do something about the numbers,' complained Aiden. 'I must have shot near one thousand kangaroos and wallabies over winter.'

Edwina's horse grew restless. She gave the animal a reassuring pat. 'They probably don't know anything about it. How could they when they don't live here anymore? Besides, the Ridgeways have their excellent manager, Mr Fernleigh, to keep an eye on things,' Edwina finished sarcastically.

'Yes,' agreed Aiden, 'excellent.'

Three miles of their dividing fence adjoined Ridgeway Station and it was this portion they now rode along. It wasn't a large border to share by any means but it seemed that size proved inconsequential such had been the disputes between the two properties over the past few years.

'I wonder who they are?' said Edwina, speculating about the twosome sightseeing on the forty-thousand-acre sheep station next door.

Edwina and Aiden took off as one, galloping their mounts along the fence line until the trees and shrubs began to lessen, revealing open woodlands patched with grazing sheep. They halted again behind clumps of prickly pear where there was a clear view of the road. Here the automobile reappeared, scattering recently shorn animals before slowing to a complete stop. The driver stepped out of the vehicle and slammed the door shut, the female passenger joining him. Edwina noted the lean silhouette of the woman's dress, the way the material, falling just below her knees, glimmered in the sunlight, and was suddenly conscious of her own masculine attire, her brother's seconds.

'A flat tyre, maybe?' suggested Aiden, as the driver examined one of the wheels.

A cooee sounded from the scrub and a man appeared on horseback.

'Who is that?' asked Edwina, taking in the heft of the man and the wide-brimmed hat.

'Who are any of them?' countered her brother.

The rider circled the automobile and then slid from the saddle in one fluid movement. The strangers talked briefly and then the driver and his companion returned to the vehicle, slowly driving away. The rider remained stationary on the narrow bush track as the vehicle was consumed by trees and bushes, the noise of the engine gradually fading.

Aiden tightened his grip on the reins, as the rider flung himself up into the saddle, turning the horse towards the boundary fence. 'He's probably seen us, E.' They nudged their mounts from out behind the cover of the prickly pear, moving directly into the stranger's line of sight.

It was impossible to make out the features of the man. He sat tall in the saddle, a hand on a hip, unmoving, observing. Edwina wanted to lift a hand in greeting, to call out hello. But something stopped her. It was as if there was more than the wire fence separating them. A lot more. Was this the eldest Ridgeway? The elusive son and heir? 'I think we should leave,' said Edwina uncomfortably. Not waiting for an answer she kicked the mare in the flanks.

'Do you think that's them? The Ridgeway twins?' asked Aiden, their horses matching stride for stride. 'I always doubted they'd ever come home. It's years since their parents died in that car accident. Father said the family made their fortune with steamboats on the Darling-Barwon Rivers. If I was them I'd be living the high life in Brisbane too.'

They rode back along the edge of the cultivation, where green plants stood thick and tall in the rich earth they'd cajoled from bands of timber and pear. Six hundred acres were planted to wheat and their father hoped for thirty bushels an acre come harvest, a not inconsiderable amount. Hoped for was exactly the right term, Edwina decided. Rain remained average for the year.

'Did you know the circus was coming this week?' asked Edwina. It was a subject she'd tried to raise repeatedly since yesterday when the ringbarker had alerted them to the imminent arrival of the spectacular.

'The Carbeen paddock will look like this eventually.' Dismounting, Aiden walked into the crop before dropping to his knees to dig in the soil with his hands. 'There's a bit of moisture there.'

'I would rather see that new area allowed to go back to natural pasture,' Edwina told him. 'I'm sure we'd do better running more livestock rather than planting further acres to wheat. There's just not the money in grain.'

The frown line between Aiden's eyes deepened. 'You're not going to start arguing with Father again, are you, Edwina?'

'Of course not; it's just that I've made some calculations and I know my idea would work.' Inside her trouser pocket were the figures she'd been working on for the last few weeks that showed the benefit of keeping their new development crop-free. Her fingers briefly touched the folded paper. 'I thought you might like to see my notes.'

'You always were keen on pen and paper,' Aiden answered. 'What were you saying about the circus?'

Edwina sighed. 'Aiden?'

'It doesn't matter what I think.'

'Of course it does. Father listens to you.'

'That doesn't mean he'll agree with me,' answered Aiden. 'Why can't you be happy with the way things are?'

'Don't you want to diversify? At the very least, introducing some cattle would make things more interesting. Why, if everything went well, eventually we might be in the position to buy more land. We certainly can't do any worse than what we are now.'

Aiden looked up to where Edwina sat on her horse. 'More land? I don't want any more land.'

'Oh. I thought –'

'That's the problem, you're always thinking. It's a hard enough job doing everything around here as it is. I don't want any more work and I don't want to read any figures,' stated Aiden. 'Now let's change the subject. What were you going to say about the circus?'

Edwina knew there was little point getting angry. Although at this very moment she felt like screaming in frustration. 'Last year I saw the Martins in town the month after Colby's came through,' she began. 'Miraculous, Mrs Martin told me. There were dancing bears and prancing horses and everyone was there,' explained Edwina. 'Mrs Martin was quite pointed about it, implying that we were quite out of step with things. If Mother were still alive I'm sure we'd attend every year.'

But Aiden was walking past the damaged edges of the crop until his palms brushed unsullied flowering heads. A pleased smile graced a full mouth and the elegant panes of a face that would have sat far more comfortably on a woman had he not been born with a deep furrow between chin and lip.

'I'd rather not shoot the kangaroos and wallabies, E.' He placed hands on hips, surveying the clipped edges of the crop where native animals fed through winter.

Edwina disliked the killing of animals, but they needed every grain.

Her brother was stepping out a square and counting the plants growing within. Obsessed, that's what he was, Edwina decided, obsessed with the growing of things that couldn't be grown, at least by them. In some ways she wished the wildlife did eat them out; then maybe their father could be dissuaded from continuing with the growing of wheat and consider some other alternative that might actually make some money. 'You know, Aiden, you might try counting the grain in one of the heads of wheat and multiplying that by the number of plants in your square.'

Her brother did as she suggested, prising free the soft green wheat. A few minutes later a look of consternation crossed his features. 'There's not much here.'

'Exactly,' answered Edwina. Maybe now he would tell their father that the harvest would be poor once again.

'I'm sure it will still be an excellent crop.'

Edwina closed her eyes in dismay.

'Are you coming?' Aiden sprang into the saddle. 'Father will be home from Wywanna by now.'

Dense trees and naturally open country gradually replaced the wheat fields as they cut cross-country to trace the creek that wound through their land. The horses whinnied quietly as they padded single file along the bank, sand flicking up from beneath their hoofs. Further along the sloping ground a goanna scuttled out from under the carcass of a sheep to race up the trunk of a tree.

Aiden drew up beside the dead animal. 'One of Ridgeway Station's escapees, I guess.' He peered at the ewe's head.

'Come on,' urged Edwina, 'it smells.'

The horses were eager to move on and they rode two abreast, the sun striking the surface of the water where the overhanging timber allowed, dabbing it with flashes of light and highlighting patches of the green-brown eddy.

'Do you hear that?' questioned Edwina. 'That noise?' It was a faraway sound, dampened by the stretch of stubby bushes and trees. 'It sounds like a child.'

'Bowerbird,' replied Aiden knowledgeably. 'You know how they like to mimic.'

'It's very lifelike.'

Birds fluttered and promenaded before them as they left the creek. The grasses, although short, were green and fresh beneath their horses' hooves as they zigzagged through saplings and prickly pear, hopping mice darting clear of the horses.

Ahead, their comfortable homestead gradually came into view. Late Victorian in style with symmetrical gable ends, the appearance of the building was much improved by the addition of slate and louvre venting covering the windows on the building's facade. The house sat in the middle of a myriad of trees, encircled on three sides by their father's impressive orchard, while the front was hemmed by a row of stately gum trees. As a child, Edwina believed the building had been placed amid the fruity grove by some mythical titan from another world. The reality was quite different. Their father was the builder, along with a workforce of men, some of them barely trained in the mechanics of construction, a fact evident on closer inspection. The walls didn't quite join uneven floors, the roof leaked and the timber boards were gappy at best. Not that the makers could be wholly blamed for such faults, for the soil beneath the foundations was a living, breathing thing, contracting and swelling depending on seasons, whether wet or dry.

The four rows of orange and lemon trees, in which thirty-eight remained of the original planting, stretched their branches out across the roofs of the weatherboard house, stables and chicken roost, boughs interlocking in an intricate web of timber, leaves and fruit. From some angles the homestead wasn't visible at all and one had to look carefully to see that the leafy mat that appeared suspended above the house was in fact its roof. The corrugated iron was almost perpetually covered with leaves and quite often fallen fruit.

'Race you!' yelled Aiden, urging his mount onwards. Apart from the orchard, there was no garden to speak of, or fence. Chickens and turkeys scattered in all directions as they raced across the papery bark discarded by the gum trees. Five large dogs bounded towards them, circled the galloping siblings, and then with a series of excited yelps raced back towards the house. The horses whinnied in protest as the collies retreated, jumping onto the verandah. They ran excitedly along the length of the floorboards encircling the building. Edwina winced as a loud crash sounded and then the dogs reappeared, skidding around the corner of the verandah. On sighting the master of the household, they slid under the house.

The bulky figure of Hamilton Baker appeared at the front door, holding a pipe, his other hand clasping a jacket lapel. Striding to the large gong suspended on the verandah, he hit it repeatedly, as if there was no sign of his children, before retreating indoors.

Edwina tugged on the reins a little more sharply than necessary as they drew up next to the hitching rail outside the house. There should have been something comforting in the familiarity of their father's ways; instead she felt a spike of annoyance. Why couldn't he just wave at them? He could see them after all.

Davidson appeared and, without a word, spat on the ground, nodding a greeting of sorts.

'Thanks, Davidson,' Aiden said with a smile. 'We won't be using the horses again this afternoon.'

The man looked at him blankly and, untying the horses, led them around the rear of the house to the stables. Edwina watched him leave. Noticed the straight shoulders and soldierly gait. It had always unsettled her having a mute working on the property, she didn't know why. Perhaps it was simply because Davidson was vital to the running of their business and yet he was unable to voice an opinion and they in turn never knew what he was thinking.

'So when Father asks,' said Aiden, 'we checked the fence and patched it.'

'I think we should tell him we haven't got to it yet,' cautioned Edwina. 'You know what he's like.'

'I'll do it this afternoon. Just for once can't you let us have a moment's peace?'

'Okay, but I'll not be responsible if he finds out we've told a fib.'

Standing forty feet away from the homestead, sitting squarely on the dirt, was the kitchen hut. Edwina and Aiden jostled each other in the doorway, calling out greetings to the cook. Mrs Ryan barely acknowledged them as she returned canisters to a wall of shelves, each tin landing with a thud and accompanied by a mumble of angry words. She paused to touch the upturned lucky horseshoe nailed to the shelving before directing her tirade at the filthy rag hanging from her apron. The single room with its large wood stove was filled with the debris of a woman whose skills didn't stretch to tidying as she worked. Dirty dishes, spilt flour, vegetable peelings and what appeared to be the innards of a number of eggs were strewn across table and workbench. Sidestepping a trail of ants on the dirt floor, Edwina and Aiden washed up in a large porcelain bowl, the water a greasy brown from the morning's cooking. They stood side by side, nudging each other playfully as they reached in turn for soap and water.

'I'll be needing more water carted from the crick.' Their cook wasn't one for asking politely. 'The well dried up this morning. Ain't a spit in the bottom worth bucketing.' She stood at the large wooden table, leaning down to clear a space with a meaty forearm. Once accomplished, she began ladling beans and potatoes onto three plates. 'About time you two were home.'

Aiden tossed the towel to his sister. 'No water again?'

Mrs Ryan blew air into her cheeks in reply. 'That'll be four wells dug these past three years. There be experts, you know. Why, my brother once told me about a man who walked the country with a forky stick.'

'You mean a forked stick,' corrected Edwina, drying her hands.

'Gifted he was. Point the forky stick he would and then he'd be a-saying, dig there,' Mrs Ryan pointed to a spot on the dirt floor, 'there be water right there, he'd say. And low and behold, a body would dig and there would be water.'

'He was a diviner,' explained Edwina.

The cook scowled. 'I can't tell you the look of the man; whether he be divine or not was not the point, young lady, but he could find water.' She gave a sniff. 'You tell Mr Hamilton that I'll not stay if he can't do something about the water.'

It was true there'd been some troubles with their water supply. The rainwater was lost when the tank bottom rotted during winter and since July they'd been relying on creek water for the washing of everything and the dwindling well with its increasingly brackish offering for drinking water.

'Hopefully we'll get rain soon.' Aiden did his best to comfort their Scottish housekeeper, reminding her that the tank was now repaired and that all that was needed was a fall of rain.

Mrs Ryan looked pointedly out the window at a blue sky. 'We've three barrels of drinking water left.' The subject of water addressed, she eyed Edwina's clothing disapprovingly. 'It would be nice for once if you two changed before sitting down to eat.' She wiped greasy fingers on her apron, before tucking wispy hair under her cap.

'It would be nice if one had the time to do so,' Edwina countered.

'It's not dignified, just not dignified I say,' the woman continued. 'It's bad enough you're out in the fields day in, day out, working like one of them factory girls in the city, but appearing like you do at table. Well, what if someone called?'

'Like who?' asked Aiden with interest.

The cook, flustered by the question, grew ruddy cheeked. 'I don't know,' she replied, slamming the salt cellar down so hard that Edwina thought it would split in half. 'Maybe one of them fancy gentlemen your father conducts his affairs with.'

'And have you ever seen one of father's business associates here at the farm?' Edwina's question confounded the Scotswoman. With a huff she carried a serving dish of roasted mutton outside, mumbling for them to bring the vegetable-laden plates. The well-trodden track between house and kitchen was freshly swept, with mouldering orchard leaves piled neatly on either side.

Edwina and Aiden mimicked the woman's gait, the long skirt swaying in tandem with the axe-handle width of her behind. The procession reached the halfway point as a turkey raced across their path. Leaves swirled, the turkey emitted a disgruntled gobble, and the meat landed with a thud on the ground.

Mrs Ryan was speechless. She stared at the meat in the dirt and then began to emit a low whine. The sound grew in intensity. The five collie dogs appeared.

Edwina, shoving the two plates she carried at her brother, shooed at the dogs and then picked up the slippery, warm meat. 'We'll just brush the dirt off, Mrs Ryan. It will be fine.'

'Really?' asked Aiden.

The cook's bottom lip began to tremble. 'I didn't do it on purpose. 'Twas the fairies what done it. I'm sure.'

'No harm done,' said Edwina, frowning at the mention of the sprites that ruled Mrs Ryan's domain. Returning the meat to the platter, she used a corner of the Scotswoman's apron to rub the dirt away, then she turned the roast upside down. 'See,' she smiled. 'Father will never know.'

The cook, clearly unconvinced, reluctantly resumed her trek indoors.

The long table was plainly set for dinner for four people, the extra setting in honour of their mother. A fine linen tablecloth, polished silver cutlery and cut-crystal water glasses were complemented by a vase of wildflowers.

Setting the meat platter at the head of the table before Mr Baker, the cook gave a quick curtsey before departing the room. Her customary description of their meal forgotten, Edwina improvised. 'Meat and vegetables,' she announced. Their father didn't make a comment. Edwina felt him studying their movements as she and Aiden placed a plate at each of the three places before sitting.

Their father began to carve. 'What was that commotion I heard?'

'Nothing,' replied Edwina. 'Did you have a good visit to town, Father?'

Hamilton concentrated on the meat. 'Reasonable. And the cacto-eggs, did you put them out?'

'Yes, in the middle of the bad patch in the Carbeen paddock,' explained Edwina.

'Good, let's hope it works. Put the rest out tomorrow, Aiden. The blasted war put a stop to the research but there have been success stories. We can only hope.'

'We saw a black automobile on the Ridgeways' place this morning,' began Aiden, as his plate was heaped with meat. 'A Model T Ford.' He tugged his napkin from the round silver holder, placing the material carefully on his lap. 'There were two people in it and a man riding as well.'

'The Ridgeway children's uncle, Mr Somerville, and his wife are due for a visit. They come up once a year to check on things. You know that.'

'Oh.' Edwina was both relieved and deflated.

'Do you think the children will return, Father?' asked Aiden. 'I remember you telling us that you thought the property would be sold.'

'Frankly, I'm surprised it hasn't been sold before this,' explained Hamilton in a rare moment of disclosure. 'The Ridgeway twins came of age regarding their parents' estate last year.'

Aiden surveyed his plate hungrily. 'You should have seen their vehicle, Father.'

Edwina kept her hand outstretched, waiting for an extra slice of mutton. 'If you intend to work me like a man, Father,' she said politely, 'then you must feed me like one.'

'Your mother was always so elegantly svelte,' Hamilton grunted, adding a further two slices to Edwina's plate. Aiden gave his sister a wink. With his own plate served, Hamilton sat in the heavy carver and folded his hands in prayer; together all three bowed their heads. 'God bless this food. Amen.'

'Amen,' Edwina and Aiden repeated, both sitting up straight as they waited the habitual few minutes while their father stared at the opposite end of the table to where their mother once sat.

'It would be good if we could have an automobile, Father,' Edwina finally suggested.

'Young women were never so outspoken before the war. Your hair is out of place.' He pointed to the windblown strand hanging across Edwina's cheek. 'Tidy yourself.' Hamilton pointed to the crystal cruet stand. 'Salt.' Dousing his meal with salt, vinegar and prepared mustard, he began to cut his food into bite-size pieces. When he'd completed this ritual and the beans, potatoes and meat were piled into little mounds, only then did he begin to eat.

'It takes so long to go into town, Father,' Edwina told him. 'Why, it's a whole day in the buggie when we need supplies. A long day. Everyone's modernising.'

Brother and sister held their breath as their father picked something from his tongue, peered at it and then deposited it on the edge of his plate. Hamilton gave each of his children a wary glance and resumed eating, this time examining each forkful of food carefully. 'Are they? Well then, maybe you should ride over to Ridgeway Station, Edwina, and ask them about this automobile of theirs, if this is something you feel keenly about.' Placing his fork down, Hamilton took a sip of water and then dabbed at his moustache with the linen napkin. 'I'm sure their manager, Mr Fernleigh, would be overjoyed to make your acquaintance again, Edwina. It must be a good two months since the man last eye-balled you across the fence.'

Edwina picked at her vegetables sullenly. Mr Fernleigh would undoubtedly throw her off the property if she took one step on that land. It may have been different if her father's diplomatic skills were more advanced; however, last winter when a large mob of

Ridgeway merinos had broken through the boundary fence and begun feasting on their crops, their father's response was to ride out and shoot the luckless animals. He managed to kill ten before Davidson and Aiden intervened.

Their father chewed thoughtfully on a bean. 'I saw Sears earlier. You didn't promise him anything, did you, Aiden?'

'Of course not, Father. He asked me to put in a word for him, that's all.'

'Apparently he wants to buy some land in Wywanna, Father,' added Edwina.

'Well, I've said no. So if he has the audacity to mention it to you again, don't get involved. Sears' team will be finishing up soon.' Hamilton changed the subject. 'And one of the men has walked off the job?'

'Ran away to the circus,' confirmed Aiden. 'Apparently he didn't like killing things.'

His father scratched at the surface of a piece of meat with his knife. 'He doesn't like killing things? What, trees? One would think he'd be more concerned about where his next meal is coming from. Still, I don't like a man leaving my employ without being recompensed for his labour, especially when the lad's father served at Gallipoli. If he does intend doing such a foolhardy thing then I imagine he'll be skulking around Colby Brothers on Saturday night.'

'The circus . . .' Edwina gave her father a beaming smile. 'We've never been to a performance, you know.'

'I have business in town over the weekend; however, I want you to go into town on Saturday as well, Aiden. Find the lad and pay him. The circus. I've never heard of a more ridiculous thing.'

'I'm to stay overnight while the circus is on?' Aiden sounded almost breathless.

Hamilton cleared his throat. 'Of course not. You will return home within the day. This is a good opportunity for you to be entrusted with this task, Aiden. Should you encounter any problems, send word for me at the Guild.'

'Can I go too, Father?' Edwina pleaded. 'Please?'

'I'd send Sears, but the rest of the men would take off as well,' their father continued, ignoring his daughter. 'I don't need the ring-barking halted because of the demon drink. Pay the boy, Aiden, and then come straight home. And I mean what I say. *Straight home*. No dillydallying, not with your sister left here alone.'

'Alone?' repeated Edwina.

'Mrs Ryan has the weekend off.'

'So it's alright for the cook to attend the circus, but not me?' argued Edwina. 'I am twenty years of age, Father, and I'm yet to make my first appearance in public life.'

'And the circus isn't the place to do it,' her father replied.

'And why should Aiden get to go when he is two years younger than me?'

Hamilton addressed his son. 'I'm entrusting you with this, Aiden. You are a man now, after all. And take Davidson with you.' Hamilton ate quickly, the steady crawl of the grandfather clock measuring the clatter of knives and forks. 'And, Aiden, you'll attend to the woodpile and cart some water as well.'

Edwina chewed the now cold food, pausing to absently study the gleaming mahogany sideboard with its empty decanters and the matching pale green bases of the kerosene lamps that lit the room at night.

'Why can't I go?' she finally asked.

Folding his napkin, Hamilton placed it on the table. 'Because, although you may choose to parade around this property dressed like a man, you are in fact a young woman. And young women of breeding don't attend such spectacles. The hurly-burly of the circus is hardly appropriate for a daughter of mine.'

'If I had somewhere to go to,' she responded, 'like the circus, I'd be quite happy to dress appropriately, but when I'm here, Father, all the time, on this half-starved block, there is little point swanning around in my mother's altered seconds. Not when I work like a factory girl, my opinions ignored.'

Edwina wondered if her father was going to have some sort of attack. He plucked at his tie and collar. 'You will remember who you're talking to, Edwina. Clearly you've had too much free time on your hands. Well, that can be rectified. Next week you and Aiden can start work ploughing the new block.'

'Father,' replied Edwina, 'I know the cost of things. The wheat undertaking is far from viable once the expense of land clearing is factored in and Aiden will tell you that having just checked the wheat the harvest doesn't look like it's going to be a good one this year. Again,' she said for emphasis.

'I think the crop looks alright,' Aiden answered his father's gaze.

'Aiden, really?' said Edwina. 'Father, we should be letting the cleared land grass up and then go into sheep or cattle. Wheat is too chancy. Our yields simply aren't good enough. We have to do something else. Try something different so that we have a chance at a better life.'

Across the table Aiden appeared to shrink.

Pushing his plate aside, their father stood abruptly. 'Are you starving?' he asked, his words clipped. 'No. Plenty are. You'd do well to remember that, Edwina. And another thing, I like to be forewarned when my meal ends up in the dirt.'

'At least read this proposal, Father,' pleaded Edwina, holding out the piece of paper she'd been carrying around for the last few days. 'I have assessed the risks, calculated the costs involved and the profit to be made. I think you'll be pleased.'

He stared at her. 'I have looked at your suggestions in the past, my girl. Have any of them been implemented?'

Edwina shook her head. 'But that is not to say they weren't good ideas or that they wouldn't have worked.'

'You are very opinionated for a young woman who has no business experience.'

'But I do have business experience, Father,' argued Edwina. 'I learn from you every day.'

Her father reluctantly took the paper and walked out of the room.

He simply couldn't ignore her this time, could he? thought Edwina. She'd been so careful with her sums, recalculating them to show differing outcomes dependent on season and prices.

With their father's departure, Aiden slouched back in his chair. 'Steady on, old girl.'

It was hard to get rid of the image of Aiden and her coaxing the horse and plough across unbroken land. Edwina could already feel the exhaustion and taste the September wind, dry dirt biting at her eyes and skin. 'Doesn't it bother you, Aiden, that we're working like slaves for nothing? Seriously, I mean if someone in the family comes up with a proposal that has the potential to benefit everybody, isn't that a good thing?'

'It's Father's decision, Edwina. You have to stop antagonising him. Look, the latest copy of the *Agricultural Gazette*'s in the parlour. Why don't you go and read it?' he said dismissively.

'Have you read it?' she asked.

He gave a lethargic smile. Aiden never read anything. Edwina thought of the number of times Aiden had abandoned his sums as a schoolboy and wondered why she'd bothered to share her ideas earlier. She doubted he would manage running a business without their father when that day came, and the thought worried her.

'Honestly, Aiden, if we made more money we wouldn't have to be outside working like navvies all the time. We could be researching new ideas for the property and making some improvements like new fences and gateways. And in our spare time we should be able to do the things that other people do, like going to the circus and –'

'Edwina.' Aiden grew impatient. 'I'm happy being like everyone else.'

'But we're not like everyone else,' argued Edwina. Their small holding was somewhat of an aberration in a landscape mainly populated by sheep graziers. To the east and south huge areas of land were engulfed by pear and to their north, only miles away, was the dingo fence. Two tangible boundaries that in Edwina's mind literally hedged them in. Why couldn't she make Aiden understand that they had to do better, that everything they did mattered, particularly when your father was held at arm's length by the district for being a moneylender. And clearly not a very good one at that.

❈ Chapter Four ❈

On Saturday morning Edwina woke to rays of fractured light patterning the soft draping of the mosquito net cocooning the bed. Around her the house creaked and groaned, as if the bulk of leaves matting the iron roof was pushing down on the building's timber frame, expanding the tongue and groove cypress boards and bulging the pressed metal ceilings. As a child, Edwina often believed that she would wake in the middle of the night, shrouded by leaves, the stars her ceiling, and was somewhat dismayed when such a disaster didn't happen. Even now she half expected to wake to a sagging ceiling. This morning she stared through the open doors to the grey-green tangle of bush beyond, watching as a moth fluttered against the suspended netting. She kept her bedroom door open to the elements, except for the coldest months of the year, and the mesh provided protection from all manner of creepy-crawlies.

The homestead was noisiest at dawn and dusk as if attuned to each day's cycle. Edwina stretched out her arms and legs, feeling the sheet taut across her toes as the building gave a final groan, a yawn of sorts and then fell silent. In its place came the sounds and smells of the household. A door closing. The pad of feet on timber. Kitchen smoke. Susan Ryan's baking accompanied by a tuneless song. Down the wide central hallway footsteps retreated to the dining room. Outside a horse whinnied. Mrs Ryan would have already set a pot of tea at her father's elbow, a slice of freshly baked bread and a silver jar filled with mulberry jam from the lone tree in the garden. Rituals. Hamilton Baker was one for procedure and habit. Edwina would never know if he'd always been so, but certainly over the past years both she and her brother had become gradually aware of their father's increasing need for routine. Everything had its place and there was a place for everything, including his children.

The black-and-white border collie lying on the floor by Edwina's bed stared at her impatiently, his tail flicking the timber boards. Despite his advanced age, Jed wasn't one for lying about. As Edwina pushed back the bedcovers and gathered the netting, securing it behind the brass bedhead, she noted that one of the wallaby hides scattered on the timber floor was partially chewed.

'Jed.'

The old dog got to his feet slowly, moving to the verandah door.

'That was my favourite.'

Jed regarded her fleetingly. The days of meeting his mistress's gaze with a knowing air were gone.

Wrapping a shawl about her shoulders, Edwina twisted long blonde hair into a loose bun, securing it with a tortoiseshell comb. A silver locket lay on the plain oak dresser and she opened it carefully, touching the delicate strand of curled plaited hair belonging to her mother, before hanging the keepsake about her neck. The dresser with its mirror, a dilapidated brocade chair and a wardrobe of limited proportions comprised the extent of the furnishings. The centrepiece of the bedroom was the fireplace. The mantelpiece held an assortment of framed pictures – dour-looking grandparents, bearded uncles of uncanny resemblance and her father photographed in front of a painted Grecian screen. The swan of the grim-faced grouping was her mother. Caroline Baker stood elegantly posed in a large picture hat, the gossamer folds of her gown sweeping elegantly in a train across the studio floor. Edwina smiled at the photograph and then, picking up the broom, began brushing out the leaves and dust carried indoors during the night.

It was an impossible task holding back the bush from the interior of the house. In summer Edwina kept many of the windows in the main part of the homestead closed and the curtains drawn in an effort to minimise the beating heat and powdery dust. But it was an unwinnable battle. They lived in the middle of the scrub and the land surrounding them could not be contained. On hands and knees, Edwina repositioned the length of material that blocked the gap between the outside wall and the floor. The space had worsened over winter and was now due to be patched with mud brick, a messy concoction of mud and straw. It must be done quickly, thought Edwina, before the snakes came out in numbers. There was a long, wide length of wood to place across the doorway, which usually kept the serpents at bay.

With the room tidied, Edwina searched through the items sitting on her dressing table. 'Where is it?' she said aloud. Her hands moved the few objects. A small glass bottle of lavender water, the silver-backed brush and mirror, and a number of empty vessels with beaten silver lids, which once held her mother's creams and potions. 'Where is it?' Inexplicably her heart gave a little flutter of anxiety. 'There it is.' The fragment of blue glass was partially concealed beneath an embroidered linen handkerchief. Edwina studied the jagged piece found in the chicken pen yesterday and, with it clasped in her hand, joined Jed on the verandah.

A rising sun skimmed the tree-edged horizon in the faraway east. Through the orchard Davidson could be glimpsed, leading her father's saddled horse from the direction of the stables, the now silent collies appearing to trail beast and man at a safe distance.

Edwina knew it was wrong to feel a sense of relief at her father's departure for town, but at times his harsh character made her feel disheartened and quite often maudlin. The splintering light glinting through the orchard distracted her thoughts, the refracted brightness increasing as the sun rose in the sky.

Between the gnarled trunks of the lemon and orange trees, her mother's decorated coolabah shimmered brightly. Caroline had been so alive, so vital. Twenty years his junior, her husband once referred to his wife lovingly as his little Bowerbird and the description was perfect. Plain in appearance but with striking blue eyes, their mother was a hoarder of magnificent proportions. Ten years after her leaving, her bedroom remained filled with clothes and novels, sketches, scrapbooks and bric-a-brac. It was a sanctuary for her daughter, but more importantly it was a reminder of how big and imaginative a life could be in the most indistinguishable and remote of places.

Edwina walked barefoot across the leaf-littered ground, zigzagging through the gnarled trunks of the fruit trees, clutching the coloured piece of glass. Jed kept close, snuffling and continually whining, as if trying to explain something of great importance. She smiled at the old dog, placating him with a pat, promising him a tasty titbit. As she drew closer to the coolabah tree the shapes strung from the branches grew recognisable. Bottles, cans and tins, many of the labels faded by age, tinkled in the morning breeze. Their mother's habit of attaching an object to the branches had, by the time of her death, grown to the depositing of items on the ground.

At the base of the tree, a pile of debris became a mass of decipherable objects: flowers, feathers, stones, mouldering fruit, coins, nails, rifle shells, and pieces of glass. The tree bridged the boundary between the homestead and the thick scrub beyond, and what had begun life as a Christmas tree, was now Caroline Baker's memorial, a living reminder of a woman's need for artistic expression, of creating beauty where there was none. Edwina carefully added the shard of glass to the mound at her feet, contemplating her own sheer lack of invention.

'Edwina!' Aiden called to her from the veranda. 'There's braised kidney for breakfast.'

'Has Father gone?' She ran back towards the house, Jed loping behind.

'Yes,' he confirmed, the skin of his brow crinkling, 'as has Mrs Ryan. Left you a mess in the kitchen I'm afraid. I must say they were both keen to leave. I'd forgotten how quickly the old girl could move when she puts her mind to it. Even Father had a spring in his step this morning.'

'The scent of money brings out the best in him,' replied Edwina.

'Edwina,' chastised Aiden. 'Anyway, you shouldn't be walking about out here in broad daylight when you're not dressed.'

'Oh, fiddlesticks.' She joined him on the verandah. 'Who is going to see me? Besides, it can't be much past six.'

Shoving his hands in his trouser pockets, Aiden gave her bare feet a disparaging look. 'That's not the point.'

'You sound exactly like Father.'

'If you keep on like this,' warned Aiden, 'I won't tell you my news.'

'News,' Edwina said eagerly, 'what news?' She shook Aiden's arm. 'Do tell.'

'Steady on, E.' He smoothed the sleeve of his 'going-out' jacket.

'My, we are dressed up.' The suit, purchased from a travelling tailor who'd measured Aiden up and then mailed the completed trousers, jacket, vest and shirts, wasn't a perfect fit, but the material was of good quality. She waited obediently, although Edwina couldn't quite stem the tug of disappointment at the new changes in her brother. It was true he was becoming quite the man. But despite his soft looks, Aiden was also beginning to cultivate some of their father's stuffier characteristics.

Hesitantly he began, 'It's about the circus. I spoke to Father about you coming with me.'

'Really?'

'Yes,' answered Aiden, not meeting her eyes. 'He said no.'

Edwina felt her spirits fall, briefly wondering if her brother had even bothered to go into battle on her behalf. 'Oh.'

'He said it wasn't the place for well brought up young women.'

'Rubbish.' Edwina walked into her room, the wire springs of the rumpled bed creaking as she sat on it. 'I've seen the papers after the circus has been to town. Everyone goes. It's a big event and family entertainment. The problem is that Father wants me to stay here for the rest of my life.'

'That's not true, E.'

'Really? And how do you know?'

Jed ambled into the room, snuffling the floorboards. A breeze lifted the leaves outside, blowing them through the open doors and sending them tumbling across the floor.

'So what's this news you have to tell me?' Edwina finally queried.

Aiden was slow to answer. 'I'm to find that Will fellow and give him the money owed. Father entrusted me, so to speak. As it's only for the day, after all. I'll be back before dark.' He cleared his throat. 'I'm taking the buggy.'

Edwina knew her eyes were popping. No-one except their father was allowed to drive it. 'You're taking the buggy? Whatever for?'

Her brother's cheeks reddened in indignation. 'Because, Edwina, being the age that I am it's more appropriate for me to be driving a buggy.'

Edwina walked across the room, crossed her arms and looked her brother up and down. 'Really? So that's why we're looking so shiny this morning. Going courting, are we? Or, more specifically, you're hoping to find someone to court.'

'Don't be ridiculous.'

'And Davidson will be, what, your chaperone?' teased Edwina.

Clearly Aiden had forgotten about the stockman's role in the day's proceedings. 'I'll tell him to wait for me until I'm ready to leave.'

'Wait where?' At the question Edwina could see that her brother's bravado was starting to lessen. In spite of her disappointment she was rather impressed with Aiden's attempt at rebellion. It was no small thing to go against their father's wishes. 'Fine, go.'

'Really?'

'Now you're asking me when you've already made the decision.'

'I thought –'

'Just be careful, Aiden. Father will be in town as well, you know. And don't delay. It's always a push to make the return journey by dark. It would be quicker on horseback.'

She was right and Aiden knew it, but he mumbled something about knowing the way by heart and the longer hours of daylight now spring was here. 'Besides, I've checked the almanac. It's a full moon. I'd take you with me, E, but if Father caught us . . .'

'I know,' Edwina reluctantly agreed. It wasn't worth the inevitable drama that would follow. Although Edwina suspected that any fault would be laid squarely on her rather than her brother. As it was, Aiden was risking their father's wrath if he caught sight of the buggy. 'Be careful. Don't go promenading down the main street.'

Aiden hugged her. 'Thanks, Edwina, you're the best. And don't worry, I promise to tell you everything when I get home.'

With Aiden's departure, Edwina dressed quickly. Although disappointed, there was something quite freeing knowing only she was left at home. Jed padded after her, down the hallway and through to the parlour where breakfast was served. The braised kidney and tea were cold. The fire in the hearth nearly extinguished. Setting the plate of offal on the floor for the dog, Edwina gathered the breakfast things on a tray and walked outside, across the dirt to the kitchen hut.

The room was a mess. Mrs Ryan hadn't bothered to wash the pots and pans. Hunks of meat were soaking in kerosene containers filled with brine, flour covered part of the dirt floor, the pitcher used for drinking water was empty and the door to the wood stove's fire box was open, the coals barely smouldering. Edwina surveyed the hastily deserted area, hanging the few clean cooking implements above the oven. Through the window she could see that the woodpile was totally depleted. The lengths of timber fetched by Aiden were still untouched, yet to be cut into usable pieces.

Edwina sat heavily at the wooden table yearning for a cup of tea, wondering if the labour involved was worth the sweet satisfaction once the hot brew was laced with sugar. Wood needed to be chopped with the axe, the fire coaxed back to life, water fetched from the barrels outdoors, then boiled. She picked at the breadcrumbs on the board. Cut a chunky wedge from the freshly baked loaf. The dough balled in her cheek.

Never would she have thought as a child that their lives would be so altered with their mother's passing. Edwina still recalled their bedtime stories and the way her father would often interrupt their telling, dragging a chair to the end of the bed and sharing his own childhood tales. England's friendly 'Green Man of the Forest' was a particular favourite, although their mother once confessed that Father concocted his own story based on an effigy carved on a tree near his childhood home. How she wished for those happy days.

In the quiet Edwina picked at the hardened calluses on her palms. Her little brother was on his first visit to town without their father as chaperone. That didn't bother her so much. Edwina understood that young women didn't travel long distances by themselves and that society demanded that the fairer sex be constantly chaperoned and cosseted. What did bother her was the way their father continued to treat her like a child.

A dirty cup and saucer was at her elbow, and beneath the cup, what appeared to be paper. She stared at the object, surrounded by other unwashed things, focusing on the size of the item, the folds, the creamy smoothness that was stained, ringed by tea. Edwina didn't want to investigate further for she knew it was her note, her projections, her ideas. Reluctantly she unfolded the paper, peeling apart the stuck notes to reveal her carefully considered sums and accompanying explanations, every word and numeral smudged. Had he even read it? she wondered. Probably not. That was what her contribution, her enthusiasm, was worth to her father – blotting paper for spilt tea.

It would have been easy to cry. To curl up in her room and wait for Aiden's return. To hear his excited stories of his day at Wywanna. The paper scrunched in her fist.

Edwina wanted to see more of the world. And she wanted to be seen. To meet people, to experience different things. She refused to be a carbon copy of her mother, relegated to the small island that was Baker's Run. But there were few opportunities available to her. Edwina was either a daughter, a sister or, in the future, perhaps a wife – although the latter wasn't written in stone for there were a few spinsters and widows in the district. Women considered old maids aged thirty. Women whose potential husbands died in the war. Young women farmed out to look after the households of married brothers or sisters. Daughters compelled to care for motherless families. Edwina chewed on the bread. Thought of the cow that needed milking. Of the butter that should be churned. Of the father that was only interested in her as a dutiful daughter content to obey his rules. What if she didn't want any of those roles? What if she wanted something more? The world was changing. Cars and planes. Shorter dresses. And a great bridge was being built across Sydney Harbour. Edwina realised that if she didn't get out soon, she never would.

❧ Chapter Five ❧

It was noon by the time Edwina reached the outskirts of Wywanna. Hot and tired, she patted Heidi-Hoe affectionately, glancing out from beneath the wide brim of her father's fedora. The thoroughfare was busy. Apart from those on horseback, the sulkies and drays, a number of automobiles motored past, horns tooting at anyone in their path. The road ahead held many travellers, with a few on foot as well. Strangers called out a friendly greeting to Edwina and she lifted a hand in reply, emitting a gruff deep voice that didn't sound quite like her own but was nonetheless, to her mind, clearly contrived. The men rode on followed by a sulky driven by a woman; it was filled to capacity with children, the youngest of which, supported on an older sibling's knee, kicked pudgy legs out the side, a tongue poked in Edwina's direction.

On one side of the road a team of men were cutting prickly pear, their lower legs protected from the death adders the plants tended to harbour by guards fashioned from kerosene tins. Ahead, an irregular line of structures rose above scattered trees. Edwina felt the breath catch in her throat. Now that the town and circus lay within her reach, leaving the property seemed like the absolutely worst decision she had ever made in her entire life. It was one thing to feel sad and sorry for oneself, quite another to rush thoughtlessly ahead without considering the consequences – one of the results of the morning's rash decision-making being the pain in her thighs and bottom. Nearly five hours in the saddle was not for the faint-hearted and it would be with gratitude when her feet eventually touched the ground. She drank thirstily from the waterbag.

'Come a-ways have you, mate?' a passer-by queried.

Edwina made a point of wiping her lips roughly with the back of her hand. 'A-ways, yes,' came her blurred response.

'Be worth it. Nothing like a circus for bringing the girls to town.' The man winked. 'I'm at the stage where I need a wife, but you, lad,' he drew his horse closer, peering at Edwina with interest, 'well, with your soft looks I'll be betting you'll be rolling around in the hay before sundown. Half your luck,' he chuckled. 'I myself was always partial to a taste of the wares. Hard to buy when you don't know what you're getting.' He sniggered and rode on.

Edwina's heart raced. She took another gulp of the warm liquid, feeling the heat of her burning cheeks. Did men really speak that way about women? And was that what was expected of young men? Was that what Aiden intended to do? The very idea of her young brother rolling in the hay with some fast girl absolutely appalled her.

Heidi-Hoe plodded onwards, nickering at every horse encountered. Heavens, she thought, the animal was like her, starved for conversation. The tall mast of the clock-tower, the pale curves of Wywanna's town water tank and a row of buildings of various heights gradually became recognisable. Her stomach grew tight. Soon they would cross the railway tracks and the narrow one-lane bridge that spanned the brown swirl of the river. It was barely a half-mile after that before they reached the town proper. Pulling her chin closer to her chest, Edwina concentrated on arranging her features into a gruff semblance of the male ancestors lining the bedroom mantelpiece. *You can do this*, she told herself, *you can do this*.

'It's a fine day for it,' a man in a dray called to her.

His wife smiled a greeting, shushing the four children in the rear of the wagon. 'Trees are flowering real pretty this year, sir,' she said.

Edwina tipped her hat and nudged her mount forward, just missing a swaggie who glared from between a battered hat and bushy beard. The dogwoods were pretty with their tight clusters of flowers. The trees were one of the features of the area but Edwina could not enjoy the spring showing. It was too late to turn back, although the ghastly comments made by the stranger had quite ruined the adventure. She realised now how silly she'd been, but perhaps it was just as well. She would have to find Aiden as soon as possible and ensure he behaved himself. To calm herself, Edwina concentrated on the people heading into town. The older women still favoured ankle-length skirts while the younger set were dressed in garments of a more tubular shorter style. Edwina was reasonably abreast with current fashion, thanks to the mail-order catalogues they received. Neatly rolled up in Heidi-Hoe's saddlebags were a pair of shoes and a beige day-dress in the current style. Purchased three years ago for the rare occasion when the family attended a funeral or town, it wasn't quite as fancy or as short as some of those currently on show but it would do. Riding dressed as a man was one thing, carrying off such a guise once she was on foot and in a crowd was quite another.

The mob was a happy one. People waved to each other, children talked loudly, some sang songs. It was difficult not to be caught up in the excitement. It was also a perfect way to enter the town unnoticed. Edwina's attire wasn't really much different from what she wore on the farm, except that the suit was comprised of ill-matching pieces. A too-big riding jacket of her mother's passed as a man's suit-coat. Aiden's waistcoat, white shirt and necktie, although firm across her bust, were more satisfactory items, as was the spare pair of trousers that arrived with his new suit.

'I can see it. I can see it,' one child on foot called. Youngsters raced to the side of the road, pointing and crying out in excitement.

In the distance the tops of two large circular tents were visible, each of which were supported by central poles. The tallest flew a bright flag, fluttering in the wind. The pounding of wood was loud and rhythmic and as Edwina watched a third tent sprung upwards, the billowing sides abutting the centre marquee and looking for all the world like a crusader pavilion from a faraway world. A cheer went up from those nearby as the breeze carried the noise of a marching band, the clattering and clash of musical instruments and a strange reverberating, almost guttural sound that was similar to a trumpet.

Instead of continuing along the road, many of the travellers, on foot or on horseback, suddenly left it, detouring across a paddock. Edwina hesitated. Automobiles, drays and buggies were continuing straight ahead along the dirt road.

'This is quicker, mister,' a snotty-nosed boy advised on seeing her indecisiveness. 'We can get through the gate and be some of the first there.'

And avoid the town, thought Edwina. 'And there's a band?'

'Of course there's a band. They parade through the street they do, telling everyone they're here. They arrived on the morning's train. Saw them myself I did. Watched the elephants help unload and then hightailed it home to do me chores.'

'Come on, Ben,' the boy's mother called.

The child ran from the road, the flapping heel of his shoe barely breaking his stride.

By the time Edwina and the rest of the travellers crossed the paddock, went through the gate and found themselves on the open river flats where the circus was located, the shadiest spots were all but taken. The boom of the circus band reached fever pitch and then suddenly stopped. Although a good half-mile away, against the faded greens and browns of the thick trees bordering the river, the colourful uniforms of the band and the white horses leading the procession appeared like something from a fairytale. As Edwina caught sight of two elephants with their grey skin and large flapping ears, children escaped their parents' clutches, running towards the parade. They couldn't get far. A rough barricade manned by burly individuals encircled the spectacular, ensuring that people could only use the main entrance and pay accordingly.

The march soon broke up with the band disappearing into one of the tents and the animals smartly corralled away from the public. A man's amplified voice announced that the menagerie would be open for viewing by the public for one hour only, from 4 pm, while tickets for the main performance were still available. Everyone settled on the grass to wait. Far from being the sizeable crowd that Edwina first supposed, she realised now that there were only thirty or so people scattered about her.

Edwina hobbled Heidi-Hoe near a tree and settled in the shade to rest. There was nowhere close where she could change her clothes and with the parade finished it wasn't worth risking discovery by walking around looking for Aiden. It would be better if she waited for the zoo to open in the hope of finding him there. Daylight travel was a priority. By 5 pm Edwina would need to start heading back to the farm. At worst she would be travelling for an hour or so in the dark before the moon rose. At best she would encounter Aiden and then they could both return home together.

A number of families took advantage of a few hours' rest before the entertainments began. Edwina observed their happy groupings as children played, young couples promenaded and friends and families picnicked. In one part of the paddock, Chinese vendors were selling vegetables, while the smell of roasting meat drew Edwina's attention in the opposite direction. Whole sheep were being cooked on spits and customers were already lining up to partake of the chop picnic. Edwina sat spellbound beneath the tree, intrigued by the sights and sounds and the sheer novelty of being surrounded by people. Soon a number of clowns arrived, wandering around on stilts and contorting their painted faces. The jesters provided much laughter, although it was their presence on the edge of a small, dusty country town that made them unique.

Some of the men were talking about industrial unrest, while church in the morning was the next social outing for many, with a picnic to follow. Others, clearly labourers, complained of their employers and the Chinese who were invading the land. Yet no matter the conversation, what charmed Edwina was the happiness emanating from these people, the feeling that these family and kin not only shared labour but also happily provided care for each other. There was a distinct feeling of mutual support, of reciprocated aid, characteristics of strong family networks that, with only a brother and a father, she had little exposure to. It was nice to be here, Edwina decided. The world was a big place and she'd not had to travel far to find it. Lulled by the warm afternoon and sated by the bread and salted mutton she had brought with her, she closed her eyes.

The ball hit her firmly in the chest. Edwina sat upright, picking grass and leaves from hair and cheek. She wiped at the thin line of saliva seeping from the corner of her mouth. There were ants everywhere.

'Mummy, that man's a woman.' The chaser of the object, a pretty child in a dress the colour of an English meadow, snatched up the ball and ran back to the arms of her mother. The woman tugged her husband's elbow.

Appalled, Edwina searched frantically for her father's ill-fitting hat. The dark brown fedora lay on its side in the grass and she snatched it up, twisting her hair underneath it. The child's comment had attracted the attention of others. While the menfolk were intrigued, the women were most definitely not. They appeared thoroughly stunned, and Edwina wondered what to do next as remarks of 'not seemly', 'unconventional' and 'fast' rippled through those grouped closest to her. It was fine to wear trousers on the farm, to dress like a man when working, for Edwina knew other farm women did the same, but such freedoms did not extend to the public arena. At least not out here.

Not very far away was the Colby Brothers three-ringed circus and here she was a spectacle in her own right. A spectacle that could well be recognised as the daughter of Hamilton Baker.

As the wave of disapproval abated, Edwina heard someone calling out to her. Edwina packed up the remains of her food, shoving the newspaper-wrapped parcels in Heidi-Hoe's saddlebags. Determined to leave immediately, she ignored the man for as long as possible.

'I say, would you like to join me and my friends?'

Edwina turned around slowly. The man before her was tall and good-looking and the cut and material of the suit he wore was, quite simply, top-drawer. He was clearly not from the country, let alone this district.

'We're visiting, you see, and, well, if you don't mind, I'm sure my friends and I would like to ask you a few questions, about being in the circus, that sort of thing.' He took in Edwina's appearance – the ill-fitting suit and waistcoat – his gaze falling on the loosened necktie and tight white shirt, the top three buttons of which were undone from her recent rest.

Edwina hastened to rectify her clothing. The man, who intro-duced himself as H.J. Bellington, was holding up paper cones of peanuts and gesturing to a group of young people who were picnicking next to a black car quite some yards away and separate from everyone else.

'I'm not –'

'Half man and half woman?' H.J. chuckled. 'I know. Too darn attractive for that sort of thing. Do say you'll come with me. We have our very own drinking bar, and I'll be next on the scrounge list for liquor otherwise if they discover I'd seen you and not brought you over. Let me tell you it's impossibly difficult to get hold of the stuff in any decent quantities out here in the sticks. But I'm sure I don't have to tell you that.'

Edwina gathered that the stuff H.J. referred to was alcohol and the invitation to his private drinking bar, as he called it, was in fact to the Model T Ford. There was nothing to do but follow him. She certainly couldn't stay where she was. The fracas regarding her appearance may have ebbed; however, that didn't stop women from giving her quite derogatory looks. 'My horse?'

'Bring him, or her. Whatever. I say, can he do tricks?' asked H.J.

'No.'

'Pity.' H.J. led Edwina through the crowd to the automobile parked right on the edge of the field. With the parade finished, people were entering the paddock to wait until the menagerie opened; earlier arrivals, having been into Wywanna to collect supplies, were parking drays and wagons near the main entrance. Edwina noticed part of the wooden fence was pulled apart, allowing the vehicle closer access to the circus grounds. Three women were lolling on a blanket in the grass while a man was searching for something on the back seat.

'Found it.' The man lifted his head from the vehicle, waving a bottle in the air. 'Beer or champagne, anyone?' The friends all cheered. He met Edwina's arrival with a look of surprise. Tall and dark eyed, he was dressed in a white shirt, bushman's trousers and worn boots.

'And look what *I* found,' H.J. announced their arrival, passing around the peanuts. 'A genuine female circus performer.'

Edwina was horrified. The most glamorous young women she'd ever laid eyes on were taking careful stock of her appearance and trying not to laugh. They were powdered and rouged, with the shortest of dresses showing their knees. And, they were smoking.

'Heavens,' one of the woman commented, 'wherever did you find her?'

H.J. whipped the fedora from Edwina's head, her long hair tumbling free. 'The local hayseeds put up a fuss when they realised she was incognito.'

'How marvellous!' A red-haired woman, introduced as Janice, sat upright. 'And does our guest have a name?'

'Edwina. And I am not in the circus.' She snatched back the hat.

Two of the women giggled.

'I've ridden quite a distance,' continued Edwina, humiliated by the way they were staring at her. 'And apart from trousers being more comfortable,' she retorted, 'it's far more sensible.'

'Good for you,' the man holding the bottles said. He was clean-shaven but there all similarities to his friends ended. There was no brilliantine slicking his hair, no smart edge to his speech. In fact, he could have been about to go out mustering on horseback, based on the casual way he was dressed. 'Are you from around here then?'

'Yes,' she answered.

'Mason usually knows everybody,' Janice advised, holding up a glass for champagne. 'And if he doesn't,' she gave Edwina a knowing smile, 'he will. Soon enough.'

'That's rich coming from you, Janice.' A blonde-haired girl with green-blue eyes smiled prettily at Edwina. 'I'm Louise. Do join us. You probably think we're the most awful people but we're not really.'

H.J. tied Heidi-Hoe to the fender of the car and Edwina found herself accepting a glass of bubbles and sitting cross-legged on the blanket. The women were all close to her age, their stylishly bobbed hair covered by snug-fitting cloche hats.

'Your skin is so brown,' Janice said pointedly. 'How is it possible, when pale and wan is de rigueur, that you can look so unreasonably –'

'Healthy.' The third woman, Debra, blew smoke through her nose, nostrils flaring delicately. 'Maybe she's from abroad. An import from one of those marvellous foreign countries like Italy.'

Mason, lounging against the side of the vehicle, was staring at her, his face unreadable.

'Rubbish, she's a farm girl.' Janice elbowed the pretty blonde. 'You know, Louise, milks cows and that sort of stuff. You can tell she's one of those capable types. Not like us.'

'Heavens,' said Louise, 'do you really?'

Edwina shrugged. 'Doesn't everyone?'

There was a moment's silence and then the group burst out laughing.

She liked champagne. Emboldened, Edwina accepted another glass when it was offered.

'A farm girl you say. I could use a bit of help on my run,' Mason told her. 'It's different in this part of the country. Not at all what I'm used to.'

'That would be the Territory,' interrupted H.J., slurping his drink. 'He's been up there on some godforsaken block tending cattle. Can you believe it? Chasing cattle for six years. Then all of a sudden he arrives in Brisbane and we're off on a road trip to see the world.'

'You didn't get very far.' Edwina took another sip of the fizzy drink.

'Wywanna,' said Mason loudly, 'centre of the universe, isn't it?'

His friends laughed.

'Anyway, not all of us can be pushing pens behind a desk, H.J.' Mason filled his glass. 'University didn't really gel. I did twelve months in an accountancy firm trying to get my head around numbers,' he said to Edwina. 'But the bush is what my family was born into. It's what I'm good at. What I like. There wasn't much point fighting it. And I got a push from an old friend, Mr Gordon of Wangallon Station.'

'Namedropper.' Janice dipped a finger into the glass of champagne and licked it. 'You've heard of them?' she asked Edwina.

'Of course.' Everyone in the bush knew of that family. 'What was the Northern Territory like?' Edwina enquired.

'I was on Victoria River Downs Station. Now that's a place you'd not soon forget. It was a Kidman run once but a British company owns it now. Thirteen thousand, one hundred square miles of undulating country, ridges and plateaux, limestone outcrops and floodplains. And the grasses, there's Flinders grass, Blue grass –'

Janice yawned theatrically. 'Our Mason just loves cows and grass.'

Mason frowned. Edwina guessed by the severity of the expression he was unused to interruptions. 'It's cattle country alright. This sheep-herding thing takes a bit to take to. I'm looking at country further north. A cattle run.'

'That's big enough for his ambition,' interrupted H.J. 'What he's not telling you about the Territory, Edwina, is that it's big and full of blacks.'

'And a bloody good lot of people they are too,' said Mason.

Edwina blushed at the blasphemy.

'Of course you get the odd bludger, the troublemakers, but you find them anywhere. It's the whites that cause the problems, mostly between them and us. I saw some messy things up there. Things that would make a white person hang their head in shame.'

'Oh please, Mason,' begged Janice, 'spare us the maudlin. I don't care about the natives or their problems. They're all meant to be on missions or in orphanages anyway. It's for their own good.'

Mason didn't look convinced. 'Many of them are stockmen. What do you think, Edwina?'

'I feel sorry for them.'

Mason pushed his hat back further. 'I don't think they want your pity.'

Louise changed the topic and Edwina listened to an account of a party the friends attended before leaving Brisbane, where a girl standing on a billiard table had danced the Charleston, ripping the felt with her heels.

'And do you do the Charleston here, Edwina, or the Black Bottom?' asked Debra.

'No.' Edwina knew of the dances, but not the steps involved. She'd never seen either done.

'Well, there's no point bothering to learn now,' Janice told her with a fixed smile. 'They're nearly out of style.' She exhaled cigarette smoke, blowing the acrid fumes in Edwina's direction.

She coughed and did her best to smile, aware of Mason staring at her.

'Drink up,' H.J. urged, 'this is meant to be a party and I'm not going back to the river to cool off any more bottles.'

'Party pooper,' complained Janice.

The next time Edwina glanced in Mason's direction he smiled.

❊ Chapter Six ❊

Hamilton wasn't one for hasty assignations. Lord, he was even speaking like Gloria, he thought as he tied his shoelaces and got up slowly from the bed. He'd scarcely been in Wywanna for two hours and already he was exhausted. He should have taken the buggy instead of riding, he decided, glancing at his reflection in the gilt mirror as he straightened his necktie. At his age, when his free time in Wywanna was happily limited by business, it was important he conserve energy. Still, he couldn't blame Gloria solely for his fatigue. He was a willing participant and, dare he admit it, quite readily led astray. Picking up her day-dress of chocolate silk, the knickers, chemise and stockings, he rested the delicate items across one of the chairs. Mrs Zane, as he occasionally addressed her when she grew tiresome, lay sprawled across the bed, her soft snores punctuating the quiet room.

Closing the door once inside the adjoining sitting room, Hamilton removed a key from his pocket, unlocking the central drawer in the mahogany desk. Inside were a number of folders which he sorted through and, with the correct one found, he withdrew to an armchair, sitting heavily. At his elbow was a decanter of whisky and Hamilton poured a nip of the amber fluid, skolling it in one gulp. 'Better,' he belched, proceeding to study the contents of the folder. The papers within held the details of his current business transactions, which were few. Loans for gambling debts and structural improvements to two small businesses located in Wywanna were the extent of his trade at the moment. Clients were finding it difficult to repay the money borrowed and the few customers Hamilton still dealt with in Sydney and Brisbane were only just managing their monthly interest repayments. Business was tough. But there was relief in sight.

Hamilton glanced over his shoulder towards the bedroom before perusing the sheath of papers. The numbers written in his neat copperplate outlined the accumulating debt on a substantial loan made to an established pastoral family seven years prior. The Ridgeways. Another month had gone past and as Hamilton ran a finger down the neat row of columns, making a brief calculation of the monthly compounding interest, he knew that a meeting with the landholders was long overdue. With the initial capital and the addition of the compounding interest the monies owed to him had grown considerably, to a sum of thirty-four thousand pounds. Why, one could build a most respectable mansion in Brisbane with that amount, or purchase a good parcel of shares, or keep a rural holding in fine running order for years.

The Ridgeways' growing debt was a conundrum. These people were of old money, the holding was large, the livestock considered of excellent bloodline and their wool clips were not to be sneezed at. While not everyone would agree with the current management of the property concerned, everything suggested that there was no reason for this debt to remain outstanding. But it did.

Closing the folder and replacing it in the locked drawer, Hamilton tapped the desktop thoughtfully. For the last seven years, he'd penned a monthly letter to the client reminding them of the interest due and the compounding nature of their agreement.

And without fail their solicitor would respond, noting receipt of Hamilton's advice with formal courtesy. And still the monies remained unpaid. It was unfortunate but at the end of this week the agreed term was up. And Hamilton expected to be repaid immediately, in full. He was glad that the debtors were finally agreeing to a meeting for it really was quite off-putting when a client's hand needed to be forced.

Leaving his rooms, Hamilton walked downstairs. Once outside, he mounted the long-suffering gelding tethered in the shade and trotted the horse down the street. He was still at odds with having to attend the circus this evening and had done his best to wangle his way out of the event. Surely Gloria could have gone with one of her bohemian friends or, better yet, they could have shared an intimate supper in their rooms. But there was no dissuading the woman. He glanced at the upstairs window, feeling outmanoeuvred through a clever mix of titillation and argument. The woman should have been a lawyer.

It wasn't the first time they'd attended one of these travelling shows, and the seats were inconspicuous. However, Hamilton was uncomfortable at public events. He was a loner by nature, a useful personality trait considering his profession, but also wary of flaunting his relationship with Gloria until the matter of a husband for Edwina had been settled. The rich and the well-bred, the two of which were rarely mutually inclusive, were terrible hypocrites.

'Get your lettuce here, bravest hearts you'll find,' yelled a young grocer from his vegetable cart.

At the corner bakery Hamilton purchased two Cornish pasties and continued his journey. Every available wall space along the street was plastered with posters advertising the circus, while the roads were littered with manure. Horses and elephants, wool wagons and parades did nothing for pedestrians he decided. And the band. If he'd heard one more fart of a noise from the wind section earlier he'd have rushed outdoors and shoved something up the dreaded instrument. How was a man supposed to attend to a lover's duties with that fracas going on?

Five minutes later Hamilton reached the corner of Chinaman and Webley streets. Here he turned right, passing the substantial brick edifice that was the Commercial Banking Company of Sydney. The two-storey Edwardian-style building with its open colonnades and domed copper roof was quite the landmark in Wywanna and yet, Hamilton thought with satisfaction, one didn't need such trappings to do business. Traffic was busy for a Saturday afternoon. Horses, buggies, automobiles and pedestrians were heading in the direction of the showground across the river where Colby Brothers had erected their circus tents. It was close to 4 pm and the organisers of the extravaganza were opening their zoo to the public before the commencement of the main show at 8 pm. Hamilton recognised some of the men and women and greeted them accordingly. As usual they were reservedly polite. Having devoured one of the meat and vegetable pastries, Hamilton whistled, throwing the uneaten food to a swaggie walking outside the iron palisade of the courthouse. The man gave him a broken-toothed grin.

Hamilton's destination, The Wywanna Guild, was situated rather conspicuously between two weatherboard post-and-slab dwellings. He dismounted sedately, spending adequate time securing his horse and dusting off his clothes. The Langer family drove past in their open automobile and he tipped his hat, receiving a similar greeting. Excellent, Hamilton thought; it was always important to be seen by those who wanted to be seen as well. And Mr Langer, one of the leading agents in the stock and station fraternity, was yet to be accepted as a member of the Guild.

Pausing at the gabled entrance Hamilton noted the number of tethered horses and the three automobiles already lined up outside. Undoubtedly it would soon be a full house, he speculated.

The Guild President was visiting town for the week and the added entertainment of the circus would be a drawcard for many. Inside he signed the members' book with his usual flourish, surreptitiously checking the names already registered, a tap of a forefinger on the lined page of the ledger the only sign of his approval. This then was the true centre of business for the region, indeed for the south-west of Queensland and beyond, for the greater district of Wywanna acted as a gathering point for some of the largest landholders. And here he was, Hamilton Baker, about to join the crème-de-la-crème of pastoral enterprise.

Hamilton handed his hat to the attendant at the reception desk. 'How are you, Andrew?'

'Very well, thank you, Mr Baker.' The youth discreetly slid a folded piece of paper across the desk. Hamilton quickly pocketed it and in return gave the lad the change in his pocket. 'Thank you, sir.' Andrew stared at the coins. 'You're very generous.'

The words *young upstart* came to mind. Hamilton placed a pound note on the desk, which the boy was quick to grab.

'Your usual table, Mr Baker?' asked Andrew, as he led the way along a short hallway lined with portraits of committee members.

'What do you think?' growled Hamilton.

⋘ Chapter Seven ⋙

Edwina held on to Mason's arm as H.J. purchased tickets for the menagerie. A gruff man was advising people to line up and be quick about it else they'd miss the chance to see the wondrous zoo within. A mix of people of all backgrounds jostled for position around the ticket counter. Edwina smelt lavender water, perspiration and tobacco but there were also softer scents like Pears soap, a heady combination blending with the press of bodies. Were she not clinging to Mason, Edwina may have felt uneasy. Never had she seen so many people in one place at one time.

They waited until the initial queue dissipated but there was still a throng of people within the man-made alley set up next to the circus tents. Lions roared, monkeys chattered and dogs barked as they entered the area bordered by gaudy red cages. Each enclosure held a variety of animals, with only the smallest and the safest creatures part of the petting zoo.

'It's feeding time,' one of the circus attendants announced to anyone who would listen. 'And some of the animals are very, very hungry.'

Mason led the way through the crowd, Edwina holding tight to his arm. For some reason she felt quite light-headed and everything around them seemed extremely funny. Together she and Mason looked at monkeys and squealing pigs, two sheep, white horses in spangled harnesses and a sour-looking donkey. These exhibits received only minimal interest from the rest of the ticketholders. Most rushed forward, eager to see the big cats and elephants.

'Grown lions eat fifteen pounds of beef every day,' H.J. shared, reading from the program as a monkey peeled a banana in a cage. 'Then they have to fast on Sundays in case of over-feeding.'

'Where are the lions?' asked Edwina, feeling a little woozy. The monkey tilted its head, ate a portion of the creamy flesh and returned Edwina's stare.

'At the end, little lady,' a bearded guide advised. 'Save the best for last we do. The best for last.'

'Have you ever drunk champagne before?' asked Mason.

'Of course.' Edwina couldn't recall how many glasses of the fizzy drink she'd consumed, nor who'd purchased the roasted meat sandwiched between bread. But the floaty sensation of earlier was starting to dissolve and she was becoming terribly thirsty. Edwina slipped her hand from Mason's arm, realising with a shudder of embarrassment that she'd been clinging to him.

'The big cats are my favourite,' said Mason.

'I really don't know if I could be bothered seeing the show,' announced Debra loudly, making a point of keeping to the middle of the path as she walked disinterestedly behind them. 'I mean if you've seen one flying trapeze artist you've seen them all. And look at that monkey. It's half bald. And no doubt full of vermin.'

They peered at the offending creature and in response the monkey threw the banana peel through the bars. H.J. and Mason laughed in amusement.

'How disgusting!' Janice lifted her feet one at a time as if avoiding something unmentionable. 'Let's leave and have dinner. I'm absolutely starving.'

'They say,' H.J. interrupted, pointing at the circus program, 'that there is a woman who drives eight ponies and that she turns somersaults on a cantering grey. I'd pay to see that.'

'The horses or the woman?' teased Debra. 'You always were one for sequins. Anyway, I like bears. I saw some bears performing in Sydney and they rode bicycles and walked on stilts.'

H.J. ran a finger down the list of events. 'There's bears as well.'

'Have you been to Sydney?' Mason straightened Edwina's necktie, warm fingers brushing her skin.

'No.' Edwina tucked her hair more securely under her father's hat.

H.J. cleared his throat. 'I say, whoever wrote this has a way with words. "Wolves from the frozen wastelands of the Arctic stand next to the denizens of the African and Asiatic jungles."'

'I heard a story once,' Janice began, 'about a donkey that was painted so that it looked like a zebra. Can you imagine?'

'My father shot one on safari,' H.J. announced. 'The poor animal's mounted on the wall. Sad-looking thing really, but nevertheless impressive.'

Mason led Edwina away from their group. 'You're looking a bit flushed. Would you like to go outside and get some air?'

'Yes, I mean no, I mean tell me about Sydney, Mason.' The thought of fresh air away from the crush of people appealed, but to walk outside with a man she barely knew, alone?

'Ah, where to begin? There are tea rooms and coffee shops and American-style soda bars where you can eat confections like banana splits with ice-cream and cream.'

Debra interrupted. 'Yes, yes. That's during the day, but at night we party. We dance and drink and stay out all hours and then we wake up and do it all again. Are you quite shocked?' Debra lit a cigarette, passing it to Edwina.

She took a puff, her eyes smarting from the smoke.

'Go on. The odd ciggy isn't going to kill you,' Janice enticed. 'I think we're quite corrupting you, aren't we?'

Handing the cigarette back to Debra, Edwina turned to view hamsters running relentlessly around a wheel. She was beginning to dislike Mason's friends. All they did was party and travel on grand ships to places like London. They did everything together, much like a pack of dogs. She couldn't understand why Mason would want to be with them.

It was noisy and congested in the menagerie. Apart from the din made by the various beasts, children screamed and laughed, the adults talked extraordinarily loudly and they were continually bumped by people trying to get as close as possible to the animals on display. Edwina tugged her hat brim lower as two matrons from the town passed by. They stared at Debra's above-the-knee dress and short glossy hair before paling at the sight of the cigarette between her fingers.

'Flappers,' one of the women announced in disgust.

Her companion, dressed in dove grey with a long string of jet beads about her neck, turned her attention on Edwina, showing a flicker of recognition. It was the widower, Mrs Hilton.

'Stuffy old busybodies,' complained Debra.

'They're probably what passes for the establishment out here,' said Janice. 'Food? The extravaganza doesn't begin until 8 pm. We can return to the boarding house and cajole that frightful Mrs Parkinson into cooking us up something edible.'

Edwina recalled the paltry piece of bread in Heidi-Hoe's saddle-bag and the lack of firewood back at the farm. 'Heidi-Hoe,' she said aloud unintentionally. 'I really should go home.'

Mason gripped her arm a little more firmly. 'No-one will take your horse, Edwina. And what is the point of going home? You said yourself your father is staying in the town tonight, so we can take you back there after the circus.'

'I can't go back there.' Overhead the blue sky was now an elongated strip of fading light.

'Why not?'

'Because I have to get home.' The return journey would be long and tiring with most of it in the dark. And Aiden? Where was her brother? Heavens, she'd almost forgotten about him. Regretfully, Edwina knew it was time to leave. She glanced at Mason, knowing the probability of seeing him again was never. 'I must find my brother and get home before it's too dark.' She tripped, falling forwards.

Mason grabbed at her waist, steadying her. When he pulled Edwina close it was more than manners required. 'Just stay a little longer; I want to ask you where you live and –'

H.J. tapped Mason on the shoulder and pointed to Louise. 'Here we go again,' he sighed. 'It's your turn, Mason. You rescue her.'

Louise, cornered some feet away between a tall man in a red jacket and white jodhpurs and a cage full of little dogs with ruffled collars around their necks, stood on tiptoe, waving in an attempt to attract their attention.

Mason, placing both hands on Edwina's waist, lifted her gently to one side, out of the crowd's path. 'Don't move. You know I really don't think I've ever seen anyone look so damn good in a pair of trousers.'

Edwina blushed. It was her first compliment. She lingered next to a woebegone gorilla who clung to the rear of the cage, watching as Mason shook hands with Louise's admirer. It would be best, Edwina decided, if she just slipped away. There was little point in putting off the unavoidable.

'Are we taking her with us?' Debra asked H.J.

Edwina knew Debra meant for her to hear the comment.

'She looks positively dreadful in that outfit,' complained Janice. 'I mean she's a nice enough girl, but do you think it's fair to Edwina to bring her along like a plaything. The poor girl's all starry-eyed over Mason.'

Edwina brushed the worn lapel of her mother's riding jacket, wishing she were somewhere else. Through the cage bars the gorilla let out a dismal moan.

Mason, having rescued Louise from the jodhpur wearer, was navigating them expertly through the crowd.

'It's Mason's call,' said H.J. 'But he looks to me to have taken quite a fancy to her.'

'He's been in the outback for too long.' Debra's tone was slightly bored. 'But who am I to stand in the way of true love for one night? You'll have to rustle up some supplies, H.J.'

'I know, I know. Candy is dandy but liquor is quicker.'

Edwina thought she would be ill. There was a connotation to Debra's words, an awful, unladylike implication. Backing away from the redhead's scrutiny, she pushed through the crowd, feeling the press of bodies swallowing the gap between the dream of the afternoon and her real life. Edwina walked the length of the menagerie, searching for the exit, coming to a halt where the big cats were caged. The lion tamer dressed in blue and gold stood before the long pen telling people to stand back or they'd be eaten alive. Five lions were prowling back and forth across a hay-strewn floor stained with blood.

'Look at that magnificent mane! That power! The strength of the beast! Don't be shy, ladies and gentlemen, boys and girls. This is the only chance you'll get to see them up close. In the cage these lions are pussycats. But in the big top, in centre ring, well that's quite another matter. Have you got your tickets for the show? You don't want to be the only person in Queensland who didn't witness the most breathtaking, the most death-defying act ever performed in the southern hemisphere? Do you?'

The smell of urine and hay mixed with the stench of offal. Edwina tried unsuccessfully to squeeze past the audience. They were hemmed in by the larger number of onlookers at the elephant's

71

enclosure, a cordoned-off area within which the elephant's leg was chained to a stake in the ground.

A slight distance away from the spruiker of all things ferocious stood a grey-bearded man with a deeply pitted face. Children pushed and shoved each other around a wobbly table, the attraction a beautiful lion cub lying on a square of red velvet.

'A shilling for a pat,' the keeper of the cub repeated continuously with a slightly American drawl. 'One shilling only.' Slapping away children's eager hands, he grabbed the mewling animal when a freckled-face youth made a lunge for the baby beast. 'Get away with you, you young rascal! I'll have the constabulary on your doorstep quicker than you can say bread and lard if you do that again. A shilling only. One shilling for a pat of this wondrous baby lion. And I've one for sale too.' He petted the cub roughly. 'Hard to raise the young in captivity it is. The lioness is a peculiar beast. She doesn't like to share. Well, I know women like that.' The comment provoked sniggers. 'Hides her babies away, the lioness does, rather than let you or I take a peek, and then what happens?' He made a slapping noise on the table with his palm. 'Squashed flat they are. And then, then she eats them.'

The assembled people were in awe. Men were fascinated. Women disgusted. Children dumbstruck. Her own problems momentarily forgotten, Edwina cooed with those around her as the lion tamer swapped the baby cub for one the size of a small dog from a cage on the ground.

'I've too many lions. I'll swap this young fellow for a black panther. Anyone? Anyone?'

A ripple of laughter swept through the onlookers.

He lifted the baby lion. 'He's close enough to weaning. Nearly four months old and already a meat eater. Anyone, anyone?'

The cub shrank back into the man's arms. Edwina thought the animal appeared weak, in need of a good feed. She guessed he was the runt of the litter.

'How much?' someone called.

'Twenty pounds.' The man nuzzled the cub, receiving an affectionate paw to the side of his face in response. 'Just like dogs they are.'

'Twenty pounds,' a townie in a tweed cap repeated. 'Anyone would think I had a regular job.'

'What do you want, a regular job or an unregular pet?' the circus man responded.

'In these times I'd take a regular job. The way things are I might have to eat the unregular pet.'

The audience laughed again. The cap wearer bartered for a time, but when it became obvious the cub holder wasn't budging on the price, one by one those watching began to drift away.

'I can give you a fiver, and work off the rest.'

Edwina observed the young man who appeared by her side. He was tall, with a twang to his voice. His suit, although clean, was roughly patched in places. Digging deep in a pocket he retrieved the fiver and, holding it by each end, displayed it proudly. His thumbnails were filthy.

'I'm looking for work. I could work for you, mister. Muck out the straw, feed the animals. Cut wood. I'm good with an axe.'

'Then find yourself a tree.' As the crowd began to disperse, the grey-bearded circus worker sat in a wooden deck chair.

'Five pounds. It's a good offer,' the young man persisted.

'A fiver for a lion?' The man stroked the cub. 'Daft, the world's gone daft.'

'He's not a lion yet,' the lad argued, moving closer to the table that separated them. 'In fact he looks half-starved to me.'

'And who are you? A big cat expert?'

The lad ignored him. 'What will you do if no-one buys him?'

'Someone will buy him eventually, and if not and the mother doesn't squash him flat,' he made a slicing motion across the animal's neck, 'kindest thing.'

Edwina gasped. 'You wouldn't?'

The young man caught Edwina's eye. 'So it's a good deal then. Me giving you a fiver and working off the rest.'

The man appeared to be contemplating the offer. He stroked the cub thoughtfully.

'You won't get much for a dead baby lion.'

'Wise little cove, aren't you?'

The lad persisted. 'A fiver is better than nothing.'

Next door, the elephant sucked up water from a bucket, spraying it at his minder. The onlookers clapped and cheered as the elephant man wiped his face and pretended to chastise the massive beast. In response, the mammal flapped its ears, blinking amber eyes. The crowd roared their approval.

'There'll be another town, sonny. Another place. That's the thing about a travelling circus. There's new towns, new people and new opportunities at every bend of the track.'

'There you are.' Mason was at Edwina's side. 'Sorry about that. Time to go. We thought we'd have drinks and dinner and then return for the show.'

'I won't be coming, Mason,' Edwina explained apologetically. 'I can't. I have to go home.'

'Really? You're sure?'

Mason actually looked disappointed and Edwina, although harbouring mixed feelings towards him after what she'd overheard, was quite desperate to let him know how much she'd enjoyed the day.

'Are we going?' It was Janice. She waited with her three friends, fingers tapping the material of her dress. It was clear by the woman's stance that Edwina's company wasn't wanted.

'I can't, but thank you, Mason.'

'But –'

'You heard what the lady said.' The would-be lion-cub purchaser placed himself slightly in front of Edwina. 'If the lady has had enough of your company, then she's had enough.'

'Is that right, Edwina?' asked Mason. 'Have you had enough?' Although he addressed her, the comment was directed to the stranger.

Awkwardly caught between the two men, Edwina hesitated. How could she possibly tell Mason what a wonderful afternoon it had been with this interfering man standing right next to her?

With her hesitancy Mason's demeanour changed. 'Then you and your friend here best make tracks before it gets dark.' He tipped his hat politely, taking in the other man's worn suit, before rejoining his friends.

Edwina took a step after them and then turned abruptly. 'Who do you think you are? Making a scene like that?'

'Me making a scene?' He gazed lazily at her attire. 'Apart from the fact you're dressed like a man,' he pointed out, 'usually when a woman has a man annoying them and a well-meaning person steps in to help, thanks is in order. My name's Will.' He held out a hand.

'He wasn't annoying me.'

One of the attendants was speaking through a handheld megaphone. The menagerie was officially closing. Edwina and Will were caught up with the departing visitors.

'Move on. Show's over, folks!' one of the circus workers yelled.

In the commotion, the seller of the lion cub bent down to pick up the cage on the ground, leaving the larger cub momentarily unattended. Quick as a flash, Will removed his coat, left the fiver on the table with a pebble on it, snatched up the lion cub and ran.

The cub owner yelled in protest as Will weaved through the remaining people, the lion hidden within the folds of his coat.

'You!' The grey-bearded man pointed a bent finger at Edwina.

'Me?'

'You're his accomplice. I saw you talking to him.'

'I wasn't. I didn't.'

'Saint Julian, you're a woman.' Retrieving a whistle from his pocket, he blew hard and the shrill noise brought a number of attendants running.

Edwina didn't wait to explain. She rushed after the thief, intent on clearing her name, aware that people were searching for her. The departing crowd provided a shield before she caught sight of a man running between two large woodpiles. It was him. She was sure of it. Edwina guessed he would head towards the river away from the town, the circus and the open paddock surrounding the spectacular.

'Stop,' she yelled, giving chase. 'Stop!'

He veered around a camp fire where a group of men relaxed. The workers looked up disinterestedly, calling out a few rough remarks. Edwina ran on. Will enjoyed an impressive lead but it was easy to pursue him. The sun was yet to set and although shadows stretched across the ground, his figure could be clearly seen. Her father's fedora now clutched in one hand, hair flying, Edwina ran past an assortment of smaller tents, a cookhouse, sleeping quarters and an ablutions area and then chased the thief, who was heading straight for the tree line and the safety of the river where he vanished among saplings.

'Ridiculous,' Edwina reprimanded herself, coming to an abrupt halt. She clutched at paining ribs, breathless and annoyed. The sun would set in a blink. The thief was gone and Aiden was yet to be found. There was nothing for it but to try and leave the circus grounds unnoticed.

Something hard struck her head and Edwina landed face first in the dirt. She lay quite still, a throbbing sensation robbing her of all sensibility. She tried to breathe and found she couldn't, attempted to roll over but her body refused to obey. Then the ground began to move and the air rushed into her lungs. Grass and pebbles grazed her cheek, branches bruised her clothed skin. With a shock Edwina realised that she was being dragged across the ground.

'Help me.' The words were a whisper. 'Please.'

She was flipped onto her back. Edwina heard material and buttons rip and then she was fighting, punching into the air, trying to hit whoever attacked her. The sting of a slap stopped her efforts.

'It'll go better for you if you're quiet. What we got here then? A trinket.'

The locket chain was pulled taut against her neck.

'You got any other fancy baubles, girl?'

Edwina gazed onto a crown of greyish hair as the man examined the locket.

Pinned though she was, her fingers scrabbled frantically on the ground for a branch or rock. Feeling something long and rough, she seized the branch. Held her breath. Lifted her arm.

A loud thwack broke her concentration and the attacker fell sideways, the weight of his body replaced by a shadow before a fading sky. The length of timber still in her hand, Edwina felt the wood extricated from her grasp.

'You're okay now, miss. You're okay.'

He was sitting her upright. Doing up buttons. Straightening clothes. When he lifted her into his arms, Edwina began to cry.

❦ Chapter Eight ❧

Hamilton's favoured position at the Guild was a corner table vacated three years ago by the passing of an aged squatter. The spot provided a clear view of arriving members, was close enough to eavesdrop on those seated nearby and yet still afforded the privacy required for business transactions. The main room was dimly lit, the windows all but concealed with heavy damask curtains. Overhead three rather plain light fixtures of six parchment shades apiece shone weakly on the occupants, some of the wealthiest pastoralists in the state.

There were fifteen men in the room and Hamilton knew exactly how much each man was worth, down to the last pound. He knew when their forefathers had arrived in the district, the size of their original and current holdings and their bloodlines. In order to be a member of this club, which the current custodians of wealth and privilege had established for those of their kind, one practically needed a blood test. When it came to the occupation of lending money, however, there were other elements that required consideration. Hamilton made it his business to know whether their enterprises were well managed and fruitful, each man's temperament and eccentricities and if he were faithful to his wife. Mistresses were not uncommon, although he was yet to benefit from any shared confidences.

The risk level was paramount in every transaction and Hamilton had not prospered in his chosen enterprise without first weighing up a client's flaws. He drew the line with gentlemen who couldn't keep their brood in hand. Reputation was everything. Which was why, after some of the scandalous gossip he'd heard regarding wayward children over the years, his own two offspring were kept safely away from the enticements of the modern age.

Hamilton returned the greetings from the clusters of men scattered around tables and at the long mahogany bar. His acceptance into this strictly men's-only domain had been granted for two reasons. Firstly, he *did* know everyone's business and had been instrumental in some middling-sized transactions of land over the past two decades, so keeping him within the circles of influence was to every member's advantage. Secondly, his great-grandfather had once sat on the board of the powerful Australian Agricultural Company in London. This fact in itself elevated him to the higher echelons and almost but not quite obliterated the stain of his profession. It was one thing for a man's services to be recognised and needed, his ancestors approved, quite another for him to be accepted at social gatherings beyond these tongue-and-groove walls.

'Hamilton,' Peter Worth, Guild President and owner of five stations stretching across the border into New South Wales, beckoned him from where he sat in the middle of the room. Hamilton recognised the President's companion, Tom Clyde, whom he'd met on two separate occasions a year ago. The man appeared in Wywanna only if something big was afoot. Owner of a large holding in the Riverina and a racehorse enthusiast of renown, when not dabbling with Melbourne Cup place-getters, he was vocal in selecting the next big thing in racing. Recent newspaper reports had the man stating that a horse named Phar Lap that placed second in the Chelmsford Stakes at Randwick only a few days ago was going to be the next horse to watch.

'Sit, old chap,' said Peter.

Hamilton joined the men, exchanging greetings. Peter Worth was not improving with age. While his frame remained sinewy and upright, gravity pulled at a face marked by childhood illness and flaccid skin.

Andrew was at their table immediately, placing a glass at his elbow, pouring a nip of whisky. 'And will you be joining us for dinner, Mr Baker?' the lad politely enquired.

'Well, of course he will be,' replied Peter irritably, scratching at a pockmarked cheek. His attention wavered between the men at the table and the far end of the room.

Tom gave the boy an encouraging nod as he walked away. 'You have them well t-trained, Peter?'

'It's a simple formula,' the President responded. 'The committee selects staff based on association and merit. Andrew's the son of the Vice-President's manager. If they breathe one word about what transpires within these four walls, well, that's it. One goes, they all go.'

'R-really?' Tom's surprise was evident.

'These days you have to lay down the law with these young whippersnappers.' Peter swirled his whisky. 'Besides, a lad like Andrew, well, being trained up by Carmichael is akin to attending a Swiss finishing school.'

Carmichael, resident chief and manager, had been persuaded to leave the employ of Sydney's Australia Hotel. Blackmailed, Hamilton decided, was too hard a term. The man should have kept his trousers buttoned.

'Hamilton grows wheat,' Peter explained to Tom. 'A waste of fine grazing land in my view.'

'A side interest,' said Hamilton, raising the glass so that the whisky barely touched his lips. 'Having spent more money than I care to acknowledge trying to eradicate that blasted prickly pear I'm not going back to clearing scrub again.'

'Sheep will keep any g-growth under control,' suggested Tom, 'once the land's cleared of this d-dratted pear. Or c-cattle. I'm quite partial to a good line of c-cow flesh.'

'Don't bother trying to convert the man, Tom,' said Peter. 'We've all attempted to make him see the light, but he's been led astray by the likes of those growers who have a penchant for being providers of bread.' He lifted his hands in mock despair.

'Th-there are many in my area who are turning to c-cropping as well,' said Tom. 'But up here in the west, well, the c-climate's too unfathomable for my l-liking. More h-hot than cool, more dry than w-wet.'

Hamilton nodded politely. The dapperly dressed grazier positively reeked of money. A scent so appetising that most people never noticed the stutter that grew more pronounced when he was excited.

'Quite.' Peter held the table's attention as he stuffed the ball of his pipe with tobacco, sucking on the end, a match lighting the weedy filling. 'But tell us, have the Somervilles arrived?' Smoke escaped with each word, his gaze settling on the rear of the members' area where a single door displayed a brass shingle claiming the room as that of the President.

Hamilton wondered what captured Peter's attention. The office was off limits to all but a select few and never without the President in attendance.

'Baker? The Somervilles?' repeated Peter.

Hamilton expected the note in his pocket to contain the details of his upcoming meeting with the custodians of Ridgeway Station. It was best not to conceal what these men obviously already knew. 'I hope to meet with them quite soon.' There appeared to be interest in Ridgeway Station from Worth and undoubtedly Tom Clyde as well, otherwise the Riverina man wouldn't be party to this conversation.

'I see.' For a third time Peter glanced at the door at the far end of the room.

'Is there something the matter?' Hamilton finally enquired.

The office door swung open and a man stepped out into the members' area clutching a folio of papers. A rough-looking individual, with a pistol jabbed through his belt, he sized the room up with an arcing gaze and then walked straight to the bar. He could have been middle aged but it was difficult to tell his face was so sun wizened. The men present backed away slowly and fell silent. Hamilton stood with the others, not knowing the reason, conscious of the scraping of chairs and then a period of wordless waiting. The stockman at the bar ordered a rum, a tumbler full, and drank it straight. Then he lurched back against the polished mahogany, perching on his elbows, a Cuban-heeled boot resting on the brass guard running the length of the bar.

The second man who exited the President's room was barrel-chested and tall. He glanced about the Guild's interior, sharp-eyed, knowing.

Hamilton felt the air leave his body as Angus Gordon, not more than thirty years of age, placed a battered wide-brimmed hat on his head and, singling out the President, approached their table.

'Peter,' the two men shook hands, 'appreciated.'

'Not a problem, Mr Gordon, anytime.'

Hamilton shuffled forward but the boy-man was already leaving, the other members clearing a path as he strode out of the club, followed by the stockman.

'Be seeing you, Pete. Thanks for the drink,' the stockman said as he left.

'No problems, Luke. Dinner next time you're in town?'

'You know I'm not the indoors type.' He smiled good-naturedly.

'Come with me, gentlemen,' said Peter.

Hamilton and Tom followed the President to the office, their progress keenly followed by the other members, Hamilton still trying to process what he'd just witnessed. 'I didn't know the Gordons were members?' he said as the normal sounds of the Guild started percolating once again.

'They're not.' Once inside Peter flicked on the light, gesturing to the men to settle themselves in the comfortable leather armchairs. Hamilton was instantly at home, reminded of the plush Sydney offices he once had. With the thought came the familiar feeling of loss.

'What are they doing in Wywanna?' asked Hamilton. The President's office was lined with darkly polished timber. A bookcase filled a wall, its contents more suited to a solicitor's rooms than a private men's club.

'Part of their wool clip is coming through here and they're looking at land. I have no idea where,' explained Peter. 'It's only the second time I've seen young Angus. Luke, on the other hand, can be relied upon to pass through here every three years or so. He never got droving out of his blood.' He sat at a large desk, its surface cluttered with rose-coloured folders tied with string, a bronze cow holding down a sheaf of loose papers.

'But he's –'

'Half-brother to Angus?' completed Peter. 'Yes, unlike most dynasties with more than one son, Luke wasn't interested in taking on the reins of the business. It makes for a much easier succession.'

Tom remarked on the age of Angus Gordon; Hamilton, however, wasn't interested in such things. Behind the desk was a map of the world, British sovereignty coloured in pink. Hamilton fixed on the place of his ancestors while contemplating Peter Worth deferring to another. The stepping stones in life may well be spaced differently but there was still water to be crossed no matter your station in life.

'Any thoughts as to the Somervilles' intentions?' asked Peter.

Hamilton could quite easily hazard a guess, but it was not any business of Worth's, at least not until he'd ascertained the most advantageous position from his own viewpoint. But he knew how to play the game, perhaps better than Peter Worth, who'd taken up his seat behind the desk with a smile verging on smug. 'No. I have a somewhat tenuous relationship with Ridgeway Station's manager. Mr Fernleigh and I are not on convivial terms.' Admittance to this inner sanctum was not to be treated lightly. There was some joy in that.

'A matter of straying stock,' the President explained to Tom. 'Still, requesting a meeting with a neighbour – yourself, Hamilton – would suggest they want to divest themselves of the property.'

Hamilton nodded. 'It's my understanding that the Ridgeway twins came of age last year in regards to the terms stipulated in their parents' will.'

'They are in their twenties?' asked Tom.

'Mid-twenties, I believe,' answered Hamilton. 'I presumed they would list the property immediately; however, the children may well have wanted some time to consider their options. Their parents were very fond of the property. Perhaps it is hard for them to sever ties so quickly.'

'Good people, the Ridgeways. You knew them, Hamilton?' asked Peter.

'Yes, reasonably well.'

'The wife was delightful, but Ridgeway senior was always a little wild. Very interested in cattle, at one stage. Had a good run in North Queensland around the turn of the century, while his brother and father ran the riverboat business in New South Wales. Made a fortune, those two did, before the railways took over, while Ridgeway eventually sold out to a syndicate and came here.'

'And he did well during the war,' said Hamilton, 'what with wool and the demand for tinned meat, but then it all unravelled. First the father died, then the younger brother on the Western Front and then Ridgeway and his wife in that car accident.' Peter poured rum into three crystal tumblers. 'The children rarely come home.'

The men raised their glasses in unison.

'Here's health. And the uncle, Somerville, he's on the mother's side, Hamilton?' asked Peter.

'Yes, but I know very little about him.'

Peter took another sip of his drink. 'I'm interested in the Ridgeway holding, Hamilton. It would link two of my properties together, giving me a chain of runs with good water.' He paused as if for effect before tugging at the frayed cord of the world map. The linen parchment furled upwards, slowly revealing another map before finally spinning closed.

Hamilton leant forward, resting the tumbler on his knee. Here was a chart he'd never seen.

'This shows the major pastoral properties in New South Wales and Queensland. Mine are in green, Tom's purple.'

'You p-put me to shame,' commented the southerner.

'And the red?' asked Hamilton, drawing attention to a land mass that outdid the President and Tom combined.

'The Gordons' of course.'

It was really quite a staggering thing to see a graphic representation of two states' agricultural land, divvied up into various sized stations by the biggest pastoralists. 'And what are those white spaces?' asked Hamilton, trying not to stare at Peter Worth's holdings, which Hamilton was sure would engulf a number of small countries on the world map.

'Anything under twenty thousand acres isn't worth bothering noting ownership.'

That, Hamilton thought, was a touch rude.

Peter pointed to his properties, then noted the position of Wywanna and Ridgeway Station. The holding was indeed in a prime position in relation to his enterprises. Hamilton could quite understand why he was interested in it. Everyone was trying to emulate Kidman and the Gordons. Droughtproof their holdings. Increase their acreage. A linking of land, or at least properties positioned along a market route with water, was the best way to accomplish this.

'As you can see,' continued Peter, 'Ridgeway would be of great value to me.'

'And I'm k-keen to see such a p-purchase,' interrupted Tom, 'for my d-daughter Eliza is to m-marry Peter's youngest, Lloyd, and I would like her situated closer to civilisation. Well, W-Wywanna at least.'

'My congratulations to the both of you,' offered Hamilton, now understanding the common ground that brought the two men together.

Peter dismissed the good wishes as he relit his pipe. 'It's early days, old chap. They are yet to meet.'

'You're n-not interested in it, Hamilton?' asked Tom.

'No, no, five thousand acres is enough for me. I shall leave the pastoral empire-building exercise to those best suited to such enterprises.' Yet, it was a sobering thing to see the apportionment of land and the few who held it.

'Good. I didn't want to have a battle on my hands, not over a piece of dirt. Not that I think you'd do that, Hamilton, now you know my intentions. Too much of a gentlemen for that,' Peter concluded before his brow furrowed. 'But if you've no interest in land, what do you do with your money? Shares. That's it, isn't it?'

Hamilton gave an enigmatic smile. He was a recent convert to the share market having invested six years ago, although his previous business ventures were far wider than these good men could ever hope to know.

'I dabble myself,' Peter revealed, 'in a very limited way. I have a great adversity to placing my money at the whim of the economy. Too changeable for me. And you know that financial expert, Roger Babson, is talking about a crash.'

'Yes, well that p-prediction did shake th-the markets,' commented Tom.

Peter studied the map before him. 'Commodity prices continue to fall, unemployment is rising. The papers are full of stories about men leaving the cities and trudging through the countryside looking for work and the economy is already stagnant. No, I'll stick to my land.' The map of pastoral ownership was concealed once again by the faded world chart.

'Th-that was a depressing outline.' Tom swirled the contents of his glass.

Peter gave his friend a perfunctory frown. 'So, Hamilton, now you know my interest, I'd like to see the matter attended to in a timely manner. There will be attention from other parties, specifically the Gordons I'd imagine, and with that in mind I'd like initial negotiations kept quiet. And to that end, if we are successful I would like you to handle the sale, arrange a deposit. In short, do what you do.'

'Of course.' Hamilton was already calculating the property's value, the size of the deposit required and the funds he had at his disposal. This was the transaction he needed. A deal to cement his reputation and boost his income. It was perfect.

'Well, I promised my wife I would take her to the circus this evening. Acrobats, lions and clowns.' Peter sounded less than interested.

'Perhaps I shall see you there,' Hamilton tested. 'I am relegated to escort duties myself.'

The President appeared impressed. 'I was wondering when you were going to dazzle dusty Wywanna with Mrs Zane's company again. The lady in question,' the President explained to Tom, 'is the grand-daughter of Lady Perpetua Wilkins of Devon.'

'Well done,' said Tom appreciatively. 'If a man is going to put his f-foot in the s-stirrup a-again, the effort must be worthwhile. It is some time since your wife's passing, isn't it?'

Hamilton was not one for the past. 'Five,' he told them, although Caroline's incarceration in an asylum was a good decade ago, making her dead to him for many years.

'You should be remarrying,' suggested Peter, 'especially with such a pedigree on your arm.'

Worth and Clyde proceeded to discuss the advantages and disadvantages of title while Hamilton enjoyed the rare pleasure of a cat-and-cream smile. Did that mean that Gloria and he would be accepted? While his lover was blessed with beauty, lineage and wealth, she did nonetheless have a rather notorious reputation. Gloria's elopement with a croupier at a casino in Monte Carlo quite startled the establishment and the ensuing years did nothing to enhance her reputation, especially when she divorced him. His lover was most commonly seen as being part of the fast set, very fast. Worse, she was a businesswoman with money, old money. Beauty, intellect and unfettered free will. A definite challenge for the English male, but perhaps not so much in Australia where women had held the right to vote since Federation.

'Keep them satisfied,' Peter advised, discussing the management of the weaker sex, 'but not so satisfied that there is expectation. And your Mrs Zane, Hamilton?' enquired Peter. 'She maintains a house in Wywanna?'

'Yes, west of the central business district,' answered Hamilton. So the President was suddenly interested in his relationship. Not that he wouldn't know everything there was to know about Gloria. The fictitious lung condition that required dry air, her house and the rooms where they met. Was he expecting an invitation? Hamilton doubted it. If Peter Worth stepped foot inside Gloria's abode it would mean instant acceptance of Hamilton and his lover by the greater Wywanna district. Worth knew how much power he wielded and he wasn't about to show such largesse unless it was of benefit to him.

'She is quite the modern businesswoman, I hear.' Peter's tone was flat, if questioning. 'And I believe her gatherings are very entertaining.'

Hamilton smiled. 'Indeed.' Gloria partied with a motley assortment of bohemians, artists, musicians and singers who literally appeared out of the woodwork, or scrub in their case, whenever she arrived in town.

'And Mrs Gloria is an acknowledged beauty,' remarked Tom with a knowing smile.

The conversation had come full circle. It was a query, Hamilton decided, as to whether he and Gloria would wed. Here, ensconced in this office, there was never going to be a better time to mention his quandary. 'I am conscious of being father to a motherless twenty-year-old daughter.'

'She needs a mother?' asked Peter, a probing look in his hazel-flecked eyes.

'A husband at th-that age,' suggested Tom. 'It is so much easier with sons.' He toyed with an unlit cigarette and sat back thoughtfully. 'If they sow some w-wild oats, well good luck to them I say. A b-bit of adventure and a few broken hearts stands us in good stead, but d-daughters. Women are my nightmare and my joy. My young g-girls in particular have been urging me to send them abroad. But Europe's not the same since the war. B-beggars everywhere. A shortage of labour. Half the world is filled with d-decimated c-countryside, bombed-out buildings and starving people; the rest, returned soldiers w-wandering around in a d-daze, with womenfolk scared of losing their jobs. And we know that's n-not going to happen. I mean, who needs to employ a verified war hero when you can keep hiring a girl for less than half price.' Tapping the cigarette on the desktop, Tom lit it with a flinty match. 'And then we have th-this t-treaty thing. If you ask me th-the G-Germans will be m-mad at us for a l-long t-time to come. Reparations is o-one th-thing, the wholesale b-bleeding of a c-country is quite a-another.'

'I certainly wouldn't send my Edwina abroad,' said Hamilton, trying to turn the conversation.

Peter voiced his agreement. Knocking out his pipe and placing it aside, he paused thoughtfully. But much to Hamilton's frustration there were no immediate suggestions. Surely they knew of some family with a second or third son who needed a wife. Money wasn't an issue. In fact Hamilton would be satisfied with a poor man of breeding. What he needed most was a good name.

'Marriages are such t-tricky things.' Tom puffed at his cigarette as if his life depended on it.

At least the word was out. In a matter of days the district would know that Hamilton Baker was shopping for a husband for his only daughter. But perhaps he needed a form of enticement that might soften the fears of aligning with a man of his profession. 'My father was a great believer in substantial dowries.'

Tom ashed a cigarette in a brass saucer, Peter concentrated on re-stuffing his pipe. For the first time since sitting down Hamilton was aware of the other members outside the closeted office walls talking, laughter at the bar, the clash of balls as men played billiards in the adjoining room. Desperate. He'd sounded too desperate. Hamilton finished his rum. How ill-advised to verbalise the one thing that no-one ever talked about. Money.

Tom finally spoke. 'A fact not to be taken lightly.'

'It was good to see you, Hamilton,' said Peter, politely dismissing him. 'You don't mind, do you, old chap? Tom and I have much to catch up on. You'll keep us informed about that other matter with Somerville?'

Hamilton agreed that he would and, taking leave of the men, shut the door to the President's office where he had experienced the extraordinary sensation of bearing witness to the dividing up of the pastoral world. Normally he would have joined another party, ensuring he didn't dine alone, but there was too much to think on.

Young Andrew appeared, taking his order for the evening meal as soon as Hamilton returned to his table. 'You're dining early this evening, Mr Baker. Do you think everyone will?'

The poor lad was undoubtedly eager to attend the entertainments on the river flats. 'I have no idea.' He ordered the French onion soup, wild bush turkey with bacon and a glass of champagne, declining dessert with the knowledge that he would have to endure a late supper.

The fact that Peter Worth called on him to act on his behalf in the matter of Ridgeway Station was cause for celebration. This was the type of transaction he'd yearned for. Working with and for a respected pastoralist. Being accepted. Trusted. Hamilton would have shouted the men at the bar were discretion not imperative. Instead he took a gulp of the champagne Andrew set by his hand, beaming into the bubbles. Then he read the note received on arrival. Somerville was due to arrive on Monday's train. Which made him wonder who his children had seen driving around Ridgeway Station in a Model T Ford? The paper scrunched in his fist. No upstart cash-rich grazier was going to get a foot in the door of Ridgeway Station without him being involved. He would have to cut the speculator off at the pass, so to speak, and somehow bring forward the meeting with Somerville. Hamilton was on the cusp of killing two birds with one stone, ensuring repayment of a significant debt and ingratiating himself with Peter Worth and Tom Clyde. And, by Jove, he wasn't about to let the opportunity slip through his fingers.

⋘ Chapter Nine ⋙

'We always get drifters and no-hopers hanging about. Travelling shows entice the worst of men. 'Course, I shouldn't be saying it with your lady friend having recently been attacked, but a woman shouldn't be out and about at sundown. Not these days. I mean the world's a-changing. Too fast for my liking. But it's a-changing. Of course, I blame the war for the state of young women today. Working in factories and the like. And it's worse out here. Most of the young women work like navvies they do. 'Course that doesn't mean a lass should be walking about unchaperoned, dressed like a man. And wandering around here, out of the public area? Well, where I come from we'd say she was asking for a bit of rough, if you get my meaning. Silly young thing.'

'As I said, it wasn't her fault,' a man replied.

'Never is, is it?' answered the woman. 'Excepting that the lass told you that she came here by herself. What woman does that, dressed like she is? She ain't like you and me, you can tell by the look of her. You can put a woman like that in a potato sack but it don't hide the quality of the goods.' She gave a weak cough. 'And you, what's your caper then? Do you make a habit out of rescuing women? Handsome young man like yourself and all. If you feel inclined you could save me.'

'I'm looking for work. I can do most things.'

'It'll take a bit to calm Riley, with you having nicked his cub. I'll be in for a right telling-off as it is, if he finds out I've helped you.'

'He only would have killed it.'

Edwina lifted the heavy compress partially covering her face, frowning at the half-light. She wasn't dreaming then. There was a man and a woman sitting next to her.

'Maybe, maybe not.' The woman belched and drank heavily from a flagon. 'Some cove would have purchased it eventually. If not out here while we're travelling through the sticks, then once we arrived at a bigger town. Either way, it ain't a pet, you know, lad. One of these fine days you'll be searching for another circus or zoo to hand it back to before it kills you.'

'And work?' the man persisted.

'There's so many looking for work. You all seem to think that a travelling circus has an endless supply of jobs. We don't, you know. We have the performers and then we have the workers who set up the tents and care for the animals, that sort of thing. There's not much in between. And there ain't much coin at times either. Of course, if you're willing to work for food that's another matter,' the fat lady explained. 'There's plenty here that work for food and the joy of seeing the world.'

'So, if I was taken on, would I get to go abroad then?'

The fat lady lowered three heavy chins. 'I was talking figuratively, lad. You'd see the bush on our regional tours. No, the days of us travelling to the likes of America are long gone. It's the filmums, you see, and the talkies. Everybody wants to see Clark Gable and watch the newsreels. No, the days of travelling overseas, well, the golden years are gone. We ain't even as popular in the cities these days. But out here, well we're still the only major entertainment you folk get.'

The man peering at Edwina was the thief she'd given chase to. He smiled encouragingly, the skin creasing at the corners of his eyes. She clutched at the blanket, rough against bare skin.

'You're awake, love? Good, good. A cup of tea with a dollop of rum always helps. That and a bit of a rest.'

Edwina was lying on a camp bed, the blanket protecting her modesty although she noted she still wore her brother's trousers and a chemise. A huge woman, barely contained within a purple gown, sat next to her. Shaped like a pyramid, white rolls of flesh grew in staggering proportions so that Edwina half expected the bottom of the lady to be pooled on the ground.

The fat lady bit a length of cotton and, stabbing a needle in a pin cushion resting on a massive thigh, held up Edwina's shirt. Tiny eyes in a pudgy face surveyed the handiwork. 'Work of art, if I do say so myself.'

The shirt was roughly stitched. Part of the shirt tail was longer than the other. The thief, Will, nodded approvingly. 'Good bit of work, eh?'

Maybe, Edwina thought, she really was dreaming. If she was it was a nightmare.

'Get yourself dressed then,' the fat lady commanded, pleasantly but firmly. 'I've done what I can for you, but this ain't no hospital.' Handing Edwina the mended shirt she pointed to a three-panelled dressing screen standing at the foot of the bed.

The screen was painted with a faded, dirt-smeared woodland scene of nymphs and castles, with her clothes flung untidily across the top of the room divider. Gripping the blanket, she sat up slowly. The pain in her head, although having eased a little, still throbbed terribly.

'Do you need some help?' Will was beside her, offering a hand.

Edwina stemmed the bile rising in her throat. Hadn't he caused her enough trouble already? She steadied herself, ignoring the man and then, standing carefully, stepped shakily behind the curtained area. There had indeed been something strong and sweet in the tea she'd drunk. It helped clear her head, but just the same, Edwina leant on a chair for support while dressing. Her head ached terribly and she'd been sick twice after Will found her; Edwina recalled that at least. The attack itself was a haze. The hit on the head, being dragged across the ground, that was quite clear. She dry-retched.

'If you're going to be sicking-up again,' the older woman sighed, 'do it outside. If there's one thing I can't abide it's sick. Takes a day to get the stink out of the place it does.'

Through the flimsy partition the outline of the thief and the fat lady appeared very close. A kerosene lamp accentuated their silhouettes wavering on the canvas wall of the tent. Edwina emerged, dressed but shaky.

'Thank you, I –'

The fat lady eased herself into a standing position, the large travelling trunk she sat upon creaking as if with relief. She waved away the gratitude, the skin on her arm wobbling in meaty chunks. 'You get yourself home, young lady. I've a show to get ready for.'

Will thanked the woman profusely.

'*You* can come back, you know, I'll feed you. A girl like that, well, she'll only be trouble.'

'Thank you, but we better go.' With a hand under Edwina's elbow, Will steered them out of the tent. Flares had been lit here and there and faceless people wandered about in the dark. For a moment he hesitated, then, with their course decided, Will whispered, 'This way.' Animals bellowed, clowns rode past on bicycles and the tempting scent of cooked mutton wafted on the air.

'Come on,' Will urged, tugging at her arm.

Edwina winced and drew back.

'I'm sorry. Did I hurt you?' He took her arm again, gently. 'We can't hang around here, miss.' He stopped as an Indian with a trailing headdress stomped past. 'I don't have a mind to be explaining ourselves to anyone else. We best get back to the public area as quick as we can.'

The pale walls of the big top towered over the smaller tents. Although still dazed, Edwina reluctantly understood that she needed Will's help. It was a dependency she wished she could avoid, for, if not for him, she wouldn't be in this awful situation. They passed canvas shelters and camp fires, people's features highlighted by flickering flames as they sprawled on the ground. One group of men were arguing good-naturedly about whether Wywanna was the best country town they'd passed through on the tour. 'Then this cove appeared with extra hay. Extra hay. No charge he said. Just wanted his little'uns to be able to pet one of the monkeys.'

'You have to keep walking.' Will drew her away from the men.

'I am,' snapped Edwina, marvelling at her ability to stay upright. The further they walked the more exhausted she became. All she wanted to do was crawl into a dark corner and hide.

Ahead the creamy sides of the big top grew near. Up close, the canvas walls were dusty and dirty, not at all the glistening pavilion that had billowed into existence earlier that day.

'The fat lady was right, you know. Whatever were you doing here dressed like that and alone?'

'None of your business.' Edwina slowed and instantly an arm was about her waist moving her forward again. It was an effort to walk, especially with the fresh air, and forced movement increasing the throbbing in her head. But she needed to concentrate. She was a practical, resourceful woman, one who often worked like a man. Now, she determined, was the time to think like one, to be strong, to get home to the farm. Edwina bit her lip; oh, but it was hard, so very, very hard.

'For someone needing help, you've got an uppity air about you. Must come from having money I guess.' Wait here.'

Will was gone before Edwina could answer, slinking past a stack of barrels and into the shadows. She waited nervously, huddling into her jacket. There was no disguising her sex now. The loss of her father's hat rendered her totally exposed to the world. Alone, the noise of the animals grew quite pronounced. Edwina listened to the chattering and growling, braying and barking as the shadow of a tree stretched across the wall of the big top. The branches crept across the surface, moving ever so slightly in the wind. It was with a feeling of relief when a few minutes later Edwina heard the crunch of gravel and Will reappeared by her side. 'Where did you go to?'

'Nowhere.'

Edwina didn't persist, she didn't have the strength, although she noted something was now slung around his shoulder.

'This way,' her companion directed, leaning slightly forward as if bowed by added weight.

Keeping the marquees to their left, they slipped under a railing and, following a short roped-off area, found themselves at the entrance to the menagerie. In the distance the faint lights of Wywanna shone. The sight of the familiar cheered Edwina, albeit briefly. Her father was only a couple of miles away and yet she wouldn't go to him, couldn't go to him. The situation Edwina found herself in was beyond her.

'Are you alright?' asked Will.

'I . . .' Edwina drew her gaze from the town, from civilisation, to the dense blackness of the bush and the direction of home.

'Look, I know you've had a bad time of it, but we have to stick with our plan and get you home.'

'I don't know if I can go much further,' she replied.

'Sure you can. A girl like you? Well, I bet you could do most anything you put your mind to.'

She could hear the smile in his voice, the kindness. Without warning, Edwina burst into tears. 'W-what p-plan?' she asked, stemming the moisture in her eyes.

'What we talked about earlier,' said Will, politely ignoring her distress. 'Don't you remember?'

Edwina shook her head, gave a weak no in answer.

'Well, don't worry. I'll get you home,' Will promised.

'B-but you don't even know me or where I live,' sniffed Edwina.

Taking her by the hand, Will led them across the paddock. 'Of course I know you. You're Edwina Baker. You rode out twice with your father and brother to where we were ringbarking last year. I remember the day because it had been a while since I'd seen a woman, and the men, well they talked about your coming. You being your father's daughter and riding about like a farm girl, dressed like a man. I guess they thought you'd be playing the grand lady at home or at least getting about in one of them fancy riding turnouts the posh people wear. But you weren't like that at all. When you smiled at us, every man to a one thought you'd smiled at them. I know that for a fact because it was argued about that night around the fire. Anyway, I saw your brother Aiden earlier. I was a bit surprised your father was so intent on seeing me paid. But I'm grateful. Not many people would bother doing right by a man like me.'

Edwina gasped. 'You're Will Kew?'

'At your service.'

'You saw Aiden?' She clutched at his arm. 'Has he left? Do you know?'

'Shush,' he told her. Will stared warily into the darkness. 'I'd imagine so. I asked if he was staying to see the show, but he said he had to get back to the farm. And then he left. You just missed him in the menagerie, you know. Why, it can't have been by more than ten or fifteen minutes.'

'You're sure?'

'As sure as a man can be.'

'Oh.' Edwina couldn't choke back the pain any longer. Her tears came in the form of gulping sobs and she found to her embarrassment that she couldn't stop crying. Will observed her distress awkwardly and then very gingerly drew her closer so that Edwina's cheek pressed against his shirt.

'Why weren't you with your brother?' he asked with concern. 'Why did you come alone? It's a fair ride for a girl.' His accusation was tinged with admiration.

'I wasn't allowed to come and I wanted to see the circus,' replied Edwina. Freeing herself from his embrace, she wiped at the tears with a jacket sleeve.

'And I wanted to join the circus, so that makes us a right pair, doesn't it? Guess I'll have to find another vocation,' declared Will with an edge of resignation. 'I'm not saying they would have given me a job but I guess I didn't do myself any favours by way of introduction either.'

Inside the big top the band could be heard warming up. From somewhere a whip cracked.

'It's very dark,' sniffed Edwina.

'The stars are out. Best enjoy them before the moon takes all the limelight.'

Groups of people waited in the paddock for the circus to start. Camp fires glowed. Edwina gave vague directions to where Mason's automobile was parked earlier, concerned as to what had become of Heidi-Hoe. It was with relief when they found the mare near the same tree Edwina rested at on arrival at the grounds. It was also a sure sign that Mason and his friends were gone.

Will put his foot in the stirrup and flung himself up into the saddle. 'Come on.' He extended a hand, an overly large swag slung across his shoulders.

'What are you doing?' asked Edwina.

'I can hardly leave you to make your own way home. Besides, I need a job.' He grinned. 'Temporary like.'

'A job?'

'Not ringbarking, no I'll not be camping with that lot again,' said Will adamantly. 'I'm thinking you might need someone to cut your wood, or make repairs to fences or buildings.'

Edwina didn't argue. The thought of having someone accompany her home was a massive relief. And once they were back at the farm, surely Aiden would solve the problem of Will Kew. Heidi-Hoe whinnied in annoyance as she added to the weight on the mare's back.

'You best move up and hang on a bit, miss. I'll not be held responsible if you slide off in the dark.'

Heidi-Hoe walked off at a smart pace. 'Thank you,' said Edwina tiredly.

'For rescuing you? Well, it's a strange thing when a woman abuses you for a good deed and then gives chase, but I'm nothing but a gentleman.' He spoke softly, a smile in his voice. 'That's two rescues today. I reckon you owe me, miss.'

'They thought I was your accomplice,' replied Edwina, feeling totally drained as they turned through the gate heading away from the river flats and the circus. 'That's why I came after you. They thought I helped you steal that cub.'

Will extended an arm, pulling her close behind him. 'I'm sorry.'

A warm bulge hit her stomach. Edwina felt the length of canvas slung across Will's back, thinking at first it was a swag. She then pulled apart the taut cloth and delving inside touched something warm and furry. 'You took the baby lion?' This was unbelievable. 'Why in heavens name didn't you return it? You could have left it with that fat lady.'

'That *fat lady's* name is Jacqueline,' said Will stiffly. 'And the cub would most likely have died. Besides, it's not much of a baby. It might be the runt of the litter, but the little fella must weigh close to twelve pounds. You needn't fear him though, miss. Jacqueline gave him a feed of meat laced with a good portion of rum. I reckon he'll sleep for most of the way.'

'You must take him back right now,' demanded Edwina.

'No.'

'You must. If someone finds us with him –'

'No,' said Will adamantly, 'I saved him. I don't like killing things or watching things killed. Or knowing they could be killed. Especially harmless things. There's just no need for it.'

Edwina recalled the conversation around their dining-room table at the farm. It seemed like a lifetime ago. 'So I've heard,' she replied testily. 'But you can't bring it with us. I mean, if anyone comes looking for it we'll all be in trouble.'

'You owe me,' replied Will.

Edwina disagreed.

'Would you like me to take you into town instead? You can report the attack, and my stealing, and explain to one of the coppers why Hamilton Baker's daughter is riding around with a worker and dressed like a man.'

Heidi-Hoe reached the dirt track leading into Wywanna and then, following her instinct, the mare turned left and began to head home.

⊰ Chapter Ten ⊱

'Wonderful, wonderful,' exclaimed Gloria as the small dogs with their ruffled collars and hats were escorted from the main ring by a sour-faced clown. Trailing this act was a woman of humungous size whose only contribution to the evening's performance appeared to be to walk around the periphery of the ring, sitting down where she could every few feet so that the folds of her body appeared to mass at her feet.

'Superlative,' responded Hamilton flatly. The one benefit of the circus was the dark interior. He didn't need to ensure that his face was arranged pleasantly, nor was it noticed when he dozed off now and then. As they waited for the next act, the flying whatevers, who promised to treat the spectators to the most death-defying of acts, he scanned the tiered benches for the tenth time, noting dismally the eight assembled gentlemen of the Guild committee, including Peter Worth, who were seated in the front row. Clearly all had booked together, with their wives. He drummed fingers irritably on a thigh as attendants began to set up a large net beneath the area where the trapeze artists would soon be spinning through the air. He'd made great progress this afternoon, but there was still a distance to travel.

Gloria clasped his tapping hand, squeezing it tight. 'Cheer up, my dear,' she said sweetly, 'maybe one of them will fall.'

If only he could be so lucky. Besides, he was trying his best. Gloria knew there were pressing business concerns which were occupying his thoughts but the woman still expected him to be the ever-solicitous, entertaining companion. Sometimes Hamilton yearned to be the desolate bachelor again.

Three rows down, the widower Mrs Margery Hilton of Hilton Station returned to her seat. The large woman, dressed in boring beige, her often-worn jet beads dangling over the shelf of her bosom, made a fuss of ensuring that her primly attired daughter and the girl's newly acquired husband were seated first. The woman then made a show of waving to those friends she knew, swivelling on her heels so that her circular field of vision encompassed everybody in the crowd. Unabashed, the matron flapped her hand about at all and sundry – that is until she laid eyes on Hamilton and Gloria.

'Bloody old battle-axe,' whispered Hamilton as Mrs Hilton ignored them.

Gloria beamed. 'Do you mind, Mrs Hilton?' she called out sharply. 'The next act is about to begin and you're blocking the view.'

Those seated around them also called out for the matron to sit. Mrs Hilton's lips compressed together grimly, but then curved into a smile, her eyes sparkling as if she were the custodian of hidden knowledge. Hamilton felt quite uncomfortable. Why on earth would the woman be giving him such a knowing look?

Turning to Hamilton, Gloria said quite loudly, 'Wouldn't you think that with all the money the Hiltons supposedly have that she could find something a little more fashionable to wear?'

Hamilton shielded his face, wishing he could make himself invisible.

'What?' she asked playfully.

Of course Gloria was correct. The country women of means from the greater district of Wywanna were, on the whole, rather dowdy and at times verged on being coarse compared to his peacock Gloria. They and their families, many pioneers, may well have prospered out here over preceding generations but distance and harsh beginnings did not lend themselves to refinement.

'Cheer up, Hamilton,' said Gloria. 'At least you can strike them off your Christmas card list.'

'I don't send Christmas cards,' he replied morosely. For every step forward there were twenty paces back.

Gloria smiled. 'Well then. No harm done.'

'I need a drink. They should serve champagne.'

'Now that,' exclaimed Gloria, 'is something I do agree with. Still I'm sorry we didn't arrive earlier to see more of the commotion. The whole incident seems to have created quite a stir.'

Apparently there had been a tremendous hullaballoo after the theft of a lion cub from the circus zoo. And the ramifications of the incident were still ongoing when the hired sulky dropped them at the circus entrance. Even as they sat in the gloomy rear stalls with the canvas walls silhouetting the heads and shoulders of the surrounding audience, the police, along with volunteers, were continuing to search the grounds and were going so far as to boat down the river. That would be the next instalment, decided Hamilton. The boat would undoubtedly run aground or someone would end up overboard in the dark. Stupidity seemed to have a habit of following foolishness.

'I would rather like to meet her,' admitted Gloria, forcing Hamilton to draw his thoughts away from the difficulties of Wywanna society and overturned boats.

'Who?'

'The girl,' said Gloria.

'Yes, I'm sure,' placated Hamilton. Some young lad steals a lion and the accomplice is a girl dressed as a man. It could only happen in Wywanna. Reason enough to keep his children, particularly Edwina, at home. Such events could be quite unsettling to impressionable minds.

'I mean, it's fascinating to think of a young man and a woman as partners in crime.' She pinched Hamilton's cheek playfully. 'There's hope for us yet.'

'Well, I hope the police catch them. It's just not on, this stealing of property.'

In the half shadows Gloria did her best to look aghast. 'But heavens, surely you don't believe such a thing. I mean all these good rural folk you do business with, haven't they all dabbled in the thieving of livestock, even if it was unintentional?'

The woman in front of them looked over her shoulder.

'Shush,' complained Hamilton.

'Oh please,' pouted Gloria. 'A sheep here, a cow there. Why that's how herds are built and dynasties are forged in Australia, isn't it?'

'Don't be ridiculous,' snapped Hamilton. 'Of course it isn't.'

'Oh do relax. I'm only teasing.' Gloria gave a little ripple of laughter.

The tips of Hamilton's fingernails poked sharply against the material of his trousers into his thighs.

The ringmaster, megaphone clutched in a gloved hand, was introducing and then sprouting the magnificent abilities of the three artists who were manning the swings overhead, much to the oohs and ahhs of the assembled crowd. Hamilton settled back to observe the whole sequin-spangled catastrophe that passed for the district's yearly excitement, as the performers swung back and forth posing like attention-seeking children.

On second thoughts, he was beginning to appreciate the theft of the lion cub, and as a silver-suited male tumbled through the air Hamilton begrudgingly thought he, too, would like to meet the young people who were leading the law on a merry chase.

It was a prank of the highest order for, after all, what could they actually do with a lion? They couldn't keep it or rear it, so obviously they intended to return it.

Overhead, the woman of the trapeze troupe performed a half-twist mid-air. Misjudging the timing, she was caught one-handed by her companion on the opposite swing. For the barest of seconds she dangled like a small fish, scales glinting, before her saviour lunged for her other arm, pulling her to safety. The crowd watched in awed anticipation and then let out a collective gasp as the young woman shimmied to the floor with the aid of a thick rope.

Hamilton found himself upright, clapping enthusiastically with everyone else.

≪ Chapter Eleven ≫

If not for the rising moon, the journey would have been more than difficult. In some places the scrub lined the track so densely it resembled a wall of tangled limbs, in others the land was sparse and empty, stretching endlessly away from them. They saw no other people as they rode through the bush, save for a slab cottage that served as an inn for travellers and drovers. Here they stopped. Assisting Edwina down from the horse, Will led the mare to a nearby trough. Sitting the bundled cub carefully on the ground he stretched his shoulders and back. A short distance away, men rolled out swags and settled around a camp fire, the lowing of cattle close by.

'You're travelling late.' A man stepped from the shadows. 'You and your missus should rest for the night.' He scratched at a long beard. 'Mrs Landry will take care of you,' he said to Edwina. 'She's a tasty stew on the stove.'

Edwina dearly would have loved something to eat and drink. She looked to Will, pleading with her eyes.

'Thank you.' Will's reply was grateful. 'But we're making the most of the moon tonight.' At his feet the sack began to move; the cub growled and Will coughed loudly to hide the sound.

'Ah, yes.' The stranger sighed, his gaze directed to the ring of trees bounding the inn and the brightening orb breasting the woody skyline. 'Once overhead she'll be a beauty. A real beauty. I've often said to Mrs Landry what a shameful thing it is to have this here inn sitting against the trees. Out on the flat it should be, so a man can see the moon a-rising the moment she shows herself. But I'll content myself knowing that once I've bedded down for the night she'll be shining her grace upon me.'

Lifting her head from the trough, Heidi-Hoe nickered softly.

'We should be going,' Will answered, lifting the concealed lion and settling in the saddle. He extended a hand to Edwina. 'Safe travels to you.'

'And you, friend,' replied the stranger.

Edwina allowed herself to be pulled up onto the horse's back. The lion cub gave a whine, half growl, half cat purr. 'Come on, girl,' Will petted Heidi-Hoe between her ears, 'let's go.'

The camp fire and inn soon dwindled to nothingness.

'I'm hungry,' complained Edwina, her stomach rumbling.

'My pockets are empty,' apologised Will. 'Besides, I think it best we keep moving, don't you?'

The cub was growing noisy. Edwina could hear the animal scratching and growling in the bag that held him. 'I'm still hungry.' She would be home by now, if not for Will's tomfoolery. Home without the sordid memory of . . . but she wouldn't think of that, not tonight, nor tomorrow.

'Shush,' Will soothed the baby animal. 'Sleep now.'

Gradually the cub settled. Their presence barely disturbed the wildlife. Rabbits and wallabies, fluttering quail and pigs all crossed their path, pausing only momentarily to gaze at the night-time intruders. Owls peered down from branches and night-birds twittered as unknown eyes glowed from among the bushes. Edwina thought of the snippets H.J. read from the circus program. Of jungles, deserts and frozen wastelands. Away from the crowds and activity, she imagined the animals of the menagerie prowling across the land and swaying through branches, hunting for prey. Exotic creatures let loose in a foreign world.

'It's a fine night,' said Will.

Edwina, her fingers clutching Will's coat-tails, reluctantly agreed.

'My mother says there is beauty in everything.'

'And where is your mother?' asked Edwina out of politeness.

'In the slums.' Will was hesitant. 'Sydney. I was ten when I last saw her. She wouldn't leave the city when my father purchased the soldier settler's block.'

'Is she still alive?'

'I suppose so. She's a fine woman. Did her best for me and the rest of the family. Made sure we all ate every day. But I guess that's something you never had to worry about?'

Heidi-Hoe walked steadily onwards. Edwina wanted to hate this man, whose actions had so impacted on her, but at the same time she was beholden to Will for escorting her home.

They entered a patch of thick timber, the moonlight momentarily fading to an eerie wanness.

'Look at that,' said Will, as Heidi-Hoe carried them free of the woody plants.

They watched as the moon reappeared again above a distant tree line, large and luminous. The great sphere was their lantern, highlighting the road with its rutted wagon tracks and blanketing the land in a soft white glow.

'It's beautiful,' said Edwina.

'Yes,' said Will softly. 'When I first came out to the bush, I'd never seen such a thing. I was . . .'

'You were what?'

'Scared of it,' admitted Will. 'Oh, I'd seen it big and white. In Sydney whenever there was a full moon the light would shine through the timber slats into my room, but I never saw it like this until I came to the bush. It's different here.' He paused. 'It fills a person up with its brightness.'

The mare plodded on, encouraged by Will's intermittent whispers, and Edwina grew sleepy with the rhythmic gait of the horse. The bundle of fur between them was now rearranged so that the sleeping cub lay cocooned on Will's lap, and more than once Edwina jolted awake to find her cheek against the breadth of Will's back. Twice Will reached around to stop her falling when sleep claimed her, pulling Edwina closer and placing her hands firmly on his waist. 'Don't,' she'd said on both occasions, uncomfortable at the intimacy of his touch.

'I won't bite, miss,' he stated, 'and it is best you hold on.'

Edwina breathed in hay and soil, wool and the faint scent of perspiration as her skin rested against the cloth of Will's jacket. The next time Will's steadying hand reached for her, Edwina didn't pull free.

The track divided into two and Will took the road to the left. Everything would be fine, Edwina decided, now they were on the final home leg. As long as she never thought about the attack. And it would be doubly fine, Edwina convinced herself, for their father was in Wywanna and there was only Aiden to contend with once they reached the house. She had done what she set out to do after all. Timing and difficulties aside, she had seen the petting zoo and returned home. And she had met a man. Mason. A handsome man she'd not likely forget. Edwina peered over Will's shoulder. 'It's not far now.' Through the timber she saw the homestead and the glimmer of whitewashed sheds circling around the house. She gave a silent prayer.

'What will you tell your brother?'

'Not the truth,' replied Edwina.

The cub made a mewling noise. 'You won't tell him about the lion, will you?'

Common sense said that was exactly what Edwina should do.

'I mean he's only here because I was helping you,' argued Will.

Edwina gave a choked reply. 'Helping me? You're helping me because of the mess you got us both into.'

'You chose to be the busybody, miss. Anyway, you agreed to give me work.'

Who did this person think he was? Why, he couldn't be much older than her, Edwina decided. 'You won't be able to stay long,' she told him firmly. 'A week at best. I mean, everyone will be looking for that baby lion. And if they find you here –'

'I understand,' said Will stiffly. 'I won't get you into any trouble. Anyway, the circus will be packed up and headed out of town come morning, so I don't think you need to fear them.'

'And what about the lion? I mean, what are you going to do with it?' asked Edwina. 'You certainly can't keep it. Once it grows up it will be dangerous. You do realise that?'

'They can be trained,' answered Will.

Edwina gave a sharp laugh. 'Like a pet? You must be joking. Where on earth would you keep it?'

'I haven't worked that out yet, but I will. Anyway, it's not your problem, is it? I'll be gone in a week and the lion cub will be too.'

Heidi-Hoe plodded onwards as the rutted track wound past the silvery grey trunks of gum trees. The homestead was suffused in moonlight, the orchard and leaf-laden roof transformed by the shiny gleam that encircled the buildings. The mare trotted a little faster over the dirt track. A weak light beckoned from a window. The dogs barked on their approach and rushed out to greet them, at first with uneasy growls and then wagging tails on recognition. The lamp in the window disappeared and a second later Aiden was at the front door.

'Where have you been, Edwina?' Setting the lantern on the veranda, Aiden moved quickly, his hand on Heidi-Hoe's reins. 'Will? What in heaven's name?'

111

'It's a long story,' replied Edwina flippantly, as Davidson appeared from the dark, a rifle in his hand.

'It's past ten o'clock,' countered Aiden angrily. 'I get home and there's no fire lit, no food, the place in darkness. Where on earth have you been? What happened?'

'So, were you concerned for me, little brother, or your stomach?'

Swinging his leg across the mare's back, Will jumped from the horse, the cub already slung behind his back so it was hidden from view. He helped Edwina down, his grip lingering on her waist. 'Miss Edwina asked me to escort her home, it being dark and all.'

Aiden, clearly baffled, turned from his sister to Will. 'Home from where?'

'The circus,' replied Edwina. 'I wanted to see the menagerie.'

'The menagerie? You wanted to see the menagerie? And you went by yourself,' Aiden's voice rose, 'unchaperoned, dressed like that?'

Edwina fidgeted with the jacket she wore, hastily buttoning it so that the damaged shirt and waistcoat were not so obvious. 'And how was your trip in Father's buggy?'

Aiden scowled. 'You look a mess, Edwina. An absolute mess.' Brother and sister stared defiantly at each other. 'I appreciate you going out of your way, Will. And I'm sorry if my sister inconvenienced you.'

'No problem, Mr Aiden. But I could use a job. Just for a week or so. Food and shelter is all I'm asking for. I had something lined up but then I had to help your sister.'

Edwina opened her mouth to retaliate, stopping immediately when she noticed the dogs. One by one they approached Will, snuffling at his trousers and boots, lifting their heads with interest at the bulging bag. Will kept his back close to the mare as Aiden whistled the canines to his side. The dogs moved away reluctantly. Davidson cocked his head to one side. He knew, Edwina realised.

The stockman guessed that all was not right, that Will concealed something.

'Of course, Will,' replied Aiden, 'and again I'm sorry if Edwina has put you out. Davidson will show you to the stables. You can bed down there for the night.'

Taking Heidi-Hoe's reins, Davidson led Will around the side of the house.

'And what do you have to say for yourself, Edwina?' Aiden pursued her indoors.

Taking a lantern from the hall table, Edwina turned briefly to her brother. 'I'm tired,' she replied. 'Goodnight.'

≼ Chapter Twelve ≽

Hamilton tethered the horse to a tree limb, then walked down to the creek. The homestead was only a mile or so away but the waterway provided a calming place in which to stop and think. This silent time was invaluable, allowing a transition of sorts between Wywanna and the farm. Quite often it was as if he led two lives and the only way he could connect both worlds was here, in this bridging space, a no-man's-land of sludge-brown water surrounded by bush and timber. He'd seen Davidson ride in this direction some years ago and made a point of following the aboriginal. It was probably the only time their roles were reversed, so self-absorbed was the stockman. By the time Hamilton reached the water his man was gone, the splash of the crossing an echo and bird flutter the only sign of a presence.

Hamilton hadn't bothered following any further that day. Who knew where the stockman went when time was his own? Besides, across the muddy-bottomed creek and beyond the twisted roots of the old trees lining the bank was a thick wall of prickly pear. Useless country that didn't entice. The black man could have it. But the loneliness of the spot, the giant roots of trees bordering the narrow stream, the rustle of critters moving about in the grass — that's what drew him. And like a lover starved of an embrace, it was the solitude Hamilton craved for, the solitude of the area, returning whenever time permitted.

The chance to sit on a fallen log as he did now, to draw aimlessly with a stick in the dirt, this was the simplest of pleasures. Birds were calling out, stretching their wings as they took to the air, while kangaroos grazed. The creek fascinated, with its varying width and tree-shaded shallows. Further downstream it grew large and generous but here it was narrow, as if the earth refused to yield to the water's force and the carving of a deeper passage. If he could stay here, if the hours could be stretched out into one long day, then Hamilton knew he'd be a happy man. It was tiring, this business of continued advancement. But life demanded money and he could never have enough of it.

Hamilton flicked at ants with the stick. In his great-grandfather's time, there'd been a grand house in London and another in Sydney. Dinners with Governor Macquarie and an audience with the Queen. There was even talk of a peerage, such was his great-grandfather's contribution to the colony. But through stupidity they'd lost it all. Lost the wealth and the prestige. Three generations on and Hamilton gained scant purchase from a direct blood association with the man who'd once sat on the board of the Australian Agricultural Company. Occasionally, this distant link could provide a useful, if brief, entrée to a world lost to him, but invariably it was the likes of Peter Worth who made use of the connection, as if by mentioning it the acquaintance could be justified.

Further along the creek, on the opposite side, partially concealed by trees, a girl appeared to squat in the muddy creek, washing herself. Hamilton gazed at her through the drooping timber. He'd not heard her approach and she was clearly unaware of his presence. Dark-skinned, the young woman cupped water, cleaning her face, the liquid streaming down to wet the shift she wore. She was pretty, with roughly cut shoulder-length hair and the type of body built for purpose. They were not like white women, these girls. They were scavengers, hunters and gatherers, inordinately suited to the wilds. Hamilton could appreciate a disposition tending to survival.

A wail, high-pitched, carried across the breadth of the waterway. The sound ripping through the stillness caused startled birds to fly from nearby shrubbery and sent the lolling kangaroos bounding into the surrounding bush. The piccaninny lay on the creek bank screaming, its plump legs pumping the air in fury.

Hamilton watched fascinated, conscious of his intrusion. They were natives, it was true, but there was something about the simplicity of the scene that he found quite entrancing. As he observed the girl, she removed her dress, a shapeless piece of material that covered a tempting body. Large-breasted with a small waist and fertile hips and thighs, she dunked the gown in the water. Hamilton watched the young woman's round backside as it bobbed up and down. It was a half-hearted attempt at washing and she lay the dress on the sand to dry, before returning to the water to wash herself more thoroughly. She used handfuls of mud as soap, scooping up the sandy creek and scrubbing harshly at her wet skin, as the baby continued to cry.

Eventually the young woman left the water and, ignoring the baby, lay down on the bank, her breasts falling sideways, legs spread comfortably across the sand. Once or twice she glanced at the mewling child, before sitting upright, her face wet with tears. Hamilton wondered what she contemplated. Whether the child was hers and who the father was and what they were doing on his land. Where they'd come from. The young woman was very upset. There was no smile for the baby, who'd now cried itself out; instead she stared at the child and sobbed.

He didn't want natives sneaking about on his land. Particularly natives like this one. The girl couldn't be more than fifteen years of age. By rights she should be in a home or have been adopted out to a white family. It was for their own good, after all. The full-bloods would die out eventually and the old ways would go with them. It was vital that mixed-blood children be integrated into white society; otherwise what good could they possibly be to anyone. The government said as much and Hamilton certainly didn't want to fall foul of the law.

The girl picked up the baby and, walking straight into the middle of the creek, stood quietly as the water ebbed at her thighs. The child was paler than its mother and lulled to quiet. A long wound marked the side of the girl's face, stretching from temple to chin, but the ugly injury was forgotten as the young woman, still weeping, tenderly touched the baby's head. Combined with the girl's sadness, Hamilton found her affection for the child captivating.

The woman shifted a little, moving about as if finding solid ground. Then she knelt, the water chest-high, and in one deft movement she held the baby under the water.

For a moment Hamilton didn't quite understand what the girl was doing. The infant was still submerged, the young woman looking at the water's surface, her anguished cries echoing along the waterway. He knew he should yell out, make her aware of his presence, stop the terribleness of the event. But Hamilton also knew it was too late. The child would be dead by now.

Eventually the woman lifted the lifeless form from beneath the surface of the water and, with infinite gentleness, pushed the little body away from her. She watched the child as the water slowly bore the baby away on the sluggish current before returning to the creek bank.

Hamilton walked quickly down to the water's edge. It wasn't his intention to speak to her. What could he possibly say? There were no words that sufficiently described how he felt. What he'd been forced to witness. And he didn't know if there were any laws concerning half-castes killing their own children. His immediate concern was ensuring that the girl knew that someone had seen her terrible wrongdoing. A shocking act committed on his land.

He waited for her to catch sight of him. To be surprised by his presence, to acknowledge her wrongdoing with entreaties for help, for sympathy. But the girl never looked back, not even to check the progress of the child, whose body continued to be borne onwards, alone. Picking up the discarded dress lying on the sand, the black girl threw it over her shoulder and walked back into the scrub.

✖ Chapter Thirteen ✖

The ride from the creek did little to calm Hamilton. He spurred the horse on until foam from the tiring beast flecked his face and clothes. The house grew larger as he imagined the baby slowly sinking, watery arms cradling the infant's progress. Outside the house he waited impatiently, his thoughts addled by the incident. Where was everyone? The house was quiet, far too quiet for his liking. Even the dogs seemed uninterested, gradually crawling out from under the house to snuffle around him. Usually on his return from a stay in Wywanna the gramophone would be playing, the dogs would be overly excitable and, after he called for one of his children, Edwina would finally appear, breathless and dishevelled from some part of the homestead. Davidson at least could be relied upon to attend him immediately. But even he was not prompt this afternoon. Something was afoot. Hamilton stretched out aching limbs, wincing at the pain caused by yesterday's voracious entertainments with Gloria and the Big Top's hard bench seat.

'Davidson!' he bellowed.

The gelding shied as the dogs settled obediently on the verandah. The stockman appeared behind him.

'Must you sneak up on a man like that? Where is everyone?'

Davidson nodded to the west and back to the house.

'So my daughter is inside and Aiden is out. Good. And the cook? Has Mrs Ryan returned? There's a reason I never give the help time off. They can never be relied upon to return when expected,' complained Hamilton. 'That's what I like about you, Davidson. You're always here, one of the great benefits of having neither family nor friends.' The aboriginal didn't blink. 'I want to ask you something, Davidson. Are there blacks on my land?' Hamilton studied the man: the erect stature, the cheekbones that hung wide and high – a spectral sight in the half-light. 'A nod will suffice. You see, I just saw one. Down by the creek. She was young with a baby. A baby that she drowned in front of me.' He watched the man carefully. 'Held the poor thing under the water she did and then watched it float away.' He saw it then, the slightest change in the stockman's unreadable nature, a hollowness, a glazing over. 'So, I'm asking you, Davidson, are there aboriginals on my land? Because if there are, you have to get rid of them. Seek them out, find them and get rid of them. If you don't, you know what will happen eventually. I will have to report them and I'd rather not do that. I'd rather the coppers weren't riding around my land looking for young half-castes who should be in homes. It's for their own good, you know.'

If Davidson could speak Hamilton wondered how the man would respond.

'Well, I said what I must. Fetch a fresh horse for me, will you, and one for Edwina; the three of us will ride to the Ridgeway boundary and check on things out there. And tie up these dogs, man. They need some discipline.'

Leaving the aboriginal to care for his horse, Hamilton entered the house, kicking at the leaves on the unswept verandah as he passed. Yes, it was definitely too quiet. He ran a finger along a dusty hall table, noting the unlit fire in the parlour. Flies were already buzzing down the chimney. What had his two children been up to? He met Edwina in the hallway, a rather poor-looking apparition with milk-pale skin and dark circles under her eyes. 'Heavens, girl, have you come down with something?'

Edwina gave a wan smile. 'Nothing serious, Father.'

'Well, you look quite undone. Have you eaten? You've a tendency to be finicky with your food at times.'

'A little bread and milk, Father, but I'm sure I will feel better very soon.'

Hamilton wasn't one for superstition, but he was always cautious with a full moon. One never knew who was travelling about at night or what effect the astronomical movement may have on the feeble-minded, or females for that matter. Why, Gloria had been all a-twitter last night, oohing at the tumbling acrobats, laughing loudly at the clowns with their yapping, jumping dogs. And when the white horses and the bareback rider appeared, well, he thought the woman would have a conniption, along with the rest of the crowd. He led his daughter into the parlour, observing Edwina carefully as they both sat in slightly battered horsehair-stuffed armchairs. The highlight of the spectacular, the theft of the lion, was the talk of Wywanna this morning and he was rather disappointed at having to leave town. Especially now he was home and subjected to his listless daughter.

'And your brother, what is he out doing? I assume he found that boy yesterday and paid him?' Opening a wooden box on an inlaid table he retrieved his tobacco and pipe and proceeded to stuff it.

'Yes, Father, he did. In fact, Will returned with Aiden. Apparently he wasn't able to get any work with the circus so he's here with us for a week or so. Aiden has him doing odd jobs in return for board and keep. I believe they are out cutting wood.'

'Young people today,' complained Hamilton, lighting the pipe and sucking furiously. 'Imagine leaving a perfectly good job with the foolhardy idea of joining the circus?' The smoke spiralled free from his lungs. 'The circus. The lad should have been sent on his way. And then, of course, to expect employment having walked off the job!' He chewed the stem of the pipe, contemplating the weakness of character in his son that undoubtedly came from the boy's mother. While his primary concern was to see Edwina well married, Hamilton worried more about Aiden's future. The boy was a gentleman farmer with limited ability. Never once had his son argued a point of view with him over anything. And while Aiden was becoming more like him in some ways, in others they were polar opposites. His only son would happily be led around with a ring through his nose, like a stud bull, while his feisty, tomboy daughter needed the strength of a good man to contain her.

'I would have turned the boy away, but in my absence Aiden must have the authority to act on my behalf. Otherwise how will he ever learn? One week then. That's all. Are you quite alright, Edwina?'

'An ache, Father, it will pass.' She rubbed absently at the back of her head.

'I suppose you sat up late listening to that infernal gramophone? Never should have purchased it. Nor that rubbish you listen to. What is it? Jazz, or some such rot?'

'Yes, Father.'

Hamilton squinted, scrutinising his daughter. 'I'm not inclined towards having a young man around the homestead, Edwina. It's not proper. Be aware is what I'm saying. No fraternising. One must know one's place in society.' Hamilton puffed on the pipe. She really did look quite peaky. 'You look exhausted, as if you've been up half the night, my girl.'

'I slept poorly, Father.'

'Ah yes. The full moon. I myself was quite activated by it. Still, what's a little lost sleep, eh?' It happened of course. Women were quite unaccustomed to being left alone. They could quickly become maudlin and out of sorts. He thought of the scene at the creek. 'It's no excuse for not keeping things in order, however, my girl. The porch needs sweeping, the grate cleaned of coals and the fire lit. The room is full of flies.' With a final puff, he lay the pipe to one side. 'Well, are you up to a ride?'

'Not really. Father, did you read the notes I gave you?'

'What notes?'

'My suggestion for the new paddock we're developing.'

Hamilton scratched above his ear. 'Not feasible. The cost of the livestock, cattle for instance –'

'Would be repaid in eighteen months when the cows calved,' interrupted Edwina.

'We'll talk about this later. I want to check the boundary. Well, come on then.' Hamilton took down the Lee-Enfield rifle from the brackets above the fireplace and walked outside, waiting on the verandah for his daughter to reappear from fetching her coat.

Davidson was ready with the horses and as Hamilton mounted the mare he noticed a smudge of a figure in the distance. 'So the Scotswoman returns,' he muttered. Forgoing his fob watch, Hamilton checked the position of the sun. There was still a good two hours of light available. He would have to refrain from admonishing Mrs Ryan for there was enough time for the woman to ready the evening meal. 'This Will fellow?' asked Hamilton of the aboriginal. 'What sort of man is he? Can he be trusted? I have to consider my daughter if he's to be around the homestead.'

Davidson gave the slightest dip of a pockmarked chin.

'Keep an eye on him. Oh, I'd like her to stay here with me for there is nothing like a daughter when it comes to the care of hearth and home. But Edwina's not a simple farm girl. She's far too complicated for that. Complicated and clever. Not that having intelligence is a boon for a female like Edwina. No, it's a troublesome thing when an intemperate woman thinks herself clever. My daughter must marry and marry well, to a strong-minded man with a firm hand, for otherwise what is the point of having produced her in the first place?'

Davidson remained impassive. Hamilton nodded in satisfaction. There was something quite liberating venting one's frustration without interruption or comment. Leaving the Winchester rifle he carried in Wywanna on the verandah, he replaced it with the Lee-Enfield.

Edwina finally joined them and the three rode off towards the Ridgeway Station boundary. Although he wasn't normally one to marvel at the landscape, Hamilton enjoyed the ride past the wheat paddocks. With the sun drooping towards the west, the rays filtered across the fields suffusing the seed-filled heads with light so that they resembled a shimmering green carpet. Hamilton found the whole farming exercise quite tedious at times and, although he liked producing things, he really wasn't very good at it. Not that he'd ever tell his daughter that. However, he could see the value in land ownership. And there was a contentment to be found in improving land and growing things, as long as there was money coming in. Thanks to Worth and Clyde, he didn't need to sell any of his shares now, allowing him the indulgence of a property that rarely covered costs.

'Look.' Hamilton directed Davidson and Edwina to a path that led through the wheat. Something had trampled the tall plants so that they lay ruined on the ground. 'Damn and blast.' The cause of the destruction, straying sheep, stood only feet away, foraging on the edge of the field. Disturbed, the animals looked up nervously. Hamilton scanned the fence line, pointing at two broken wires and the telltale tufts of wool caught there. 'Why wasn't that repaired?'

'Aiden said he would fix it,' answered Edwina.

'That'd be right.'

Extricating the rifle from its holster Hamilton loaded it, aimed and pulled the trigger at the fleeing merinos. The gelding backed up in fright as two of the sheep disappeared into the wheat while the third, shot in the hind leg, tried to follow its companions. 'Blasted animals,' Hamilton protested, 'they're either eating it or knocking it over. Get that animal, Davidson. Cut its throat and string it up on the fence as a warning to that so-called manager next door.'

'Father,' Edwina complained, 'you can't do that.'

'My land. My wheat,' answered Hamilton, holstering the weapon as Davidson took off after the wounded sheep on foot. The black man ran lightly through the wheat in a wide circle, then rushing forward made a grab for the animal, catching him by a leg. Although the sheep was large in frame, Davidson hefted the animal with ease and carried him to the side of the field. Unsheathing a knife he cut roughly at the struggling beast's throat, an arc of blood spurting through the air to land in globules on the ground.

Hamilton watched the procedure with satisfaction as Davidson dragged the twitching carcass across to the boundary shared with Ridgeway Station. Once there, he heaved it over the top of the fence, sitting it on the ground. Next he tied each front leg to one of the strands of wire so that the dead sheep was outstretched, sitting on the ground, blood still draining from the fatal wound.

'Excellent. Excellent job.' Hamilton turned to his daughter, but Edwina was already riding away. He should have waited for Aiden, his pleasure momentarily eroded. Aiden would have appreciated the incident. The stockman was cleaning the knife, rubbing the blade with dirt. 'Well, Davidson, what are you doing dawdling, man? Go after those other two sheep and change their ear-marks from a v to a block, and this time remember to put a slash in the tip of their ear.' Removing ear-marking pliers from his saddle-bag, Hamilton threw the implement across to the stockman, who caught the object one-handed. Hamilton watched and waited as the aboriginal set out on horseback after the stragglers. Pursued across the paddock, the sheep led Davidson into the ridge on the far side, horse and rider disappearing in the timber. Hamilton noted down the two live animals in a pocketbook and then estimated the damage to his crop. On his calculations, Ridgeway still owed him five head for the damage done to the wheat over the season.

'And what the blazes do you think you're doing?' The rough individual glaring at him from across the fence was the Ridgeway manager, Fernleigh.

Hamilton feigned indifference although his thumb tapped nervously against the horn of the saddle. Fernleigh carried more hair on his face and body than one of Hamilton's collie dogs. Thick, grey, matted hair. Hamilton tried not to grimace. He hated beards. Always had and was pleased that being clean-shaven was back in fashion. Whenever he saw Fernleigh he couldn't help but wonder how much food from previous meals was deposited in the long fuzzy strands that hung down from the man's face.

'Good afternoon, Mr Fernleigh.' Hamilton tipped his hat. 'We have our usual problem of straying stock.' He looked at the garrotted sheep spread-eagled on the dividing fence and already gathering blowflies. 'Confronting though this may seem, Mr Fernleigh, this need not happen again. If we can check this fence on a regular basis then perhaps *you* could extend yourself to do likewise.'

The manager spat on the ground. 'Or what?'

'Well, I'm assuming you don't have many dingoes coming onto the station.'

''Course we don't. That fence is kept in good repair.'

'Then why, man, can't you do the same on this boundary? My crops are damaged every year by your sheep and not once have you offered compensation.'

'I'll not be spoken to like I'm a simpleton.' Fernleigh walked his horse closer to the fence.

'We ensure the fence is in good repair.' Hamilton gestured to the manager. 'And *you* ensure the fence is in good repair. It's a rather easy solution, don't you think?'

Mr Fernleigh laid a rifle across his thighs. 'The fence *is* in good repair.'

'Then why are we continually mending it?' replied Hamilton conversationally as he too clasped the stock of his gun.

'Maybe there's another problem,' the manager suggested through a clenched jaw.

'Yes, there is. You're overstocked and they're hungry. Therein lies the problem, Mr Fernleigh. Your sheep are literally eating my money.'

'Really? Every year come shearing the tally don't come out the same. It's always this paddock, right here, that is missing sheep. Strange coincidence, don't you think?'

'I do,' Hamilton agreed, 'think it strange that you're insinuating I could be at fault when your complaints began when the weather turned dry. I don't see you chasing after your own stock or lowering numbers to compensate for the season.' He heard the subtle click as the manager cocked his rifle, aiming the gun at Hamilton's chest. 'I'm sure your employers will be very happy to hear that you've shot the owner of the adjoining property.'

'You're an arrogant man for a money-lender.' The statement was hissed. 'A money-lender on a block of land that wouldn't even match one of the smaller paddocks on Ridgeway.'

Hamilton's teeth ground together. He was inclined to shoot the man here and now and be rid of the obstinate individual. 'At least I own it,' he said pointedly. Lifting the rifle he slammed the magazine into the breach, resting the butt on a thigh. 'Guns at twenty paces, is it, Fernleigh?'

'The thing is, Baker, we both know I could take you here and now and no-one would be the wiser for it. I wouldn't even need to bury you. I could drag you out to the dingo fence and drop you over the side and those wild dogs would clean you up inside of a week.'

The saliva collected in Hamilton's mouth. He swallowed and pointed the rifle. It was said that the bolt action of the firearm combined with its ten-round magazine enabled a well-trained rifleman to perform the 'mad minute' firing, twenty to thirty aimed rounds in sixty seconds. But Hamilton wasn't a veteran of the Great War. In fact the closest he'd come to fighting was with the ownership of the gun in his hand. At this distance they'd both be shot, the reality of which didn't bear thinking about. Across the fence the manager pressed the weapon into his shoulder. Hamilton hesitated. He could shoot first of course, but even with his connections, murder was murder.

A twig snapped and Davidson walked his horse out from behind a tree. The black man was less than ten feet from the manager, his rifle directed at Fernleigh's back.

'That's enough for today I think, Fernleigh.' Although Hamilton tried, he couldn't keep the patronising tone from his voice. 'I'll be sure to mention your enthusiasm for your work to your employers when I meet with them to discuss the future of Ridgeway Station.'

The manager grunted and with a cark of his throat spat a large glob onto the ground at Davidson's feet. Holstering his rifle he walked his horse into the trees.

Hamilton ran a finger between shirt collar and skin. 'If not for your arrival, Davidson, I fear I may well have ended up like that poor sheep.' And it may yet happen, Hamilton considered, wiping a slick of perspiration from his brow, if he didn't do something about Mr Fernleigh first.

⊰ Chapter Fourteen ⊱

On Monday morning Edwina was sweeping the leaves from the verandah outside her bedroom when Will emerged from the fruit trees ringing the homestead. She'd been thinking of her mother's locket. The loss of it upset her deeply. Apart from its value, being of fine sterling silver, and the lock of hair within, the necklace was her mother's favourite. At the sight of Will, Edwina grew uneasy. They'd not seen each other since their night-time ride back from Wywanna two days before. Edwina concentrated on the broom moving across the uneven timber boards. She'd had time enough to recover from yesterday's pounding headache, and to try to forget the fateful trip to town. But with Will's appearance the memories of that afternoon and night immediately returned. Because of him her locket was gone, and Mason had left abruptly. Because of him she had no idea where Mason lived and a stolen lion cub was secreted somewhere on their run.

He looked different in daylight. Taller, with a sun-tanned face and the greenest of eyes. Edwina guessed he would think her quite the fool, regardless of his part in the day's events and she rather wished Will Kew would vanish back into the trees and never show his face again.

But Will didn't vanish, even though Edwina ignored him as she concentrated on completing her chores, the broom circling the growing pile of plant life. She didn't need to look in his direction to know that the man was watching each swish of the broom across the verandah, the desultory stab at cobwebs matting the wall. Edwina knew she should speak first. He was an employee, after all. However, there was a growing tightness in her stomach as she re-swept a section of the veranda, her gaze falling on his dusty boot resting nonchalantly on the edge of the veranda.

Will tipped his hat in greeting. 'How are you, Miss Edwina?' He wore an old pair of trousers and a pale blue shirt, the sleeves rolled to the elbows.

Jed walked from the bedroom directly to Will, receiving a prolonged pat as reward.

'Busy.' The leaves swirled as Edwina swept the pile off the timber boards and onto the ground. They'd shared more than she cared to remember and yet the man before her, with his unruly brown hair and bristly chin, was a stranger to her. 'And you?'

'Cutting firewood, carting water. I didn't realise you grew sheep as well.'

'We don't, we only keep a handful of killers for meat.'

He ignored this, his gaze taking in the plainness of her bedroom with the sagging bed and patchwork quilt. Edwina immediately closed the doors to her room, feeling somehow invaded.

'And you're feeling alright now? I mean after what happened at the circus?'

'I'd rather not talk about it.' Edwina leant on the broom, keeping the sweeper directly in front of her body, a boundary of sorts. She lowered her voice. 'What did you do with the baby cub?'

'That's what I wanted to speak to you about.' Will removed his hat, twiddling the brim between his fingers. 'I've had him hidden

130

in the stables but it's a right thoroughfare in there at times what with Davidson coming and going and your brother. I think Aiden knows we told him a pretty story. And that black of yours, well, I reckon he's on to me.'

Her father would never approve of such shared intimacy between a member of his family and the hired help. 'Forget about Aiden. He won't say anything. He took Father's buggy without asking. And Davidson can't speak.'

Will relaxed a little. 'Then there are your dogs. They're always sniffing around. So, I was wondering if the cub could stay with you today until I find somewhere else to hide him. Maybe in your room. He wouldn't be any trouble and he'd have some company what with this old dog of yours.'

'With me? In my bedroom?'

Will stepped up onto the porch and squatted, scratching Jed on the neck. 'He's a baby, miss, as you well know, and it would only be for a few days. When my time is up here, I'll be on my way.'

'A baby? He's the size of a dog! Anyway, I can't. I couldn't. If my father found out –'

Will stood up. 'I'm sorry. I didn't realise.'

'Realise what?'

'That you're scared of him. Scared of your father. If I'd known I wouldn't have asked. I know what it's like to be flogged.'

'Flogged?' repeated Edwina. Resting the broom against the verandah wall, she crossed her arms. 'I am not afraid of my father. And he has certainly never hit me, if that's what you think.' She lifted her chin. 'We're not like that.'

Will shoved his hands in his trouser pockets. 'Of course you're not.'

'It's just that there is a difference between right and wrong,' continued Edwina, 'no matter how righteous you may feel about something. Anyway, you simply can't expect me to look after stolen property. Especially when you involved me in the theft.'

131

'I did nothing of the sort. You just got caught up in the moment,' Will told her. 'That wasn't my fault. Besides, you're not really worried about the baby lion; it's the thought of your father finding out about your visit to town that's giving you the willies.'

Edwina's nails cut into the soft flesh of her palms.

'If you ask me, if anyone's to blame for Saturday night it's your father. I mean what gives someone the right to stop a person going to the circus?' mumbled Will.

Placing the blame on her father for the zoo debacle was not something Edwina had considered. But as Will stood before her, his green eyes bright and clear, it occurred to her that Will did have a point.

'I can see I've riled you and I'm sorry for that. I shouldn't have bothered you or even asked. You've already done me a favour letting me stay here.' Turning abruptly, Will began to walk away.

One minute ago, she was fuming at this man. Now, as Will weaved through the knobby trunks of the orchard, she felt quite at odds. How was it imaginable that this man could make her feel bad when he asked the impossible? Jed got to his feet and ambled after him.

'Jed, come back here!' called Edwina. 'Jed?'

But the old animal didn't respond. The dog padded straight ahead, following Will.

Edwina caught up with Will under one of the oldest orange trees, under the pretext of ensuring her dog didn't wander away. 'Traitor,' she said to Jed who sat nearby. She was determined to explain herself, to make Will realise the difficulty he placed her in, even though the man was outspoken and impolite and thought he knew everything. As she marshalled the courage to speak, Will was gathering a handful of leaves and rubbing them briskly between his palms. He held them towards her, encouraging Edwina to smell the offering.

'No, thank you.'

'Go on,' he urged. 'You're very pretty when you're angry.'

Edwina thought him the most irritating person she'd ever had the misfortune of knowing.

'Go on,' he enticed.

He clearly wouldn't leave her alone until she did so. Edwina reluctantly leant over his cupped hands.

'Close your eyes,' he invited, 'and breathe.'

The bruised leaves were both sweet and sour in scent, but she could also smell something else – him.

Will's smile revealed a dimple. 'Best smell in the world,' he declared, throwing up the leaves so that the breeze caught them. 'Here.' He reached for her hand, lowering her mother's locket into the palm.

'You found it?'

'I would have given it to you sooner, if there'd been an opportunity.' He didn't give her a chance to say more, for as Edwina hung the locket around her neck he asked her about the orchard.

'Father planted the fruit trees years ago. My mother complained awfully that they were too close to the house, but he insisted.' Behind them the homestead roof was littered with vegetation. Beige and yellow interspersed with green mottled the iron roof, which shone silver in some parts, rusty in others. 'I worry that one of the trees might get struck by lightning and fall on the house, but it's never happened.'

'I'd worry the roof would collapse under the weight of those leaves,' commented Will.

Edwina spun towards him. 'That's what I always think. Especially when the gums lose their leaves as well.' She looked back towards the homestead, tempering her enthusiasm at the shared thought. 'Some years the orchard hardly loses any leaves at all. Father says it's a combination of things. If we have a cold spell and there's been little rain, the leaves fall off. And, of course, when

it doesn't rain in the summer quite often all the trees turn yellow.'
When Edwina turned to face Will, he was staring at her.

'Yellow gold leaves. I can see you surrounded by gold.'

Edwina blushed.

As if suddenly aware of what he'd said, Will pointed to the tree at the end of the garden. 'Tell me about that one. Why has it got all those things hanging off it?'

With a sky patched by cloud, the usually glimmering plant was dull and lifeless; worse, it appeared quite out of place. 'It's nothing,' replied Edwina. Having never needed to explain the plant's significance, nor the items strewn at its base or tied to the branches, she felt awkward at trying to rationalise its existence.

'Nothing is never nothing. Come on,' urged Will as he moved in the direction of the tree.

Edwina had little choice but to follow Will as he led her past the stables and the building that garaged the buggy. Her mother's tree claimed the space between the homestead surrounds and the dense scrub beyond, but what had been a tangible link with the past now made her uncomfortable. This man would think her an idiot, thought Edwina, as they approached the object-laden branches and the pile of refuse scattered on the ground. Worse, she didn't want to share this special place.

'I like glass,' Will announced, squatting by the pile.

Edwina watched as he sifted through the mass of broken odds and ends. Objects that had been set purposely by her in a specific place. 'Don't,' she said.

Selecting a dark blue square, Will lifted the glass to the light, examining it. 'Are you the bowerbird then?' he asked.

Edwina took the fragment from his hand, laying it carefully back on the pile before meticulously rearranging the disturbed pieces.

'Don't tell me you have a spot for every bit of this stuff?' asked Will.

His cheeks became square when he spoke and then dropped naturally into softer planes. Edwina felt her breath easing. He was asking her about the tree. Repeating his question of who the bower-bird was in the family.

'It was my mother's idea. It started as a Christmas tree, which my mother kept adding to over the years. I continued the habit in her memory, I guess.'

'And where is she now?'

'She died.'

'Well, it's a fine tree,' Will said approvingly, 'and you're very good at it.'

'Whatever do you mean?'

'Collecting things,' said Will. 'Finding and saving bits and pieces that nobody sees value in. You found me,' he explained, 'even if it wasn't intentional. Here I was ready to leave the district and instead I find myself back where I started. Except this time I have a roof over my head and I'm standing beside a pretty girl who collects broken thingamajigs instead of hair ribbons.'

The bottles and tins hanging from the branches tinkled in the morning breeze. If her mother were still alive Edwina guessed she would have liked this young man who stood next to her. A poor boy, trustworthy enough to return her locket.

'Edwina?' Hamilton Baker's voice reverberated through the orchard.

'It's Father.'

Will winked. 'God save us all,' he whispered with a smile.

Hamilton located them and, with a quizzical lift of an eyebrow at finding them together, spoke without addressing either. 'Ah, yes. My wife's, may she rest in peace, monument to feminine nonsense. So, Will, you ran away to join the circus? Rather ridiculous in hind-sight, I'm sure you'd agree, especially in light of the fact that my son said those showpeople turned you down. I'm sure that ring-barking doesn't seem such a bad profession now.' He paused. 'And here you are, back in my employ.'

'Yes, sir. I appreciate the opportunity, Mr Baker.'

'Aiden seems to have kept you busy enough,' confirmed Hamilton.

'Yes, sir, he has, Mr Baker. Sun-up to sun-down.'

'Well, as this is the first time I've laid eyes on you since your inglorious return, you must be earning your keep.'

Edwina saw Will through her father's eyes – the dusty, damaged boots, trousers threadbare at the knees.

'My son tells me you can shoe a horse, make saddlery repairs? Is that right, Will?'

'I'm a blacksmith by trade, sir, yes, Mr Baker, but my leather work comes a poor second.'

'Then you must practise. The only gift God gives us after life is time, my son. And that time should not be used precipitously, but wisely and with dedication to the task at hand.'

'Yes, Mr Baker.'

'With that in mind I have a task for you. Our well has dried up and you, my boy, are going to dig down until you find water. After that I've a whip that needs re-plaiting.'

'Yes, Mr Baker. I will do my best, sir.'

'And, Will, as you don't appear to have been able to afford the services of a barber, my daughter will cut your hair.'

'Me?' said Edwina.

'And you will make good use of a cut-throat razor and clear that fuzz from your face. Place a chair on the verandah, my girl, and give this man the short back and sides required.'

'But . . .' Edwina tried to interrupt.

'Hair. I can't abide hair. It's over your ears, man, and scraping your collar and I'll have no man about this house whose appearance isn't suitable. Are we clear? And, Will?'

'Yes, Mr Baker?'

'Don't speak to my daughter again unless it be to ask for instruction or to receive it. Are we understood?'

'Yes, Mr Baker.' Will waited until his employer left. 'I've never dug a well.'

136

'Father's right. We shouldn't be talking. It's not proper.'

'Perhaps, but it seems you still have to cut my hair.'

Edwina pressed her lips together. She was well aware of her father's fastidiousness. A characteristic she felt was more suited to the regular churchgoer than a man who was happy to read the Bible occasionally at home on Sundays, but was far from interested when it came to travelling to Wywanna for a service. Returning to the house in silence, Edwina consulted her father on the mechanics of hair-cutting as Will, supplied with razor, soap and water, shaved.

Scissors in hand, Edwina set a chair on the veranda with a thud, wrapping a towel about the stiff-backed man.

'I am sorry about this,' he said, pushing the bowl of shaving water to one side with the toe of his boot. Jed clambered slowly onto the veranda to sit at Will's feet.

Edwina's answer was to sit a cooking pot on his head. 'Now don't move a muscle, otherwise you'll be all higgledy-piggledy.'

'What are you doing!' complained Will, immediately removing the pot and standing abruptly.

Edwina snatched the vessel from his hand. 'It's how Father said I should cut your hair.'

'I know the basin cut,' replied Will angrily, 'and I'll not be going about looking like a boy from the slums.'

'I'm sorry?'

'If you put that damn thing on my head and cut around it, how do you think I will look?'

Edwina tried to envisage what he described.

'Well?' persevered Will. 'I'll tell you. You'll follow the rim of the cooking pot above my ears, in a straight line, all the way round.' He grabbed the container from Edwina's grasp. 'I'll not look like that again. You'll just have to do your best without it.'

Edwina hadn't thought about how Will would appear. Her only concern was obeying her father. 'If I had a choice I wouldn't be cutting your hair at all.'

In response Will sat back down in the chair and, with the pot clasped firmly on his lap, he told her to get on with the job and be quick about it.

'What, no pot? Let's hope you can cut straight, daughter, otherwise your customer's self-esteem will suffer.' Her father placed a chair on the veranda and crossing his legs waved a hand for his daughter to begin. Lifting the scissors, Edwina rested them against Will's neck.

'Don't cut me,' said Will.

'Be quiet, young man,' replied Hamilton. 'Well, get to it, Edwina.'

Nervously Edwina pushed Will's head slightly forward with her hand. The warmth of his body seeped into hers. Uncomfortably aware of her audience, Edwina's gaze moved to where her father sat.

'Don't look at *me*, Edwina,' advised Hamilton. 'A drawing of blood is not recommended.'

Keeping equal distance between hair and shirt collar, Edwina did her best to curtail the thoughts that came with each snip of the scissors. Novelty mixed with self-consciousness, as her fingers grazed sun-burnt skin. She cut slowly and methodically, noticing the twirl of his ear, the thinness of the lobe, the fine creases on a neck that for some inexplicable reason she wanted to touch, and all the while brown hair fell in clumps onto the towel about Will's shoulders. She dusted away the thick locks, blowing softly on his neck, watching as the silky tufts fell to the ground.

'Stop fussing, Edwina,' complained her father.

This was the second time Edwina had been in close proximity to Will. She was reminded of the strength of his touch as they'd ridden home together and then, later, his grip about her waist strong and sure as he helped her from the saddle. Stop it, Edwina berated herself. Was she really so sheltered, so keen for the company of someone beyond that of her father and brother that she would ponder over an inappropriate stranger?

Will began to whistle, softly and melodiously. Heavens, thought Edwina, he's enjoying this, enjoying her discomfort. He sat with his legs outstretched, with a pleased if drowsy expression, an attitude that rather infuriated her. She straightened her spine, before getting to her knees so that she was at exactly the right height and angle, level with him.

'Stop that,' she hissed into his ear.

'Don't you like music?' asked Will, his head never moving.

'Hurry up, Edwina,' stated her father, walking inside the house.

'You have to do the sides as well,' whispered Will. 'Not straight across but a bit of a curve around my ears. I don't want the girls thinking I had my hair cut by an amateur.'

'Shush,' came Edwina's reply. She wanted to ask what girls he referred to, but instead she shuffled sideways, wincing at the discomfort of the boards against her knees. With her hand steadying the sideways tilt of Will's head, she continued cutting, stopping occasionally to check her handiwork. Having got over her initial apprehension, Edwina quite enjoyed the challenge of the task set her. She was one for doing things properly, carefully.

'I'll not look like I can't afford to visit a barber,' Will told her, his voice low.

'But you can't,' said Edwina quietly, stating the obvious.

'That's not the point,' replied Will a little more loudly.

Edwina looked to the door leading into the house. 'Keep your voice down. For someone with *no* money, you're very proud, aren't you?'

'And for someone with *a bit* of money you're very haughty. I'd not expected that of you, not after the caper you pulled at the circus.'

'Hold still,' she replied brusquely, wondering if a little nick to his ear would be so terribly wrong. Finally satisfied, Edwina stood. 'Look at me.' Will did so and she blinked away his scrutiny as she cut the fringe of hair that fell across his brow, noticing the healthy glow of freshly shaven skin.

'Now that I'm presentable will you walk out with me one day?' he asked.

Edwina frowned at the audacity.

Will scooped up some of the cut hair. 'You can put that in your locket as well if you like.'

Edwina was about to tell the young man what he could do with the locks when her father reappeared.

'Are you finished?'

Edwina answered her father, 'Quite finished.' Will winked at her.

'Good,' replied Hamilton. 'And you can use a rifle, Will?'

Will shook out the towel, handing it to Edwina. 'I know how they work, sir.'

'Then we'll do very well indeed.' Hamilton passed Will a jacket and waited until he'd put it on. 'That will do nicely. Well, come on, lad. Aiden and Davidson are waiting.'

'Where are you going, Father?' asked Edwina. 'Into Wywanna?'

At the mention of the town, a troubled look crossed Will's face. Through the orchard Davidson could be seen readying the horses. Her father left to join the aboriginal, Will following with a shrug of his shoulders.

'No, my dear,' Hamilton called back, 'I'm going to pick a fight and then stop it before it begins.'

≪ Chapter Fifteen ≫

With the men's departure, Edwina decided that there was no reason why she shouldn't take a peek at the cub. After all, visiting the baby lion didn't mean she agreed with Will's theft. It was simply a case of checking on a creature who, through no fault of its own, suddenly found itself bereft of a mother and the environment it had been born into. Besides, Edwina reasoned, she didn't have to tell Will what she was about to do. An important consideration when he was likely to view her interest as concern and then further cajole her into caring for the animal. Not that she was drawn to doing any such thing. In fact, the less contact she had with the cub, the better.

Walking through the orchard, Edwina reached the stables, sliding the heavy bolt open. 'Stay,' she told Jed, before closing the door behind her. Edwina waited for her sight to adjust to the dim light, half expecting the stolen cat to appear out of a shadowy corner to growl hungrily at her feet. But there was no movement within the building and, apart from the odd bird scuttling across the iron roof, no doubt picking through the leaf-litter, the shed was quiet. Bright angles of sunlight filtered through the timber walls, highlighting the row of boxes that stabled the horses. Opposite were a number of crates holding oranges and lemons, while at the far end a stack of hay was piled against the wall. It was in this direction Edwina walked, sidestepping lumps of manure, noticing that each of the stalls were already mucked out and strewn with fresh hay.

Will's belongings, a narrow furled swag, were sitting neatly on the ground near the hay but there was no sign of the lion. Edwina peered into each stall, checked under a pile of empty hessian wheat bags and behind the oat-filled feed bin. The only place she hadn't investigated was the hay stacked next to where Will slept. Stepping onto one of the bales, Edwina climbed up the shaky pyramid-shaped mound. Once at the top she steadied herself and looked over the edge. By the drag marks in the dirt below it appeared that the bales had been recently rearranged so that there was a gap next to the wall and in the semi-darkness she could just make out a container that held water. A crease formed above Edwina's nose. There was no sign of the cub. That was all they needed – a baby lion running wild on the property.

Then she heard it. A noise. Similar to a purr but almost like a snore. It came from the adjoining tack room where all the saddlery items were stored. In her haste to climb down the stack of bales, Edwina stumbled, rolled awkwardly to one side and then fell, landing heavily on the ground as a number of the bales fell down beside her. Shaking her head to clear her thoughts, Edwina got to her feet slowly, holding her lower back as she walked out of the stables, shielding her face from the morning glare.

Outside the tack room, she met Jed, who was busy sniffing the ground. 'Found something, have you?' The dog immediately sat, waiting patiently. Edwina drew the bolt as quietly as possible and stepped inside. At first it was far too dark to make out anything and she left the door slightly ajar, allowing a slither of light to enter the room. Gradually the surrounds came into focus. Saddles were lined up along one wall on an A-shaped stand. Yokes, harnesses, leads, saddle blankets, ropes and reins hung from a beam and in another corner sat a variety of parts for their various horse-drawn vehicles, wagon, dray, plough and the buggy. Wheels, snigging ropes for dragging logs, broken lengths of leather and two piles of horseshoes, old and new, was just some of the gear Edwina identified. The air smelt of grease, oil and leather and dust particles floated in the air, illuminated by streaks of sunlight that criss-crossed the room through numerous gaps.

Edwina scanned the walls and floor, finally noticing that one of the saddles was lying on the ground. The surcingle had been chewed, teeth marks visible in the well-oiled leather. After examining the damage, she looked carefully under the row of saddles next to the dividing stable wall. A deep hole made a neat tunnel under the wall and staring out at her from the other side was a pair of eyes. Edwina's breath caught in her throat.

Within reach of the lion was a sack. Plainly the cub was not willing to wait for a meal for the bag had been dragged close to the hole and a meaty bloodstain marked the canvas. Edwina slowly reached out a hand and picked up the bag. It was clearly stamped with the name Colby's Circus. When she next looked up, the cub was sitting a couple of feet away, regarding her with large inquisitive eyes.

'Oh my. You really are very beautiful.'

The creature before her was covered in tawny fur with white spots that Edwina could only describe as being slightly faded. The cub surveyed her steadily, its amber-coloured eyes unblinking.

His nose twitching, the lion moved a little closer. Edwina slowly upturned the bag, shaking the material to empty it, and a few chunks of dark meat fell to the ground. The animal reached out a paw, scrabbling across the dirt, and with a lunge pulled one of the pieces of meat towards him. As he ate Edwina moved the remaining flesh a little closer to her. The cub seemed to regard her thoughtfully, tilting its head just slightly as if weighing up the outcome of moving closer to the last of the meat.

'I won't hurt you,' said Edwina. They remained quite still, regarding each other quietly, before the cub slowly got to its feet. This time the cat moved deliberately towards her, baring its teeth on approach. Edwina wanted to tell the animal that he could trust her, but noting the lion's obvious caution remained silent. Eventually temptation gave way to action and the cub moved quickly, snatching up the meat and swallowing it immediately.

'You'll have to go back inside your hidey-hole,' said Edwina, turning to see Jed by her side. Having pushed through the door left ajar, the old dog stared at the cub and then sat tiredly, his tail wagging happily. 'I'm not sure he'll want to be friends, Jed,' warned Edwina. The animals regarded each other with interest until the lion cub backed away, scrambling through the tunnel and out of sight. 'Just as well,' commented Edwina, moving to gather up some of the broken leather and old horseshoes and using the material to block the entrance.

Outside Edwina wondered what on earth Will thought he was going to do with the lion cub once he left here. The animal was already built like a small dog. In a few weeks she guessed he'd be far too heavy to cart around on horseback, let alone have running or walking beside Will as he wandered the countryside in search of work. As she called to Jed to follow her back to the house, Edwina hoped the week went quickly so that Will and the cub could be on their way. There was a sinking feeling in her stomach. She just knew that with the lion cub holed up only feet away from the homestead things would become worse before they got better.

≺ Chapter Sixteen ≻

I t was nearing noon by the time Hamilton reached Ridgeway
Station homestead. The building sat squarely in an area cleared
of trees, the bush kept at a distance from the house by the continual felling of timber. Hamilton had visited the homestead on
two previous occasions and, as before, he was immediately struck
by the imposing building which spread low and long across a
flood-safe ridge. Made of mud brick and plastered with whitewash,
the structure still carried the telltale signs of early settlement.
There were small holes in the outside walls made for rifles and the
outbuildings were situated some distance from the house, ensuring
that should a structure be fired, such a disaster did not spread
immediately to the other buildings. It struck Hamilton that, for all
the station's impressiveness and endurance, having survived intact
through the years, it remained a lonely looking place.

A lawn, patchy but recognisable, was the extent of the garden,
except for the line of trees that bordered the stone path leading to
the front door. On a previous visit, from within the dark interior
of the gloomy station office, Hamilton had once glimpsed a substantial vegetable garden through the window, being tended to by

a Chinaman of advanced years. He wondered if the plants still thrived or if the lack of a family at Ridgeway over the last decade had rendered the plot redundant.

'It's grander than I imagined,' announced Aiden as Davidson lifted the latch on the gate. The men rode through in single file, Will at the rear. 'Bit of a waste though, isn't it? With no-one living here permanently.'

'Remember what I told you all,' said Hamilton, halting briefly. 'If Fernleigh appears, a show of force is all that's necessary.' His initial inclination to give the upstart manager a lesson by having Davidson punch the man squarely in the face was regrettably replaced with the decision to report the altercation to the local constabulary and Somerville. This was a far better approach. Firstly, it would hopefully deter the manager from carrying out his threat and, most importantly, the incident provided the perfect opportunity to catch Somerville on the day of his arrival under the guise of complaint and in doing so discover just who exactly had been inspecting the station last week.

'I won't be involved in any shooting, Mr Baker,' Will reminded his employer as they stayed their mounts at the verandah's edge.

Hamilton frowned. 'So you've said.' Now was not the time to give the young whippersnapper a lesson in talking back to one's employer. 'But I do expect you to sit astride your horse and look the part, Will. Otherwise you'll be back in Wywanna by nightfall.'

'Yes, Mr Baker, sir.'

Hamilton admitted that the lad was much improved by a haircut and the addition of a coat, but he still didn't like him. Boys such as he were fine to employ as ringbarkers and odd-jobbers, but he could tell this one was an opportunist and a smart talker to boot, based on his recent ability to coerce Aiden into giving him a job. And the very fact he'd left a man's job for the circus suggested a tendency to laziness. Hamilton was not partial to having him near his daughter for long. Edwina was quite removed from the wiles of the modern world and, although she was generally a sensible girl, even the epitome of females was not immune to advances from the male sex. Hamilton knew that from bitter experience. He'd already decided that once Will completed digging out the well he would be on his way.

The men were lined up appropriately. Still on horseback, Davidson held his rifle, cocked and ready to fire, while Aiden and Will flanked the aboriginal on either side. 'Good,' stated Hamilton, dismounting. Wrapping the reins around the rail, he climbed the two slab stairs, crossed the verandah and, pounding the brass doorknob, stepped to one side. 'Don't hesitate to shoot, Davidson, if the recalcitrant comes to the door armed. Leg wound only, mind.'

A young woman dressed in a rather old-fashioned maid's uniform of white and black answered the door with a curt, 'Good afternoon. Can I help you?'

'Hamilton Baker to see Mr Somerville.' He thought the girl looked a bit too pale for country life, her tone was citified, the gaze coolly professional. She was quick to take in his attire and those of the men waiting on horseback.

'I'm afraid Mr Somerville isn't in, sir,' the maid announced.

'What do you mean he isn't in?' Hamilton thought back to the note handed to him by Andrew at the Guild. It clearly stated this was the day of Somerville's arrival. 'I have it on good authority that he was due to arrive on this morning's train.' Hamilton made a show of checking his fob watch, wondering if the Western Mail was late.

'I'm sorry, sir, but Mr Somerville was taken ill. His nephew is here, however, if you would like to see Mr Ridgeway.'

Excellent – the son and heir. Hamilton offered the girl his most gracious smile. 'I would indeed like to see the young master.'

Cumbersome footsteps in the hallway heralded the arrival of Mr Fernleigh. He pushed past the maid. 'Ah, if it isn't the money-lender,' the manager said with a leery tone, scratching his beard.

'And look, Donella, the Englishman's brought his black factotum, the white-eyed crow.' Mr Fernleigh reached inside the hallway and walked out onto the verandah clutching his rifle.

Twenty feet away Davidson lifted his own firearm in response.

The maid moved a little, increasing the space between herself and the manager. Unsure as to what to do, she waited for Mr Fernleigh to take charge of the situation.

'I'm here to see Mr Ridgeway.' Hamilton directed his request to the maid, ignoring Mr Fernleigh.

The girl looked at the three men on horseback as the manager took up a position in a squatter's chair, the rifle resting casually across his thighs.

'You best come in.' The maid stepped back, allowing Hamilton to pass.

'Come here, Aiden,' bellowed Hamilton, leaving the stockman and Will to face off with the manager.

Hamilton followed the girl the length of the hallway, scowling at his son to keep pace when the boy stopped at one of the bearded portraits that lined the dark passage. The place smelt musty and was sparsely furnished with a few occasional tables. They passed the door leading to the station office, left the entrance hall and then turned down a series of smaller halls that gradually suggested more frequent habitation. Music and laughter could be heard as the maid led them through the rabbit warren of rooms and passages. Some of the walls were tongue and groove, others cracked mud brick, while the floors were a mix of worn stone pavers and timber boards. The homestead had seen many changes over the decades and Hamilton guessed that most of the rooms would have long been invaded by spiders and cobwebs, the furniture sheathed in dust sheets. Aiden was right. It was a waste of a fine home.

Donella opened a door and they entered an airy room filled with white wicker furniture. Clearly this was the living area the family inhabited when in residence. The timber floor was covered in rugs and a mixture of furniture filled the room. Round gilt mirrors, large Chinese patterned vases and silk-covered cushions were prominent along with the tasselled throws on the scrolled arms of the daybed. He recognised the tooled leather desk from the station office, placed in a sunlit corner, an item he'd coveted on first sight some years prior, and wondered at the character of the son and heir, who was clearly responsible for the altered state of the house. It certainly wasn't to Somerville's taste. The little Hamilton knew of the man suggested he wasn't the type to be bothered with such rearrangements. Especially to this extent. He could only guess at the number of rooms that had been ransacked to create such a semblance of cluttered eclectic sophistication. Gloria would undoubtedly be quite impressed.

'You're to sit in on this meeting, Aiden, and learn. And what you hear is not to be repeated, especially to your sister. Edwina is impressionable. I am taking you into my confidence, into the workings of my business.'

'Yes, sir. What a marvellous room,' replied Aiden, distracted by the furnishings and the long sideboard which was crowded with bottles of alcohol. 'So, this all belongs to the son. Lucky guy.'

Hamilton nodded.

'Good morning, I'm Charles Ridgeway.'

Turning, Hamilton shook the outstretched hand of the young man who had appeared. The heir to an indebted forty thousand acres, Charles was tall, well-bred by his symmetrical looks, but not at all what he expected. He'd thought to meet a well-dressed citified type, with the kind of healthy countenance that suggested he'd been good at sports at school. But the man before him was nut-brown and hard-muscled with a handgrip that brought tears to the eyes. 'Hamilton Baker,' he announced, rubbing briefly at his hand. 'And my son, Aiden.'

The man gave a disarming smile. 'Welcome, Mr Baker, Aiden.'

'What are you doing?' a female voice called from outside.

Hamilton followed Charles' gaze out the window to where three women and a man of similar age reclined on blankets in the sun.

'My friends,' he explained. 'Donella, can you please take out a round of drinks before they start throwing things.' The maid went straight to the cabinet and began lining up crystal glasses. 'I think they expected a little more excitement, but I'm afraid I've only had the circus to offer as entertainment. Although the theft of that lion cub provided some conversation.'

'An unfortunate happening,' replied Hamilton, noting the casualness of Charles' attire, a shirt and open waistcoat.

'We've been taking bets on who would give up first, the girl or her partner. You haven't heard anything, have you?'

'Nothing.' Hamilton discreetly elbowed Aiden, drawing his son away from the picture window framing the pretty young women clustered outside. 'I expect they'll be found soon.'

'We heard the circus owner posted a reward for the safe return of the cub. Apparently they're worth a fortune,' explained Charles. 'Of course, the thieves have to get it somewhere where it can be sold first. I would have thought that would be a problem in itself.'

Expecting to be led to the comfortable settee and matching cane chairs, Hamilton was a little amused to find the young cove playing Lord of the Manor. Charles sat behind the large leather desk in the corner, gesturing to the seats opposite. A good sign perhaps, Hamilton considered. Does the boy know the difference between business and pleasure, or is he just trying on his new role as heir for size? Hamilton settled back in the chair and crossed his legs, noticing the filthy wide-brimmed Akubra sitting on the desk.

'It is a pleasure to meet you, Charles. You're here with your wife?'

'No, friends, Mr Baker. It's been some time since my sister and I came home. I've only just returned from the Territory.'

'I thought you were based in Brisbane.'

'Not for some years. The outback beckoned.'

'That would have been an experience,' said Hamilton, impressed by the man's fortitude. Would that his own son had the ability.

'Yes. It's a big country. Anyway, I coerced my friends to join us with promises of adventure. My mistake and their boredom. I'm afraid I never was a great partygoer, but I forgot how much they are.'

'Nothing like travel, hey what?' Hamilton responded agreeably. So the young man was unmarried. The loan document was in his top pocket should an examination of the outstanding debt be required, and if it wasn't? If Charles had funds at his disposal, well then, that was quite another matter. Here then was what Hamilton had been searching for – a young man of good breeding who would very soon be debt free and cash rich. There were possibilities here if Charles proved amiable. The boy would be thankful for Worth's offer to buy the property, and then there was Edwina. A good marriage was in the offing. That's how dynasties were made.

Charles made a point of offering them morning tea and when the maid returned from carrying the drinks outside to his companions, he asked her to fetch the beverage for the three of them.

'I knew your parents, Charles. We met on a number of occasions. I was sorry to hear of the accident.'

'Thank you, Mr Baker. My father loved automobiles as much as he loved a party. Anyway, it's a good twelve years ago now and I rather think that if he'd not been turned down by the army for being too old he would have been killed over there anyway, considering the casualties.'

'A harsh assessment,' answered Hamilton.

Charles shrugged. 'I was fourteen when they died. I barely remember what they were like. They loved Ridgeway Station though. As did Louise and I. When we arrived here the other day it really was like coming home.'

'It's a bit different to the Northern Territory I'd imagine,' said Aiden.

151

'It is, mate, yes. There's so much potential up there. So much space. So many opportunities. It's quite a thing to be walking alongside thousands of head of cattle bringing them into the nearest yards. Makes this sheep business boring in comparison. Anyway, I believe, Mr Baker, that you and Mr Fernleigh are having some difficulties. That's why you're here, I gather.'

So much for niceties. Hamilton's eyebrows drew together. 'Boundary problems, yes.' The manager was clearly on good terms with the family, his presence inside the house on their arrival evidence of this.

Charles drew a ledger from a drawer and flipped the pages until he'd located the information required. 'Substantial problems, I'd say. We seem to be missing some sheep.'

Hamilton wasn't here to discuss lamb roasts, but he was prepared. 'And I am missing income from the damage done to my crops. I have noted the loss over the years in terms of yield and done my best to seek compensation as Mr Fernleigh refuses to oblige.' Hamilton opened the notebook showing the dates and numbers of sheep that had wandered onto his property.

Charles tapped the page. 'I see. And these numbers are?'

'The acres damaged each year and the sheep I have kept as payment for the destruction. I suspect that Fernleigh keeps cutting the boundary fence in order to feed your livestock. In your absence of course.'

'Really?' Charles sounded unconvinced.

'Your manager threatened me yesterday, which is one of the reasons for my visit this morning.'

Donella arrived, setting a cup and saucer before each of them and pouring strong black tea.

'Thank you, Donella.' Charles waited until the maid left the room. 'Yes, Mr Fernleigh did mention the incident. He's obsessive in his role, but harmless.'

'It didn't feel harmless,' countered Hamilton, wondering how the lad could have the slightest idea of his employee's ability or personality. 'And with due respect, Charles, with no family member here on the station to keep an eye on things, the man has been allowed to run quite unchecked.'

'But you weren't the one who had a native pointing a rifle at your back, were you, Mr Baker?' stated Charles.

They eyeballed each other across the desk. 'No, Fernleigh's rifle was pointed at my chest, but I'm sure he didn't bother to share that with you.' Hamilton didn't wait for a response. 'The best fertiliser is provided by the footprints of the owner, Charles; management of staff is imperative to the running of a business, and a manager is a manager, after all. Fernleigh should remember his place.'

Charles appeared entertained. He leant back in the chair, crossing his leg so that an ankle rested on a knee. 'And you're here to offer me some friendly advice as to the management of my staff?'

'Your property is overstocked. That's the reason your sheep are hungry. And I don't see any of your staff out there patching up the fence. It's always us that must tend to it. We are the ones suffering damage and it has gone on far too long.'

'I see.'

'The incident will be reported to the authorities. But I trust that while you are here visiting you will instil in Fernleigh the necessity to behave like an enlightened human being.' He stopped momentarily, pleased to see Charles' irritated expression. 'In the meantime I am here to discuss the substantial monies owed me by the Ridgeway family. As I am aware you have now come of age regarding the estate and with your uncle's illness,' Hamilton lifted his hands, palms up, 'unfortunately it falls to us to discuss such matters.'

Charles closed the ledger, replacing it in the desk drawer, his movements brisk. 'I am aware of the outstanding loan. I would like to extend it.'

'It is with regret that I am unable to do so.'

'Why not?' Withdrawing a tin of tobacco from his breast pocket Charles crushed the leaf between large palms before deftly rolling it in paper. Hamilton caught sight of the man's hard-skinned hands as he tapped the end of the cigarette on the table, lit it and exhaled the smoke thoughtfully.

'The contract clearly stipulates –'

'Contracts can be amended,' Charles answered, 'we both know that. Don't take me for some schoolboy, Mr Baker.'

'Not a single interest payment has been made over the term of the loan and the amount outstanding is very large.'

Charles inhaled deeply.

'And nor was the possibility of an extension noted in the terms of the agreement,' explained Hamilton. 'I'm sorry, but I have been informing your family for a number of years now. You have sighted the correspondence forwarded to your solicitor?'

'Recently, yes. As I explained, I've been away.'

'So you said,' Hamilton replied equally crisply, 'running after someone else's livestock.'

Charles crumpled the cigarette in an ashtray. 'You should be able to relate to that.'

Hamilton didn't appreciate the implication. He could only conclude that the wilds of the north had been the fatherless lad's undoing. Studying him now he could clearly see the rough-and-ready stockman barely hidden behind the remains of a private school education and the chance of being born into a well-known pastoral family. If this was the new breed of landowner, the likes of Peter Worth had their work cut out in the future. 'You know that you have until the end of the week to make good on the transaction.'

'The end of the week? But I thought . . . And if I can't?' responded Charles, a definite edge to his voice.

'Then unfortunately you will need to dispose of some asset in order to meet your legal obligations,' said Hamilton carefully.

'You understand that I don't want to force a sale but time is up. In any case I would have thought your solicitor would have advised you accordingly, no matter where you were.'

'My uncle handled our family's affairs.'

Hamilton considered the limited options available. He could suggest a partial sale of the station but Peter Worth wanted the entire property. Besides, the situation presented the perfect transaction. Hamilton would have the loan repaid to him in full and benefit from doing business with the Guild's President. And eventually the monies received would go towards enlarging his share portfolio.

'And you really won't consider an extension?' asked Charles.

Hamilton dipped his chin. 'My hands are tied.'

Charles, distinctly unimpressed, pushed his chair backwards, the timber striking the window behind. 'I did wonder why my uncle didn't approach a bank,' he said, standing, 'instead of using your services. I suppose he wanted to keep things private but your interest terms are pure highway robbery. If that's all, Mr Baker?' he said dismissively.

Hamilton wasn't prepared to be spoken to like that. 'Charles, I do understand the difficulty this presents but I was under the impression from your uncle that there was unlikely to be another generation of Ridgeways here on the property. That being the case and with this matter pressing then may I offer some advice? If you have no other saleable assets then you must consider selling Ridgeway Station.'

'No.' His voice was firm.

Hamilton tried to remain calm. Years of grovelling to the Guild members, of trying to better his place in society, of being accepted, and it all came down to this moment and the young man opposite him behind his father's desk. He had to close this deal. 'So then we return to the question of how you intend to repay the loan.' Careful, Hamilton warned himself. Debtors could turn skittish in an instant. It was time for a little fact finding. 'Have you received any expressions of interest?'

Charles remained standing. 'No. I'm not selling.'

Hamilton paused. 'Aiden saw an automobile on the property last week and –'

'So that was you?' commented Charles to Aiden.

Aiden looked over the rim of his teacup. 'Yes, my sister and I were out riding.'

'Well, don't worry, Mr Baker, it was me, on my land.'

Hamilton ignored the proprietorial air. Had he been less of a gentleman he would have plugged young Ridgeway in the nose. 'So you can either place a mortgage on the property to repay the debt owed or sell and recoup. If you do choose to sell I have an interested party. Do think carefully, Charles. As a friend of your father's I am trying to do my best for you and you know what they say, pride cometh before a fall.'

'Are you threatening me, Mr Baker?' Charles' fist curled.

Hamilton hoped something could be salvaged from the meeting, but that now appeared unlikely. 'I'm simply a businessman stating the obvious.' He waited, hoping Charles would see reason.

'You could extend the loan if you wanted to,' argued Charles.

Yes, he could; however, Hamilton made it a practice never to delay settlement and only in the most extraordinary of situations did he extend credit beyond the initial agreement. He drank the now cold tea in three gulps. 'Well, I can see that you're not interested in discussing options. Please be advised that the monies are due by 5 pm this Friday. If not received by this time you will be in default and I will commence legal proceedings immediately.' Hamilton stood; Aiden followed his lead. 'It's probably worthwhile remembering that it was your family that came to me for the loan, Charles. Take that under advisement the next time we speak. This is Queensland. Not the Northern Territory. We're civilised here.'

'I'm sorry. Am I disturbing you?' A young woman appeared, smiling prettily.

Hamilton observed his son as Aiden, standing next to him, stood a little straighter.

'My sister, Louise,' introduced Charles. 'Mr Baker and Aiden were just leaving.'

'Oh, from next door, but you must come over and visit us. We're starved for company, aren't we?' Louise didn't wait for an answer as she walked forwards, resting a hand briefly on Aiden's arm.

Hamilton cleared his throat as laughter streamed in from outside. 'Thank you, but unfortunately we must be on our way.'

The girl pouted charmingly, looking to her brother for support.

'We mustn't keep Mr Baker from what he does best,' replied Charles sarcastically.

'Then if the mountain won't come to Mohammed.'

'This is Queensland, Louise,' Charles said sternly to his sister, 'a most civilised part of the world. One must wait to be invited.'

Hamilton noted Louise's questioning expression, when the expected invitation to visit the Bakers' property did not materialise. Their leave-taking was stilted, and as they walked through the house Louise could be heard cross-examining her brother.

'I didn't know you lent money to people like the Ridgeways,' whispered Aiden.

Hamilton looked at his son's gaping mouth and prayed he'd not been staring at Charles with that same shocked expression for the entire time. 'Well, now you do. And you will keep this matter to yourself, Aiden. Remember what I said earlier.'

'Yes, Father. I thought he may have reached over the desk and grabbed you by the collar at one stage. Are all your meetings like that?'

'Not usually, no.'

'Is it a lot of money that's owed?' asked Aiden.

'Enough.'

'Do you think you'll get it?'

'I have the law on my side.' His son didn't respond and Hamilton wondered if he thought as he did – that with Charles and Fernleigh in a similar frame of mind, the law might not be enough. They were quite a handful to have brooding on the other side of a boundary fence.

Outside, little was altered between the men. Davidson still sat astride his horse with the rifle directed at the manager, while Mr Fernleigh was his mirror image, although the hairy stockman lounged in the squatter's chair as if his spine was incapable of supporting his body.

'Come on,' said Hamilton gruffly to the waiting men, mounting his horse and ignoring the manager's unsavoury comments.

'Don't come back again unless you've an invitation!' the manager yelled.

This time Hamilton didn't have a suitable retort. Fury blinded him. Everything he'd worked for lay in ruins thanks to the Ridgeway upstart, unless Charles had no other option but to sell. He'd not said he intended to stay on; however, with his experience up north he would probably be more than capable of running the station. Either way it would become unpleasant now. He could feel it in his gut. When he had arrived at the property, Hamilton had appeased himself with the knowledge that, no matter what happened, Peter Worth would get the land, he would get his monies and the unqualified friendship of his latest client, and Fernleigh would undoubtedly be out of a job. Now, as Hamilton spurred his horse, he wasn't so sure. The financial laws were one thing; Charles Ridgeway quite another. He was sorry he'd even considered his daughter's union with such a man.

≪ Chapter Seventeen ≫

Dropping the kindling for the fire outside the kitchen door, Edwina backed away before Mrs Ryan asked her to fetch something else. The Scotswoman was in a right foul mood on account of having to cook for Will and complained that a joint of mutton was missing from the food safe. The cook wasn't the only unsettled one in their household. Her father and brother had returned from Ridgeway Station an hour earlier, with Father stomping into his study and slamming the door, before immediately heading out on horseback again with Davidson. In contrast, Aiden was dawdling about the place with a dreamy expression she'd not seen before. It seemed that Mr Somerville had not ventured north to the property and that in his place were the visiting Ridgeway children.

'And that's who we saw last week with the car?' probed Edwina once their father was riding away.

'It was,' Aiden told her. 'It was a business meeting, E. Really, you wouldn't understand.'

'I wouldn't understand? Did you?'

Her brother shoved both hands in his pockets.

'Well, as Father slammed the door to his office, I assume it didn't go well.' Really, her brother could be so painfully exasperating at times.

'No, it didn't,' he admitted, then in a rush of beneficence Aiden explained that their father was owed a great sum of money and the Ridgeways had no choice but to pay by the agreed deadline, Friday. 'The son, Charles, will put up a fight though. He's that type of person.'

'So you didn't like him?'

'No, I didn't. He's different. I got the feeling he thinks he's better than us. By the way, I was thinking we should block the creek so we have a bigger waterhole near the new paddock we're clearing. Some people spend an awful lot of money scooping out dams and that would be a lot cheaper and easier, don't you think?'

It was impossible to work out how Aiden's mind functioned at times. 'And what happens to those people depending on the creek further downstream?' asked Edwina. 'Not to mention we already have a bore drain out there which is currently only watering the wildlife.'

'I'll speak to Father about it.'

She shook her head. 'You do that.'

Edwina walked back to the chicken pen musing on the shiny Ford and the man that had made her feel so uncomfortable when she and Aiden had come across the party while out riding. Now she understood why. Not that it mattered, for there were more important things to think about. Firstly, her brother's admittance into the holy sanctum of their father's world outside the property. Secondly, the surprising news that their father was involved in business with the Ridgeways and that they owed him money.

The hens squawked in annoyance at her intrusion. Racing towards the rear of the coop to their timber roost, they soon lost interest in Edwina as she began scooping shovelfuls of dried manure, dirt, grass and hay into a bucket. She wondered how many other people her father had loaned money to. Not the small-time clients which he alluded to occasionally, but the large landowners, the prominent graziers like those who owned Ridgeway Station. Those people had money. Generations of money. And if their father was doing business with the likes of these people, then it only stood to reason that he would undoubtedly be making money from such associations.

How many times were she and Aiden told that they must live sparingly, that every enterprise must pay for itself, that they were fortunate to have the comfort of a home and food on the table? Edwina always believed that a money-lender made a modest living. And their lives were certainly frugal. But perhaps she'd been naive.

Closing the latch on the gate, Edwina walked across to the vegetable garden and began scattering the manure she'd raked from the chicken pen across the recently turned earth. Something small and round caught her attention and, scraping the soil away, Edwina snatched up the marble with a smile. 'A cats-eye,' she murmured, pleased at the find. The yellow-green interior glinted prettily and Edwina happily pocketed the object. There would be no last-minute search tonight for something that could be left at the base of her mother's tree tomorrow morning.

'Edwina, have you got that washing yet? And what are we doing about the water?' Mrs Ryan stood with her arms crossed, her laced shoes planted shoulder-width apart. Aiden called it her angry stance and today the woman was making good use of it.

Sitting the bucket on the ground, Edwina rubbed at the back of her head. There was still a lump from the attack at the circus and the residual dull pain was yet to totally disappear. 'I just have to finish up here first, Mrs Ryan, and Aiden fetched the water. See?' She pointed at the barrels lined along the outer kitchen wall next to the food-keeper. 'Will is to start on the new well any day now.'

'Well, any day now we could be dying of thirst,' replied the older woman. 'And I'm telling you now that not a body in this house will last one minute drinking that brackish muck once the heat comes. And when it does we all know who'll be the first to complain – your father. His Lordship doesn't like the taste of his tea, his Lordship finds his lemon cordial quite spoilt, his Lordship –'

'Yes, Mrs Ryan,' answered Edwina abruptly. 'We're all well aware of our water problems.' The cook, red-faced from the oven, returned inside the kitchen. Why couldn't Aiden handle these types of issues? As usual, it would be left to her to address the water problem. To remind her father that work needed to begin on the new well immediately. Flinging the remaining manure across the wilting vegetables, Edwina wondered absently who would fertilise and water the vegetables if she wasn't here. Did her father ever think of that? No, he was too busy with his trips to Wywanna and dining with his business associates at the Guild.

The Guild. And who were the members of the Guild? Some of the most prominent landowners in the region and beyond. Edwina thought of the fine shirts in his wardrobe, the suits, quantities of neckties and socks and those stays in Wywanna at the guesthouse where rooms were retained. With a start she realised her naivety. This property was more hobby than business. One didn't have to be a mathematician to understand that their outgoings may well be far greater than the money made from the farm, but that wouldn't matter so much if there was access to another income. An income that allowed their father to indulge in wheat growing, nice clothes and overnight stays in rented rooms. Was that why he ignored all her suggestions regarding the property, because it was a sideline to his main interest? Well, she'd shown him her plans. And it was a strategy that she was sure would make their holding successful. It was a simple formula that involved branching out into different commodities so that they didn't have to rely on grain for an income. It might take three or four years before results could be seen, but Edwina knew it was the right decision. The only decision that ensured continued viability.

On hands and knees, she began pulling at the weeds between the onions and turnips. She tugged fiercely at the intruders, crawling between the rows as her anger grew, the soft soil collecting under ragged nails as she plucked out the offending plants, tossing them aside. The afternoon at the circus now seemed a terrible mistake. A mistake that never would have occurred except that her father forbade her to attend. Mason's friends were right, of course. What woman dressed in second-hand clothes and disguised herself as a man. And what man would want to be seen with someone like Edwina unless it was to either make fun of her or have some fun. Some inappropriate fun. Without thinking, Edwina bit her lip, drawing blood.

'Edwina, come.'

She looked up from her task, brushing her hands free of dirt. Will beckoned her urgently from the safety of the orchard. Not now, she frowned, waving him away. If her father had let her attend the circus in the first place, she never would have been placed in such an embarrassing predicament.

'Edwina?' persisted Will.

After the awkwardness of the morning's haircut and Will's delight at her discomfort she was not in the mood for more of his tomfoolery.

'Edwina, please.'

With a sigh Edwina checked her handiwork before brushing the dirt from her clothes. 'What?' Having walked through the trees to meet him at the stables, she said, 'I was busy. Couldn't you see I was busy?'

The smile on his face fell. 'Sorry.' He kicked at the dirt, bending to pick up a stone which he passed from one hand to the other. 'No-one's about and I just thought.' He gestured in the direction of the tack room. 'You saw him, yes?' he said hesitantly.

The lion, he was talking about the stolen cub. Edwina thought of the fallen hay bales that she'd neglected to tidy.

'I didn't think you'd be able to stay away,' he rushed on. Ignoring her attempt at a response, Will stepped inside the tack room. 'Come on.'

Edwina peered into the gloom. There was still the washing to bring in from the line and the hallway to mop. There really wasn't time for this. 'Shouldn't you have made a start on the well?'

'Come on,' said Will, taking her arm and dragging her inside.

'Will, stop it.' She rubbed at her forearm.

He let her go instantly and sat cross-legged on the ground, patting the earth beside him. 'You really want to see this.'

'See what?' she said curtly.

'Come on, I know you're not really as grouchy as you sound. And this is really something.'

Edwina wanted to leave straightaway, but, intrigued, she joined Will, sitting on the cold, packed earth beside him with a deliberate huff, just so he knew she was doing this under sufferance.

'See, I told you they'd be friends,' stated Will.

Under the row of saddles in the shadows lay Jed, side by side with the lion cub. The cub's head was resting on the soft under-belly of the dog, Jed's front leg draped protectively across the animal. Occasionally one or the other would yawn and press a paw against his companion but otherwise the two animals dozed together in the afternoon heat. The baby lion was only slightly smaller than the collie dog and Edwina wondered how Will had managed to carry such a weight the night they walked from the circus grounds.

'The little fella seems happier with some company.'

Edwina wouldn't admit it but she was sure that her old dog would be pleased for a friend as well. The other collies ignored him these days and if they did pay Jed any attention it was only to annoy him.

'What happened at the Ridgeway place?' asked Edwina as they sat companionably watching the animals. 'Aiden didn't say much.'

'Don't know,' replied Will, 'but your father and Mr Fernleigh sure don't like each other. And your father was really mad when we left.'

It had been something of an adventure for Will. Edwina sensed his thrill at having been a part of the proceedings. She thought of the return of her precious locket. 'Were you always a ringbarker?'

'You mean was I born with an axe in my hand?' Will laughed. 'I did my apprentice as a blacksmith not eight year ago but lost my job. In the big cities a lot of people have automobiles now; people want petrol pump attendants or electricians to fix their shiny new appliances. The horse transport industry isn't what it used to be.'

'Everyone uses horses out here. Surely someone would take you on.'

'Me and the rest of those children who were dragged out to the middle of nowhere with their hero father in search of a better life? Do you have any idea how many people are looking for work? If asking for a job earnt money I'd be a rich man.'

'Your father saw service?' asked Edwina.

'Regular Anzac, he is. From the slums to Gallipoli to a block of dirt that could barely grow a tree. My pa had no background in farming, no money for help or to buy machinery. That was his reward from the government.'

'You did have a job,' reminded Edwina, trying to steer him towards more positive thoughts.

'You've seen that camp. Would you work there? Anyway, I've not had much luck with jobs in the bush. I did a stint at a boot factory but they let me go on account of my soles being skew-whiff.'

Edwina giggled.

'The manager suggested I'd be better suited as a boot-catcher, one of those boys who works at inns pulling off patrons' boots and cleaning them. My ma raised me better than that.'

'All mothers want the best for their children.'

'Here, you better take your brother's coat with you.' Will removed the wool jacket, folding it carefully. 'Last time a person lent me a suit and trousers it was my father.'

Edwina took the still warm garment. 'You didn't have one of your own?'

Will laughed. 'What – with seven of us in the family? There was only one suit in our house and when it was needed for something special, me pa lent us his. Of course it had to be a real special reason because he had to go to bed.'

'Why?'

''Cause he had nothing else to wear. Ma reckoned that's why he signed up. Never had such flash clobber and a hat as well.'

Edwina drew her gaze from Will back to the two sleeping creatures. 'It must be very hard to be that poor.'

Will flicked at the dirt floor with a finger, the soil spraying a short distance before settling on the ground. 'When you're born in a slum there's always someone worse off than you. And if I hadn't been born the way I was, and if me pa hadn't gone to war, then we never would have settled up-country and I wouldn't have ended up knocking about the bush, odd-jobbing here and there, and then I'd never have met you or rescued Jim-jam.'

'You named the cub Jim-jam?' Edwina thought the choice of name very funny.

'Well, I thought about Pickle,' said Will, 'seeing as he was in one, but I figured Jim-jam was better.'

'Yes,' Edwina laughed softly, 'it probably is.'

'You smell of chicken poo, you know.' Will brushed a strand of hair from her face.

Edwina drew back from his touch. 'Don't do that.'

'Why not?' he asked.

'I'm dirty,' said Edwina softly.

'So am I.' His fingers touched her chin.

Will's face grew closer until his features blurred. Edwina closed her eyes instinctively, knowing he was about to kiss her, understanding she would let him. His mouth touched hers. Gently at first, testing, and then the pressure increased and his tongue tenderly parted her lips, lapping and flicking. She opened her eyes at this unexpected penetration, readying to push Will away, but his eyes were firmly closed, his arms protectively encircling her body, dragging her towards him, until one of Edwina's legs was across his lap. Edwina relished the sensation that she could barely explain, delighting in the moment. So this is what it felt like to be kissed.

The door to the tack room opened with a bang. Will was standing in an instant, fiddling with Aiden's spare coat, which lay on the ground, and mumbling about not having found the rasp he'd dropped.

Edwina got to her feet immediately. 'Not there,' she said as if she too had been scrounging about in the dirt for the missing tool.

The figure in the doorway stepped forward. Edwina's shoulders sunk in relief as Davidson dropped a length of rope in the corner of the room and left soundlessly, closing the door.

Will let out a loud rush of air. 'Well, that was close.'

Edwina didn't know what to say or where to look. Snatching Aiden's coat from Will's grasp, she opened the tack room door. 'I, I better leave.'

Will reached in front of her, shoving the door closed before she could escape. Edwina turned slowly to face him, not knowing what to say, noting his palm on the door. She was caught between him and the timber door of the tack room and her chest began to heave at the thought of what may happen next. 'Let me go, Will.' Her words were a whisper.

He studied her carefully. 'I'm not good enough, am I? Oh, maybe for a bit of fun, but that's all, eh?'

'Will, don't say that.'

'Isn't it the truth?'

What could she say? A boundary had been crossed that shouldn't have been crossed. Surely he knew that. She was Edwina Baker, after all, and he was just a worker on their land. A young man from nowhere with nothing to offer, a man who'd caused her trouble.

With an expression that could only be described as wounded, Will stared at her for a long moment, before opening the door and stepping back.

Edwina wanted to explain. Needed him to understand the wrongness of what they'd done. Instead, she turned and walked away.

⋙ Chapter Eighteen ⋘

Hamilton pushed through the merinos to the far end of the makeshift yard, muttering under his breath as they brushed his legs, occasionally off-balancing him. The sheep enclosure was situated on a ridge a good distance from the house. With the area surrounded by a forest of prickly pear it was a difficult place to access, unless you knew the route and had Davidson to guide you. The pear filled the understorey of the timber surrounding them and had been so difficult and costly to control in this area that Hamilton had abandoned attempts to clear it. Instead he concentrated on the periphery, trying to stem the spread of the weed, while silently deciding that with this well-hidden location finally some good was coming from the uncontrollable plant. He hoped, of course, that the famed cactoblastis would destroy the prickly pear but he wouldn't mind so much if this area remained undisturbed.

The enclosure was partially contained by towering trees on two sides. And those woody monsters with their knobbly bark and interlacing boughs provided a natural barrier, concealing what lay within while also providing support to a section of Davidson's version of a post and rail fence.

Initially Hamilton had expected to eventually return the sheep in exchange for a payment for damages, but there'd been no-one to deal with at Ridgeway Station over the years except the manager. Somerville certainly wasn't interested in livestock matters and it seemed Charles Ridgeway did not realise how untrustworthy Fernleigh was. So here he was, the owner of some three hundred sheep that needed to be sold.

Suddenly Davidson was at his side and pointing into the distance. Hamilton looked across the grassy plain in the direction of the road that led into the farm.

'I see them,' said Hamilton following Davidson's line of sight to where three men on horseback trotted in single formation. The men were clear of a ridge of timber and followed the road towards the homestead. 'Come on,' Hamilton said irritably, wondering how in the hell the aboriginal man knew there were strangers approaching and more importantly who the interlopers were.

They rode cross-country, manoeuvring through the wavering grass on the small tree-less plain, a continent in itself surrounded as it was by scrubby bushes, prickly invaders and dense stands of trees.

Davidson didn't slow and as they rode closer to the road, Hamilton understood why. This wasn't the Chinese who he'd been expecting any day. These were mounted police. Hamilton stole a look at the stockman. He was yet to report Fernleigh to the constabulary. Maybe the manager had got in first.

'Damnation.' Hamilton choked back the spittle catching in his throat. An impressive array of excuses sprung to mind, none of which were plausible. A man could explain that he was owed recompense. Couldn't he? He did have detailed notes, with dates and times, good enough for any court of law, but still . . . 'Can they find those sheep, Davidson?'

The stockman gave the usual stony stare. Sometimes, just sometimes, it would be helpful if the aboriginal could talk.

The three policemen, having caught sight of them, waited patiently on the road until the two groups met. A swirl of dust swept past the law officers, dissipating on the choppy breeze. Hamilton wondered if the policemen would drop any charges in exchange for a couple of killers. Three apiece perhaps. Or maybe funds were required. There was usually an angle to be had there. Fancy dresses for wives and mistresses, tickets to a show in Brisbane. Improvements to the police station. There were always ways and means. Always. The problem was in being able to gauge whether the intended recipient was receptive.

'Mr Baker?'

'Yes,' replied Hamilton on halting the mare, noting the clipped tone of the ruddy-faced sergeant. He was English with the type of accent that suggested a dedicated attempt to hide poor beginnings, a short but perfectly waxed moustache not helping his impersonation.

'I'm Hamilton Baker and this is my stockman, Davidson,' he explained.

'I'm Sergeant Fredericks. I have received information regarding a theft that I wanted to discuss.'

'A theft?' Hamilton did his best to sound noncommittal. So Fernleigh had put him in to the coppers. Well, the hairy ingrate would pay for this. Pay well and truly. There was no doubt he was a reprobate of the highest order, a man unqualified for the role of manager, uneducated, unkempt and, Hamilton decided, undoubtedly a buggerer of boys – and if he wasn't, Hamilton would make it his business for the world to think Fernleigh was.

'What theft?' asked Hamilton, with the air of concern befitting a leading citizen. 'It's a bit late in the day for a house call, isn't it, Sergeant?'

'You did attend the circus at Wywanna on Saturday night, did you not? Along with a . . .' The sergeant consulted a pocketbook. 'A Mrs Zane.' He read. 'And your son and daughter?'

171

'What?' Hamilton stuttered a yes to Mrs Zane's presence as he processed the pleasing revelation that the policemen's visit was nothing to do with his merinos. Well then, this was quite different. Clearly the police were investigating the theft at the circus and were interviewing everyone of note. Hamilton should have known that Fernleigh didn't have the necessary gumption to complain to the law. A grubby manager trying to outwit a land-owner. Ludicrous.

'Your children, Mr Baker?' the sergeant pressed.

'Yes, of course,' answered Hamilton. 'My son was at Wywanna on business during the day. Well, Davidson was with him. Weren't you, Davidson? Can't speak I'm afraid.'

The aboriginal remained impassive.

'Can't or won't, Mr Baker?' The sergeant's mouth curled a little at the corners.

Hamilton wished he could give the nod to Davidson. One gesture from him, just one, and the policeman's mocking tone would quickly be replaced by a punch to the face.

'Don't take blind obedience for intelligence, Mr Baker.' The two young constables flanking the sergeant looked along the road where pigeons strutted about in the dirt, tail feathers fanned and wings outstretched. 'Dogs have more ability than these natives do. Even a half-caste such as Davidson here. He's been with you for some time I believe?'

'Many years. He simply walked in from the scrub, didn't you, Davidson? So I gave him a job.'

The officer stared at the stockman as if weighing up Hamilton's words. 'Very well. Perhaps we could discuss things further on the way to your homestead.'

'Of course.' Hamilton was in no mood to entertain, particularly at this hour. The sun was close to throwing afternoon shadows and they were not a household used to receiving guests. However, there was no choice but to offer hospitality, particularly as it seemed the sergeant was not the type to be induced. And so they trotted their horses along the rutted road.

'You've been busy I see,' noted Fredericks, ensuring his horse kept pace. 'Sheep work, yes?'

Hamilton bristled. 'Why would you say that?'

'The smell, the stench of wool and dust. You'd think that being surrounded by sheep and woolgrowers in this district I'd be accustomed to it.'

'Yes, quite.' Hamilton wiped at his dusty face with a handkerchief, pristine in its whiteness. 'We only keep a handful for killers.'

He was relieved when the house came into view, although the denseness of the orchard darkened one side of the building so that it appeared small and rather nondescript.

'You like trees, Mr Baker?' asked Fredericks.

What sort of question was that? 'Well enough.'

'Everyone is intent on clearing their land of them. I'm glad to see you appreciate the odd specimen, in your garden at least.'

'The land's unviable enough as it is what with this blasted prickly pear, without a tree-covered paddock to contend with as well.'

'And yet you plant them,' noted the sergeant, as the green of the orange and lemon trees grew recognisable. 'As for the pear, Captain Arthur Phillip's determination to create a cochineal industry in the colony has certainly left a legacy.'

'Well, your countrymen have always liked their pretty red uniforms,' responded Hamilton thoughtlessly.

'I believe they are your countrymen as well,' Fredericks retaliated. 'The early colonies were a vast social experiment, Mr Baker. An attempt to create a whole society through forced labour at an extraordinary distance from the civilised world. There were bound to be a few hiccups. Could we have done better, you and I?' He paused. 'I think not.'

Hamilton was still trying to formulate a response as they rode between the silver-barked gums. The dogs rushed out at their arrival, growling and barking at the unknown men, snapping at the heels of the strange horses, drying leaves swirling into the air. Hamilton shooed the canines to quiet as he dismounted. Unasked, Davidson called the dogs away to be tied up as the men tethered their mounts at the rail. 'You and your men will have some tea, Sergeant Fredericks?' He led them up onto the verandah, offering the three men seats.

'Please,' Sergeant Fredericks interrupted, 'we are not here to disturb your household. I would, however, like my men to take a walk around the grounds if possible. Inspect the buildings.' He brushed dust from the tabletop as he sat.

The request was quite unexpected. 'Why of course, but may I ask what you are looking for?' At the nod of the officer-in-charge, the younger policemen quickly walked around the corner of the house.

Seated at the verandah table, Fredericks turned the pages of a notebook. 'A number of witnesses can confirm the fact that your son, Aiden, attended the circus menagerie last Saturday.'

'The menagerie?' Hamilton repeated.

'Yes,' confirmed the sergeant. 'Oh, and they said he was accompanied by an aboriginal and that your son left the showgrounds in a buggy.'

'A buggy? Davidson, what high jinks have been going on behind my back?'

The aboriginal, untying the reins of his horse from the hitching rail, met the two pairs of querying eyes, barely pausing in his movements.

'And your daughter?' continued the sergeant.

'My daughter was home all night,' Hamilton responded, frowning at his employee, who left, leading their two horses. Was it possible that Aiden attended the circus?

'Actually, it appears she wasn't,' the officer corrected. 'A Mrs Hilton stated that your daughter Edwina was also seen at the menagerie, dressed as a man, in the company of, shall we say, some quite modern young ladies.'

'I've never heard anything more preposterous,' said Hamilton. 'Never.' Where was this gossip coming from? He'd done nothing to deserve such troublemaking.

'Yes, well, I believe the young lady caused quite a stir.'

A feeling of dread leached its way into his body. Hamilton recalled the expression on the face of the Hilton matriarch at the circus. The busybody knew something was afoot that night, he was of no doubt.

'Are you aware that a lion cub was stolen from the circus on Saturday night?'

'Of course I am,' answered Hamilton brusquely, swatting away a fly. 'Everyone was talking about it.'

'Well, Mr Baker, it seems that a young woman matching Mrs Hilton's description of your daughter was seen moments before the animal was stolen and then again running after the culprit. One of the circus performers admitted to helping the young woman when she was injured after a supposed attack.'

'Which woman?' demanded Hamilton.

'A Miss Jacqueline April. The fat lady.'

The pillar of lard that passed for entertainment. He didn't mean to laugh. 'You can't be serious.'

'I'm quite serious,' responded the sergeant. 'There were drovers camped at Mrs Landry's Inn on Saturday night. They recalled seeing a buggy go past trailed by an aboriginal. Later that same evening one of the drovers recalled speaking with a young couple who stopped to water their horse. They were riding double, Mr Baker, and the girl accompanying the young man matched the description given of your daughter.'

'Impossible,' stated Hamilton.

'The problem with beauty is that it tends to be recalled.'

Hamilton knew he should be able to respond intelligently. 'I don't believe it. It must be a case of mistaken identity.'

'And the man seen with your daughter? I assume he returned her home? Do you know who he was?'

'I wasn't here, Sergeant. However, I assure you that we have no new employees.'

'I have to search your premises, Mr Baker; you understand that, I'm sure. If we do find anything I will have to interview everyone on the property.'

This was a disaster. An unmitigated disaster. The man actually thought the stolen lion cub was here.

'Do you think it possible that your daughter was involved, Mr Baker?' the sergeant probed.

What could he say? The facts suggested a terrible truth. 'She has always been so obedient. Edwina has only just turned twenty and is yet to be introduced to public life.'

The sergeant considered this. 'If she was involved, Mr Baker –'

The man didn't have to utter the words. Stealing. His daughter a thief. Edwina would be ruined. He would be ruined. The family would be ruined. Good Lord, was it possible?

'I do understand the ramifications of this for a man in your position.'

The sergeant was still talking. Hamilton heard nothing. He watched the man's lips beneath the thick hair as the word ramification kept repeating itself in his mind. He tried to compose himself, but the best Hamilton could do was to remember to breathe. If Edwina had disgraced herself – and the coincidences were almost too great to doubt – they would have to leave. Sell up. Move interstate. No-one could remain in this district with such a stain besmirching their name. And Gloria. Would his beloved gather up her Egyptian trinkets and disappear as well? He needed to salvage what he could. Immediately. He was sorry for it but what other measure could be taken? 'I find it difficult to believe that my daughter could do such a thing.' There was only one excuse he could use to save the family from disgrace and his daughter from her own terrible waywardness, if indeed she was implicated in the matter. 'It pains me to say it, Sergeant, but if, *if* my daughter was involved in this dreadful event I can only put it down to the fragility of Edwina's mental state. My daughter,' he stretched the words out, 'takes after her mother. And Caroline, my dear Caroline, spent her final days in an asylum.'

'I see.' Sergeant Fredericks closed the notebook.

'It is not common knowledge.'

'So you believe that if your daughter was involved in this incident that it was a case of misadventure, of a young fragile woman being misled?'

'I know my daughter, sir,' answered Hamilton. 'She is erratic in temperament. Equal parts melancholic and forthright.' He thought of Edwina's obsessive attitude towards Caroline's tree, of her outspoken nature, the facts reinforcing certainty. 'However, I do not believe that she rode into town dressed as a man with the intention of attending the circus when she has never left this property unless accompanied by myself or her brother. If she did. If what you say is true, then it shocks me to the core and I can only say, with the heaviest of hearts, that reason left my daughter and someone else must be held accountable for that.'

'And you had no-one employed on the property that may have coerced your daughter if that is what indeed occurred?'

Hamilton said no immediately. Will Kew was still among them, his reappearance coinciding with the circus weekend. But to mention the boy's name was to entice further investigation.

'If my men don't find anything, Mr Baker, I will not implicate your daughter in the theft. The reward for the return of the lion cub is substantial and it is the cub,' he said more kindly than Hamilton would have expected, 'that is my primary concern, not harming the reputations of our delicate womenfolk.'

Hamilton appreciated the sentiment and said so; however, the damage was already done. People would talk. The sergeant to his wife. The wife to a friend. The young constables to lovers or family members. They waited for the search to be concluded as a lifting wind blew the earth in waves across the ground.

'The district could do with a fall of rain,' remarked the sergeant. 'I am sorry for your troubles, Mr Baker.'

Hamilton met the man's gaze. 'As am I.'

'If the cub is found, your daughter –'

Hamilton lifted his hand for silence. 'Please.'

The young constables reappeared, their boots crunching the leaf-litter. Hamilton knew as soon as he saw their expressions that they were empty-handed. That was something at least.

'We found nothing, Sergeant,' the elder of the two constables stated.

'And you searched all the buildings thoroughly?'

'Yes, sir.'

The knot of apprehension sitting in Hamilton's chest untwisted itself just a little. 'You will stay for supper,' he said, dreading an evening in the company of these men with his children at the table. 'I can offer you a roof over your head, Sergeant, and your men the relative comfort of the stables.' It took an inordinate amount of willpower to remain composed.

'Actually we have already availed ourselves of beds at Mrs Landry's Inn, but I thank you for the offer.' He stood to leave.

'It is I who thank you.'

He waited until the policemen were some distance away, and when they were out of earshot, Hamilton bellowed for Davidson. The stockman appeared promptly and Hamilton wondered if the man had been eavesdropping. 'You let Aiden take the buggy to town and allowed him to attend that infernal petting zoo? What the hell has been going on around here, Davidson? You know Aiden isn't allowed to use the buggy. And what's this nonsense regarding

Edwina's supposed involvement? Did you see her? Is there any credence to what the sergeant said? The man practically accused her of theft. God's holy trousers, I turn my back for one minute and the world's gone mad. Well, what are you still doing here? Get back to those blasted sheep and let them out of the yards.'

Hamilton observed the black man as he rode away. This was one of those times when he would have liked to have been able to shake the words from the aboriginal's mouth. To learn what things were left unsaid that should be told. If the sergeant was right, and clearly Aiden Baker driving a buggy with an aboriginal in tow was an easy sight to recall, then it was also true, based on the witnesses, that Edwina had gone to the circus as well. Davidson either carried little authority with his children or the stockman didn't see guardianship as part of his role. As of this moment, Hamilton realised that Davidson was somewhat of a liability.

He bashed the table with his fist, his mind teeming with images: of Aiden driving into town, of Edwina disobeying his express orders and riding into Wywanna alone dressed as a man? And who were these modern women she was seen with? Did they all think him a fool?

Hamilton strode back and forth along the verandah, his hands clasped behind his back, as the anger inside him grew. The more he stomped across the floorboards, the angrier he became. And with each stride, his fury transformed itself into resentment. Everything he'd done in life was for the advancement of this family. What man could have done more? And a family that he'd committed to raising alone when his once young, beguiling wife had lost herself to self-pity with the excuse of loneliness. As if it were his fault that she couldn't adjust to country living, away from family and friends. Caroline. Caroline. Caroline. Caroline and her blasted tree. Caroline and her exasperating, dreamy, fragile nature. Caroline and her melancholy. Caroline, mother to his rebellious, thankless children.

Without realising, he'd walked away from the house to stand among the eucalypts, kicking at the strips of papery bark littering the ground. He was exhausted. Sweat plastered his brow and his hands tremored. He sighed at the homestead, large and solid among the wooded grove, the blasted orchard planted with such pride. It was a nuisance now, with its ground-splattering rotting fruit, the rancid sweet scent, the annoying hiss of wind through the leaves, the creak of knotted, too-old boughs. The dirty, decaying mass of leaves that swirled and piled and matted the ground, worse than any dust storm.

Will.

Was it him who brought his daughter home that night? He recalled Edwina's sickly demeanour the following day.

He would say nothing to Aiden or Edwina of the sergeant's accusations. He needed time to decide what must be done and, while Hamilton thought on the problem of his daughter, he would wait and watch and see what morsels of truth were revealed by those he loved and once thought he could trust.

⚹ Chapter Nineteen ⚹

Two days later, Edwina nervously set the salver on the table next to where her father sat on the verandah and poured tea into a white-and-blue patterned cup. He'd been inordinately quiet at dinner the previous evenings and even Aiden commented on their father's sullen disposition. An empty rum bottle was discovered outside as if pitched from the study window and a good part of the day he could be seen stalking around or inside the house. As if he were watching or waiting for something. Even Will detected a change in his employer for Edwina saw him skedaddle around the side of the stables mid-morning, saying something about having moved the cub the day before. No further opportunity arose to question Will about his nervousness and even Mrs Ryan was reticent when Edwina queried the cook about her father's mood.

Having barely spoken to him since Monday, Edwina hoped his disposition was improved. She'd arranged his favourite lard biscuits in a circular design and as an added touch set a vase of wildflowers on the tray. Her indecision towards questioning her father about his business affairs had kept her awake most of the night. But her resolve was firmed the more she thought about his association with the Ridgeways and reinforced every time she looked at her rough-skinned palms. They were scratched today from the extra coil of barbed wire she and Aiden had run along the Ridgeway boundary early this morning.

Edwina waited patiently for her father to acknowledge her presence, perhaps note the extra effort gone into preparing the tray. It was a warm spring afternoon and Edwina focused on the grass wavering in the tepid breeze, the way the sunlight haloed the seeding tufts as a haze of silvery heat hugged the paddocks, causing the distant tree line to twist and warp. Edwina understood that her world would be altered following the conversation she planned to have. And for the briefest of moments she clung to the present.

'Are you going to sit down, Edwina, or is it your intention to stand there like a statue?' Her father didn't look up from the pages of the book resting in his lap.

'Will I pour for you?' she offered, still standing.

'No, thank you. Don't you have something to do?' He scribbled numbers in the ledger. 'What about the rest of those insect eggs?'

'Aiden and I put them out yesterday afternoon. Father, Mrs Ryan is wondering about the new well?'

'Yes, yes. We'll get to it.'

'Perhaps Will should start on it tomorrow.'

His look was sharp and Edwina wondered what she'd said. She liked Will. And the liking was difficult to admit considering the circumstances under which they'd met. The thought of their shared impulsive kiss made Edwina blush but it was hard to deny her enjoyment of it. If ever there was an illustration of incompatibility for a young lady of her station, Will Kew was that person. And yet she would be sad when he left. He'd been a pleasing addition to the monotony of a life bordered by duty and shadowed by the movement of the sun.

Her father made another note with a stubby pencil. Edwina wondered what sums he analysed, pinching the inside of her wrist when she gave thought to the possibility of entering the study and reading his papers. It had taken most of the last two days to gather enough courage to speak to him and she knew it must be done before that courage failed her.

'Father?' she said softly, watching as Jed padded towards them to lie on the floor.

He added two lumps of sugar to his tea, blowing on the surface of the liquid. She was not unprepared. Firstly, she would outline her ideas for the property and then, if her father still refused to listen, Edwina had decided that she would leave the district and find employment where her contribution would not only be appreciated but also valued.

'Father?' said Edwina more loudly.

'What?' he snapped in reply. Clearly irritated, he closed the book and spread the linen napkin across a knee.

'Father, I wanted to discuss my suggestions for the property. You said on Sunday that you'd read my notes so you know that I feel it would be a good idea if we purchased one hundred cows and two bulls next year and started a herd. We could run them on the country that's being cleared once it's grassed up. Even with an eighty percent calving rate, in two years' time we'd recoup the initial outlay. If you –'

'Enough, Edwina. Why can you not confine your thoughts to more womanly tasks? The management of a property does not fall to women. It is men's business and men know best,' he snapped.

'So you won't even consider it?'

'It's been considered. I discussed the matter with Aiden.'

'And he of course said no, didn't he, Father?' asked Edwina. 'That's because he's not comfortable or capable of doing anything beyond what we're doing already, but –'

'Enough,' he replied. 'I'm not interested in pursuing this conversation.'

'Even if it means making more money?'

'I will decide how we make our income and how it is spent.'

That was it then, Edwina decided. 'If there is money enough, I would like to travel to Brisbane and become a secretary.' There – she had said it.

In response he took a bite of a biscuit, the crumbs sprinkling the linen. He chewed slowly, pushing the dough back and forth from one cheek to the other.

'There must be money for a rail ticket at least,' she persevered, feeling the knot in her stomach grow, 'because you're doing business with the likes of the Ridgeways. And a family with forty thousand acres clearly has to have money. And Aiden told me that they owe you money. A very large sum, in fact.'

Finishing the biscuit, her father took another sip of the tea, placing the cup gently in its saucer. 'You are very knowledgeable today, daughter,' he answered pleasantly. 'Do continue, Edwina. What else do you know?' He turned to her for the first time. 'Come now, you have obviously given some thought to this conversation.'

A thin eyebrow lifted as he spoke. It was tufted with thick grey hairs. Her father was ageing. She would reach out a hand and stroke the cracked leathery skin spotted with dark patches would the gesture not be waved off. 'Yes, of course I have, Father.' Edwina thought of the rehearsed words, of the way her features stiffened as she practised her speech in the mirror. 'I am now twenty years of age,' she explained with renewed effort, 'with no immediate prospect of marrying.'

'Go on,' he encouraged, sipping the hot drink.

'Well, I don't think it is right to be worked day and night,' she persevered. 'Especially when every suggestion I offer regarding the running of the property is ignored.'

'And?'

'I am a young woman and yet I wait on you and Aiden hand and foot. I'm not allowed to go anywhere or do anything and I am yet to be presented in public life. It's just not fair.' When her father didn't interrupt, she rushed on, 'Especially when you have fancy clothes and rooms in town and important clients. Why, everyone else gets to do things like have nice dresses and go to the circus or perhaps even visit the seaside. But no, not me, I have to work like a hired hand. Look at me.'

Her father did indeed look at her. Edwina felt his thousand-yard stare boring into her from the worn but polished laced-up boots, trailing the length of her trousers, shirt and waistcoat until he reached the frayed collar and faded floral scarf tied about her neck. Edwina flinched under the harshness of his glare and busied herself by tucking a length of hair beneath a felt hat.

'Yes, it was a pity you missed the circus. It was rather enjoyable. But you like those clothes, don't you? I mean it was your choice to go about dressed up the way you do.' He didn't wait for a response. 'You'd be happy enough to wear them into Wywanna, Edwina, wouldn't you? Incognito?' A nerve above his upper lip twitched, jerking the mouth in a series of tight upward movements.

Edwina thought she would faint. 'I have no idea what you're talking about, Father.' Beads of sweat formed on her brow. 'But you know why I wear these clothes on the farm.' The words sounded stuttery, like a child hiding the truth. Did he know about the circus? Surely not?

Her father narrowed his gaze and smiled pleasantly. 'If you need new clothes you only have to ask.'

Of course he didn't know. How could he? 'That's not what I mean,' she answered with relief.

Her father poured more tea, studying the blackness of it. 'This is a rather rushed decision, isn't it, wanting to move to Brisbane? Anyone would think you were running away.'

'I am not running away, Father. I simply want to make my own way in the world. Doing something I enjoy, that I know will make money. Where I will be appreciated. I do have a brain and I'd like to be able to use it.'

'If you are unhappy with your circumstances, Edwina, then may I suggest you look to yourself for the reason.'

'Myself?'

'As a child you skinned mice, pegging them out on the ground to dry in the sun so that you and your brother had hides to trade for your silly games.' He paused for emphasis. 'You progressed to daring your brother to jump on our horses bareback and twice he broke his arm. Oh, and as for being forced to contribute to the family business, if I recall correctly it was you who whined when you weren't allowed to come out riding with me. It was you who elected to dress like a man. You who were happy enough to work in the field alongside your family. And now you complain?'

Edwina was momentarily struck dumb that he could think so poorly of her. The days and weeks following her mother's removal to the sanatorium remained embedded in her mind along with the sadness of the empty house. Of course she didn't want to be left alone every day when the men went outdoors. Edwina had explained as much to her father and brother at the time. But for her father to assume that the days of toil spent under his direction was something that would continue on into adulthood was simply unfair, especially when the only contribution wanted of her was labour. Not once were her ideas or needs considered. She had to make him understand. 'I –'

'Have I starved you, beaten you or forced you to sleep out in the open? No.' Her father's face was growing puce. 'I have protected you and your brother from the whims of society. From the modern ways of today's world. And I may add what you are doing here is no different to what any other able-bodied woman does on a property in this district or any other for that matter.'

'I'm sure the better families on the stations don't have their womenfolk working the way I do. Anyway, maybe I don't want to do it anymore. Maybe I'm tired of being ignored and running myself ragged when the property could be doing so much better than it is. Maybe I want a better life.'

'A b-better life,' he stammered in anger. 'I have done everything humanly possible as a father to ensure your wellbeing and you have the audacity to question me about my business affairs and demand money for some inappropriate, foolhardy scheme. I agree that you no longer belong here on the farm. I have seen your discontent, bore witness to your outspokenness, but now I find my concern and disappointment at your ungratefulness goes beyond your petty complaining to the very heart of our reputation.'

Edwina blanched. 'I, I don't understand.'

'Clearly you need the guidance of a husband, and do not worry, my dear, I have been doing my very best to find you one. For, in spite of your complaints, and my clearly insufferable treatment of you, I only desire your happiness.'

'Then why will you not let me go away from here?' Edwina's hands curled into tight fists as her eyes moistened.

'You can't go gallivanting off to Brisbane, Edwina. It just isn't done.'

Edwina stamped her foot loudly on the timber boards, the vibration rattling the teacup in its saucer. 'Why not?'

'Because it isn't right. Young women of breeding must live by certain standards regardless of whether you're inclined to do so or not. God, would that your mother were here. Unstable though she was, as a member of the weaker sex I'm sure she would know how to handle you for I am at my wits' end.' He stood abruptly, the linen napkin fluttering to the ground. 'I am doing my best to find you a suitable husband, before you ruin this family and become unmarriageable.'

'And is it very hard to find one for me, Father? Me being the daughter of a money-lender? I imagine it must be for we never entertain, and we are certainly held at arm's length on the few occasions I'm allowed to accompany you to Wywanna. If it is too difficult, I tell you now to save yourself the trouble. I would rather be my own person than have my guardianship placed in the hands of another male.'

The slap caught Edwina squarely on the side of her face. She staggered backwards, tripping over Jed and landing heavily on the veranda. The dog howled in protest and limped away.

'You are just like your mother, Edwina. Wilful and spoilt.'

Edwina got slowly to her feet, steadying herself on the wall of the house. A shooting pain was burning the side of her face.

'I will find you a suitable husband,' her father stated, retrieving the napkin and throwing it on the tea tray. 'And you will marry. I promise you that. Did you think I wouldn't find out about the circus? That's right. I know all about it. You and that no-hoper, Will. I know he's involved in this somehow. Sergeant Fredericks came here two days ago. *Came here.*' He slammed a hand on the table, upsetting the crockery on the tray so that the cup overturned, spilling its contents. 'Did you steal that lion?'

'N-no, Father.'

'Did Will?'

Edwina couldn't lie, but if she told the truth she'd be implicated in the theft. 'I don't know.'

'You don't know?' he yelled.

Edwina's nose dripped blood.

'Regardless of whether they find you guilty of stealing that blasted animal or not, there were witnesses, my girl. The damage is done. The gossipers will already know of your tawdry behaviour. So yes, I will try and find you a husband, and quickly before you can disgrace us further. Before you can ruin yourself, your brother and me.'

Edwina couldn't breathe properly; she clutched at her stomach.

'Oh do sit down and collect yourself, girl, before you create a spectacle. The men are coming.'

Edwina dazedly reached across the table to tidy the tea things as Davidson, Aiden and Will approached the house on horseback. The mark on her cheek clearly showed for Will took one look at her as he dismounted and stared furiously at her father.

No, she mouthed, having caught Will's attention. *Please*, she pleaded through clenched teeth. Edwina blinked with the pain. Blood came away from her nose, dripped onto her blouse. Although clearly agitated as to the course of action he should take, Will kept his silence.

'I say, Edwina,' said Aiden, 'are you alright? What happened?'

'She fell,' answered Hamilton. 'That old dog's always in the way. He should be put down. Now what news? You three arrived in a hurry.'

Davidson pointed to the north-east and the road that led towards the homestead. There was something moving in the distance. A trail of dust hung in the air.

'Chinese, Mr Baker,' said Will curtly.

Aiden was quick to continue. 'We caught sight of them coming in from out east. There's about fifteen on foot plus a wagon.'

'A gang of Chinese, eh?' her father stated, directing the comment to Davidson. 'Excellent. Finally Mr Sears and his ringbarkers have some competition. And a wagon.' Hamilton tugged at the waistband of his trousers, pulling them a little higher. 'Well, they'll have stores to sell. We could use some fresh vegetables to make up for that scraggly patch of yours, Edwina. And you must show them the oranges in the stables as well. No point letting good food go foul, not when the almond-eyed celestials are keen buyers of what they can't grow themselves.'

Edwina was beginning to feel cold and slightly dizzy, but she was aware of Davidson's scrutiny. What did he think of the scene before him, she wondered, for the aboriginal alternated between staring at her and his employer.

'You may get that new dress you're hankering for after all,' her father announced.

The visitors were getting closer. The drably clothed walkers were accompanied by two men on horseback and, behind this initial grouping, a wagon.

'Clear the table, Edwina, and tell Mrs Ryan to make some tea for our guests. Well, come on, girl, get a move on,' her father commanded.

Hands shaking, Edwina carried the tray to the kitchen. Inside the room was a furnace. The wood fire burned hotly and the scent of roasting meat hung heavily on the air. Mrs Ryan was in the process of peeling potatoes and the earth-encrusted vegetables vied for space on the table with cooling bread draped with muslin and a pan of freshly rendered mutton fat.

The cook didn't take her eyes from the task before her. 'You can take that lard out to the food-keeper. It'll just as likely melt in here, along with me.' The Scotswoman rubbed roughly at the vegetable in her hand and then with a mutter began to cut away the skin with a knife. The peel landed on top of a substantial pile of shavings and the incompletely skinned tuber was dropped from a disinterested height to land with a splash in a water-filled pot.

'Mrs Ryan, can you please make some tea for –'

'That would be right. A person doesn't have a moment to herself. No sooner has his Lordship been favoured with tea and biscuits than the daughter appears demanding the same. Not for her the lowly task of boiling water or steeping leaves. No, we'll leave that to the cook. For Susan Ryan has nothing better to do than run after the likes of the Baker family. A woman might as well still be married.' Lips pressed firmly together, she narrowed her gaze at the potato she held. 'Might as well not have run away from the back of a husband's hand.' She stabbed the blade into the tuber, prising free a black eye. 'Might as well –'

Edwina dropped the tray on the kitchen table, the fine porcelain cup and saucer falling and smashing on the ground. 'Can you please just make some tea?'

Mrs Ryan loooked up from her task. 'The Almighty save us,' the cook muttered, dropping the vegetable. Wiping her hands carefully on a rag, she led Edwina to a chair. 'Was it that Will fellow that done it, Edwina?' she asked, pushing her firmly on the shoulders so that Edwina sat heavily. The woman lifted Edwina's chin, tilted her cheek towards the light. 'I've seen him mooning after you. As if he were good enough for Mr Baker's daughter. Never liked the boy. Moment I saw him I said to myself, now there's one who's been dragged by the scruff of his neck through the sewer.' Dampening the corner of her apron in a bowl of dirty dish water, she wiped at Edwina's face. 'Oh he's a pretty one but ever since he came here things haven't been right. There's meat missing from the keeper every day and when I goes out and about, well he's always skulking about the stables. Sly, that's what he is. And currying favour: "Can I help you with that washing, Mrs Ryan?" he says to me. "Do you need more wood, Mrs Ryan?"' The woman tutted, pressing her fingers along the bridge of Edwina's nose and cheekbone, repeating the process when Edwina flinched with the pain. 'Irish Nationalist I'd say. He's done his best to water down that accent of his, but I can pick them, I can. Troublemakers that lot are, through and through. Always have been.' Wiping her hands, she rested them on her hips. 'Nothing's broke. So there's some good to be seen. But there's blood.' She examined the discoloured material and then her handiwork. 'But the worst of it has stopped. There'll be a fine bruise on that cheek of yours, a very fine bruise. Now you sit there and I'll go tell your father. He'll have that damn rascal with the coppers in Wywanna quicker than you can say lickety-split.'

Edwina reached out, grasping the cook's arm. 'It wasn't Will, Mrs Ryan. It . . . it was father.'

191

The older woman frowned as if unable to comprehend what she'd been told. 'Your father?' She sat, the chair beneath giving a single ominous squeak.

Edwina nodded. 'We had an argument.'

Mrs Ryan studied Edwina thoughtfully. 'I'd have never thought it of the man. Well, I'm sorry, lass. I've felt the back of a man's hand and it's not a pretty thing to be used as a punching bag.' The cook retreated to the stove where she poured tea from the large pot into a chipped cup. 'Drink that. It's boiled with sugar. Feed your blood it will. Make you get your strength back.' She rested the back of her hand against Edwina's brow. 'You're burning hot. Well, it would be the fright of it. Just goes to show you can have more than some folk but that don't mean you're any better. Any better at all.' She clucked her tongue.

Edwina wiped at welling tears. 'It was my fault.'

'Now, I'll not have that. Don't go making excuses for it. It's the excuses that make things worse. He did wrong. Leave it at that. A man should know not to hit a woman, unless she's done something horrid. But a father . . . he's taking advantage. Of course a girl like you, well you should be married by now. Out of the house and away from here. Oh I know it's a daughter's duty and there's plenty that do it, staying on as the domestic, working the farm, but there's plenty not suited to the task as well, and with a father like Mr Baker, well,' she gave a snort of condemnation, 'he ain't got any excuse not to ensure you're well married.'

From outside came the noise of garbled speech. The cook thrust her head out the door and recoiled in fright. 'It's a Chinese deluge,' she said in fright.

'They're ringbarkers, Mrs Ryan,' explained Edwina, feeling a growing tightness across her cheek. 'That's why Father wants the tea.'

'I see,' the cook answered coolly, 'so now we're to entertain the likes of them. Two days ago I thought we'd have to have the

Wywanna coppers to dinner.' She blinked. 'Wasn't meant to say nothing about their coming. Your father swore me to keep mum. He said they were here about Will. That I was to keep an eye on him. I weren't surprised one bit.'

'Don't worry, Mrs Ryan, I know about them,' replied Edwina tiredly. For a moment the circus debacle had been forgotten.

'Well, that saves me from worry. Of course your father's never been too fussed about who he keeps company with. White, yellow, black, brindle, rich, poor and that woman.'

'What woman?' Edwina looked up from where her palms cupped the hot tea.

Mrs Ryan chewed at a thin lower lip. 'Chinese, eh? At least I'll be able to buy some spices. Nearly out of cloves we are and you can't run a kitchen without cloves, or cinnamon for that matter.'

'Mrs Ryan,' persevered Edwina, 'what woman?'

'The woman your father's been seeing. I thought you knew?' she said hesitantly. The cook busied herself filling a large boiler with water. 'I'm not feeding them. I've nothing against yellow men but I've enough to do as it is.'

'*What woman*, Mrs Ryan?'

The Scotswoman wiped her hands agitatedly on a rag. 'There's a woman,' she began slowly. 'She comes to Wywanna every year on account of your father.' She lowered her voice. 'A divorcee. They say the husband worked in Monte Carlo and that she's the daughter of a lord or somesuch. Terribly rich she is with a house in town.' The cook nodded. 'Mixes with the wrong sort of people, she does. Artists and such like. Your father took her to the circus last weekend. Dressed she was in silk and satins, with a strand of pearls as long and as large as a rope of pearls could be. 'Course your father tried to keep her hidden, but I saw her. She's very beautiful.'

Edwina took the cool compress Mrs Ryan offered, pressing it against her cheek. The faintness was yet to lessen, making it difficult to grasp what the older woman was saying. Would her father really be walking out with a divorced woman of dubious background? The cook must have misunderstood.

'Of course a man can't be expected to stay alone forever. It's not in them. They're not capable. They're needy, helpless creatures despite their blather. Still, that don't mean you can't have principles.'

'You're saying my father is seeing another woman?'

Mrs Ryan's muscled forearms folded across her stomach. 'Yes.'

'How long? How long has he been seeing her for, Mrs Ryan?'

'Now don't go having the vapours, girl.' The cook fiddled with the pot of peeled potatoes, jabbing at the water-covered vegetables with a wooden spoon. 'Ever since I came here,' she admitted, meeting Edwina's gaze. 'It wasn't my place to tell you, although I thought you'd probably guessed what with your father visiting the town so much, at certain times of the year,' she concluded.

'Like now?' asked Edwina.

'Yes,' said Mrs Ryan. 'I heard about their . . . friendship,' she said delicately, 'in town I did. Not that I'm a gossiper. No, miss, a telltale I'm not, but a person hears certain things and then sees particular things.'

Edwina pushed the cup of tea aside; if she consumed any more of the sickly drink she would be ill. 'And what else have you heard?'

'I really shouldn't say.'

'He is my father.'

Mrs Ryan sat the vegetable pot on the stovetop, the water splashing across the surface and sizzling loudly. 'They say,' she said with an air of confidentiality, looking out the window to ensure no-one approached, 'that she decorated his rooms in the town.'

'And?'

'Like one of those places that gentlemen frequent, for *company*,' the cook said knowledgeably.

Edwina was beginning to feel very hot. Hot and sick.

'All reds and pinks and a bed with silk sheets,' continued Mrs Ryan, her speech gathering momentum. 'And there's crates of champagne and special titbits to eat, all delivered regularly on your father's say-so. Your father paid Mrs White the landlady a handsome sum to rent those rooms from her and it was the divorcee, Mrs Zane, who selected all the furnishings and had them freighted to Wywanna at great expense. Chests of drawers and fancy mirrors and rugs wove from silk.' Mrs Ryan looked about the messy kitchen. 'Apparently your father has fancy tastes, not that we see it here.'

'Mrs Zane?' Edwina repeated slowly. 'That's her name?'

'Yes. Please don't say anything on my account, Miss Edwina.'

Edwina leant unsteadily on the table as she stood, her neck and head aching from the force of the slap. 'I appreciate you telling me, Mrs Ryan.'

Edwina carried the congealing fat outside to the cooler eastern side of the building. The timber-and-wire-mesh food safe was sheltered under the awning and she lifted the damp hessian bag to open the door, placing the lard in the cool interior. The galvanised tray atop the safe was nearly empty of water and she topped it up with trembling hands using the pitcher stored nearby, ensuring the hessian stayed wet and cool.

There was a gap in the wall of the kitchen hut. Edwina concentrated on the deep fissure, half wishing she could fall through it and never come out. Maybe that's what her mother once wished. That she too could escape into another world away from the harshness of the man she married. If so, then Caroline made sure that desire came true.

⋙ Chapter Twenty ⋙

'So it's agreed?' asked Hamilton of Han Lee, as they sat at the verandah table. The Chinaman was a savvy operator, living up to his reputation. Hamilton had first heard of the man two years ago, when the oriental and his men began to undercut established ring-barking teams in western New South Wales. The newcomers were not greeted favourably by those who'd enjoyed a monopoly on the business for a number of years. And when it became immediately obvious that the landowners' loyalties lay with those who could do the job the quickest and the cheapest, there were fights and the burning of Chinese property in retaliation.

'Mr Baker. Yes. We will do your ringbarking at this price.' Han Lee lifted the china teacup, an extended pinkie emphasising a long tapering fingernail.

Four hundred yards away, Han Lee's team sat cross-legged in rows on the ground, the wagon and horses at a standstill. Hamilton wasn't used to an audience when conducting business and he rather felt as if he were performing on a stage. If Gloria were here she would undoubtedly remark on their sphinx-like expressions, a most disconcerting image when combined with their number and the sombre-coloured pants and long tunics they wore. Waiting slightly apart from the visitors were Aiden, Davidson and Will. Now the Chinese were here, the boy could be on his way. There was no need of him anymore.

'We wish for land to grow our vegetables.' Han Lee sipped the hot drink. 'My extended family owns the Emporium in Wywanna and with an established garden we could supply this business more advantageously.' He spoke melodiously, his almond eyes unblinking.

The ringbarking rate was very reasonable. Far more economical than expected. Hamilton guessed the clan was keen to get a foothold in the district and with the prices they offered that was assured. 'You already stock a large range of goods,' said Hamilton, recalling the silk scarfs and other small items purchased for Gloria.

Han Lee finished the tea, wiping his face fastidiously with a napkin. 'Yes, imported from Canton and Hong Kong. But vegetables and fruits –'

'Are always in high demand,' Hamilton completed the Chinaman's sentence. 'And there is good money in market gardening.' The statement was left unanswered. 'There is available land around the town, but you would have conducted your own enquiries.' He poured more tea.

'This is true, but unfortunately,' Han Lee dipped the long nail in the cup, stirring the black tea thoughtfully, 'we have found some difficulties in acquiring it.' He sucked at the wet nail.

'Your English is very good. You were born here?' asked Hamilton.

'Yes. My grandfather and father were sojourners from our village and their descendants followed. We are businessmen, Mr Baker. We come here to make money. We stay, three years or thirty years, but we eventually go home. I have heard you are a man who helps others. That is why I have come to you.'

Hamilton leant back in his chair and tapped the table thoughtfully. 'There are two plots of land on the outskirts of the town.

One is next to the tannery, the other a small orchard. Do you need financial assistance?'

'No, Mr Baker. Quong Howe attends to such things.'

Quong Howe owned the Emporium and was a headman of sorts, for on those Sunday mornings when Hamilton rode out of Wywanna after sampling the delights of Gloria's many charms it appeared as if every Chinese in the district converged at the shop. 'So you simply need me to broker the sale.'

'We would pay for such assistance.'

'Seven percent of the purchase price. I believe that is the going rate,' offered Hamilton.

'Mr Baker, you are a very tricky man,' replied Han Lee. 'I hoped for latitude in consideration of the generous rates we have just agreed. One percent,' he countered firmly.

Hamilton took a sip of the now cold tea. 'My dear man, I couldn't possibly –'

Han Lee remained unblinking. 'Two.'

'So then we cannot do business,' admitted Hamilton with only the slightest of misgivings. It was a paltry transaction and at the moment there were larger matters to occupy his thoughts.

'Three percent. My final offer,' said Han Lee.

Hamilton now understood why the Chinese were considered unknowable.

'The land is important, Mr Baker, but with its purchase must come honour. If I were to agree with your terms I would be considered, how do you say it, fleeced.'

The Chinaman amused him. And God only knew after the sergeant's accusations and Edwina's outburst he could do with some diversion. 'My daughter needs material for a new dress.' He couldn't go shopping for an appropriate catch if the goods were not presentable.

'Ah, yes.' Han Lee allowed the slightest of smiles to pass his lips. 'And perhaps a case of rum for your kindness.'

'I believe we can do business, sir,' announced Hamilton, shaking Han Lee's hand. 'You can begin at the end of the week. Aiden will show you where to make camp. There's a creek nearby. A good shady spot. I'll have to finish up the current team first and then I'll show you the paddock. One out, another in, so to speak.'

'They won't take kindly to our arrival,' Han Lee stated the obvious.

'The bush needs more competition and more investment in terms of money and labour. At the right price. The sooner everyone realises that the better for all concerned.' Hamilton walked the Chinaman from the homestead. 'If you wish to keep your men employed, we have plenty of prickly pear to be cut.'

'You don't believe in the success of these insects?'

'Results first,' replied Hamilton, 'belief second.'

Han Lee's followers stood immediately as their headman rejoined them. 'Aiden, please show Mr Han Lee to the creek. They'll make camp there until they start work.'

Aiden nodded. 'Of course, Father.'

'That toffy-nosed Chinaman hasn't worked a day in his life,' muttered Will as Aiden mounted his horse and rode off.

Hamilton pivoted on his heel, grateful that the head of the new ringbarking team was out of earshot. If Edwina had disgraced herself at the circus, Hamilton knew in his gut that this young man was involved.

'I'm just saying —'

'Say nothing.' Hamilton couldn't believe the little ingrate was actually continuing to speak; the boy was talking about earning a pittance trapping rabbits while the Chinks banked twice as much from their market gardens. 'I didn't ask for your opinion, Will.' Give a monkey a fur coat, he thought furiously, remembering the jacket the boy was lent on Monday.

'And is that what happened to Edwina?' Will practically spat out the words. 'Did you not ask for her opinion either?'

Hamilton caught Davidson's eye and seconds later the aboriginal's fist struck Will in his midsection, the boy doubling over in pain.

'It takes a man to hit a man,' Will gasped, clutching his stomach.

Hamilton knew the lad would be trouble. Sensed it the moment he'd taken off, leaving a good job to join the circus.

The aboriginal took hold of Will by the forearm. Struggling, he stomped on Davidson's boot, trying to pull his arm free; however, the stockman didn't move or retaliate. Standing ram-rod straight he kept a steely gaze levelled on his captive and a hard grip.

'Keep him here until there's a bit of distance between Aiden and the Chinese, Davidson,' Hamilton said sourly. 'Then get him off my land.' Guilty or not, it would be one less lead for the sergeant to follow. One less irritant. The boy barely paid for his board and keep as it was.

≈ Chapter Twenty-one ≈

Edwina turned over in bed, feeling the lumpy mattress beneath a hip. It was difficult to sleep with her face swollen and a sadness enveloping her thoughts. But sleep must have come for the waning moon was high, its glow sending a beam through the leaves of the orchard beyond. The stream of light formed a circular patch on the timber boards, illuminating the room ever so slightly. Edwina lay still, grateful for the haven of the bush and the peace it offered.

Yet something wasn't quite right and it took a minute or so for the haze of sleep to fade and for her thoughts to clear. Edwina stared at the doorway, trying to think what bothered her. Then she understood. The door was closed after Mrs Ryan brought the tray to her room. She'd done it herself. Determined to shut out the world and to fall into a dreamless sleep.

It certainly wasn't shut now.

The timber floorboards creaked, a sound at odds with the usual moans of the house. This was a footstep, ever so slight. Someone was in the room with her. Edwina was sure of it. She pressed back into the pillow and waited. The surrounds were altered by the netting boundary and the weak moonlight. It highlighted the dressing table and chair, haloing the bed and her body lying within the white sheets, but the corners of the chamber remained dark and impenetrable. She rubbed at sleep-gummed eyes. There it was again. The same noise.

She sat upright, lifting the sheet to her chin. 'Who's there?'

Maybe it was her imagination. Jed lay on one of the wallaby hides, sleeping soundly, and although he was old, surely he'd wake and start barking if there was an intruder. But then how could the door have opened itself?

The noise sounded again. This time a soft thud. There was definitely something in her bedroom and by the direction of the sound it was over near the dressing table. As she waited, sheet clutched to her chest, the lion cub appeared. With a start Edwina watched as the animal walked silently across the floor, moving from the dark to the light, padding cautiously as if on its toes. Tail extended so that the tasselled end was obvious, the animal halted and looked upwards. The moonlight reflected onto the young lion's face and Edwina drew back from the eerie shine in the cat's eyes. Then the cub was moving again, circling the collie sprawled on the floor, snuffling the dog until Jed lifted his head. The cub pounced on the old animal, grabbing at his neck. Jed snarled and snapped and the baby lion growled back. Then both settled down next to each other on the wallaby hide.

'Heavens,' said Edwina, lying back in the pillows. Her heart was racing.

'Did I wake you?' Will stepped out of a shadowy corner.

'What are you doing here?' Edwina said sharply, sitting upright again. 'You've scared me to death. You shouldn't be here.'

'I've been here most of the night, Edwina,' admitted Will. 'I was worried about you.'

'I'm . . . I'm fine,' she replied, drawing her knees to her chest. 'Now, please go.'

He approached the bed, walking slowly around the perimeter, his fingers brushing the mosquito netting, rippling the material. 'No you're not,' he argued. 'Who would be?'

'You should go. If anyone found you in here . . .'

Will began lifting the netting, gathering it up as if he were a fisherman hauling in his catch, the material bunched in his hands. In an instant he was ducking beneath the folds.

'What are you doing? Stop,' she said loudly, shifting sideways away from him.

'Do you really want to wake the house? Your father and brother?' Unasked, Will sat on the edge of the bed, folding his hands in his lap. 'You've certainly managed to cocoon yourself in here.' He draped the mesh so that once again it contained the sleeping space and now him.

Edwina's breath caught in her throat.

'Are you alright?' asked Will. 'I don't mean you any harm; you know that, don't you, Edwina?'

'Yes,' she answered meekly, moving carefully away from him so that the brass bedhead dug into her shoulders. 'Please leave.'

'Mrs Ryan was very worried.'

'You must go. It's, it's just not proper, you being here.' She felt his eyes on her and was conscious of the thinness of her nightgown.

'I'm only here to help. Been sitting there in the corner since the house quietened I have.' Will gestured to an undistinguishable space. 'Must get cold in here come winter. There's a gap over there you could fit a child through.'

'Have you really been here for most of the night?' The thought of a man sitting in her private room watching her unnerved Edwina.

'Someone had to keep an eye on you. Make sure you were alright, and besides, that cranky old Scotswoman said you didn't eat your supper.'

It was true; she'd picked at the cold cuts of mutton, the congealed fat making her dry-retch. 'I wasn't hungry.'

'I don't blame you.' Reaching out, Will took her hand in his.

'You shouldn't be here,' said Edwina, only half-heartedly trying to pull away from his grasp. The heat from his touch made her heart race.

'I know what it's like to be flogged,' admitted Will. 'You try your best, and still it's never good enough. Everything has to be their way. As if we owe them. They make us feel ashamed as if it's *our* fault. But it's not, you know.'

'It's different for me, Will. You don't understand.' She felt his breath on her skin, warm and moist.

He clutched her fingers more firmly. 'It's not different, Edwina, that's the problem. That's what we tell ourselves to survive. But the thing is, once they start hitting they usually can't stop. They have to have everything their way, all the time.'

'He's never done it before,' she sniffed, wiping her nose with the back of a hand. He was so close to her, too close. 'Father knows, Will. He knows about the circus. The police came.'

'The coppers? Here? Why didn't he turn me in?' His eyes were sharp, calculating in the moonlight. 'Of course, because then you would have been dragged into it and the entire family involved. And we couldn't have the Baker name associated with a petty criminal.' Will tugged absently on the hanging netting. 'Blood's thicker than water, eh?'

'You forget, Will, I was at the circus unchaperoned, dressed as a man. People will talk. I have quite embarrassed my family.'

'And that's why he hit you, because of reputation?'

Edwina wished he would leave, but at the same time she found herself thinking of their shared kiss in the tack room, of the whorl of his ear when she'd cut his hair. 'You wouldn't understand.'

'No,' agreed Will, 'you're right; I don't. There's never a reason good enough to strike a woman. He's a hard man your father. If he tells a person to jump you have to ask how high. Why would it be any different for his children when he treats his help so badly? I've sure earnt my keep and more. It's probably just as well I'm not staying to dig a great bloody hole for his water. I don't know nothing about water and wells. But I've heard about walls collapsing, about men dying inside. I know that much.'

'You're going?' asked Edwina; his leaving brought up contradictory emotions in her.

'He fired me. I reckon that was the easiest way to keep the coppers off the trail and get rid of me. Davidson even escorted me to the boundary. Your father was worried I'd upset those chinks he's brought in to do the ringbarking, taking jobs away from good honest men. I don't understand the thinking of it. Anyway, one of those chinks will dig the well. Cheaper. No complaining. That's why your father likes Davidson so much. That's his idea of a perfect worker – one that can't talk back.'

'My father's a businessman, Will.'

'Don't spruik his good nature or the ability to make some jingle. He hasn't done any favours by you, has he? And you know why, don't you, Edwina? It's because you're a woman and women aren't supposed to have wants and needs or answer back.' He gave a wry grin and moved a little closer to her on the bed so that their bodies touched.

'And you think we should?' Edwina trembled. It would be very easy to simply lean into his arms.

'Everyone's got an opinion.' He ran a finger along the length of her arm. Fine hairs rose in response. Edwina's skin prickled. He simply had to leave; they'd already gone beyond the conventions of polite society. And yet . . .

'We're alike, you and I, Edwina. You know that, don't you? Oh not with things like money, that's for sure, although you don't live in high style here.' He gave a small laugh. 'But other things. We're sentimental – me rescuing that cub and you with your mother's tree. I've watched you. You'll spend an age searching for some

205

trinket for it. It's like your world is there, but that's only because you've not found something better to replace it with, and you're certainly not getting any help from your father, are you? We hope that our kinfolk will understand and support us, but they have their own problems, you know. I don't blame them; I don't blame my father for the drinking or hitting me, 'cause eventually I fought back. But I hate him for what he did to my mother.'

'Will –'

'You want a better, kinder life. You want something more than this. That was why you went to the circus, wasn't it? To find something better, only you didn't realise that at the time. It was more than just escaping your father, wasn't it?'

'Maybe.' A vague sense of unease began to worry Edwina.

'My ma once said that goodness only comes to a person if they chase it. Well, I'm chasing mine. We belong together.'

Edwina shook her head adamantly. 'It would never work, Will. It can't work.'

'You went to the circus when you shouldn't have and I was there and we met. Some things are just meant to be.' He lay down on the bed, his head on the pillow.

'You can't stay, Will. I want you to leave.'

'Do you know how long it's been since I slept off the ground? Lie down, Edwina. Come on.'

Kicking back the bedclothes, Edwina scooped up the netting and ducked out of the bed, then ran to the far side of the room. This was wrong. Terribly wrong. Did Will really think that she would lie with him? Her head was pounding, the skin across her cheek stretched tight with pain. 'You can't be here,' whispered Edwina, 'you simply *can't be here*.'

'I'd always care for you, Edwina.' Will spoke into the dark. 'Always. I might not be much now, but soon I'll be a self-made man. I've got prospects I have. Things will pick up. There'll be work to be had. And once that happens, I'll come for you. You're not promised to anyone, are you? So what have you got to look forward to, but a life of caring for your menfolk, and when your brother marries you'll have to care for his wife as well. Is that what you want?'

The bedsprings creaked. Edwina glanced out the door. She could sleep on the couch in the sitting room; surely he wouldn't follow her in there.

Will had turned on his side. 'You're a skittish thing, aren't you? I guess that comes from being kept here on the farm. I've heard your brother and father talking, I have. You don't really think your father will find you a husband of note after what happened at the circus? I mean, you said that people will talk.'

Edwina sat near the dresser, curling her feet under the night-gown. Will was right. Once her involvement in the circus theft began circulating around the district few families would consider her possible marriage material. The way the family kept to themselves, as well as her father's profession, meant they were removed from the community, and now she had added to their oddness by way of an action that was impossible to wipe clean. Edwina was reminded of her childhood. Of learning to write copperplate, first with a pencil and then with ink, of the deliberate, painstaking strokes required to form cursive letters, of her many mistakes and the wasted paper. Now there were no fresh pages left on which to practise. Or were there? Will wanted a new life, as she did. He cared for her and she liked him. Why should she stay on the property and wait for her father to find some stranger for her to marry when Will was offering her a way to leave?

'Wait for me, Edwina. A month or two at the most. I'll find us a place first so you don't have to stay here a moment longer.' He flipped up the netting, his boots landing on the timber boards with a loud thwack. 'I'll be back. Back for you, Edwina, and you don't realise it now but you'll be thankful for it.'

There it was: the assumption that she would simply agree and be grateful. Why did every man Edwina know feel compelled to tell her what to do?

Moments after his leaving, a low whistle, a signal of sorts, came from the orchard. As the cub and Jed ran from the room, Edwina rose quickly, shutting the door.

❧ Chapter Twenty-two ❧

Edwina woke the next morning groggy and sore. Her cheek ached terribly and it was difficult to open her eye. Probing the tender skin, she was suddenly wide awake at the memory of Will sharing her bed. She lay quite still, rigid with uncertainty. Heavens, she thought nervously. He'd come back during the night. He was still here, beside her. The warmth of him could be felt against the small of her back. She began to move towards the edge of the bed, inch by inch, trying not to move too fast, hoping one of the rusty springs wouldn't squeak.

As she painstakingly made her way across the mattress she tried unsuccessfully to still her rattled thoughts, absently observing the flickering pattern of the trees on the timber floor. Outside the sound of the wind rustling the orchard leaves carried the rise and fall of a distant thumping. With the slowest of movements she lifted the bedclothes and the netting, and crept from the bed. She turned back, expecting to see Will.

'Will?' she said softly.

But the bed was empty, save for the lion cub and a cheeky Jed, lying top to tail on the sheets. The door was partially open, the outside brilliance a harsh awakening. The cub gave a yawn and snuggled closer to Jed, their muscles twitching in sleep. Will hadn't returned and she was glad for it. Glad he'd not tried to take advantage, as she knew if he had she would have truly doubted her ability to control her emotions. There was an attraction there – one that she never could have imagined would take hold of her in so short a time. And yet it was strong enough to consider his proposal. For his offer was more than just an opportunity for them to be together; it was a means of escape.

The pounding of her heart lessened as Edwina shut the bedroom door so that the animals couldn't get away, and then reached for yesterday's clothes scattered on the floor. The shirt was spotted with blood and she cast it aside. Opening the wardrobe, Edwina sorted through her scant garments and, choosing an ankle-length skirt of beige, matched it with a clean white shirt of her mother's. Edwina rolled the sleeves up, added a tight-fitting waistcoat in pale yellow that had been relegated to the too-small drawer, and then sat down at the dresser. She wasn't working in the fields ever again.

Jed and Jim-jam, disturbed by the noise, jumped from the bed and began rolling around on the floor as Edwina looked at her reflection in the mirror. Eyes rimmed with darkness and crusted blood around her nose, a blue-black bruise accentuated the swelling across a cheek. The person before her was unrecognisable. As was the individual within.

Pouring water into a bowl from a pitcher on the washstand, Edwina splashed her face. She'd thought a lot about her father in the hours before sleep found her. About what Mrs Ryan knew, about the woman, Gloria Zane. She wasn't the only one in the family to cause harm. Her father was a hypocrite.

In a drawer Edwina found scissors and with a thick thatch of hair in one hand she lifted the blades. By cutting it she would be transformed into a modern girl. A flapper – admired by many and despised by the wowsers like her father. A new woman for the new age that her father was clearly so intent in keeping her from.

But could he keep her from it any longer? For she doubted there would be a fitting suitor here in the greater district of Wywanna. And what did it matter anyway when Will Kew was offering her freedom? The hair Edwina grasped was thick and glossy. Heavy and long. People sold their hair for wigs. For money. Her fingers closed tightly around the scissors.

After a long moment, Edwina sat the cutters on the dresser. Her circumstances were not that changed. A semblance of the girl she'd been before the bite of her father's hand, before his wrathful, nasty words, still existed. But things would never be the same between them again. And Edwina doubted her ability to forgive.

Outside, a dull, continuous thud sounded. Edwina tied her shoe-laces then walked onto the verandah, meeting Mrs Ryan, who cradled a pannikin of tea. Edwina quickly closed the bedroom door on a curious cub.

'You're up. Good. Good. I was worried, after yesterday's horrors. Haven't you missed all the fun and games.' She passed Edwina the tea, studying the rarely seen skirt with a querying gaze. 'Well, aren't you gussied-up?' The question hung. 'The Irish boy's gone,' she said with an air of good riddance. 'Was fired yesterday. Davidson escorted him off the property. Imagine that. Gone in a flash he was, then snuck back to ask after you. Made a favourite with him you did, eh?' Mrs Ryan stared at Edwina's skirt. 'I told him to skedaddle before he was caught and your father put him in for trespass. Just as well he's gone. Can't have a lad like that sniffing around. No good can come of that. No good.'

'No, no good.' Edwina took a sip of the tea.

'Something attacked the fowls last night. If I haven't spent the morning counting dead hens. Three. Dead as doorknobs and killed for the fun of it. I'd blame the dogs but they were all in their kennels. Feathers everywhere and mangled necks, but it

211

doesn't look like whatever attacked was after a feed. No,' the cook scratched her head, 'doesn't look like that at all.'

'That's strange,' mumbled Edwina, thinking of the baby lion and last night's open bedroom door.

'Well, we'll be eating those birds regardless. A person can't be wasting good meat like that and it was a cool night so you can be assured the meat won't be bad. In the boiler the first one is. Soaking the others so they'll keep another day. Lucky for you, my girl, you were poorly. The morning I've had. I never imagined myself a full-time chicken-plucker. My mother would say the Ghillie Dhu was up to no good. My wordy. That's what she'd be saying.' She coughed and spat over the edge of the veranda. 'Elves. Troublesome they are. That's a pretty bruise you'll be wearing for a few days, girl.' The cook cocked her head in the direction of the rhythmic noise. 'That's the Chinese your father's got digging the well. It's a good quarter-mile from the house. Out on the flat, straight past your mother's tree. That headman of theirs swears there's pure drinking water in that spot. If they find fresh water I won't have a problem making them the odd cup of tea. No, by Saint Andrew, I'll be right pleased to do so.'

'And where is everyone else?' asked Edwina.

'Your brother's gone out with Davidson to tell Mr Sears that his team will be finishing up at the end of the week. He asked me about you. About what happened? And I told him to keep his nose out of father–daughter business. As for your father, he's gone to Wywanna. Left in the dark.'

'Wywanna?' said Edwina.

'Now don't frown like that, Edwina. You know the truth of things now but that doesn't mean you can share your opinion. You promised me that. Remember.'

'I remember.'

'Anyway, I expect it's something to do with them coppers riding out to see your father. Yes, I expect that's it. Though it makes a body wonder, it does. What that Will got up to.' Mrs Ryan clucked her tongue disapprovingly. 'You've a bruise and a half you have, my girl. Hat and a scarf is my advice. No need to advertise what can't be helped.' The woman turned to leave. 'And that reminds me. When you've a chance, go down to the Chinamen's camp and fetch me these things for the pantry.'

Mrs Ryan held out her hand for the mug and Edwina exchanged it for a piece of soiled paper with its scribbled items of foodstuffs.

A distinct chopping noise reverberated through the orchard towards them.

'What's that?' Edwina whirled on a heel towards the sound.

The cook sucked her cheeks in. 'I couldn't say anything.' The air rushed out from between rubbery lips. 'It wouldn't have done any good anyway. Really it wouldn't. You know what your father's like.'

Lifting her skirt, Edwina stepped from the veranda. The Scotswoman was saying something about it being for the best. That a person can hold on too tightly to memories and be lost in them, like a coin down a well with no chance of the wish in repayment. There was an urgent voice inside Edwina telling her to run and she did so, slowly at first, weaving through the lemon and orange trees, then as realisation grew her shoes kicked up leaves and soft soil as she gathered pace. Beyond the stables, where her mother's tree grew, two men were visible.

They worked alternately, their arms swinging rhythmically in wide, smooth arcs, their torsos twisting at the waist as each spun their bodies towards the target.

'No!' she screamed. 'No, stop!'

The blades of their axes flew swiftly through the air, hacking at the trunk, the vibrations stirring the keepsakes strung from the limbs above. Items began to fall to the earth as the tree's tremors grew. Old bottles, pieces of broken crockery crazed by the heat and old lengths of faded material, ribbons and lace.

'Stop, please,' she begged.

The axes grew shiny with sap. Branches trembled and leaves fell.

Edwina collapsed on the ground as the Chinamen sliced away at the green wood, their brows slick with sweat below brimless caps. Each cut sent great shuddering waves up the tree's trunk, resonating through the ground to where Edwina watched on in a useless huddle. Every graceful slice was matched with effortless motion. Feet braced shoulder-width apart, a single plait swinging pendulum-like across their backs, each man's cut reaching deeper into the plant's heart.

Finally, one of the oriental men stepped back and the lone axeman gave a single strike. The hatchet bit deep. A terrible splitting noise came from the heart of the tree and then the woody plant buckled and fell. It landed with a thud in a flurry of wind-blown dirt, leaves and relics from the past.

Edwina lifted a tear-stained face.

The axemen poked and prodded the slain timber, talking in garbled tones as they picked through the debris of their handiwork. Finally one of the men approached Edwina.

'Rotten,' he said, showing a mouth with too many teeth. 'It start in a crack or rabbit burrow or maybe from lightning strike. It rise slowly even as tree reach for the sky. Then one day it starts to lean. Who knows how long before the earth pulls at it and it falls. It is good to cut down before the badness takes over. You plant another tree. Like orange tree.' He pointed towards the house. 'Orange tree very good. It will bring you very much happiness.'

The smiling man pointed towards the orchard. Edwina was sorry for his ignorance. He really had no idea. They went back to their work stacking the lengths of wood. Still sappy with the remnants of life, the flames came quickly when they set it alight, aided by kerosene. The smoke, a whitish sliver, grew fat too soon.

Edwina got to her feet. There would come a time when her father would wish he'd been fairer, kinder. There would come a time.

≪ Chapter Twenty-three ≫

'Is it true?' asked Gloria on arrival.

Maybe it was his imagining, but the rooms seemed less welcoming today. They moved from the sitting area to the bedroom where Gloria leant on the windowsill, his favoured position. There was little point in querying what the woman alluded to. He'd not bothered with champagne, there'd been no welcoming kiss, simply a far from prompt arrival after Hamilton sent a runner with a note to her door. Gloria Zane clearly wasn't of a mind to rush over and see him today. She was yet to remove her day coat or the absurd thing of a hat pulled low over her forehead. If he didn't know Gloria better, he thought she may have been ill. There was a pallor to her skin and an air of preoccupation.

Hamilton waited awkwardly at the foot of the bed. 'You've heard, based on your less than enthusiastic arrival.'

Undoing the single button on the marl grey coat, Gloria flung it on the bed, narrowly missing him. Hamilton was glad he'd already brokered two plots of land with the widower May Cummins on behalf of Han Lee. He doubted he'd much feel like negotiations after this.

'It's terribly fun until the person involved is someone you know. It *was* someone I know, wasn't it, Hamilton? It was Edwina? That's what people are saying.'

'No charges have been placed. It's all innuendo. Mistaken identity.' Hamilton offered a cigarette, lighting hers and then his.

Gloria wiped the tip of her tongue clean of a shred of tobacco. 'A world of people saw her, Hamilton. Everyone's talking of it. I wouldn't be surprised if it's in today's *Wywanna Chronicle*.'

'Yes, yes, she went to the blasted petting zoo but anything else, any other implication, is just hearsay.'

'It's bad enough that she would go by herself, dressed as a man.'

'She dresses that way on the farm, Gloria, for ease of movement.'

'No, Hamilton. She was *disguised* as a man. There is a difference. And people say Edwina was drunk, Hamilton. Drunk and smoking in public. The world may have changed, but it hasn't changed that much out here. They are calling her a flapper. This isn't a city. There are no masses to hide in. No bright young thing to rock the establishment tomorrow and make Edwina's antics seem unimportant in comparison.'

'I'm surprised you are so concerned. You haven't exactly led the quiet life yourself.' Hamilton ran his thumb and middle finger from the bridge of his nose across his eyebrows.

'This could ruin her if they find that animal and link her to it.' The cloche hat joined the coat on the bed. Gloria patted her hair. 'At least as far as someone can be ruined in Wywanna.'

'There's no need to be glib.' Hamilton loosened his necktie. 'Edwina has never smoked or drunk liquor in her entire life.'

'Your daughter, by your own account, hasn't done anything at all. How could she with you keeping her under lock and key, chained to that piece of dirt? No wonder she disobeyed you. And no wonder she was easily led when she found herself among strangers. How on earth did you ever expect to find a husband for her? Word of mouth?'

Hamilton bit his tongue. He would tell Gloria to mind her own business, but arguing with the woman was a waste of time. Across the room, his sweetheart appeared decidedly sour. 'Edwina never took the creature.' Stubbing out the cigarette, Hamilton fiddled with the silver container, flipping the lid open and closed. 'There's no proof.'

'You suspect her?' Gloria's voice rose an octave.

'Truly, I don't know what to think. I can't understand what possessed her to do it. To go to the circus alone. To actually ride into town by herself. Edwina wanted to go.' Lighting another cigarette, he exhaled in a short, sharp puff. 'She was desperate to go. I said no, for obvious reasons.'

Gloria ashed her cigarette, and moved to his side, giving him a kiss on the cheek. 'My poor Hammy, caught between the two women he loves.' She gave a little tut. 'That is a pathetic excuse. You should have told them about me by now. But you've always been so concerned that our relationship might stymie Edwina's chances of a good match, not to mention have an effect on your own position in the district.'

'I wanted to wait until she turned twenty,' he argued.

'Everyone has their eccentricities. Although from what I hear of your daughter's looks you would have done far better to parade her around town if you wanted her married.' Gloria took a quick puff of the cigarette. 'You did want her married, Hamilton? Or was she more useful to you on the property?'

'What a thing to say.'

'Well, it doesn't matter now. If you keep someone in a box long enough, my dear, eventually they will want to escape.'

This was not what he'd expected. The conversation was double-edged and, knowing Gloria the way he did, Hamilton knew he must salvage it.

'It didn't bother me until now,' said Gloria, almost businesslike, so erect in the smart navy dress without a hint of frippery. There was no seed pearl brooch or silk scarf, no butterfly hatpin with jewelled eyes. 'After the circus I realised that being hidden in the cheap seats was getting wearisome. In fact I'm very tired of it. It's no fun anymore.'

The room seemed inordinately small.

'I'm sorry. And you're right. But you have to understand, Gloria, Edwina is a problem. The girl's obsessed with her mother. She spends half her life searching for bits of rubbish to hang on a tree in memory of Caroline. You have no idea how difficult she can be at times. Anyway, the tree business ends today. It's being chopped down.'

'Excuses.'

Gloria almost sounded disinterested. Hamilton was beginning to get quite fed up with the women in his life. Daughter and lover expected far too much. Did no-one ever think of him?

'You are obsessed with money, fanatical when it comes to your need for acceptance by who you deem to be the right people in society, and fixated with finding an appropriate husband for your daughter, knowing a good match will shine a light on you as the father as well.'

'You make me sound terribly provincial.' He laughed, dreading what was to come next. 'Do go on, my dear.'

'I am not an idiot, Hamilton; you and I both know you have a less than spotless past. Yes, I know about your shady dealings in Sydney. I would hardly get involved with a man without having checked his credentials.'

This was unpredicted.

'I was prepared to take you as you are,' said Gloria more softly, 'on face value. I chose to forget your past and concentrate on the future, but that's impossible for you. In your quest to regain a little of your family's former glory you have become moody and controlling and now you have a major scandal to contend with. You will not find a husband for your daughter now, not here. At least, not the one you hoped for.'

'And I will never be accepted properly by Wywanna society, either. That's what you're really saying, isn't it, Gloria?'

'Yes, I suppose it is.' She played with the jewelled rings on her fingers, twirling them. 'And honestly I don't understand why you care so much.'

'And I don't understand why you don't. I'm not content to circle the periphery as you are, Gloria.'

'There is nothing to circle in Wywanna, Hamilton, but if you feel so left out, stop depending on titbits from the Guild members. Create your own centre of power. Then see who comes to you.'

But he had done that very thing. Peter Worth was the one who made the initial approach and now it was all ruined thanks to Charles Ridgeway. 'You do me a disservice, you know, my dear; I am not the self-centred buffoon you paint me as. You don't know Edwina. How could you? You have no children. Heavens, you barely have any relatives left that I know of. The child is wilful and ungrateful. She takes after her mother. Why, Caroline had the attention span of a gnat. Edwina never thinks of consequences or reality for that matter; she only thinks of herself.'

'Really? In that department,' her reply was brittle, 'you are much alike.'

'This is the end then, I presume.' Hamilton sat resignedly in the brocade chair. He could use a drink now, a double.

Gloria approached. Tilted his chin, smiled prettily. 'I can't see you staying here, Hamilton, not now. I know you too well. You will fixate on this dilemma and it will drive you into the ground. Prudence would suggest you sell up. Move elsewhere. Start again.'

'I see. And you?'

She walked about their boudoir, examining the fine curtains, lifting one of the delicate crystal bottles on the glass dresser. 'I had a telegram from my broker. It seems I've lost half my fortune. The London Stock Exchange crashed.'

'It did what?'

'Clarence Hatry and some of his associates have been accused of fraud and forgery. Really, he was such an unhealthy looking little man that one hardly thinks it possible. Wonderful house though. He lives in Great Stanhope Street in Mayfair,' Gloria explained, 'near Princess Mary. It's very luxurious really. He has a swimming bath on the principal bedroom floor, and a stone-floored Tudor-style cocktail bar in the sub-basement. That's why I invested in his companies. Because he'd done well. Was doing very well. He was, as one of his American friends used to say, a sure thing.'

'Who on earth is this Hatry? And how much have you lost?'

'I've lost enough to make it more than worrisome. As for Hatry, he's a corporate financier. Apparently Clarence was on the brink of a merger of steel and iron concerns that was to become the forty million dollar United Steel Companies. That is until the Stock Exchange Committee caught him borrowing one million dollars on worthless paper. Terence, my broker, says the whole thing's a catastrophe. I've directed him to sell all my shares in America. You should do the same.'

Hamilton thought of his exposure in the American market as he took Gloria's hands in his. 'My dear girl, what can I do?' He needed to send a telegram. He needed to sell, and quickly. Nearly everything he owned was invested in shares. 'Do you really think America will feel any repercussions? I mean, you said yourself that London wasn't the financial centre it used to be.'

'Of course you must consider your situation, make your own decisions.' She squeezed his hands, promptly releasing him. 'I've booked passage home.'

'But there's nothing you can do,' argued Hamilton. 'Surely this Terence fellow can keep an eye on things.'

'Terence was my broker. He does not manage my estate or my finances.'

She took a step backwards. Hamilton sensed the gap was more than physical.

'I'm on Sunday's train to Brisbane.'

'Sunday's train. Listen to me, Gloria. Stay. Don't rush off. We can look into your losses. See what can be salvaged.' Hamilton was all too aware of how this would be perceived – Gloria leaving immediately on the heels of Edwina's all too public disaster. 'I'll ride down to the Telegraph Office, send my broker a message asking for an update on the market, then I'll be back. We'll talk. Spend the night together as we always do.'

Draping the day coat over an arm, Gloria checked the angle of her hat in the dresser mirror. 'Even without this monetary setback, you know I've wanted to go home. I miss England, Hammy.' Turning away from the reflection, her lips stretched taut. 'It's so terribly brown and dry and lifeless out here. I want green and cool.' She kissed him on both cheeks. 'This has been a wonderful interlude.'

'An interlude? Five years,' he called after her as she walked away. 'Five years and you leave just like that? On account of losing a handful of pounds?'

At the entrance to their rooms, Gloria turned on her heel, the line of her dress showing off her slim ankles to perfection. She looked around the sitting area. 'It was more than a few pounds, Hamilton. As for the five years, what can I say, except four was too little,' she blew him a kiss, 'and six years,' she shook her head, 'would have been far too much.'

≪ Chapter Twenty-four ≫

Hamilton turned the brass key in the lock not knowing when he would return.

Gloria Zane had been a lover, a friend, his confidante at times, but more than that she'd been a salve to his ego. Oh, yes, he got carried away with the titillation at times, with the bordello intimacies that kept them both entertained, but he did care for her. By God, he really could strangle her.

Outside, Hamilton gave his horse an absent-minded pat and shoved the business folders and share notebook from the sitting-room desk into the saddlebag. Light-headed from the half bottle of rum he'd consumed, he began leading the mare down the street, oblivious to all other traffic. For some reason the blasted animal wouldn't walk straight and Hamilton veered to the left and the right before grabbing hold of the thick chestnut mane and searching for a fixed point in the distance.

On the street corner ahead a figure moved. The shape was yelling and holding something aloft that fluttered in the breeze. Hamilton's teeth ground. Children ran past him, pointing and pulling faces.

'Local girl steals from circus, read all about it.'

Head angled, shoulder squared in dogged concentration, Hamilton managed to reach the young boy, who followed his progress with a quizzical gaze.

'Are you alright, mister?' asked the paperboy.

A stitch was tracing ugly steps up his side and across his chest. Hamilton was grateful for the shade and, looking upwards, saw the provider, the awning of Lee's Emporium. 'Of course.' Hamilton frowned at the child. 'Here's a pound,' he dug into his pocket, 'take it and call out something else.'

The boy snatched at the money and then passed a paper. 'But that's the headline, mister.'

'I don't care if that's the bloody headline. Talk about the crash in London. That's far more important.'

The boy looked out from under a raggedy cap. 'My father says blasphemy is for non-believers. You'll be struck down, you know, mister. That's what my dad says.'

Hamilton figured that was the least of his problems. 'And did he also tell you not to argue with your elders? If you do, you'll definitely go to hell for that.'

Playing with the satchel strung crossways over his body, the boy thought on this.

'Just do what I say, young chap. Alright?'

The boy hunched his shoulders. 'Alright,' he agreed, walking to the kerb. 'London crashes. Read all about it.'

'That's better.' Hamilton edged his way back to where the horse waited patiently, the pain in his chest yet to disappear. 'Don't look at me that way,' he said to the animal, reaching for the waterbag. It took a long drink and a number of anxious minutes waiting for his eyes to focus before Hamilton could consider reading. He bypassed the front page. Just for the moment. He wasn't sure he could trust his stomach to behave if the article on Edwina and the family read as badly as predicted. Instead Hamilton turned the pages to the financial section. The editorial confirmed Gloria's disaster, briefly outlining the loss of confidence in the London market following the collapse of Hatry's empire.

Dragging a finger under the newsprint, Hamilton read as quickly as comprehension allowed. The gist of the editorial appeared as bullet points in his mind. Some economists were concerned. The world markets were jittery.

'Yes, yes.' The column was boringly long.

Sporadic selling was taking place in America where there were signs of trouble, the journalist wrote. Steel production was showing a decline, construction was sluggish, and consumers were building up high debt thanks to easily obtained credit. The Sydney Stock Exchange was monitoring the situation. Hamilton disregarded the negativity of the editorial. The piece told him nothing – at least nothing of substance – until the very end.

He read the final sentence, once, twice and then checking to ensure no-one was observing, Hamilton read the paper for a third time.

The price of American stocks had gained more than twenty percent since June.

Carefully folding the paper, Hamilton slipped it beside the business documents in the saddlebag. Gloria shouldn't have run out on him so soon. He was still a very wealthy man.

So much for Peter Worth's prediction that a crash was coming. Men like that knew little, their world view skewed by the limits of their interests. Hamilton was sorry for Gloria of course, but women were skittish, untried players. Only good in business to a point, then with the first problem their stomachs grew fluttery and they ran home. Were Gloria equipped with good sense, she would have seen what was so blatantly obvious. A loss was suffered, yes. But this was the correction the world's markets had to have. It was quite healthy. In fact it was a buying opportunity.

The ride through Wywanna was not one to be enjoyed. Tipping his hat where required, Hamilton kept his path straight and unhurried, feeling the pointed stares, hearing the whispers and guessing at the spoken words.

He would have the last laugh of course. They could refuse to welcome him as an equal, blacken his daughter's name, turn their backs on him; however, he knew how to do business. With the surge in share price the glorious days of his ancestors were almost in reach. By heavens, he may even be able to purchase a vacant British title and join the aristocracy. It was all within his grasp. Only the matter of Ridgeway Station and the unlikeable Charles soured the moment. Still, some good could come of it. He would report to Peter Worth about Charles Ridgeway's disreputable attitude. The Ridgeway boy would be compelled to pay his debt and the lad would quickly discover that if he elected to stay in the district his acceptance would not be as he'd hoped. Hamilton would ruin him.

Hamilton stood to one side, allowing a woman to leave the building before he stepped into the cool interior of the Post & Telegraph Office. With the morning rush and lunch hour over, the postmistress was absorbed in the task of stamping and sorting mail, placing envelopes into black pigeonholes and correspondence bound for outlying properties into large canvas mail sacks. The woman greeted Hamilton with a brief hello and he pointed amiably to the telegraph operator at the end of the room.

Hamilton approached the middle-aged man, waiting patiently as the operative converted the beeping sounds coming through on the telegraph machine into a written message. The paper was then folded, placed in an envelope and the addressee written on the front.

'Can I help you, sir?' He pushed at the peak of the cap he wore, revealing a craggy, sweaty brow.

Hamilton nodded. 'I'd like to send a telegram please.'

'Of course. Would you mind writing it out for me, sir?' He placed the recently received message in a pile at his elbow. 'Usually I'd do it, there being no queue, but it's been a busy morning. There was a problem at the Brisbane office. I had to resend the daily weather observations and then one of Mr Worth's sale results came in. The man has more cattle than the population of Queensland.'

'Yes, yes.' Hamilton took the slip of paper and pencil offered, noting the name and address of his broker. In the message portion he wrote:

Keep 10,000 pounds aside STOP Invest remainder of savings across share portfolio STOP Immediately STOP Provide financial position by return mail STOP
    Hamilton Baker

The operator took the coins offered, quickly reading the message. A shade of interest touched his office-white face. 'No problem, Mr Baker,' he replied tentatively.

'It's not true,' said Hamilton. 'About my daughter. Mistaken identity.'

The operator studied the written lines, as if a letter or word was incorrect. 'Yes, sir. I really wouldn't know, Mr Baker. Sir.'

As the clock tower struck three, Hamilton took the road out of Wywanna that curled past the river flats, his stomach churning as the site of the circus came into view. Beneath the wooden bridge boys fished for yabbies in the yellow-green swirl, a mother hollering at the group to come home and do their chores. The wind gusted hot and dry across the fringes of the town. Grasses bending. The sky a razor's edge of blue steel. He pushed the mare onwards, his limbs heavy. Palpitations came and went in little ticks of feverish anxiety. When he gave thought to Gloria the heat in his body rose.

The mare soon refused to keep pace with Hamilton's demands. The horse slowed and stayed slow, doggedly refusing attempts to be urged. Finally Hamilton gave up using the spurs, gave up trying to decipher a feasible plan from the wreckage of ideas spinning around in his head. Now he was sobering, the greater ramifications of Edwina's antics became clear. Would Peter Worth still be inclined to do business with him, and what of Charles Ridgeway? Would the man pay up in a timely manner?

The road that freed him from Wywanna curved to the right, bending through a frill of silent timber. Trees bordering the road grew sparse, allowing glimpses of life. Sheep feeding in the gritty breeze, chickenhawks chasing a small brown bird, circling and diving, and the flat surface of cleared land, throbbing shade-less under the sun.

Hamilton held the reins loosely, the horse's pace edging back. There was noise ahead. The gravelly taste of dirt on the air. Ahead, the ball of dust balancing between sky and road grew into the ambling shape of walking cattle. Hundreds of cattle. The dust rose to hang feet above the herd as they plodded south. The thrash of hoofs on brush and the crack of stockwhips, steady and reliable in the heat. Hamilton counted two men tailing the mob and more on the wings ensuring the animals kept a steady pace. They were some miles from Mrs Landry's Inn and Hamilton knew the drovers would be pushing to make water by nightfall.

It didn't take long to catch up with the herd. Hamilton drew level with one of the men, suddenly hungry for company, for the comfort of a stranger's words. A furry-faced man with round dust-puffy eyes glanced in his direction, pulling a triangle of dirty cloth away from mouth and nose.

'G'day.'

'And to you. Travelling far?' Hamilton brought hand to mouth. The dust was thick. 'You'll have a thirsty mob,' he commented, noting the inverted PW brand that marked the livestock as belonging to Peter Worth.

The man's face was grime-free and white where the cloth protected fairer skin. 'Not far, mate, no. Heading to Ridgeway Station. Taking the shortcut past Woodville's waterhole.' He winked. 'A bit of free-range grazing along the way. We'll camp there I reckon. Man and beast alike could do with a breather. It's filthy dusty and summer's come. I could do with a swim myself.'

'Ridgeway?' Hamilton didn't understand. 'But they're in sheep.'

The drover yawned, showing cracked yellow teeth. 'Well, there's a story there. I was meant to be droving these girls over the border for the Boss, but the young fella on Ridgeway's just back from the Territory. A true son of the saddle he is now, I hear. Ride anything. Hates sheep, he does. Wants to buy cattle. Just bought a spread further north, the boy has. Beyond the dingo fence.'

'But he hasn't got any money!' blurted Hamilton.

The drover's eye twitched.

'I mean that's what I heard. Something about the place being foreclosed on,' Hamilton hedged.

'I dunno nothing about that, mate. Excepting that he's a tough nut the lad is. Knows his mind.' He yelled at a soil-crimped dog snapping at a cow's heels. 'There's talk of him having sheep lifted by a neighbour. The coppers will be on to that right quick.'

Things were as bad as they could be. Even with his detailed notes of fair exchange for the damage done, he didn't need the district to get whiff of another problem. They'd think the worst. Hamilton let the drover walk on, wondering who Ridgeway's backer was. However, the stockman wasn't letting him have any peace. He slowed his horse, drawing abreast with Hamilton, eager for conversation.

'They say the Ridgeway boy knows his cattle. They say he's got a fine eye for big beefy types and he's gone and bought this here mob.'

'Peter Worth sold these cows to Charles Ridgeway?'

The drover's head tilted solemnly, clearly equally taken aback by the news. 'I might tell you too, friend, that the Boss isn't too

228

pleased by the turn of events. Nope, he's none too pleased at all. Between me and that gate post over there, I think he was fixing on buying the station. He booked me up a while ago for the next twelve months in order to shift cattle from one run to another.'

Hamilton felt his throat begin to shrivel and close.

'I only got told of it myself last night. But a sale is a sale and in the end the Boss ain't never been one to poke an eye when he can tend a fire.' One of the cows darted away from the mob. The drover whistled and a dog appeared out of the grasses tufting the side of the road. The cow was brought to heel with a couple of barks.

Hamilton was stunned. After all the wrangling and careful positioning he'd crafted, how on earth could this have occurred? How had the insufferable Ridgeway and Worth ended up conducting business together, without him, when it was he, Hamilton Baker, who was meant to be acting as the go-between? He'd been inches from accomplishing a major sale for the highly esteemed pastoralist. Had come so close that, after years of plying his trade, he'd finally gained admission to the President's office. Only the final step was required to seal his favour with Peter Worth. Now it was all destroyed by that damnable Ridgeway. There would be no opportunity to even wreck Ridgeway's reputation now he was in cahoots with Worth.

This final piece of news quite took the fight from him. Hamilton doubted he would mount another charge amongst the custodians of privilege, well aware that it might be years before an opportunity presented itself again. Besides which, after Edwina's recent performance, the level of acceptance he'd previously enjoyed in Wywanna could no longer be relied upon. There would be no advantageous marriage now. No private discussions in the President's office. The only consolation was knowing that Peter Worth's aspirations were also crushed. Hamilton felt tired. The earth dragged on his bones.

'Word is the Ridgeway boy's got himself a backer of note.' The drover tapped the side of his nose. 'And this is a man no-one says no to. Not even my boss.'

Hamilton chewed at powdery black soil and bile. 'Grazier?'

'You could say that,' replied the drover evasively. 'Pastoralist is the term I'd use. Never met him myself. But I know plenty of men that work for the family. Now there's a man that knows the land.'

There were a handful of pastoralists in Australia who commanded that type of respect. Hamilton blinked away the grime, his eyes watering. He thought back to that extraordinary day at the Guild, when the man himself had arrived. If one was going to be well and truly felled, it might as well be by a consummate axeman. 'Who is it?'

'It's Mr Luke Gordon himself of Wangallon Station.'

❧ Chapter Twenty-five ❧

The Chinese camp was a neat assembly of tents pitched within a clearing. From a distance the area was all angled surfaces of canvas alternately caving in and billowing out like lungs against the push of the wind. Thin trails of smoke tangled with the leaves of overhanging boughs from a number of fires and as Edwina approached she saw the ground had been swept clean of twigs and branches. A man stirring a large copper with a stick lifted a pair of trousers from the steaming water and hung them over a makeshift line. He looked up as Edwina passed, bowing politely. Men were honing axe-heads, iron gleaming under swift, brisk strokes. Another fitted a fresh handle to a blade. These were the country's new artists. Craftsmen from another place and time who would chisel away at the ancient timber, creating new land from old.

On any other day Edwina may have felt anxious entering the camp alone, but after hours of staring at an unyielding sky a dragging listlessness had leached into her bones. Sitting by the stump of her mother's tree would not return the plant to health, nor would thinking on her father be of any good.

The wagon was in the centre of the clearing. She rode towards it, listening to men talking as they went about their tasks. A water carrier with two buckets appeared from the direction of the creek, dumping his load near one of the camp fires. Another man skinned a rabbit, a pile of glassy-eyed carcasses on the ground beside him. Each man attended to his role with deliberate movements. Even the group of card players sitting cross-legged under a gum tree were quiet in their laughter. They could have been here for a year, such was the feeling of permanency. Wet clothes, the smoke of green timber, tobacco fumes and the heavy scent of spice thickened the air. Nearing the wagon Edwina dismounted, smoothing the skirt she wore and tying the horse so it couldn't wander. Two men sat at a table by the wagon talking animatedly, a fire nearby. They rose on her approach, the taller of the two smiling cautiously, as the second Chinaman was subtly dismissed.

'I am Han Lee.' He bowed.

'I have come to fetch some stores,' replied Edwina awkwardly. Even though, with his roundish face and almond eyes, he looked different to her kind, Edwina could tell from his features that he was a good man.

'You are Mr Baker's daughter?'

'Edwina, yes.'

He gestured politely to one of the chairs. 'You will take tea, Edwina, and then we will see to your needs.'

She didn't want tea, but Edwina sat politely as Han Lee poured hot water from a billy into a teapot patterned with Chinese calligraphy. He swirled the liquid around before throwing it on the ground, then added a spoonful of green leaves from a canister and more hot water to the pot. 'Now we wait, a few seconds only; there is enough bitterness in life I fear,' he said, examining her face, 'without drinking in such things.'

Embarrassed at how she must appear, Edwina lifted a hand to the brim of the hat she wore.

'I have an ointment that will help with the bruising.' Han Lee poured the pale green tea into two handle-less earthernware cups. 'You will think that I am very British, but the Chinese developed tea thousands of years ago.' He studied her face. 'Drink it. It is restorative.'

He observed her over the rim of his cup as she sipped the liquid. When Edwina put the cup down he topped it up with hot water.

'It is said that Shennong, an Emperor of China, was drinking a bowl of just boiled water when a few leaves were blown into it from a nearby tree, changing the colour. The Emperor took a sip of the brew and was pleasantly surprised.' Han Lee smiled. 'Better?'

'Yes, thank you.'

He rose to stoke the camp fire, selecting lengths of cut timber from a stack of wood. Pouring water into the billy, he set it on the embers, adding a handful of rice from a cloth sack to the water. 'Now what do you need, Miss Edwina?'

Mrs Ryan's list in hand, Han Lee began sorting through the goods. A set of scales was produced and he began weighing the spices selected from a series of small drawers that were fitted to the wagon, placing the contents in small paper bags. Canvas sides could be rolled down to protect the contents of the dray, which included a stack of cloth and hessian sacks and a number of wooden crates.

'Rice, some potatoes and a little flour,' Han Lee explained, noticing her interest. 'You would think to have such staples would suffice but I miss my mother's noodles,' he admitted.

'When were you last home?'

'Years. But I should be happy here in this jade-and-gold world. That's how this land is seen by my people. It has always been so.' Han Lee busied himself with a basket containing dried herbs. 'You will understand, Miss Edwina, that I do not carry the normal wares of a hawker. If you asked me for household linen and feather dusters, these things I do not have.'

'You don't much look like a hawker,' admitted Edwina, thinking of the fruit and vegetable seller in Wywanna with his catchy phrases. Han Lee was dressed in clothes that her father would wear and she noted that, unlike the rest of his clan, he didn't have a long plait hanging down the length of his back.

'I am only here to oversee the team. A new area requires a certain diplomacy. Here.' Unfolding a parcel wrapped in brown paper he displayed a quantity of pale blue silk.

'It's very beautiful.'

'It is yours.' He saw the doubt she harboured, for he quickly added, 'Your father wanted you to have material for a new dress.'

Edwina accepted the cloth reluctantly.

'For the purposes of this trip I only have foodstuffs, herbs and spices. The lengths of silk I always carry and a few other oddments, but these things for your kitchen I can help you with.' Placing a quantity of ginger aside he deftly peeled a knob, chopping it directly over the billy so that the pieces fell into the simmering liquid. A pinch of something dried was added along with a bunch of herbage that looked to have been pulled fresh from the ground. 'And salt?' he asked.

'Yes, please.'

'I only have the type for the curing of meats.' Han Lee walked around the side of the wagon, returning with a solid lump in his hands. The piece was as long and as thick as his forearm, coloured a dirty white. 'You must break it up of course, but it is very good. Very pure.' Laying the piece of salt on the table he wrapped it in newspaper and placed it in a hessian sack along with the herbs and spices and the rewrapped length of silk. 'It is from south of here at Rocky Creek in the hills of New South Wales. The last time I was there kangaroos were inside the cave licking at it. It hangs down from the roof in columns –'

'Like stalactites?' offered Edwina.

'Exactly. A woman from the Rocky Creek sawmill told me about the caves many years ago. She said wild horses and cattle were fond of eating the salt as well, but the place is almost ruined now. People go there for picnics, driving their automobiles where there are no roads, cutting the salt down as keepsakes.' At the fire Han Lee partially drained the rice, setting a portion aside in a porcelain bowl. 'I want you to eat this, Miss Edwina. It will heat the blood and help with healing.' He pushed the bowl across the narrow table.

There was no spoon offered. She didn't want to offend.

'Drink, drink,' he urged.

The concoction resembled muddied water. Lifting the bowl, Edwina drank it, tasting the sharp spice of the ginger and the earthy tang of the herbs. The rice slid down her throat and she tipped the vessel, sweeping the smooth dish with her tongue.

'You have not eaten this day?' Han Lee waggled a finger like an indulgent mother. 'You must eat.'

Edwina gave a guilty smile. 'I better go.'

'Wait.' Producing a tiny metal pot, Han Lee unscrewed the lid, showing her the glutinous contents. 'Twice a day, morning and night.' He closed her fingers over the container of balm. 'For the bruising. Be well, Miss Edwina.'

Han Lee assisted her onto the horse, tying the bag of goods to her saddle. She gripped the reins, thanking him for his kindness.

'Come and visit us, Miss Edwina, we are always in need of the sight of a pretty woman.' Han Lee bowed before walking back towards the wagon.

'Well, Heidi-Hoe, let's go home.' The mare backed up and whickered softly, walking sedately along the trodden path away from the Chinese camp. The light of midafternoon shone through the bush, silhouetting the timber so that the branches appeared to curve between track and sky, forming a leafy tunnel. Edwina's aches began to ease gradually and she wondered at the mixture she'd consumed, for the warmth Han Lee spoke of was spreading through her limbs. She stopped to apply the balm to her wounded skin, nose crinkling at the aromatic scent. Things would get better, she thought. They had to get better.

An answering internal voice queried, how?

Leaves crackled. 'Who's there?' She was not so far from the Chinese but already the scrub had folded around her, as if the leafy shaft between the camp and the road home was momentarily blocked. Ahead a horse and rider walked onto the path a few hundred yards away. Edwina hung back, unable to tell if it was Aiden or her father. 'Hello?' The reins felt slippery in her grasp. The rider didn't reply.

Behind lay the camp and Han Lee. Heidi-Hoe would return her there in an instant. But what was she running from? It could be her father back from town early and it would be just like him not to reply. The stubborn figure remained impassive. Finally Edwina kicked Heidi-Hoe lightly and the mare trotted onwards. The rider remained in the centre of the track. Stationary. Waiting. Of course it was her father. Edwina steadied herself for another tirade. Answering back would be pointless. She would do as her mother undoubtedly had – build a wall of silence and seal herself from his fury.

The space shortened between Edwina and the horseman.

It wasn't her father. The man before her sat taller in the saddle and didn't carry the weight that he did. Edwina rode on, doubting, anticipating. And it wasn't Aiden. Heaven knew, her younger brother could afford to gain some pounds. Questioning who the stranger might be, Edwina tempered her speculation. This land belonged to her father and anyone who wasn't invited or who wasn't known was an intruder. She would be quick to tell them to be on their way

'Hello, Edwina.'

Heidi-Hoe stopped of her own accord, wary of the pale gelding and the man on his back, one hand resting over the other, a cigarette glowing between his fingers.

Edwina edged her horse a little closer. She knew this person. 'Mason?'

He tipped his hat and grinned.

⋘ Chapter Twenty-six ⋙

'I wondered if it was you. When the housekeeper told me that everyone was away except for the daughter.' Mason paused. 'When she said your name, I thought I should find you and know for sure.'

'But I don't understand, I thought you were travelling through Wywanna?' They sat astride their horses, their animals pointing in different directions, Edwina still adjusting to the sight of a man she never thought to lay eyes on again.

'It was to be a short visit but I've been here for over a fortnight and having found my plans changed through circumstance, I'll now be staying longer. A lot longer. I've quite taken to the country. It's different to the Territory but . . . let's just say I like the area.' Flinging a leg over the saddle, he slid to the ground, holding out a hand to her. 'And the people.'

Edwina ignored the courteous offer, recalling the words of his friends at the menagerie. There was pleasure in seeing Mason again, but she was also wary. Wary of his coming to the property and of the offensive innuendos spoken by Janice and H.J. that suggested that the man before her was not what he appeared to be.

Edwina held tight to her skirt to prevent immodesty and got down from Heidi-Hoe of her own accord.

'Better.' Mason pointed to her skirt. 'Not that I minded you as a man.'

She felt her cheeks colour as he came nearer.

'What on earth is that?' He moved to touch her face and Edwina flinched, backing away from him.

'An accident,' she murmured.

'That's no accident,' replied Mason. Before she could stop him he was removing her hat. 'I know the strike of a hand when I see it.'

'Please,' Edwina took the hat from him, stepping away from his concern, 'it's nothing.'

'That is not nothing. It wasn't that boy at the circus, was it? I worried about you being in his company. But you were determined to leave.'

'I had to leave, Mason. I shouldn't have gone to the circus in the first place.' Edwina smiled tiredly. 'And the man,' she said with emphasis, 'was Will Kew. He was working here, but he's gone now. And no, it wasn't him.'

'Well, that's different I suppose. He looked a bit down-at-heel, but he did step in and ensure I wasn't annoying you. I guess people are a bit wary of opportunists these days, Edwina. Times are hard. There's plenty of men looking for work and willing to take the advantage if they see an opening.' He took a step towards her. 'So who did hit you, Edwina? For we both know the wrongness of the act.'

'You're a stranger here, Mason. Please, you must let this be,' she warned. Edwina was grateful for his concern, but more indebted to his thoughtful silence. Having such a thing done to her was one thing, attempting to give an explanation, quite another.

'If there's anything I can do?' he said gravely.

They began to walk back through the bush, leading their mounts. The trees became sparse and the wind increased with the loss of the thick timber break.

'Where have you come from?' asked Mason.

'The Chinese camp. They start work on Saturday.'

'And you went alone?'

'Of course.' She patted the bag tied to the saddle. 'I had to pick up stores for Mrs Ryan.'

Mason plucked a length of grass and began chewing the stem. 'It's a good distance to the homestead, Edwina. You shouldn't be riding around by yourself. Where's that brother of yours?'

'I can look after myself, but how do you know Aiden?'

'He should be with you,' said Mason, ignoring the question.

'My father's in Wywanna and we are our own people when he's away.' Her brow puckered. 'What are you doing here anyway?'

'Actually, I came to see your father.' He appeared to expect a response. 'But I'm more pleased to be seeing you. I had no idea you were Hamilton Baker's daughter.'

'You know my father?'

'A little.'

'But how did you meet?' queried Edwina. 'At the Guild?'

Mason flicked away the grass he chewed. 'At Ridgeway Station.'

'Ridgeway Station? But I don't understand.'

Mason ruffled Heidi-Hoe's mane. 'There was a disagreement over some business.'

They stepped over rotting timber, edging around the mound of an ant's nest. Edwina was in no doubt that the meeting with Charles Ridgeway had not helped her father's mood, nor her own cause. 'My brother was there,' she said to Mason. 'He didn't mention you.'

Mason drew back. 'Really?'

'I gather you're a friend of Charles Ridgeway? If you are, I must ask you to tell him that the money borrowed must be repaid. My father is a businessman and your friend should know better.'

'Charles . . .' repeated Mason carefully.

240

'Yes. I am sorry for his troubles. His and his sister's. I know of their parents' deaths, but it is no excuse for such behaviour.' Edwina was puzzled by Mason's expression. Was it possible that, like her, he knew little of the detail involving the dealings between her father and Charles?

At a sparse-leafed tree they sought shade, Edwina feeling the pinch of the sun on her cheeks and neck.

'You're right of course, but perhaps my friend found himself in a predicament that was unexpected,' replied Mason. 'Maybe he thought a little latitude could be given considering the situation, instead of a talking-down.'

'I am not interested in your friend's problems, only in the happy result of the monies being repaid,' snapped Edwina. The muscles in his jaw contracted. 'I'm sorry, I should not have spoken like that.' He wasn't responsible for Charles Ridgeway's behaviour.

'He has a temper your father, doesn't he? As do you, I see.'

The wind stayed constant, smacking at the clouds as if shooing them away. Edwina always hated the spring winds. They pushed and pulled at a person, foretelling the coming of summer with its heat-withering days and baked-earth smells. A reedy branch overhead trembled as a single bird settled in the boughs. 'I'm sorry, Mason. You've caught me out of sorts today. So you're staying at the station with the Ridgeways?' she tried more amiably.

'Yes.' Swinging up into the saddle, Mason stared down at her. 'I was sorry when you left the circus early.'

How should she reply – that having seen him again she too was glad? Unsureness kept Edwina silent. She was not a plaything, as his friends had alluded, and Mason's host was not a neighbour to be admired. 'Are your friends still with you?' It was the only thing Edwina could think of to prolong the conversation.

'They leave tomorrow. I don't think it was quite the adventure the girls thought it would be. But then nothing ever quite turns out the way we hope it will. Does it?' He tipped his hat, clucked to the gelding to be on their way. The horse walked off sedately.

Edwina clutched at Heidi-Hoe's reins. If rudeness were a gift then surely she'd just shown herself to be overburdened by the talent. The space between them grew. Maybe she'd been too hard on Mason. He'd sought her out after all and in a few minutes he'd reach the homestead road. Edwina knew he would keep riding in a northerly direction, reaching the tree line that divided this grass paddock from the wheat beyond. The jagged contour of timber was barely ten minutes ride away. Ten minutes and then he would be gone. She thought of Will and stamped a foot on the hard ground in annoyance. She should let Mason leave . . . but she couldn't. What if this time she really didn't ever see him again? Edwina's skirts swished as she began to move through the grass. This is ridiculous, she muttered. She couldn't believe she was actually walking after a man. Heidi-Hoe threw back her head as if in disagreement with her actions. 'Mason?' Edwina finally called.

Horse and rider halted. Edwina steadied her breath, shushing at Heidi-Hoe to stop her carrying on.

There was a definite pause before Mason pulled sideways on the reins, the gelding spinning around as directed. Edwina waited, but neither Mason nor the horse budged. For a moment they simply faced each other across a bridge of air-stooped grass. Her clammy hand opened and closed on folds of her bunched skirt. A sliver of perspiration trickled across her stomach. He was making her pay for her rudeness. Edwina walked on.

What should she say? That she was pleased he'd come? That she wished they'd met under different circumstances? That she'd like to see him again? Surely a woman couldn't be that audacious. She pushed the thought of Will to the back of her mind. There was nothing wrong in being friendly.

'Yes?' Mason drawled, when Edwina was close enough to see moisture patterning the hair under one of the gelding's eyes.

She wet her lips. It was clear he wasn't going to make this easy for her. 'Thank you for coming.'

Mason gave the slightest incline of his head. 'Maybe I'll come again.'

He gave her a lazy smile before nudging the gelding to action. Edwina observed him until the hedge-work of ridge timber concealed horse and rider from view.

≪ Chapter Twenty-seven ≫

Edwina and Aiden ate the chicken pie with its mashed potato topping and then took tea in the sitting room. Mrs Ryan could be heard banging around in the kitchen, the clash of pots resonating across the short space between the two buildings in the evening air. The woman was vocal in her annoyance that their father had not bothered to let her know he would not be returning that night. She'd gone to great trouble to make his favourite dinner, claiming it might calm his temper. Her irritation amused Edwina, considering the number of mangled chickens in the meat safe. The fowls couldn't be wasted.

'Mrs Ryan didn't seem convinced it was a fox,' said Aiden, alluding to the attack as he set a lantern on the inlaid table next to their father's empty chair.

'What else could it have been?' The thought of the dead birds reminded Edwina of the lion cub. Will's departure left her sole custodian of the stolen animal for he'd not taken it with him. What on earth was she supposed to do with it? The animal had been locked inside her bedroom all day.

'Did you know Father wasn't coming home?' Aiden poured tea, handing a cup and saucer to his sister.

'No, I didn't know he was even going to Wywanna until Mrs Ryan told me.'

'He usually tells us if he's staying overnight. He talked about speaking on behalf of the Chinese to the owner of that land they want to buy. But I didn't think it was that urgent or that he'd need to stay overnight.'

Edwina wasn't that fussed if their father returned or not. The thought of him doing unmentionable things with that woman made her sick. Did he have no respect or love left for their mother? Through the parlour window a dusty pink formed a backdrop to rippling rows of fish-scale cloud.

Aiden took a sip of the milk-less drink. 'I saw Sears today. He's not very happy about losing out to Han Lee's team. I thought he might have an attack of the fits he was that annoyed. I was half expecting him to punch me or at the very least confront the Chinese on the way out.'

'But he didn't and you paid him.'

'Yes.'

'Well, then it's just as well he's gone. I think Han Lee's men will do a good job.'

The pink sky darkened. Edwina watched the dogs sprawled in front of the homestead chewing on kangaroo bones left over from their dinner.

Aiden lit the wick of the lantern. 'And does that go for Will Kew as well? Are you pleased he's gone?'

Edwina stopped stirring the sugar in her cup. 'What is that meant to mean?'

'I saw you with him a few times. Sneaking around the stables and the tack room.'

The spoon clattered on the saucer. 'How dare you. I don't sneak, Aiden. I should be asking you why you were spying on me.'

Aiden shrugged, settling back in the sofa with its faded embroidered cushions. 'No need to get riled, Edwina. I saw you. That's all

I'm saying, and Father didn't take much to having a young bloke like him in close proximity to you. He asked me to keep an eye out when I could. Anyway, I thought that maybe there was something between you, especially after he brought you back from Wywanna last Saturday.'

'There was nothing between us,' answered Edwina. 'How would there be?' She sucked at the teaspoon, aware that her brother was watching her carefully. It was the first time the subject of the circus had arisen since the weekend, Aiden's taking of the buggy keeping his silence. 'He was a strange boy.'

Eventually Aiden smiled, as if satisfied. Edwina thought of her brother's detective work on behalf of their father. The days of their sibling secrets were over.

'Well, Will's gone now so we don't need to worry about him. But the man who came to the house today while I was out? Did you see him? Mrs Ryan said she sent him down to Han Lee's camp to find you.'

In the past Edwina would have shared that she'd met Mason at the circus, that she liked him and thought it surprising he was friends with Ridgeway. 'Yes, he's staying with Charles Ridgeway.'

'Really?'

'Came to see Father apparently,' answered Edwina. 'But I have no idea why. You didn't meet him on Monday?'

'No.'

'He spoke as if he'd met you.'

'Ridgeway was travelling with friends. They were outside in the garden, talking and drinking liquor and it couldn't have been much after midmorning. Imagine taking alcohol in the morning.'

'Yes,' Edwina smiled. 'Imagine drinking it at all.'

Aiden topped up his tea. 'Well, Ridgeway has until tomorrow to repay the monies owed and then he'll be served. Perhaps he hoped to delay the payment using his friend as a go-between.'

Edwina tucked her feet up on the horsehair chair, the porcelain cup warming her hands. 'Perhaps.' They sat in the growing semi-darkness, the fire in the hearth and the single kerosene lamp providing two patches of dismal light.

'I didn't really fall over Jed that afternoon.' He had a right to know what had happened. 'Father and I had a serious disagreement.'

Although it was a warm night, Aiden rose to put a small length of timber on the fire to keep the flies at bay. 'Are you telling me that he struck you?'

'Yes.'

He stopped to study the yellow-green swelling of her skin before returning to his seat. 'Why?'

'Because I'm not happy, Aiden. I'm tired of my suggestions regarding the property being continually ignored and yet Father seems to feel it's quite alright to treat me like a labourer. Well, it's not. And now we know that Father has more money than he lets us believe. Which means we don't have to live like this.' As soon as the words spluttered forth, Edwina knew that Aiden didn't share her sentiments.

He leant forward, resting the cup on a bony knee. 'Father says that it's time you were married with your own home and children.'

Aiden addressed her so succinctly that for a moment Edwina imagined that it was their father speaking and not her earnest younger brother.

'He says that women get maudlin, that you need something else to occupy you.'

'Something to . . .' There was a ribbon-edged pillow cradling her back and Edwina tossed it at Aiden, striking him in the arm and upsetting the tea he held.

'Now look what you've done,' he complained, wiping at the spilt liquid.

'I'm already occupied, working. That's all I ever do here. Really, Aiden, I never imagined you would sit there like a parrot on a

247

perch and repeat what Father's fed you. It's not 1900 anymore, you know.'

'Everyone has to contribute, Edwina.'

'And I have and do,' she argued. 'It would be different if there was something to look forward to occasionally, a trip to town, the circus. It's not much to ask for. It's called life, Aiden. I want a life.'

'Well you must have made him very mad.' Aiden's lips pressed together, emphasising the cleft of his chin. 'It was awful cutting down Mother's tree. I was sorry that happened. That you made him so mad that he did it,' he accused. 'It meant something to me too, you know.'

Edwina sat the tea to one side. 'I know. I saw them do it. You blame me, but Father gave the order. Don't you think that killing Mother's tree was rather mean of him? Disrespectful of her memory?'

'I think you're the one that needs to show some respect,' countered Aiden.

'I angered him and he has the right to destroy something important in retaliation? I'm loyal to a point, Aiden, but doing something like that is petty.'

'Edwina, I'm disappointed that it's because of you that the tree Mother loved had to go, but I do understand why Father did it. For pity's sake. Every morning you place an object at its base as if you're leaving an offering at a holy shrine. Every morning,' he reiterated. 'Do you know how you look with your sheer shift and shawl, barefoot at dawn? It's time for you to grow up, sister. I miss Mother too, but she's gone, Edwina. Gone.'

Shuffling in the seat, Edwina stared into the fire.

'You haven't been yourself the last few months. Always complaining, going to the circus unattended, riling Father until he's fit to strike you. I'm telling you this for your own good. Father sees similarities in your behaviour to Mother and I shouldn't have to remind you that she ended up in an asylum.'

Edwina visualised hitting her brother across the face, her palm stinging with the effort. 'I can't believe you just said that.'

Aiden's brow smoothed. 'You'll just have to put up with things the way they are. I mean, until you marry and have a place of your own.'

'So I can do the exact same thing on another property?' answered Edwina.

Aiden stared at her. 'But that's what women and men do, Edwina, they marry. The women have babies and the men run the businesses and –'

Edwina rose to stare at the fire. The flames curled around the few pieces of wood, creating a thin line of smoke. 'Maybe I want to run the business. Contribute ideas. I do have a brain, Aiden. I wanted to do something different, that's all. I thought of getting a job, perhaps training to be a secretary.' She faced him. 'Don't you want to be your own person? Earn your own money? Be free to spend it as you wish and do as you wish?'

Aiden finished his tea. 'I know you think that Father's been hard on us, Edwina. But he's done his best. Anyway, the property will be mine one day. It mightn't be my choice, but it's all I know and I'm grateful for it. For the living.'

'Maybe if I was in your position I'd feel differently.' She rested a hand on the mantelpiece where a pair of emu eggs decorated the polished timber. The carvings were amateurish. Tiny stylised trees etched into the hard shell and painted by their mother. 'And maybe if you bothered to put yourself in my position you wouldn't be so harsh.' His silence gave Edwina courage to go on. 'The property, this life, Father's controlling ways . . . none of it is enough for me, little brother. You might be content to keep living the way we do but I'm not. Not now. Things will never be the same between Father and me, Aiden. He said some things to me. Awful things.'

'Then you will have to regain his favour. Be the pleasant daughter that's expected because he'll never let you leave here unless it's to be married. Better that you let Father find you a suitable husband. You'll be happy once you've settled down with a good man.'

Edwina stoked the burning wood with a brass poker. 'He will never find me a good match in this district, Aiden. It's an impossibility.'

'Rubbish, Edwina. That's pretty much all he's talked about the last couple of years. Seeing you well married. Then me. Father's hopeful. Very hopeful. A good marriage for you will be the making of this family, that's what he says.' Aiden placed his cup and saucer on the tray.

'The making of him, you mean.' Hanging the poker back in its cradle, Edwina clasped her hands tightly together. Forgiving Aiden wasn't difficult. Her brother was young, a giddy colt still trying on the boots of manhood. In the interim he followed the role model offered, the man of the house, the person who'd taken on the task of being mother and father to a heartbroken eight-year-old boy. Hamilton Baker was better with his son than with his daughter. There was an affinity there, a shared knowing that manifested in a wall of unfathomable men's thinking and patriarchal inheritance that Edwina could never hope to breach. However, her tolerance didn't extend to maintaining Aiden's ignorance. It was time he grew up.

'You know some of the reasons why it will be difficult to find a good match for me, Aiden.' Edwina spoke firmly, an elbow resting on the ledge above the fireplace. 'Our father is a money-lender, first and foremost. He is not a pastoralist or a grazier, nor a true farmer. We are a breed apart to the people of this district. If we were not we would be invited to functions. We would have friends.'

'Friends?' repeated Aiden.

'Yes. You and I have never had one, either of us. Think about that.'

'Well, I guess –'

'And while you try and convince yourself of some good reason why we find ourselves in this sorry, friendless state, there is something else you should be aware of. Something Mrs Ryan told me.'

'What?' Aiden edged forward on the chair.

'Father has been seeing a wealthy divorcee in Wywanna for a number of years now. They meet in Father's rooms, which she apparently decorated at great expense. All of it paid for by Father. There are rumours about the woman's background – undesirable gossip that is clearly well known if our cook is aware of it.' The fire grew warm. Edwina returned to her seat.

Aiden's arm slipped from where it lay on the armrest to dangle limply.

'You didn't know then?' she asked, half expecting for the confidence to have been shared between father and son. Edwina picked at the hem of her yellow waistcoat, the stitching unravelling. 'So you see what Father says and wants for us and what he does are very different things,' she cautioned. 'Frankly, he's a hypocrite.'

'A divorcee? Do you know her, this woman?' Aiden's solemn intrigue was replaced by rounded eyes.

'No.' Edwina was sorry to be the one to fracture her brother's opinion of their father. 'Father took her to the circus last Saturday. Mrs Ryan saw her. Her name is Gloria Zane. The relationship has been ongoing for a good many years.'

Aiden said the woman's name, stretching out the foreign sounding letters so the consonant buzzed as if spoken by a child learning his words. 'That accounts for not wanting us to go.'

Edwina gave the strand on the waistcoat a final tug. The thread came loose and she wound the stray cotton tight around a finger, the tip growing red. It was a relief to share their father's secret relationship. 'I understand how you're feeling, Aiden. I was very shocked and disappointed when Mrs Ryan told me.'

'Old Mrs Ryan should have kept her thoughts to herself.'

'Why?' countered Edwina. 'Why should we be kept in the dark when this sordid affair affects the entire family? If it was all above board Father wouldn't have kept the relationship a secret, would he?'

'So he's there with this Mrs Zane now?'

Edwina knew that tone, what it meant. Aiden was still weighing up the information, measuring it against what he knew, what he believed.

'Maybe that's why he wanted you to be married, so he could bring her here as his wife. Father knows how much you still miss Mother, Edwina. The tree was proof of that. Maybe he thought you'd make things difficult if he remarried. Maybe that's why he kept her a secret.'

'What?'

'You heard what I said.' Aiden rose. 'You've always been jealous because Father favoured me over you. He probably thought you'd be jealous of her as well. Well, I'm sorry you're not happy with your life, Edwina, but maybe you should be grateful for what you do have instead of causing problems.'

A howling dog drew Edwina to the window. The grassy crest at the front of the homestead was invisible. Sensing movement she closed the shutters, latching them securely. 'Someone's outside.'

Aiden lifted the lantern, the weak light illuminating the knotted tongue-and-groove walls as it swayed in his hand. 'You're sure?' Not waiting for an answer, he took the rifle down from above the mantelpiece and, handing the light to Edwina, he loaded the firearm.

Outside the barking ceased.

'Who do you . . .?'

Edwina was shushed with a finger to her lips. 'Quiet.'

The knock was sharp. Two brash heavy thumps.

Aiden stepped past his sister, hurrying to the front door. 'Keep close with the light,' he directed. Edwina did as she was told.

At the landing Aiden flung the door open, lifted the rifle. 'Who's there?' he called.

Leaves showered from the roof above. Air swished through the trees, warm and dusty, as the light from the lantern made a dim circle in the tarry dark.

The silhouette of horse and man grew visible.

'Who's there?' demanded Aiden, stepping forwards.

Edwina's mouth dried as Aiden cocked the rifle. An indecipherable figure grew out of the night. It was as if the stranger was bereft of features; only his clothes, the garb of a stockman, were discernible. A horse whinnied softly. Leather creaked. There was a noise of sorts, a soft groan. In reply the dogs began howling again.

The man moved onto the verandah, boots sure and steady. Aiden lifted the firearm and aimed at the approaching figure. 'I'll shoot,' he warned.

The figure emerged in the light of the lantern. Davidson faced them, unreadable. His dark eyes glittered as he pushed past them, carrying their father in his arms.

≪ Chapter Twenty-eight ≫

The stockman strode ahead, boots striking the uneven boards, Hamilton's arms and legs dangling like a child's. Behind him Aiden guided Davidson's path as best he could, the lantern throwing silhouettes on the wall. The aboriginal's shadow stretched to the ceiling while their father appeared as a lump with four appendages. How had her father become so very small?

'Mrs Ryan?' Edwina shouted. 'Mrs Ryan!'

Edwina pushed ahead of the men, yanking the quilt from the bed. 'What happened, Davidson?' she asked, lighting the wick of the lantern on the dresser and replacing the glass flue. Davidson lay their father on the bed.

'More light!' Aiden demanded.

Edwina took another two lanterns from the cupboard in the hallway then returned to their father's room. Lining up the pale green glass lights she lit these as well.

'Mrs Ryan?' Edwina yelled again as the room grew brighter.

'Edwina, stop screaming.' Aiden took her firmly by the shoulders. 'Clear head. Alright? Keep a clear head.'

'I wasn't screaming. Mrs Ryan knows some medicine.'

Edwina looked to Davidson. The aboriginal was sliding off their father's boots and covering his legs with the discarded quilt. Then together he and Aiden removed their father's coat and waistcoat. He was covered with dirt and dust. A bloody cut to his forehead was pitted with dirt.

'He must have fallen from his horse.' Aiden addressed the stockman. 'Is that what happened, Davidson?' he asked slowly. 'You went looking for Father and you found him on the ground?'

They waited.

The stockman gave a single incline of his head.

'Right. Thank you for bringing him home.' Removing his shirt they checked for bruising. There were no other injuries that they could tell.

The aboriginal dragged a hardwood chair from a corner and sat next to the bed.

'Look at his face, Edwina,' said Aiden. 'There's something wrong with his face.'

Pouring water into the bowl, Edwina wrung out a rag, wiping the grime from their father. Apart from the nasty wound and the cranial lump, Aiden was right. One side of their father's face appeared to have slipped. The cheek drooped on the right, the lip appearing as if it were being pulled down by a piece of twine. 'It must be the way he's lying,' suggested Edwina, looking to Davidson for answers.

Mrs Ryan appeared at the foot of the bed, chest swelling with air, a gnarled hand clasping a brass bedknob. 'What by all that's good and right has happened here?' Peering at the prone figure she muttered something unintelligible. ''Tis the palsy to be sure,' she told them. 'To be sure your father has been struck.'

A spatter of leaves hit the corrugated iron roof.

'Davidson found him. He'd come off his horse. What do you think, Mrs Ryan?' asked Edwina hopefully. 'What should we do?'

The patient moaned.

'I don't have the learning to help him. Broken bones and cuts, that's the extent of my knowledge, not doctoring to do with this. If it's the palsy he won't be able to move. I've seen it before. Years ago. No,' she shook her head, 'there's nothing to do for a body, especially when it's so afflicted.'

Aiden looked at the figure on the bed. 'It's too dark to ride to Wywanna and fetch the doctor. I'll wait and leave at first light.'

'If he lasts the night,' the Scotswoman warned.

'That's enough,' Edwina complained. 'You might as well go to bed, Mrs Ryan, if you can't help; there's nothing that can be done till sunrise.'

'I'm telling you straight.' Mrs Ryan's mouth grew thick and bunched like a knob of cauliflower. 'If he lives the night,' she said doubtfully, 'get him up and about. Let him get his senses back. That's the only hope you have.' She pointed at Davidson. 'And him? He's to stay with your father under the self-same roof?'

The stockman, elbows on knees, stared at his boss.

''Tis a bad sign, it is,' Mrs Ryan began to back out of the room, 'having him here.' She crossed thick arms. 'It's not right, not right I say. You don't have a black keep guard. Not with their unfathomable ways and him not being able to speak. I'll not be keeping with this, young Aiden, no, I –'

Davidson hissed at the cook. The woman bolted, her steps retreating down the hall.

'I'll sit with Father,' offered Edwina, covering his chest with the quilt.

'No,' Aiden corrected, 'Davidson and I will stay with him. You go to bed.'

'But –'

'I doubt when he wakes that he'd be pleased to see you, Edwina, not after everything that's happened. And after the way you spoke tonight, I couldn't allow it.'

Surely he joked? Aiden held the door to the bedroom, his knuckles whitening on the doorjamb. Edwina looked at their father, to a disinterested Davidson. Words of argument formed as Aiden moved towards her, effectively pushing her out of the room.

Furious, Edwina shoved back against the timber. 'If I were a man I'd hit you,' she spat.

'But you're not a man, sister. You're a woman.' Aiden slammed the door in her face.

≪ Chapter Twenty-nine ≫

A weedy patch of light flickered, fattening and then fading before rising to fullness again. Hamilton watched the irregular shapes as they weaved and bobbed, crossing a surface of long pale lengths defined by joins. It could be a figure. Maybe it was. All angular limbs and bulbous head. A shape-shifter of strange proportions, unrecognisable except in worrying dreams. That's what this was, Hamilton decided. A dream.

The air was cool, laced with smoke. Was he still in the dirt? Where he'd fallen. Face down. Strange, but now the ground felt softer as if it had opened up, cradling or, more worryingly, eager to accept the offering. How he'd come to be lying in the dirt was a loss to him. The road ahead was clear after the drover's mob packed the earth hard on the way to the waterhole and, in the grimy atmosphere created by their leaving, Hamilton recalled squinting into the confluence.

The track led homeward, away from a hoard of difficulties towards an unknown ending. But it was still a home. Of sorts.

Four winds. That's what he remembered. The four winds from a yellowing map once hanging in his parents' home.

Puffed cheeks. Old eyes.

East wind, west wind, north wind, south wind.

Four faces blowing out wind from their mouths.

And his mother explaining that they were leaving their fine house for something smaller. A house in the woods that they could afford. And no, Father wasn't coming. He'd gone back to his family and their estate. Where there was money.

Before he fell. After the drover. That's the remembering needed. There was a conversation. Someone speaking. Harsh words spoken at the crossroads with a man.

Hamilton felt the man's hate, recognised his own.

There were no rifles. There wasn't time. One of them punched first.

It wasn't him.

Then the pain came. A terrible headache. Worse than could be imagined. The weakness struck him on the left side of the body and the countryside began to close in, tapering, dulling. His thighs loosened their grip on the mare's warm body. The ground rose up and it seemed to Hamilton that he met the hardness of the earth too soon, mid-air.

The mare nuzzled an ear, nudged at a shoulder.

The man was gone. Bits of soil collected in his nostrils. With each breath the grains accumulated. The land shrank to a narrow pinprick.

The Green Man stepped out of the dense foliage to squat by his side. Hamilton craned his neck, his body useless. His mother said the Green Man wouldn't harm him. That his leafy face carved in trees and on churches was a happy sign. Hamilton didn't believe her. He would pull himself up and confront this creature with his grassy features, but instead, Hamilton felt himself slip away.

And now there was only the incessant smoke and the warming breeze. And a gentleness beneath him, a cushioning for old bones.

259

Light. Hamilton fixed on that point. Straining. Remembering. The pale background was boards. Tongue and grooved. Rough. Hand-hewn.

Found then. Someone had found him. For surely he'd been lost.

Smoke billowed. It streamed over his body and he watched the cloud grow in size as it moved from his feet towards his head. There was a noise accompanying this strangeness. A mumble of words, ancient, longing. A song, if it could be called such. The smoke moved, wafted. Hands held the smoke and the face above it was streaked with whiteness.

He knew this person.

Davidson. His Green Man had followed him from England.

≼ Chapter Thirty ≽

Edwina woke at daylight, a damp circle of saliva on the pillow. Rubbing at salty eyes she struggled upright, re-buttoned the waistcoat, straightening her skirt – yesterday's clothes. In the faint glow of dawn she could see that the room was a mess. The lion cub and Jed, restricted to the four walls, were a disastrous twosome to have left contained. They'd mangled wallaby hides, teethed on the linen, and swung on the netting hanging around the bed, ripping the material.

The stuffy room held the sour stench of urine and poo, while every surface bore the messy trail of animal investigation. The pitcher on the washstand lay on its side and the bowl was empty. One of the creatures at least had drunk. Chunks of hard bread had satiated the little monsters last night but the cub could not be contained again. He'd slipped past her, through the door into a night undeserving of bright sparkling stars.

The lion cub would survive she hoped, far away from here, and with the thought of its leaving, she briefly closed her eyes. She was sorry for the young lion, and worried at the danger it could pose as it grew older, but she wanted it gone. Everything changed on the cub's arrival and since then some things were now irretrievable, such as her mother's tree, a father's regard, a certain innocence of life. A daughter's expectation. Edwina poked tentatively at yellow-green skin as she applied Han Lee's balm. Her face appeared a little better. She wondered what Will was doing. Where he was. Had he walked into her room at this very moment Edwina would have found it extremely difficult not to rush into his arms. But he wasn't here. She dabbed at watery eyes. Now wasn't the time to feel sorry for herself.

Tidying the room was a stinking task. Edwina did it quickly. Scooping up poo and rubbing at stained timber. Setting items straight. Folding and tucking. Throwing the refuse in the dirt outside. Contrition was not one of her attributes, especially now, standing on the back verandah staring through the orchard to the place she'd visited every morning for years. There was a gap there now. An empty space. A hollow.

Edwina pinched at her wrist. The pain was good. Clarifying. There was anger but what she felt more keenly this morning was tiredness. There was a desire to fold. To simply give way to those who thought themselves better, believed they knew better. It would be uncomplicated, to be accepting. Like her mother. To wilt away gradually. To disappear. Except for one thing. The shame Edwina felt was for her family. For a way of thinking. For a dictated life. It didn't have to be this way. She at least could do better. Be stronger.

Outside her father's bedroom door she met Aiden. An inverted horseshoe was nailed to the wall. She recognised it as Mrs Ryan's.

'He's awake. I made tea.' Aiden's words were sharp.

'How is he?'

'He's sitting up, yes. But he's not speaking.' Grudgingly, Aiden stepped aside.

Inside, the room was gloomy. Weak light streaked the floor where it sneaked through the shuttered window. A lamp on the dresser struggled, its fuel almost spent. Beside the lantern sat a number of candles, the wax melted and pooled in a series of solid creamy puddles on the dark wood. The huddled form of their father was propped up with pillows. The scent of smoke was pungent. It was almost as if someone was burning off indoors. There were a sundry other smells, each fighting for dominance – thick sweat, something sickly-sweet and vomit.

'Heavens, are you trying to suffocate him?' she complained, holding a hand to her nose. She opened the shutters and the day streamed in through the orchard. Among the trees the collies waited, upright, silent, the dogs watching the window of their master's bedroom. Edwina stepped back from such absolute loyalty as Aiden wiped up vomit from the floor. A metal dish filled with ash sat in the middle of the room. 'What is that for?' she queried.

Aiden didn't answer. Davidson held a cup to their father's lips, a hand supporting his shoulder. In the initial darkness, Edwina hadn't noticed the aboriginal. He was shirt-less, scars crazed his chest, the dark of his face streaked with a grey-white substance that looked like powder. Their father slurped noisily from the vessel, a sag of skin drifting downwards. Edwina turned to her brother.

'Men's business,' he said in answer to her widening eyes.

'The blacks' ways are not ours, Aiden,' she cautioned, wiping her hands nervously along the seams of her waistcoat. She daren't look at the stockman. At his nakedness. In the warm room his skin glistened. There were notches etched into a forearm. Five thick welts. As if he were keeping count – but of what?

'Can it hurt?' her brother replied. 'Could you do better?' He sat the sick-cloth on the dresser. Beside it was a large brown leather book with the words *Domestic Medical Practice* written on the cover. Edwina flicked the pages until she reached p for palsy.

'I've read it. They don't know what they're talking about,' said Aiden.

The words under symptoms and complications seemed to lift off the page. 'Facial paralysis? Brain damage?' Edwina looked into her father's bottomless eyes. Somewhere within was the man they knew. So many thoughts welled up, so much unhappiness. 'We'll never know what happened, will we?' she finally asked, controlling her fears.

'I think we have a fair idea.' Aiden handed her a newspaper that was sitting on the end of the bed. 'I found this in his saddlebag along with his papers.'

Edwina read the headline, her stomach collapsing.

'Makes for interesting reading, doesn't it?'

There it was in inky print. The lion cub. The girl dressed as a man. The local daughter accused of bringing the wanton ways of the city to Wywanna. The drinking of liquor in public. Smoking. And something far more damaging – a reference to an unstable mind. Who could have said such a thing . . . 'Aiden, I –'

'It's dated yesterday,' her brother continued, 'so I think we can safely assume what caused Father's attack.'

'But –'

'I'm not interested. I'm not interested in anything you have to say anymore. If I was the head of this household I would throw you out. Give you the money you so desperately crave so you could leave here and make your own place in the world.' His gaze dropped to her feet and he glared at Edwina as he travelled the length of her. In that singular moment she was reminded of their father. 'You are surely the most ungrateful daughter a person could ever have the misfortune of knowing.' He looked as if he'd eaten something rotten. 'You have embarrassed this family no end. You've given our father a dreadful blow.'

'You're upset, Aiden. I am too, but there is no excuse for you speaking to me in that manner.'

'Leave.'

'But you must let me explain what happened. It wasn't my fault. It was Will Kew, it was –'

'Don't you understand? It doesn't matter what happened, Edwina.' He snatched the paper from her. 'This is what the district thinks.'

'I'll speak to you when you have your senses about you,' Edwina countered, her voice wavering. 'I'll go and see Mrs Ryan and –'

'She's gone,' Aiden told her. 'The old woman left in a flurry of complaints, talking about Davidson being allowed in the homestead and Father striking you. She said she'd had enough. A mighty fall from the Lord's grace, that's how she put it, as if Father's illness was of his own making. I'm pleased she's gone. I never liked her anyway. It's amazing none of us were poisoned the state she kept that kitchen in.'

Across the room Davidson sat silently. It was impossible to know what he thought about any of this. Were the stockman not a mute he may well have spoken as her brother did, but Davidson's allegiance remained with his employer and Edwina guessed that the rest of them could be damned such was his interest in the siblings before him.

'You will have to take her place. Do your share. Father needs soup. And don't whine about it, Edwina.'

'And the doctor?'

'There is no point sending for him. There are no broken bones. What ails Father is beyond medicine. Davidson and I will get him up and about in a couple of hours. A walk will help. Fresh air.'

Edwina doubted this.

'But,' Aiden lifted a finger, a sharp nail poking harshly at her chest so that she felt the spike of both word and action, 'I want you to stay away from him.'

'So you will be both son and nursemaid?' declared Edwina, pushing aside his hand. 'What a pretty picture. You don't have to try that hard, Aiden; you are his favourite after all. And as you said, all this,' she lifted her arms, the gesture encompassing the room, the house and their land, 'will be yours one day. Maybe,' her tongue was slick with spittle, 'sooner than you think.'

265

'I think you should leave,' replied her brother.

'Davidson,' said Edwina, 'we appreciate you staying with Father; however, I need you to go and see Han Lee and –'

'I spoke to him yesterday,' interrupted Aiden.

'And did you show him the way to the Carbeen paddock and tell him where we wanted his team to start?' asked Edwina.

'No,' he admitted.

'They need to know. Davidson, could I ask you to do that please?'

The stockman rose from his seat and with a final glance at his employer walked out the door. Edwina followed.

❧ Chapter Thirty-one ❧

Edwina fed the wood stove until the kitchen hut emitted torrid waves of heat, the blast of hot air eventually sending Jed to seek a cooler place to rest. There were recipe books somewhere belonging to her mother and she scrounged for them until the mouse-eaten relics were found under a large tin of castor oil. Dirt-rooted vegetables sat in a basket on the freshly scrubbed table. Edwina chopped carrots and potatoes and then, after consulting the recipe books, selected ingredients from the canisters, jars and bottles stored on the shelves, until chicken soup simmered and two slightly burnt fowls appeared from the oven. Aiden came to the kitchen three times to check her progress and on the last occasion, with the food prepared, the pots scrubbed clean and the entire kitchen disinfected with lysol, she told her young brother to serve up what he and their father needed when required, tidy up after himself and ensure the cooled, leftover fare went into the food safe when he was finished.

There would be no setting of the table, Edwina informed him. No laundered napkins rolled into individual silver rings and no sister playing slave to a younger brother. Aiden parted with a bowl of soup and a chicken leg, obviously prepared by his lack of argument to concede that if he wanted to eat he would only do so her way.

Edwina rushed through the remaining kitchen duties with one thought. And that notion eventually led her back across the short patch of dirt into the house and to the rarefied confines of their father's study.

Closing the door with a wince as the knob squeaked, she rested her shoulders against it. It wasn't the first time she'd been here. But it was the first alone. Edwina almost expected the screech of the rattan-backed swivel chair, the impatient questioning of a man disturbed. In its place were tracings of cobwebs in corners, the grind of boot-carried soil underfoot and a soft-falling dust forming a leaden patina. It fell to Edwina to sweep and brush the office thrice weekly and she did so with the timely reliability of the grandfather clock in the dining room, never speaking unless spoken to. Now, with the room stark in its emptiness, she was struck by its coldness without the presence of its usual inhabitant. Then again, perhaps the chill had always been there. Edwina thought of her father, of the man he was, of the father he could have been, and began to weep.

It took time for composure to return. She wiped at puffy eyes, trying to recall the last time she'd cried so hard – perhaps when her mother died – but today things were different. The room was sparsely furnished like most of the homestead, but the quality of the velvet curtains, the thick rug and the two leather-backed chairs that fronted the locally made desk with its red-seated swivel chair were handsome pieces that in Edwina's mind were quite wasted. Aiden would like the room. He would be lost if the worst happened, but he would enjoy what the saddest of circumstances would bring. Until he mismanaged what was left of their father's legacy.

Her father's saddlebag rested on one of the seats. Placed there by Aiden, she presumed, after the retrieval of the newspaper.

There was nothing that could be done about that now. Only the present and the future could be changed, and then only through action. Sitting in her father's seat, Edwina ran her palms along the edge of the desk, across the timber with its three equally spaced paperweights, writing paper and short stack of envelopes. The sun angled directly onto the leather chairs. The morning light revealed tiny lines where the leather hide was crazed and cracked by years of heat and she wondered at the spoiling of the barely used objects, at the waste of decorating a room for clients who never called.

The desk drawers were what she'd come for and Edwina opened them, removing the contents and reading the papers as quickly as possible. Her mind fixed on the letters and bills, absorbing what she could while listening for the most minuscule of noises in the house. Twice she glanced at the door and twice lung-locked air was released. Her father couldn't reprimand. Not at the moment. Maybe not ever again.

It was the ledger she searched for. The ledger that would reveal how much money was at their disposal. What their debts were. Aiden, absorbed by concern for their father and anger at her, was forgetting the one thing that Edwina had not – their financial situation now that the breadwinner was indisposed. Oh, she knew they'd survive. The Chinamen could be put off and they could easily live off their vegetables and wild game if needed, and there was plenty of flour in store. It was her father's second life that piqued her curiosity and Edwina wanted to know, demanded to know, exactly how much their father was worth. And she wanted to know now, before Aiden. For with their father's injury, Aiden would expect to take his place at the head of the household.

'If I was the head of this household.' They were Aiden's very words and with their father's illness he was already the head, by default, by chance of birth. But it was a position granted by cultural norm, by expectation, not by ability, recommendation or reason. No matter that Edwina was older and more suited to the task. The

269

reality was that her brother wasn't capable of running the property. It wasn't his fault but he was a dreamer like his father, without the mitigating ability of fulfilling the role of money-lender. And he was already treating her poorly. As if she were worthless. Edwina was furious, with both of them, brother and father. Aiden was barely capable of adding a row of figures and with their father's illness, the land and any monies saved were the only certainty they had. She couldn't depend on her brother, for anything. Not now.

Edwina located the ledger in the bookcase, a three-shelf structure that extended six feet along a wall and held numerous volumes of farming manuals and handbooks as well as magazines. She'd barely glanced at the covers for her father always ensured he was present when her whirlwind domesticity was permitted. Once a month he would leave the latest copy of the *Agricultural Gazette* in the parlour after he'd finished with it and Edwina would snatch it up hungrily, reading the contents. Now she selected a hefty guide on the clearing and management of land, setting it aside and relishing the quiet moment when she could read it.

Resting the ledger on the splintering windowsill, Edwina turned the thick lined pages in the sunlight, wondering at the reason it was secreted away. The breeze teased at her hair as she checked each column's figures, which were accompanied by her father's meticulous notes in the bold copperplate she'd tried to emulate in years past. Wages constituted a large expense, with the outgoings of the property far greater than their income. Based on these figures alone, they were quite broke and would have been on the brink of disaster three years ago were it not for a regular monthly deposit, its origin only described by a series of numbers. A bank account.

Closing the hardcover, Edwina walked slowly around the study. Other records must exist. Reports and transactions pertaining to the account that kept them viable. She assumed that their father's main business assisted in the propping up of their block. It was the trade of lending money, the profession she hated, the role that separated them from the rest of the district that clearly sustained them. But why remain on a property that was losing money? Why come to the country in the first place when his talents seemed to lie in the financial realm? Edwina knew little about her father's life before he came to the district of Wywanna. He'd been in business in Sydney, met his wife and then suddenly packed up and moved north to Brisbane before heading inland. There were stories of wealth lost in England. Of a grandfather who'd walked away from his family, returning to the money he'd been born into, only to lose it all. But the details were murky, except for the turning point in Hamilton Baker's life, when he sought passage to Australia in 1890. Edwina wondered what came first – the farmer or the money-lender – and realised it didn't matter. All she knew now was that they were failing on the land and with their father bedridden they could no longer depend on the secondary income stream to keep them afloat.

At the window, Edwina stared out at the pale-barked gum trees and the rise and fall of land that sank into obscurity with the setting sun. How difficult was it to make a living from the land? Was her father really so hopeless at the business of farming, or was it simply a matter of acreage? The bigger graziers, the pastoralists, appeared to make a good living from their larger holdings. In Edwina's mind, it wasn't difficult to see where they were going wrong, battling the all-engulfing costly prickly pear and trying to grow wheat when for some reason, no matter the effort, their results remained limited.

A square of colour moved into her vision. Davidson walked through the trees leading a horse. Clothed as normal, it was difficult to equate the stockman with the native who'd kept vigil beside their father's bed, with his scars and burnt offerings. He sprang effortlessly up into the saddle. Sensing her, he wheeled the dark gelding, the land between them shrinking as he looked in the direction of the study before riding away.

At her father's desk Edwina sat in the swivel chair and pulled the saddlebag towards her. The leather closure was hardened by use and weathering but she lifted the stiff flap and went through his belongings.

There were documents and a book. Edwina upended the contents on the desk, giving a whispered harrumph of accomplishment. A manila file was roughly folded in half. Inside was documentation relating to the monies their father had lent locally, including the substantial sum owed them by Charles Ridgeway. Her eyes popped at the thousands of dollars outstanding and she now understood why her father was so keen to ensure the debt was repaid. Looking back through the duration of the transaction, she saw he'd been inordinately fair about the lack of repayments. Had the management of the loan fallen to her, Edwina knew she would have been firmer, that is, until she read the compounding amounts. Her father wasn't stupid. With every month the debt remained unpaid, the interest component ignored, the money owed increased substantially. This then was how one conducted business. The end result was harsh, the process demonstrably fair. Edwina placed the flat of her hand on the desk, pride for her father's acumen inching through bitterness. The loan document, which she held, was co-signed by both parties and the debt, as Aiden said, was to be repaid today. There was no doubt that the proceeds would keep them viable for quite a few years if the worst occurred.

The smaller book was more notebook than ledger. It listed a large number of business names Edwina knew nothing of together with a series of dates and numbers. In the absence of any other information she put it aside.

Leaving the study with the Ridgeway documentation safely stored in the saddlebag hanging over a shoulder, Edwina took the Lee-Enfield rifle from above the mantelpiece in the parlour. She wasn't sure if the debt would be void if the worst happened to their father and she certainly wasn't going to wait to find out.

She found Aiden by their father's side, reading aloud.

Father and son looked years apart. One shocking to see, almost withered overnight by events, the other still dew-fresh with possibility.

'I told you –'

'I'm going out,' interrupted Edwina, ignoring her brother's glower. Their father stared blankly.

'Where? What are you doing with that rifle?' The book on his lap fell with a thud to the floor.

'While you tend to Father, I shall tend to our business,' she replied, her anger prickling.

Gathering up the novel, Aiden frowned. 'What are you talking about?'

'Ridgeway Station. The debt owed?' She couldn't help the sarcasm. 'I'm going over there to ensure its collection. It's due today.'

'But you can't go there, Edwina,' Aiden complained.

'Why? Why can't I go there on behalf of our father? I have the paperwork,' she argued. 'I know what's owed.' She walked to the bedside. A thin line of glistening drool of spider web fineness hung from her father's chin. The chicken soup was only partially consumed. 'This property is broke and who knows what may happen over the next few days. We have to protect what's ours.'

'Broke?'

'What did you think was going to happen with the cost of the clearing and you and father persisting with the growing of wheat? It's only the lending of money that's been keeping us afloat.'

'But how do you know all this?' asked Aiden.

'I've read the ledgers.' Edwina wiped away the clear liquid with her hand. Did her father blink? Edwina was sure he did. 'What is that bruising on his face?' she asked. 'Is it from the fall?'

Aiden, thrown by the change of conversation, hesitated, as if trying to find his place. 'I think someone punched him. We think that's how he fell.'

Edwina stepped closer. There was a definite swelling on the side opposite to the sagging skin. 'He was attacked? By who?' she said loudly to her brother.

'How would I know? Davidson's gone out to investigate, after he's spoken to Han Lee of course.'

Edwina rolled her eyes. 'Investigate? Fat lot of good that will do when he can't report back on what he finds.'

'Maybe it's better not to know,' said Aiden. 'Maybe it's better if he just takes care of things. He cut his palm in front of me with that knife of his. Whatever needs to be done, he'll do it. Davidson made a blood pact.'

'Why didn't you stop him, Aiden? For heaven's sake.'

Aiden shook his head. 'Stop Davidson? Impossible.'

They considered each other across the single bed. Her brother was right. Davidson wasn't a man to be stopped. 'Do you think . . .?' Edwina didn't want to say what she thought.

'That he'd harm Father's attacker if he found him? That he'd kill a man?' said Aiden. 'Yes, I do.'

'Who would have done such a thing?' asked Edwina.

'He wasn't robbed,' replied Aiden. 'Honestly, I can only think of one person that might have done it.'

Edwina could guess. 'Fernleigh?'

'Yes. You should have seen the hate in Fernleigh's eyes when we were over at Ridgeway Station on Monday. I wouldn't put anything past that man.'

'Davidson isn't the law, we should –'

'What?' interrupted Aiden. 'Tell the police? I don't think we need them out here again, do you?' He glared at her pointedly. Their father lay quietly between them. 'Besides, Davidson knows what he's doing.'

'And we never will,' finished Edwina.

Aiden thought on this. 'Exactly.'

'But it may not be Fernleigh.' Edwina considered the many men employed on the farm over the last few years. Many left disgruntled, a state they'd arrived in. Returned soldiers questioning their survival and trying to find their place in a changed world. Youths and young men searching for work when there was little to be found. However, the men who worked on the property were always paid and fairly treated. Edwina imagined Hamilton Baker's enemies to be few. 'You said Sears was annoyed?'

'Yes, he didn't take kindly losing his job to the Chinese and he'll be more annoyed when he hears that Father agreed to broker a deal for Han Lee to purchase land on the edge of Wywanna when he asked for assistance to do the same.'

'Mr Sears needed financial backing. Han Lee only needed a good word put in on his behalf,' argued Edwina as they moved to the foot of the bed.

'That won't make any difference to Sears. The end result is the same. Anyway,' Aiden explained, 'he's not the only one with a grudge. Your friend Will Kew wasn't exactly happy when he was fired. I saw Davidson punch him as I rode away with Han Lee.'

'He is not my friend.' Edwina didn't dare share with her brother that Will had told her he would return. For her. How could she? 'Well, I suppose there's nothing we can do for the moment, except wait for Davidson to come home.' The room smelt fresher. Edwina wedged a cloth-covered stone against the door to keep it from closing. 'I only came to tell you what I was doing.'

Aiden threw the book on the end of the bed. 'For heaven's sake, you didn't meet Charles Ridgeway. You don't know what he's like. And another thing, Edwina, if Fernleigh did attack Father how do you think he'll take to you showing up on his doorstep?'

'Come with me then?'

'Me?' answered Aiden. 'It's Father's business, not ours,' he said uncomfortably. 'Besides, you don't know anything about money-lending.'

Edwina thought of Mason. She had an ally there, she was certain. 'I know what I'm doing.'

'But you simply can't ride over there and demand that money, Edwina. It's just not done.'

'Why on earth not?'

'Because you're a woman.'

'That,' said Edwina, 'seems to be more of a problem for you and Father than it's ever been for me.'

⤜ Chapter Thirty-two ⤛

Hamilton used his one workable arm to leverage his body upright. The haze of past and present was clearing and he recognised up from down. Understood where he was. Could distinguish day from night and knew that at last he was free of the middling world that momentarily claimed him. He wasn't mad, dreaming or dead. There was no Green Man, his mother was long gone and Ross, his best friend from his youngest years, had been a Lord who had died on the *Titanic*. True, some of Hamilton's parts weren't hinging properly – it was as if he'd been snigged to the draught horses and dragged across a paddock – but he knew what was going on around him and that was a start. Davidson's foul smoke had startled him back to consciousness. Hamilton thought he would smell it for the rest of his life, a tangible thread linking him to the aboriginal to whom he owed his life for a second time.

Slurping down the leftover muck that was meant to pass as soup, his eyes watered at the pain in his jaw. It had been a fair punch but Hamilton's mind was not so clear that the attacker could be recalled. That would come, he reasoned, with time. Taking a breath he swung one leg from the bed onto the floor, then the other.

His toes moved at his bidding, grounding him, and although his head felt weighed down as if tethered by an anchor, he managed to stand, leveraging his weight on the dresser and allowing the dizziness to pass. For it would pass. He damn well willed it.

Dressing was another matter. His left arm was useless but he managed well enough to open the wardrobe and select a shirt, buttoning it up in a skew-whiff manner, hit and miss, slow and painful, grateful that he still wore trousers. The hallway, distant and dark, briefly flummoxed Hamilton but he limped the length of it, scowling, swear words circling his mind as he crabbed the wall for balance, a shoulder scraping paintings, dislodging one, which fell to the floor.

At the entrance to the parlour, teeth grinding, Hamilton staggered forward unaided. The first chair he reached became a saviour. Sweaty and breathless, he buckled into it. By the Lord, he craved tobacco, the comforting familiarity of a pipe, a mouthful of water. The building was quiet with no-one about to help. Not that it mattered; for the moment Hamilton was satisfied. Trees were visible through an angle of window, a square of washed-out sky, a strip of yellow curtain. If he could walk to the window his wheat would be standing tall, a green flush with beige borders.

'Back,' he said with difficulty, the word stretching out long and slow. 'Back home.' Under the floorboards the collies could be heard squirrelling in the dirt, tunnelling their way towards him, fat bodies striking the timber with thumps as they growled and snapped their way to a place beneath their master. He tapped a foot on the timber, comforting, comforted. There was life left yet in the aged carcass.

Hamilton may have stayed in bed were he not party to the extraordinary conversation in the sickroom. His daughter had gone to do men's business while his son had become nursemaid. There was something terribly wrong with the state of things. A man was non compos mentis for a few hours and the whole world went mad.

There were things he could have done. A cough, the lifting of an arm. And yet as he listened to his offspring, heard the bickering, noted the reversal of roles, Hamilton reasoned that admitting to a recovery of sorts was pre-emptive when a man could learn so much in such a short space of time.

Edwina was quick to enter the study and search through his personal papers and he was not so befuddled as to be incapable of registering the concern at the debts, at his illness, at the attacker. What irked the most was his daughter knowing his business and dealing with the unlikable Charles Ridgeway. As a female, it wasn't Edwina's place, but with Aiden's lack of enthusiasm it fell to her. The monies were obviously due today and Edwina was quite right to ensure the debt repaid. Although disappointed Aiden hadn't offered to go in her place or at least accompany her, it was with a sense of confession that Hamilton admitted his daughter did have brains. The girl was quick, smart. She was formed in his image, not her damaged mother's. What a pity she'd been born of the weaker sex.

The yellow curtains swayed in the breeze. The dogs began to growl. Their rumbles and roars were definable. Something had disturbed the collies. Hamilton tapped on the boards. Looked to the mantelpiece and the empty rifle rack. The animals were fidgety; they yapped and barked, bumping heads and spines as they rushed out from under the house. Hamilton listened to the pad of their feet, to the crash of dog versus table as they ran along the verandah. The barking and growling grew in pitch and frequency. Hamilton's good hand clasped the rubbed edge of the seat.

A head appeared at the partially open window, then a body. The animal was tawny-coloured with large amber eyes. It looked like a cat. Except it wasn't a cat. It was a . . .

'Lion?' Hamilton scrunched both eyes tightly shut before refocusing.

The creature sprang down from the sill and then jumped up onto the armchair opposite him. His chair. Outside, the dogs woofed and howled, as the cub circled the hollowed-out cushion.

'Lion.' Hamilton chewed on the word like a piece of leather. The thing sat on his chair, licking its furry hide. At first he thought the creature was a vision, a delirium conjured by a mind made temporarily feeble, but the damn animal was only eight feet away, shifting and pawing at already shoddy material. Then it was crouching, as if readying to pounce.

Edwina. That was the only thought in Hamilton's mind. 'Edwina,' he cursed, 'Edwina.' His daughter's name was a whisper, a whisper that grew in fury, taking on a life of its own. The vowels and consonants twisted and tumbled on Hamilton's tongue until thick with overuse he spat the name out in an angry roar.

The cub leapt onto the ground, skidded on the timber boards and fled the room.

Aiden arrived breathless. 'Father, how did you get out of bed? Are you alright? I heard you yelling. You can speak?'

Exhausted, Hamilton fell back. 'Water,' he said with painstaking slowness.

The boy was quick to fetch a glass. Hamilton drank in slurps and splutters. 'Lion?'

Aiden took the vessel from his lips. 'I know,' he said with concern. 'I saw the newspaper you brought back with you from Wywanna. I'm well aware of Edwina's behaviour.'

Hamilton slapped a thigh with his good arm. 'Lion. Find it.' Aiden's eyes held the same sobering stare reminiscent of his mother's. Overrun by fatigue, Hamilton closed his eyes.

⋘ Chapter Thirty-three ⋙

Once through the corner gate and onto Ridgeway Station, Edwina began to regret her rushed decision. There was business to attend to; however, a fresh change of clothes should have been considered. Creased and slightly soiled from the hours in the kitchen, this was their second day of wear, and she'd slept in them. Edwina knew she appeared decidedly down-at-heel. Added to which, the bruising on her face was only marginally improved. This was not the impression she wanted to create, skirts bunched up in an ungainly fashion as she rode astride, the lace-up shoes replaced with riding boots, her pale calves visible. The mission demanded a certain level of professionalism, and her appearance was anything but that. Charles Ridgeway would think her poor and rough-natured. And what of Mason? For that man alone a change of clothes was demanded.

'Too late.' Edwina patted Heidi-Hoe as they walked through the timber. 'Too late to turn back now.' Although she wished for her own sake that she were a little more prettified, this was a chance to prove her capability. The importance of securing the funds owed them did not escape Edwina. For not only did she worry about her father's recovery, this was an opportunity to show she could handle their business affairs as well as any man.

The bush was a tangle of prickly pear and thin-limbed trees. Tufts of wool were sticking to the pear where sheep had strayed too close. Edwina chose a northward-leading sheep track, the narrow depression dark brown and powdery from ceaseless trampling. The trail showed the defining marks of shoe-clad horses and she followed, knowing the riders' path would meet up with a road that led to the homestead. There was only one gate between the two properties and the prints belonged to her father and the men who'd ridden out on Monday to meet with Charles Ridgeway.

Too soon Edwina was on the road where she and Aiden glimpsed the automobile and horseman last week. Here and there patches of pear appeared to be ailing. It was as if the water was being sucked out of their fleshy parts, leaving them to wither and brown. She wondered at the sickness ailing these few plants and Edwina peered at the cactus, speculating if the cactoblastis was responsible.

On the next rise sheep grazed in the distance, their greyish bodies speckling the grassland. There were hundreds of them pushing eastwards into the wind. She rode onwards, the heat tickling sweaty skin, the sun mounting the sky with increasing swiftness. Edwina licked the beads of perspiration from her lip, squinted into the glare, her nervousness growing.

Passing among the next grouping of knitted timber, she could see the iron roof of a homestead shining hard and bright through the leafy canopy. Edwina thought fleetingly of retracing her path, of heading back to safety, as she ducked under a bough. So absorbed was she by the steely corrugations of the house, the commotion to her left went initially unnoticed. They were a distance away, a half mile or so, but it was clear an event of great industry was occurring. Men were unloading lengths of wood from carts and in the midst of the action a chugging sound came from a steam engine.

'Are you good with a saw then, Edwina?' Mason rode towards her, his clothes browned by dust, a coiled rope over a shoulder, a pistol on one hip. 'I could do with an extra hand. I'd apologise for my state, but then,' he gestured to her clothes, 'I see you don't stand on ceremony either.'

Edwina felt her cheeks grow hot. 'I'm sorry to have come unannounced.'

'You don't need an invitation here,' he replied.

Clearly Mason and Charles Ridgeway were firm friends for him to be so welcoming. 'I came to see Mr Ridgeway. Charles,' Edwina reiterated when a prompt reply wasn't forthcoming. 'About the money he owes. It falls due today and as we have not heard otherwise, I find myself in the awkward position of having to meet with him.'

'We are straight to business, aren't we?' Mason scratched the side of his face. 'He's not here.' Then more quickly, 'Gone to town actually.'

So she wasn't to meet the elusive Charles Ridgeway after all. Edwina was relieved but also just a little disappointed. 'To pay the debt he owes my father?'

'And here I was thinking you'd ridden all this way to see me.'

He knew he was embarrassing her. Edwina combed Heidi-Hoe's mane with her fingers. 'It's due today,' she repeated.

'So you said. Then I'm sure that's what he's going to do.'

'So you don't know for certain?' What was she to do – wait here for his return or come back tomorrow? 'I would have thought he'd have seen to his debt by now. A person shouldn't have to go chasing for it.'

'How do you know it hasn't been paid?' Mason swatted away flies. 'Anyway, maybe he's been busy, Edwina. He has been caught up in other affairs.'

'Affairs that are more important than repaying a substantial amount of money owed to my family? Perhaps you should tell your friend to get his priorities in order for I see he is not without the necessary money to make improvements.' She nodded to the labouring men. 'If the money isn't repaid today I will be forced to settle things with the help of the law.' The noise from the steam engine grew. A distinctive whirring sound cut the air as the powered saw struck wood.

'You're very hard on Charles considering you barely know him and aren't aware of his circumstances.'

'I don't know him at all,' corrected Edwina.

'Why are you here anyway? Shouldn't your father be attending to these matters?'

Edwina considered telling Mason what had occurred, but with the debt still unpaid and Davidson out in the scrub hunting for the unknown attacker she knew it was best to keep quiet.

'What's happened?' asked Mason.

Edwina rolled her lips. 'You can't tell your friend, Mason, promise me. I need to make sure the debt is repaid.'

Mason walked his horse closer. 'If papers were signed the debt will be honoured.'

'But if something happened to Father . . .' she faltered, worried too much had already been shared.

'Then it would fall to his estate. Edwina, please, tell me what's going on.'

'Father fell from his horse yesterday. It's thought it could be the palsy.'

Mason slipped from his horse in one languid move. 'Here.'

Edwina dismounted, his hands supporting her waist. They stood like that for the slightest of moments before Mason stepped away.

'I'm sorry. Is there anything I can do to help?'

What could anyone do? Her father's slap, the angry words. The terrible Gloria Zane. His illness. Mrs Ryan's leaving. Aiden's attitude towards her. 'No, there's nothing . . . it's just . . .' To her dismay Edwina started to cry. She brushed away the tears.

'Hey, don't be sad. I'll help in any way I can. Just say the word,' offered Mason. 'Have you sent for a doctor?'

Edwina shook her head. 'No, Mrs Ryan our cook said it was the palsy and the best thing to do was to get him up and moving about when he woke. Aiden was in agreement with her.'

'Give him time to heal, Edwina.'

'And if he doesn't?'

Mason took her hand. 'As I said, I'll help any way I can. Just let me know.'

'Thank you,' she sniffed.

'Come on, let me show you my new project.'

They walked towards the men and lumber. Holes were being dug, first with the breaking of soil with iron post hole diggers and then with shovels. Twelve-foot lengths of timber held by three men were stood upright in the deep hole. Once positioned, two workers held the post steady as others began to shovel the excavated soil, replacing the dirt in the cavity, packing it down hard.

'Cattle yards,' explained Mason, 'big enough to hold four hundred head. Not quite as big as the yards I worked in up north, but big enough for Ridgeway.'

'But I thought Mr Ridgeway only grew sheep.'

Mason cleared his throat. 'Yes, well, not anymore. The whole lot will be gone very soon. I never took to them to be honest. Even as a kid I always preferred cattle and, although there's not much money in them at the moment, the market will eventually improve.'

Perhaps Mason was to be a manager of sorts for he certainly appeared to be taking control of the running of the property. 'You're staying then?' She didn't want to appear nosey.

'Yes. Come and sit in the shade.'

'I should be getting home.' But Edwina followed Mason across the flat to the shade of a tree, far enough away to give them privacy yet allowing Mason to keep an eye on the yard-builders. They sat on a log watching as three men placed another post into a hole.

'You need that money quite badly, don't you?' asked Mason, sketching a rough design of the cattle yards in the dirt.

'My father likes growing things, wheat in particular. It just costs so much clearing the land of pear and timber and ploughing it.' Edwina shrugged. 'And now he's sick.'

'You'll be getting your money. Just be careful with it.'

The relief was immediate. 'Of course.' Edwina knew she shouldn't have depended on Mason for help and yet she'd known he would be an ally.

'Your father invests heavily in the stock exchange and the market is quite unsteady at the moment. The London exchange has done badly over the last few days.'

'Did Mr Ridgeway tell you that?' asked Edwina.

'In country districts, everyone knows everyone's business.'

'Do you know mine?' She picked up a twig so that Mason couldn't see her face.

It took time for him to answer. 'I've seen the paper, yes, but I've also heard that your father runs a strict household when it comes to his children. That's the thing about country people, Edwina; they hear the bad and the good.'

Edwina gave a tentative smile. 'So you don't think I'm this unstable person who has shamed my family forever?' Was it possible that Mason could think so differently?

'Of course I don't. But not everyone in the district will be impressed by your adventure. You made quite an impact last Saturday, Edwina, dressed as that tomboy. You could never in your life pass as a man. It was a brave thing you did.'

'And foolish.'

'Well, if you remember, I did ask if you were sure you wanted to go home.' Mason stretched his legs out in the dirt, crossing his ankles. 'So will you tell me what happened that night? What happened to the lion cub?'

286

'Will stole the lion. I was standing nearby when he took it and the circus people assumed I was with him.'

'You were in the wrong place,' said Mason. 'So did you really brush me off that night because you had to get home?'

'Yes,' answered Edwina, 'and besides, your friends didn't want me hanging around.'

'They said that?'

'I overheard. Anyway, everyone was yelling and pointing at me, as if I were involved. I didn't know what to do, so I ran after him. In the end Will helped me, Mason. He escorted me home and in repayment stayed for a week's work. Father fired him but he left the lion behind.'

'He brought the animal out to your property? So where is it now? Don't tell me that there is a lion cub roaming inland Queensland?'

There was a steely spark in the way Mason looked at her.

Edwina grimaced. 'It escaped into the bush. But it's only young, Mason. About four months old. The runt of the litter. It wouldn't hurt anything.'

'Yet.' Mason was unimpressed. 'It should be trapped, Edwina. For everyone's safety as well as the livestock.'

'You're right. With everything else that's been going on I never thought about it. I'll speak to Davidson about it.'

'When you catch him, tell Davidson to bring him over to me. I can take the cub into town and say I found him along the way somewhere.'

'And if it can't be caught?' asked Edwina.

'Then we'll have to try and shoot it.' He looked at her expression. 'A last resort,' he promised. 'And how about your run? Do you need a hand with anything?'

'No, everything's fine, thank you,' answered Edwina. 'Han Lee's men have taken over the ringbarking and I'm thinking of asking them to stay on and help with harvest.'

Mason smiled. 'I figured you'd have things under control.' He leant forward and kissed Edwina full on the mouth. It was short and hard, more like a branding of ownership than a slow, lingering caress.

Edwina didn't know why she slapped him across the face. Except that he hadn't asked and it wasn't expected. 'I'm not one of those girls your friends talked about at the circus,' she exclaimed. Edwina was on her feet, hands on hips, scowling.

'I never said you were. Come here.'

'No.'

Mason stood. 'Come here.'

Edwina stamped her foot. 'Why did you do that? Take advantage? I thought you were different.'

One of Mason's eyebrows skewered upwards in a quizzical v. 'So, the lady has been kissed before and I gather it was not to her liking?'

'I never, I didn't –'

'We can rectify that.'

Mason was at her side in two easy steps. Edwina pushed at his shoulders, fighting the embrace, struggling to free her body from his strength.

'Stop fidgeting.'

'No,' Edwina said forcefully.

'God damn it,' he complained, 'this is never going to work if you don't do what I say.'

Edwina stomped hard on his foot in response. He kissed her again. Not with the fledgling tentativeness of Will Kew but with an intensity Edwina could only describe as desire. 'Why did you do that?' she asked breathlessly, when she finally broke free of his embrace.

'Because you're a difficult woman who wouldn't have said yes if I asked.'

Edwina couldn't believe what she'd just heard. 'If I wasn't a difficult woman, would that make it alright for you to behave like that?'

'I'm sorry, I didn't mean to –'

One of the hands from the yard construction was yelling at Mason, asking him to check the measurements. Interrupted, he in return was calling back, cupping hands around his mouth, funnelling the words across the expanse of ground. Edwina took the opportunity to mount her horse as the yard-builder walked towards them.

'Wait, where are you going?' Mason called.

Edwina flicked the reins, motioning Heidi-Hoe to move. 'Home.' The horse went from walk to trot and then to a canter with a swift change of stride. This time Edwina didn't look back. She'd received an assurance that she would get what she came for. Edwina was sure of that. What she hadn't reckoned on, had never expected, was that with her coming to Ridgeway Station she would leave with not one thing, but two. She rode hard to the boundary, catching a glimpse of a rider ahead in the trees. It was Davidson. Instinctively she put hand to mouth and took a breath. 'I didn't see him there,' she muttered. 'I saw nothing.' When next she looked in the rider's direction he was gone from sight.

≪ Chapter Thirty-four ≫

The house was quiet on Edwina's return. Astonished to find her father asleep in the parlour, Aiden dozing beside him, she went straight to the kitchen. Food and drink were the highest of priorities. That is, until she entered the hut to find a young black woman at the stove and Davidson washing bloody hands in the basin. To Edwina's knowledge he'd never set foot in the kitchen before.

'Miss.' The girl gave what passed for a curtsey.

Edwina glanced from the copper-sheened water and the man at the sink back to the girl.

'He fetched me he did, to cook and clean. Said you needed help.' The girl rolled her bottom lip under her teeth. A long recent scar traced the right side of her face, the edges still puckered with healing. 'I don't eat much and I can do other things, like chop wood, bucket water, feed them fowls of yours. Anything you like. I'm Constance.'

She didn't look more than fourteen or fifteen years of age and she was ebony black, darker than Davidson, who was drying his hands by rubbing them down the front of his shirt. Edwina shook her head, trying to clear her thoughts. 'Where did you come from?'

'The –'

The stockman bashed a fist on the kitchen table. The girl fell silent.

'Where did you come from?' asked Edwina more firmly.

'He asked me to come, miss, he did. I do as I says. I won't be no trouble and I don't want none.'

Edwina wasn't so sure about that. The girl was a full-blood, of that she was almost certain. As such, she should be reported to the authorities straight away. Either she would be reunited with her people on one of the missions or sent to an orphanage.

'I threw that soup out what was in the pot, miss. It was awful bad. Must have gone off in the heat.'

Edwina reached for one of the roasted fowls cooked earlier. Half of it had already been devoured and she pulled off a drumstick and began to eat. The flesh was greasy but good and Edwina blessed the cub and his playtime, tearing free a wing. She would question the girl's presence, but she'd already decided to take advantage of the much-needed help, at least in the short term. 'I suppose I'll never know if you found the man that attacked my father,' she said to Davidson, picking the meat from the bone, thinking of his recent return from the Ridgeway boundary. 'Do *you* know anything?' she asked the girl.

The stockman sat down at the table and began sharpening the knife he carried. The blade moved diagonally across the whetstone, gathering in speed as the edge scraped across the rock.

'No, miss, I weren't there. I was still at the camp.'

'What camp?' asked Edwina.

The crackle of the fire broke the silence. The girl studied the pot on the stove. Davidson's blade struck the whetstone.

She wondered now whether the white-eyed crow was not the loner they'd thought. If, like the bird he was named after, he too returned to his people at various times, to forage together. The new girl mentioned a camp. Had Davidson led them here? Away from white law. A Promised Land of sorts.

Edwina recalled the sightings of blacks on the property. Stories Aiden and she attributed to tired men working long, lonely hours in the bush. She knew then in her heart that Davidson had most probably delivered his tribe to safety. 'Your people are on our land.' It wasn't a question, more a confirmation of fact. 'Hide them well, Davidson, for I'm sure you know the law.' The stockman concentrated on the blade in his hand. 'I want her to tell me the truth.' Edwina gestured to the girl. 'Go on.'

'We've been down near the crick.' She glanced at the stockman. 'On the southern side. Been there nine years we have.'

'Nine years.' Edwina thought of the stories of aboriginals having been sighted on the property. 'How many of you are there?'

'Twenty-seven, miss. Some of the men, well, they work on other runs and come home on their days off. They want be with their families without having to travel back and forth to the mission to see them. It's too far.'

'And you're one of their children?'

'Yes, miss. I didn't want to be taken away from my family so we all stay together. Davidson says your father is a good man and he wouldn't make us leave.'

Edwina felt the stockman's stare. 'My father doesn't know,' she pointed out. 'Are you related to Davidson?'

'Yes, miss. He's my husband.'

She tried not to appear surprised; however, the knowledge that so many of Davidson's kind had been living unknown on the property, that their stockman was married, made her feel foolish. They'd been taken advantage of and yet Edwina couldn't feel angry. 'And do you have children?' To Edwina's dismay, Constance began to weep. 'I'm sorry. I didn't mean to upset you.'

'My baby died, miss. But I did it because I had to. Because if I keep it maybe it will be taken away. If it was found,' she looked to her husband, 'if we were found.'

'By the authorities,' completed Edwina. She didn't like the sound of this. Had Constance killed her child on Davidson's order because they couldn't bear the thought of it being taken from them?

'So many children have been taken before.' Constance rubbed at her eyes. 'I'll have more babies, with Davidson.'

'And the baby you lost,' asked Edwina, 'are you saying Davidson wasn't the father?'

'No, miss. It was a white man. He saw me one day when I was out near the main road and he ran me down and had me. I still loved the baby, but he was half-white.'

'And a half-caste child, if found, would be taken from its mother. I'm sorry, Constance. One day I hope things will be different.'

'So do I, miss.'

How many laws did the world have to have? It seemed to Edwina that both she and Constance were bound by a society that felt justified to dictate how they should live their lives. 'And what of the man that attacked my father?'

'If Davidson did find him, miss, he be floating down the crick by now. Reckon he'd be further than an emu can run in a day by this,' said Constance.

Not having been blessed with the ability to speak was one thing, but Davidson's general demeanour did little to endear. He was a tough, wiry sort, born under a tree for all they knew. It was the bush he returned to at night, although no humpy of his was ever discovered. Now Edwina knew otherwise. But Davidson's loyalty to his employer could not be doubted. His bedside vigil was the proof of it, if the fact needed validation. And only he had the ability to track their father's attacker down. And if indeed the assailant was dead, then Davidson's loyaly was doubly proved.

Edwina sucked on the chicken bones and thought about the blood on his hands. Had he killed and what would it mean for them? Nothing, she prayed. No doctor was called to the house and Davidson couldn't bear witness. Whether anyone else could was another matter. Across the table, the stockman pushed a thumb against a glinting blade. She shoved the plate of chicken in his direction. 'Eat,' she said, and he did. Now here she sat, Edwina Baker, breaking bread with her father's man. The black factotum, the white-eyed crow. And possibly a murderer? She could never condone his recent actions, but she respected the stockman and was grateful for his guardianship.

There was a hessian bag on the dirt floor. Davidson opened it, stabbed the knife inside and drew out a piece of prickly pear. It was wilted, clearly dying, like the specimens seen this morning at Ridgeway Station.

'I saw this too,' said Edwina. 'It must be the cactoblastis. Do you know what this means? It means we're saved.'

Davidson showed a tooth by way of a smile. It was the most animated the black had appeared for years.

Edwina prodded the withered plant. She knew there were large tracts of land made worthless by the pear's infestation – land that would eventually become fertile and useable again, once the pear died. The *Agricultural Gazette*'s articles were detailed in the damage done by the plant and the acreage involved across Queensland and New South Wales. Some owners, like them, were nearly broken by it. Edwina stabbed at the plant with a bread knife, twirling it thoughtfully. What if those owners wanted to sell but couldn't find a buyer because of the uselessness of the land? Would there not be an opportunity to buy up a large tract of acreage for a low price, knowing that eventually the pear would die and the land be returned to them?

'I want you to show me where you found this, Davidson?' said Edwina.

'Oh, he show you,' said Constance. 'You boss lady now.'

⪻ Chapter Thirty-five ⪼

Having risen early and dressed with care, Edwina drove into town in the buggy, accompanied by Han Lee and Davidson. They'd left at daylight before the opportunity arose for Aiden to stop her, before she could think better of what she was about to do. The previous evening had been arduous. Placating Aiden in regards to her Ridgeway Station visit and sharing her hopes of a positive outcome did little to improve his attitude. Aiden continued to rebuke her for her involvement in the circus crime and showed no sign of understanding or forgiveness. The one bright point was the arrival of the aboriginal girl, Constance. Aiden didn't care where she came from as long as she was capable of cooking and cleaning house, so she was yet to share the news about the presence of the aboriginals on the property.

The road was quiet. A brown track rutted by the passage of wagons and horses. A cloud-patched sky and the stretch of bush on either side. Close-knit in places, as if intentionally secreting what lay beyond, at others, opening out to allow the passer a glimpse of life. Cattle, sheep, a hay-filled corrugated iron shed leaning dangerously to one side, the remains of a dwelling, all fallen brick and timber, only part of the fireplace remaining. Edwina clasped the side of the buggy as they traversed a particularly rough patch of the road, wishing she'd brought more than the rolled shawl to cushion her lower back. They passed Mrs Landry bucketing water onto an ailing sapling outside the inn, the old woman turning her back as they passed. At the sight of this landmark Edwina couldn't help but think of Will's kindness. If he did return, she was now not so sure how she would greet him. Her father's illness filled most of her thoughts and Mason the remainder.

'You are quiet.' Han Lee slowed the horse as a kangaroo bounded across their path.

She smiled in reply. Edwina thought Han Lee would be a talkative companion, and was pleased to find they'd both been content to travel in silence. Until now.

The Chinaman looked over his shoulder at a trailing Davidson, clearly uncomfortable by his presence. 'I still would have preferred to have seen your father, Edwina. I may be able to help. You should have told me of the accident sooner.'

'I'm sorry, my brother took control of our father's needs,' she answered. The Chinaman's skills were never considered, an error on Edwina's part considering how her face had recovered. 'He is sitting up and managing some speech. A great improvement compared to how Davidson found him.' Han Lee, although willing to act as chaperone on her trip to Wywanna, had been more than reluctant to leave without seeing his new employer. 'It is possible it isn't the palsy and that Father's injuries are directly related to the fall from his horse.' Her father was improved but clearly agitated. He spoke in blustery strings of words like an oncoming storm soon to blow itself out. To the ignorant his babble meant nothing, suggesting some mental incapacity, but he was coherent enough for Edwina to guess that the lion may have made an unwanted appearance at the homestead. A not unlikely event as the little animal was probably hungry.

'I hope so and I am pleased to hear that, for one of the men brought news yesterday that your father proved successful in the brokering of land on our behalf. I am most grateful for his assistance.'

Edwina knew little of this business but was happy her father was able to help Han Lee and his people. He was a good man and Edwina was pleased to have him by her side this morning. Coming to town was difficult enough without doing so unchaperoned, again, although undoubtedly her companion would set tongues wagging afresh.

'I will give you tea for your father.'

'Thank you.' Edwina wondered at the mismatch of remedies, Davidson with his acrid smoke and black man's knowledge and the man beside her from across the sea.

Han Lee gave a single nod. 'This is not my business, but I wonder at why you must travel to Wywanna, Miss Edwina, when your brother could do so in your place.'

'Is it so very unconventional?'

'For certain stations in life, yes. My apologies. This is not my world. It is yours.'

Yes, it is, thought Edwina. Or it could be. A world with many possibilities. The dying prickly pear, great swathes of which were pointed out to her by Davidson on an adjoining property yesterday, presented an opportunity too great to be ignored.

'If there is anything I can do?'

'There isn't, Han Lee, but thank you. Thank you for agreeing to accompany me.'

'I think you must walk in your father's footsteps,' said Han Lee. 'This is an admirable quality.'

Was it? The past week was one of mixed emotions. Annoyance, sadness, shock and bitter disappointment permeated Edwina's thoughts, altering her beliefs and skewering forever the relationship of father–daughter. Now, however, she couldn't help but wonder if she and her father were more alike than she cared to admit. The startling idea she'd arrived at after seeing the demise of the prickly pear offered every possibility of being a sound venture, an investment that would free them from the life they knew, although Edwina recognised it would take some years. And yet something else propelled her to Wywanna, thoughts that went beyond her concern for Aiden's lack of business acumen and she acknowledged the force of it. This was an opportunity to prove to her father that she was more than a daughter who'd made bad choices. She may be a woman, but she too was capable of great things.

By mid-morning the town grew slowly in size, changing from a horizon of indeterminate buildings to more recognisable struc- tures, the water tank and clock tower, the peaked roof of the two-storeyed Royal Hotel and the golden dome of the bank. Han Lee flicked the reins and the horse trotted sharply across the town bridge. Davidson overtook them at the other end and, turning his mount south, followed the dirt track that bordered the slow-moving river.

'He does not come with us?' asked Han Lee.

Davidson rode under a dogwood tree, shirt tail flapping.

'Don't worry, he'll be watching from a distance.'

They turned into the main thoroughfare, a haphazard assort- ment of weatherboard and brick buildings most single storeyed, some two, lining the street. Two vendors were doing their best to entice customers to their carts of fruit and vegetables, their voices competing for dominance as they sold their produce in the cooling shadows of the awnings. It was a busy Saturday morning bustling with horses, drays and pedestrians, the scent of baking bread and the tangy stench of manure overriding all. Ahead a bullock wagon was lumbering along the road. Taking advantage of the wide street planned specifically for their movement, the bullocky cracked a whip and let out a warning yell before coercing his team and the load of wool bales to turn left at the next intersection.

'Where would you like me to take you?' asked Han Lee.

'The Post Office, please.'

They halted outside the building and Han Lee assisted Edwina down from the buggy. She straightened the calf-length skirt and fitted jacket of serviceable brown wool, tucking a length of blonde hair beneath the straw hat. The clothes were far from fashionable, having belonged to her mother, but they were tailored and of good quality, more suited to this expedition than the lone tubular dress she'd taken to the circus in the saddlebag and never worn. 'Han Lee, could I ask you please to go to the Lands Office? I need a map of soldier settler blocks in Queensland. I specifically want to know what the current price is for land infested with prickly pear and who might be willing to sell. Cheaply.'

'Is this your father's wish?' The Chinaman appeared doubtful.

'Of course. Anything you can find out about land prices, location of properties, the quality of the soil before the pear infestation, grasses, carrying capacities –'

'This is not something I have knowledge of, Miss Edwina.'

She touched his arm. 'Please, Han Lee, just find out what you can for me. It's important.'

'And this venture of yours, I mean your father's, Miss Edwina, is there a place for me, in a business capacity?'

He was shrewd. Edwina removed her hand from the warmth of his arm. 'In a business capacity,' she repeated, knowing intuitively that she could trust him, that she would forge ties with not only this man but also the people who followed him, 'yes.'

'Then I will find out what you need, for I think you are an uncommon woman.'

'And you, sir, are the most uncommon of men.' They shook hands, agreeing to meet in two hours further down the street.

Edwina felt the stares of loitering bystanders as Han Lee left. A white woman with an oriental as her companion was not a usual sight. And as she was an infrequent visitor to Wywanna, most people probably considered her a stranger. There was comfort in that. Head erect she walked into the Post Office building and straight to the bank teller who handled accounts for those customers not in business with the edifice across the road. Having announced her name, Edwina asked to see her father's passbook. She knew it was kept in the safe here for she'd accompanied her father last year, waiting quietly in one of the chairs lining the wall as he checked his deposits.

The teller stared at Edwina with more than a passing interest. 'I can't just show it to anyone, miss,' he told her, dabbing at the perspiration on his face and neck with a ratty handkerchief.

'I'm not anyone. I am his daughter.' She tugged off her mother's too-small leather gloves. 'And I wish to see his passbook as a deposit is to be added to his savings.'

'You're his proxy then, are you?' The teller, white-haired and jowly, appeared satisfied. 'I'll be needing a letter of authority.'

'I have no such thing. My father had an attack of the palsy last Thursday and is invalid. Surely you can help a daughter attend to a father's request.'

The teller rose reluctantly. 'As it's for a deposit and not a withdrawal . . .' he mumbled, his tone suggesting he had better things to do as he selected a document from a stack of papers and then walked to a large cupboard, inside which sat the safe. Pencil clenched between his lips, he rummaged about the interior then returned to the counter with a bundle of passbooks. 'Yes, monies have been deposited.' He ran an ink-rimmed nail down the list he read. 'To a Hamilton Baker.'

So then, Charles Ridgeway was a man of honour. Mason's friendship with such a person now seemed right and proper.

'Would you like me to write the amount in your father's passbook?' He sorted through the pile. 'Here we are, H. Baker. Baker's Run.' He looked across the counter. 'There is quite a substantial withdrawal as well, miss, made yesterday morning. I'll write that up too.'

The teller began filling in the passbook in tiny cramped writing, his face bent close to the counter. 'So, there's ten thousand pounds remaining,' he said discreetly, showing her the entered figures, 'plus the addition of the sum recently deposited.'

'Who withdrew the other money?' The amount was considerable.

'I really couldn't say, miss.'

'But you must know. I mean this has been withdrawn while my father has been ill.'

'I only have dates and amounts, miss, but I would imagine he gave authority for the withdrawal before he took ill.'

'You understand that as his proxy I don't want any money being withdrawn unless I say so.'

A short, curious queue of customers was lining up behind Edwina. The teller placed his hand on the passbook, but Edwina claimed it before the man could return the document to the safe. 'I'll keep hold of it, for my father,' added Edwina, slipping the bank record into her handbag. 'Now please, you must be able to tell me who made that withdrawal?'

The man looked over her shoulder, then back at Edwina, his voice ingratiating. 'I can help you if you tell me what happened to that lion. For instance, your father was here on Thursday. Saw him I did. He sent a telegram and chatted to young Tufty over there.' He gestured to the telegraph counter.

Edwina's grip tightened on her mother's purse. 'So I should speak to him?'

'The lion?' he encouraged.

There would only be the slightest of chances that the telegraph operator would recall the contents of the message, and even if he could there was undoubtedly some regulation preventing him from disclosing the contents. 'I didn't take the cub. I was simply in the wrong place.' The press of bodies grew closer. If there was ever a time to attempt to clear her name, this was it. 'Besides, if I were guilty don't you think the police would have arrested me by now, especially if I'm unstable?' The men and women in the stuffy timber room were talking softly, but not quietly enough for her name to be mistaken. Her voice grew louder. 'Do you think I would be in town attending my father's business a mere week after the event? No. Of course I wouldn't. I hope the story has given the town and district much to talk about, but surely there is another tall tale to think on now.'

With a frown, the teller stepped sideways. 'Next,' he called.

Edwina pivoted on a heel, the abruptness of the movement startling the two women who stood uncomfortably close. A large bosomed matron scowled at her. Edwina recognised the lady but couldn't place her until someone called out a greeting and she answered to the name of Mrs Hilton. Edwina ignored the scathing look of condemnation as she bypassed the queue.

'Miss Baker.' The post mistress called from the other side of the room. 'Your mail, dear.' She slid a handful of letters across the bench. 'The postal rider was late yesterday so he missed the delivery to Mrs Landry's Inn.' She leant confidentially across the smooth timber counter. 'I never did think it likely a woman would do such a thing. Not out here. Don't you listen to the gossipers.'

Grateful for the warm words, Edwina moved to the end of the counter and proceeded to check the mail. There was a monthly account for food stores and kerosene and a telegram. She opened the letter as quickly as possible. The contents were brief.

Instructions carried out. All monies invested. Please advise if further transactions required.

The sender was noted as a Mr P. Harrow of Harrow Investments, Brisbane.

Mason was right. Her father was investing in the stock market and heavily, according to the recent bank withdrawal. The significance of the notebook with its names and numbers now appeared clear.

At the telegraph counter Edwina quickly wrote out a return cable.

No further transactions required.

She signed on her father's behalf, paid the shilling fee and left the building. Once outside, she passed two men who were discussing something with great animation.

'Heard it this morning,' the first man said. 'Disappeared sometime yesterday they say, for he didn't return to the homestead nor was he at his hut. The coppers were sent word but as Fernleigh was a bit of a rover at times they told Charles to give it another day and then they'd send out a search party.'

Edwina hovered near the two men, her chest beginning to pound.

'Fernleigh's been manager there for years,' replied the second man. 'He's just as likely to have camped out and will be home in time for supper.'

'Maybe,' the first man said with thinly veiled scepticism. 'But if he doesn't, forty thousand acres is a lot of bush to search.'

Edwina hurried away, a feeling of dread sitting in her stomach. There was nothing she could do except keep quiet on the subject and hope that Fernleigh was never found. She knew Davidson was responsible; seeing him at the Ridgeway boundary yesterday and then in the kitchen afterwards washing his hands only confirmed what she knew to be a certainty. Davidson had avenged their father.

She wandered up and down the streets, keeping to the more residential areas and away from the morning shoppers. There was still over an hour to fill before she met with Han Lee and the minutes ticked by slowly as she strolled around the town, pausing in the shade of trees lining the street. Finally she headed towards Dogwood Creek and down to Chinaman's Lagoon where water-lilies patterned the surface in shades of green and pink. Across the still water a horseman stood silently. Davidson. There was no need for acknowledgment and Edwina turned away and headed back towards the town.

With no errands to run, no friends to visit and the couple of shillings she'd found in the brass tray in her father's office saved for food and drink before the return journey home, the waiting nagged at Edwina. She began to question her proposed plan. What if she were wrong? What if the venture failed and they ended up poorer than when they'd begun? The thought of the Brisbane-based broker stymied such fears. Gave her hope and courage, for there was money, should things go awry. But deep in her stomach, Edwina knew it wouldn't.

At twelve noon Edwina approached the only place where she believed she may find someone willing to offer her sound advice. It was a risk to do such a thing and as her raised hand acknowledged a waiting Han Lee, she wondered anew at the audacity required, at the rashness of her decision that spurred this undertaking only two days into her father's illness. But that was one of the reasons for the speed. She would forever worry when it fell to Aiden to manage their financial affairs and, on the other hand, if their father did fully recover, Edwina knew nothing would change. And things needed to change, at least for her.

'I have what you asked for.' Han Lee passed her a rolled map and a number of papers. 'As for the quality of the land, I am very sorry, but I could find no-one able to provide information of this kind. Or at least no-one willing to share it with me.'

'Thank you, Han Lee.'

'Are you very sure, Miss Edwina, that you wish to go in here?' He gestured to the building they stood before, with its extensive verandahs and steeply pitched tiled gabled roof. There were a number of horses tethered under shady trees, three sulkies and an automobile. 'I am not sure it is appropriate and I worry that –'

'Don't worry on my account, please. I will be fine.' Edwina felt far from composed as she opened the gate.

'I will wait for you.'

The narrow path ended far too soon. Edwina hesitated before the door of the men-only domain and then, with the briefest of pauses, opened the door and walked inside the Guild.

❈ Chapter Thirty-six ❈

There was something about being anchored to a chair in the parlour for two days that intensified Hamilton's senses. He'd refused to allow Aiden to relegate him to an invalid's bed, and last night he'd come to understand the frailty of the human body, the consequences of which set him at the mercy of the unknown. In the hours when a man should be oblivious to the workings of the dark, Hamilton stayed awake, listening. Gone was the pleasurable warble of the evening birds, the quietening of the homestead, the deepening lull that formed a bridge to sleep.

It was as if the house were a giant bellow sucking in and exhaling, the rooms creaking in complaint, the iron roof stretching and constricting overhead. The musty earth rose through the floorboards to waft about windows and doors, as the papery crinkle of leaves tumbled on the iron above. The window showed too many stars. It unsettled Hamilton, all that space. The unseeable slithering and crawling things. The unrecalled face of his attacker, out there, somewhere.

Then in the grey hours before dawn, he saw Caroline sitting near the window painting the emu eggs. He'd called to her; however, it was Edwina who responded, arguing with her brother about who'd won at marbles.

Now, in the daylight, Hamilton's eyes were clear and focused. The fuzzy memories that claimed the long hours were gone and everything drew his attention in the dust-layered interior. A scuttling mouse in a corner and a ceiling-lodged spider adding to the weave of webs draping the room. The lizard that snapped up moths above the window and Edwina's dog, the collie having taken up residence by his feet. Cracks and gaps in floors and walls now appeared particularly bad and he wondered at not noticing the repairs needed before. It was his hearing, however, that had come to the fore when his body would not. Hamilton knew there was a new girl in the kitchen who liked talking out loud and that the bad-tempered Scottish woman was no longer with them, long before Aiden told him.

The girl he'd seen. Were it not for the scar he may not have known her. But the disfigurement, the youngness of age, the pot belly of a recent birth. Hamilton knew Constance from the creek. The killer of children. Knew what she'd done. Slept with a white man and been told to get rid of the paler-skinned child. Probably under Davidson's orders, as she was now ensconced in his kitchen. It was their business, and he needed a decent cook. It was best to forget the stockman shouldn't be hiding blacks on his land. Needs must.

Known too was that Edwina's trip to Ridgeway Station appeared to have been successful, not that Aiden was prepared to give his sister any kudos. The boy was too busy berating her. He must do something about that. What he didn't know was where Edwina had gone to before first light. If his son did not sleep like a child he would have woken at the first turn of the wheels and rushed to check on the commotion. Instead they were both left to ponder the reason for her trip. She was a busy girl, his Edwina.

Hamilton sensed the approaching rider, long before anyone appeared. The grandfather clock heralded noon and in the midday quiet the dogs could be heard pulling on their chains, paws finding purchase in the dirt as they strained forwards. It wasn't the baby lion, a snake or a goanna. There was no tentative growling or barking yet something disturbed them. Jed began the tedious moves of an old dog trying to stand. Hamilton waited and listened. Aiden usually whistled, made a noise of dismounting. Davidson. Well, the stockman made no damn sound at all.

He heard the horse walking through the grass, the soft creak of oiled leather, a low whinny, then, the slight roll of the saddle as the rider dismounted and the quick tight flip of the reins on the hitching rail. Hamilton leveraged his body upright in the chair, wishing he could cross the short distance to the mantelpiece and take down the rifle. He would make it, but doubted strength would be left to handle the gun.

Was it his faceless attacker, come back to finish the job? Fernleigh? Saliva pooled in his mouth. Aiden was out checking on Han Lee's team and Davidson appeared to have gone walkabout.

It was a man. Tall and broad. Hamilton caught sight of a cream shirt and open waistcoat as the veranda was crossed. Not Fernleigh then. Someone else. Then the knock came. Once. Twice.

He summoned his strength, pushed the chamber pot under the chair. 'Come. In.'

Footsteps. Loud. Assured. Hamilton saw the boots first and then the man.

'Charles Ridgeway, Mr Baker. I hope I'm not disturbing you?'

What the hell was he doing here?

The lad waited awkwardly in the doorway. 'I heard of your troubles. I was sorry to hear of your accident.'

Was he? Maybe the man was here to confirm what Hamilton wondered, that Fernleigh was responsible for the attack. Maybe he knew nothing about it. Maybe it wasn't Fernleigh, but who else?

'Rum,' said Hamilton, pointing towards his study. He'd expected the worst and instead was faced with the unexpected. 'Cupboard.'

Ridgeway glanced about the room, clearly missing nothing, and then went to the study. Hamilton heard him rummaging about, returning with a decanter and single glass. The young man poured him a measure, then as an after-thought added another good dollop.

Hamilton accepted the glass with difficulty and grunted at a chair. Ridgeway sat the rum on a table, filling the worn horsehair chair opposite with his ropey strength.

'I wanted you to know, Mr Baker, that the debt has been repaid. In full.'

Guilty then, the boy felt guilty at having been prompted by a woman to fulfil his contractual obligations. Edwina had done well. 'And?'

Ridgeway sat back in the chair, the hat perched on a knee. 'And that I'm sorry for any ill-will between us. You really aren't going to make this easy for me, are you?'

Hamilton took a sip of the rum. Maybe he did have the energy to take down the rifle.

'I didn't know the mess my uncle made of my affairs. He was in control of the estate while I was away. I trusted him implicitly.'

Why would Ridgeway consider him even mildly interested in his affairs? A person would never get anywhere in the world if they weighed up the contract from the other person's viewpoint. And one soft response could easily lead to problems with other clients.

'You rather threw me arriving as you did last Monday,' continued Ridgeway, breaking the quiet. 'I have to say I was surprised by your –'

Hamilton held up a palm signalling for silence. 'Not interested. Luke Gordon?' he said with effort.

'News travels quickly,' Ridgeway said wryly. 'Let's just say that, as you are obviously aware, I won't be needing to sell the property, in fact, I'm expanding. I'm sure that's not something you or Peter Worth wanted to hear? However, your debt has been paid.'

He spoke politely enough, but Hamilton saw through the veiled words. Ridgeway was finding it difficult to retain the patina of civility, but if the boy hoped for a response he would be disappointed. What interest was any of this when all his plans were dust and it was thanks to this upstart lounging opposite? He didn't want to have anything to do with Charles Ridgeway, let alone have the boy sitting under his roof paying a courtesy call, a visit that was unneeded and unwanted. Hamilton hated him then. A young man yet to reach his prime. A boy really, only in his mid-twenties. Born of money and name. Bestowed with the chanciest of gifts – ability. God, yes he hated him. Hated his vigour, the sense of entitlement. Hamilton stared at him, long and hard, unblinking, silent. The boy twiddled a hat between his fingers as if uncomfortable. Good, Hamilton thought, slurping at the rum.

'The second reason for my visit,' Ridgeway began, twirling his hat again, 'is to ask for your permission to court your daughter Edwina.'

The glass dropped to the floor and Hamilton coughed violently. He brushed Charles Ridgeway aside when he came to his aid, and the boy picked up the glass, cradling it.

'Can I get you anything, Mr Baker? Are you alright?'

Hamilton composed himself. What had happened at the station yesterday?

Ridgeway sat the tumbler on the table. 'Water?'

Of course Edwina was a beauty and with his name and contacts Ridgeway clearly believed he could marry who he wanted. He was mistaken. Hamilton knew what Ridgeway thought. What he saw. That Hamilton would be grateful for such a union. That it was a fine match for the daughter of a money-lender, living on a pear-ravaged property, in a creaking house, with a namby-pamby for a son.

The boy towered over him, finally backing away to take up his seat.

It was a marriage to rank with Peter Worth's offspring, perhaps surpass it, considering the lad was clearly friends with the Gordons. And wasn't this what Hamilton aspired to? A well-placed union for his lovely daughter. The radiance of a good match shining on father and son, an acquisition of respectability, not possible with money.

Ridgeway waited patiently for a response. Hamilton knew he wouldn't push his case. There was too much pride involved, as well as a level of expectation. No doubt the boy would think him grateful for the offer.

'Mr Baker?' said Ridgeway.

Hamilton thought of the friendship that may have been forged with Peter Worth and then he considered the neighbouring property. For in the end, all transactions came down to the return. All that acreage. With its fair share of prickly pear. Charles Ridgeway was undoubtedly worth a reasonable amount, but now he was beholden to the Gordons and they would want their pound of flesh. Which meant, quite simply, that Hamilton was worth more than the landed stockman who currently waited for a response.

He could be reasonable, grateful, magnanimous, if he chose, but Hamilton didn't choose. Even if he didn't despise the man he'd hardly subject Edwina to another weed-infested block. In its day it had been a fine property with its sprawling ridges and rich soils, its thousands of sheep. Not now. It had been left to decay in the hands of an imbecile while the roaming irresponsible heir chased cows in blackfella country. No, his daughter could do far better.

'Mr Baker, sir, I asked you –'

'No,' answered Hamilton with more satisfaction than any deal had ever given, pleased by Ridgeway's reaction, a slightly open mouth.

'Do you mind telling me why not?'

Hamilton stuttered. 'I may appear poor,' he rose painfully slowly, a breathlessness matching each move of his body, 'but I've more money than you,' he gasped, planting his feet firmly on the floor.

'Maybe,' replied Ridgeway, sitting the hat on his head. 'However, we both know money hasn't got anything to do with your decision. You're a man who doesn't like not getting his own way.'

Gritting his teeth, Hamilton placed one foot in front of the other until he reached the hearth. Here he leant on the mantelpiece. 'Get out.'

Charles stood, his face hard. 'I think the decision falls to Edwina, sir. I only came here out of courtesy.'

'Get out,' repeated Hamilton.

'With pleasure.' He strode out of the room. The door slammed.

⫷ Chapter Thirty-seven ⫸

'You can't come in here, miss, it's not allowed.' A young man rushed out from behind the desk, blocking the entrance foyer. 'I have to ask you to leave immediately.'

Behind him the occupants of the dimly lit room ceased talking to stare in Edwina's direction.

'I just wanted to speak to someone. To ask their advice,' she said politely, unaware her presence would cause *quite* such a fuss. 'I certainly don't mean to disturb anyone.'

Men moved from the long polished bar in order to gain a better view of the intruder. Edwina noted the electric lights hanging from the ceiling in the adjoining room and the pale gold of the painted walls.

'But you *are* disturbing, miss,' said the attendant curtly. 'This is the Guild. It's for men only. Women aren't allowed. Please, you must leave. Now.'

The gentlemen in the adjoining room began talking animatedly.

'But surely an exception can be made? I simply want some advice. Business advice,' Edwina pleaded. 'My father's a member here, Hamilton Baker.' She glanced at the portraits lining the vestibule, hollow-cheeked men with withering eyes. 'He suffered an attack of the palsy last Thursday.'

'I wonder then he did not send his son?'

The reproach came from a grey-haired man. With the interruption the attendant was distracted and Edwina stepped past him, walking quickly down the two stairs, the narrow entrance hall opening up into a large, oblong room hazy with cigarette and pipe smoke and at least fifteen men.

'I tried to stop her, sir, but –'

'It's alright, Andrew,' replied the stranger as Edwina reached him.

Andrew loitered for a few moments and then returned to his post.

The men in the room complained immediately at her presence. Edwina's sweaty grip tightened on the papers she held. Perhaps this wasn't such a good idea. Some of the diners seated at damask-covered tables stood at the intrusion while others clustered together in condemnation. Only one man remained disinterested in the disturbance. He stood at the long bar, back to the room, running a tumbler in circles across the counter.

The man in front of her introduced himself as Tom Clyde, a friend of her father's and visitor to Wywanna. 'I'm s-sorry to hear of your father's illness. Is he v-very unwell?'

Edwina smiled gratefully. 'Restricted to the house, Mr Clyde,' she tried to ignore the stares, 'but improving, hence the reason for my visit.'

'Well, unfortunately Andrew is r-right, Miss Baker, this is a m-men-only establishment. You probably sh-should leave.' He indicated the front door.

His was a fleeting appraisal. It contained no hostility, more a certain amusement at what Edwina knew was her boldness. In comparison, the other members were not so courteous. The word *outrageous* was mentioned and then, to Edwina's embarrassment, the phrase *circus theft* was uttered. Surrounded by the keepers of

313

the town and greater district, Edwina knew she should not have come to this place. Nor should she have considered going behind her father's back and embarking on such a foolhardy venture. She was only a woman after all, and where a daughter may be silly enough to pit herself against a father's wrath, engaging a roomful of judgemental men was quite another thing.

'S-surely there is a family friend who could counsel you, M-Miss Baker,' said Mr Clyde kindly. He waved distractedly around the room with its silver cutlery, curtained windows and disgruntled inhabitants. 'Th-there are no committee members here this weekend. Perhaps in th-three weeks when the monthly meeting is s-set you could leave word for the President, Mr Worth.' He took Edwina's arm, directing her with a gracious determination towards the exit. 'Who knows, your f-father may be much recovered by th-then.'

'Wait on there,' the loner called from the bar, skolling his drink and moving nonchalantly towards them.

Extricating herself from Mr Clyde's grasp, Edwina stared. A line of grit showed on the brow of the nuggetty brown-faced stockman where dirt and sweat had recently dried. Edwina smelt rum on his breath, perspiration, saw the shadow of a beard hinting at an early rising.

'This is Luke Gordon, Miss Baker.'

'Hello.' Edwina couldn't help feel she was face to face with a legend.

'I was just t-telling Miss Baker, Luke,' explained Mr Clyde, 'that sh-she had t-to leave.'

'You've a problem, have you, miss?' asked Luke.

Mr Clyde cleared his throat in irritation.

'Edwina, Edwina Baker. I just wanted some advice. My father is sick.' It was difficult not to appear as desperate as she felt. To be escorted from the Guild without having received any assistance would be the most horrifying of results. If she thought she was the subject of town gossip now, wait until this was discussed.

'You better come and have a talk with me then, Edwina Baker. It'll be right, Tom, you can tell Peter that it was me that broke the Guild's rules.' He gave Edwina a wink. 'I'm not a member anyway.'

The office Luke led Edwina into displayed a brass plaque with the word President etched into it. He offered her a seat in one of two large leather chairs before perching on the edge of the substantial desk.

'Thank you, Mr Gordon,' said Edwina.

'It's Luke. They can be like a pack of dingoes, but they're harmless enough.'

The room was grandly furnished with books and paintings and a large map of the world. Edwina sat like a reprimanded schoolchild, clutching her belongings, her spine ramrod straight, her eyes darting about the study.

'One of the benefits of association,' said Luke, alluding to his famous surname as he tapped the mahogany bureau. 'Not that I'd want to be a member. My brother does the hobnobbing and, frankly, he's much better at it than me. I never could stand the pretension that comes with the burden of supposed class, not in this land. If a person wants to be a toffy-nosed Englishman go back to the mother country I say.'

Edwina gathered her courage, recalled the humble origins of the Gordon family's beginnings in Australia. 'Your family were from Scotland?'

'Crofters, poor-as. Started in the goldfields my father did. But most people know my family's story. As for you,' Luke crossed his arms, staring at her with interest, 'I'm trying to fathom where you fit in, Miss Edwina Baker.' He eyed her shrewdly. 'Are you interested in climbing the bush hierarchy or just a woman needing some help? I'm hoping it's the latter for after the exhibition you just put on you've made a poor start with what passes for this district's establishment.'

'I wanted some advice,' her voice quavered.

'On what?'

'Land,' Edwina said hopefully.

'The buying or the selling of it?'

'Buying.'

'Go on.'

Edwina paused. What if, in sharing her thoughts, Luke Gordon took advantage of her knowledge? Worse, what if she were totally ignorant of the issues involved and he laughed in her face.

'If you don't tell me I can't help, can I?' said Luke.

She had to place her trust in someone. And so Edwina began explaining her idea of buying a prickly-pear-riddled property at low cost in the hopes that once the weed died she would be a wealthy landowner for little outlay. 'It's not that I want to take advantage of other people's misfortune.'

Luke rubbed at the stubble on his chin. 'Ever since that insect started to make a dent in the pear in '25, people have been considering the possibilities. Now, don't look like a child that's about to throw the toys from her cot.'

'I'm sorry. I thought –'

'That you were on to something?' Luke moved to the chair behind the desk. Rolling a cigarette, he lit it, exhaling thoughtfully. 'You are. There is undoubtedly land available and owners desperate to sell. And people will be keen to sell you anything, Edwina. You realise there's no money in the bush at the moment. Hasn't been since around 1920 what with the slide in prices and the particularly wonderful dry weather that seems to have taken a liking to our country.'

'We only grow wheat and hay.' She admitted her ignorance.

'Croppers, eh? Well, there are plenty living off rabbits and a few vegetables out here. Compared to folks in the city, we're well off.'

'Do you really think so?'

'You're not starving, are you? You've got a roof over your head. There's plenty in the cities that don't.'

316

Edwina hadn't come to the Guild for a lesson in gratitude. She didn't feel fortunate, although compared to some she obviously was.

'As for your land, you have to consider a few things. Firstly, anything with a lot of pear is pretty much worthless even if it is starting to die off. Secondly, there's no saying that this insect will kill all of it. Or that it won't come back again. I've heard talk of large areas of pear dying but you have to know there is a risk. Then there's the length of time involved in waiting for the plant to die and for the country to become productive again, fertile. No income,' he emphasised. 'Quite frankly there's not much of an income for anyone in the bush at the moment.'

'Except for you?' Edwina knew she shouldn't be so outspoken, but the Gordons owned huge tracts of land and ran thousands of cattle.

He blew smoke into the air. 'Say what you think, don't you?'

Edwina didn't reply.

'I'm all for straight talking.' Stubbing out the cigarette, Luke lifted a leg, resting it across the edge of the desk; a clump of manure was stuck to the sole of his boot. 'We've made plenty. Cattle producers were contracted to the Empire during the war. Bully-beef they needed and we gave it to them. Twenty pounds a bullock. But the gravy train finished with the end of the bloodbath in 1918. Now cattle are worth a pittance. It's the same with wool. So, say you buy yourself a pear block on the cheap, Edwina, but commodity prices remain dirt-low. How long are you prepared to wait for a return on the money invested? For an income? Can you afford to?'

Edwina looked at the papers in her lap. How was she meant to answer all those questions?

'If you've not the stomach for the risk, I'll understand. It takes guts to work the bush, Edwina, and more than a sprinkling of good luck to make a go of it. Do you have money?' asked Luke.

'Yes. Quite a lot.'

'You'd need around forty thousand pounds.'

Edwina wasn't willing to share how much money was at her disposable, at least not yet. 'Go on,' she said.

Luke gave an interested smile. 'A woman with looks and money, and you're not married. Considering the shortage of women in the outback you're a curiosity, to say the least.'

'What would you do if you were me, Luke?' asked Edwina, ignoring the probing question. 'I mean, I have money and I wanted to put it somewhere safe. Somewhere worthwhile.'

Luke wrinkled his nose a couple of times, moved his leg from the desk, the manure dropping onto the floor. 'Buy land. There are banks and shares and businesses, but you're relying on other people to take care of your funds, and what happens if they can't? If they go bust? Sure, you can live off a bit of interest and stare at the cash figure in a ledger, or you can stash it in a tin under your bed, but what have you got? What are you contributing to? What are you leaving behind when you've gone? Have you made anything, grown anything? Tended anything? Tried your best to stake a claim in a wild land? Because I have, and by God it's the greatest thing I've ever done. These are the questions you have to ask yourself. And when you do, and if you're still interested, remember this well, Edwina. The bush is like a brown snake. If you're not careful it'll strike when least expected. And out here the bite is fatal.'

Edwina suppressed the bubble of anxiety rising within her. Setting the papers on the desk she walked about the room, conscious of the pair of eyes watching her. Good sense told her to thank Luke Gordon for his time and leave. But another part of her, the part that wanted to prove her ability, was tantalised by his words. She envisaged the sun setting over thousands of acres of untamed country. It was possible. The Gordons had done it. Why couldn't the Bakers?

'What do you want to grow, sheep or cattle?' Luke was lighting another cigarette.

'Either, I suppose.'

'Well, I'd be the last one to go against cattle, but they're tough to keep alive in a drought and even my brother can't say what the future will bring when it comes to prices. And unlike our operation, you'll be without the benefit of a number of runs for rotation and water as well, so I'd grow wool. I've never taken to lice feeders but if you want to make a go of this and you want my help that's what I'd advise, take it or leave it.'

Edwina stopped pacing. 'You would help me?'

Luke took a drag of the cigarette. 'Why the hell not? I know who you are, about the caper you pulled at the circus, and I know your father's a money-lender, and that you have a brother. I'm not condemning you, Edwina. A man sees a lot in life, but what he doesn't often see is someone willing to have a go. A woman buying a station, well, I for one would love to be a part of that.'

'I'll not be anyone's novelty.'

'And I'm not coming along for the ride. If you purchase a station I'll help you find a manager and I'll keep an eye on the books, make sure you're not swindled. But I want rights to keep two hundred horses there. We bred them during the war for the mounted troops and my half-brother, Angus, wants to be rid of them now. I like my horses. He doesn't. I'll lease the country from you. Now you better show me those papers you've been hanging on to for dear life.'

Ten minutes later Luke was circling an area on the map Han Lee had procured from the Lands Office. 'Get away from the farmers with their crops and dairy cows. And the further west you go the further you are from the pear as well. Here.' He tapped at the circle with a filthy ragged nail.

The location was west of Miles, past the town of Roma. Edwina studied the area. 'But that's miles away.'

'About a hundred and fifty miles or so I'd reckon. It's a good run, Edwina. The place grows Mitchell, Flinders and Blue grass and there's fine herbage in an average year. The property was part of the government's state-run pastoral empire, but many of the stations are up for sale. Gone broke through mismanagement. The rot set in with the cattle slump in 1920. They've been trying to sell them for the last few years. Priced too high they were but some of the smaller ones are now going for a song.'

'How do you know so much about it?'

'Just inspected it, last week, but Angus has his sights on a larger block further north. How much money do you actually have?'

'How much do we need?' countered Edwina, feeling conspiratorial.

'Well, with Condo Station you'll get around ten thousand head of cattle. Which we'll sell and then buy in sheep. The fences are in good repair. The woolshed needs some work. There's water frontage and a decent house. You'll need extra funds for a manager and staff. And a bit in reserve, for who knows how long it will be before the markets improve. And if a dry spell hits you need enough to cover that as well.' He held up a dirt-creased hand. 'And don't ask me how much, because my answer will be how long is a ball of twine. And if you decide to do this, don't complain if your arse is out of your pants in a decade. Oops, slip of the tongue, apologies. I'm not used to dealing with women.'

Edwina was already thinking of Han Lee and the contribution his men could make. 'You haven't said a price, Luke.'

'You haven't said how much you have.'

Edwina bit her lip and then withdrew her father's passbook from her handbag, sliding it across the desk.

Luke raised an eyebrow at the name on the passbook, before flipping through the pages.

'Well?' Edwina was beginning to feel sick with anticipation. 'Is there enough?'

'Yes,' answered Luke, 'there's enough.'

⋙ Chapter Thirty-eight ⋘

Hamilton was sitting by the parlour window when Edwina finally returned home. He squinted in thought as Han Lee assisted her down from the buggy and Davidson got down from his horse as if he'd been riding shotgun. The three stood together talking.

'Where have you been?' called Aiden from the porch.

Edwina acknowledged the query with a wave.

'I said –'

This was an interesting development. The Chinaman was staring blatantly at his son, with an expression that quite distinctly told him to be quiet. The boy obeyed. Only when Edwina's business was finished did she walk towards the house as her companions left.

'Where have you been, Edwina?' asked Aiden again as they entered the parlour.

'Hello, Father. How are you feeling?' Edwina knelt by the chair, took one of his hands in hers.

'Better.'

'Good, I have seen the doctor.' Edwina removed the gloves she wore. Hamilton noted they were her mother's. When had his daughter become a woman?

'You could have told us what you were doing instead of sneaking off,' Aiden said in annoyance.

'Aiden, you have done nothing but treat me poorly since Father took ill. There have been things requiring attention and as you took it upon yourself to take on the position of nursemaid, I had to assume the role of head of the household. Now, if you have nothing helpful to add, do be quiet.'

It was wrong to be entertained by squabbling children but Hamilton couldn't help but be amused. Not only by Edwina's new-found authority, which he was in two minds about, but by Aiden's fury, which showed in pinking cheeks.

'The doctor said we must get you up and walking about. Twice a day at least, Father, and he's prescribed this tonic to purify the blood as well as Beecham's Pills. And Han Lee has tea for you. An oriental concoction that he is sure will help you feel better.'

Hamilton grunted at the medicinal offerings. He could never quite take to the knowledge invested in a man who proposed himself an expert on the human body when everything he knew came out of a book. The Chinaman's tea, however, was another matter. That he would drink. 'Han Lee?' asked Hamilton.

'He came with me, Father, as did Davidson. Best I thought to have a proper escort.'

How proper it was to have an oriental driving the buggy for his only daughter Hamilton didn't know. Edwina, however, was right in ensuring she was accompanied to Wywanna.

'Should it be needed,' continued Edwina, 'Han Lee has agreed to help with harvest. He feels it may come in early with the growing heat and lack of rain and although it's undoubtedly a good month away I felt it important to ask his assistance, although I'm sure you will be fully recovered by then. We will also only do half of the planned clearing. The cactoblastis seems to be working. So we'll save our money and see how effective the insect is.' She turned to her brother. 'Aiden, you of course will oversee the work. We have to remember there is no money in the bush at the moment and with low prices and without the benefit of the secondary income provided by Father we have to be careful with our costs.'

Aiden flopped down into one of the chairs. 'And now that you have so diligently taken over the running of the property, dear sister, what exactly do you intend to be doing?'

Hamilton felt the warmth of his daughter's hand on a shoulder. 'What I normally do, though outdoors my role will be more managerial.'

'My, we have assumed all the trappings of leadership,' Aiden quipped, looking to his father for backing. 'I am the head of this household until Father is recovered. Isn't that right, Father? As the eldest son it is my responsibility to assume the role. To run our business, to organise and instruct the workers.'

'Then you should have done so,' answered Edwina. 'There were things that needed to be attended to, such as the debt owed by the Ridgeways, which has been paid, Father. And as I recall, Aiden, you didn't even offer to accompany me. So I'm sorry for your anger, but what's done is done.'

'Father?' queried Aiden. 'Father, tell Edwina to stop bossing me around. It's not right.'

The two of them were like the polar caps. One north, the other south. Each pulled by a force that neither could control let alone comprehend. They were arguing now. Aiden's voice hard and angry, Edwina's patient, perhaps a little bored. He'd missed their growing. Specifically his daughter's. He could see how she could catch the eye of a grazier, even one as unlikeable as Charles Ridgeway. There was a spirit to her. A knowing. Troublesome characteristics for a female, but women could be moulded. There was time, for both of his children, and still much for them to learn. A lifetime really.

And, although it went against everything he knew and believed, for the time being Edwina was the one to take control of the business. Giving her the responsibility would bring her back to his side and eradicate the nonsense ideas and, hopefully, behaviour of the past weeks. Yes, the girl had strayed, done wrong, pushed at boundaries that were not meant to be assaulted, but hers was the stronger intellect. Edwina's success in recouping the debt owed proved her ability and he believed after everything that had transpired that she would not do anything foolhardy now. For the girl was in charge, for the time being. As for Ridgeway, if Edwina could capture the interest of one pastoralist after the circus debacle, there would be others. All was not lost.

'Leave her be, Aiden,' ordered Hamilton.

His son's jaw trembled. 'But –'

'Leave Edwina be.' Hamilton urged to say what he thought but his ability to draw the words forth at will remained limited. It was as if his brain slept, only waking to allow the utterance of the barest snippets. Surely it was unnecessary to speak the obvious. The boy played a part in his care and the sister attended to business; for the time being things should stay as they were. Hamilton expected Aiden to mount an argument, to put up more of a battle – as his only son it was his right.

'Very well,' retorted Aiden stiffly, 'if that is your wish.' He glared at his sister and then left the room, furious.

The boy had no idea how much he was like his mother. Caroline was never one for confrontation. Hamilton shut his eyes against the disappointment. He was still so very tired. One side of his body refused to function properly, lagging behind like an irritated child.

'He will not forgive me, Father,' Edwina said softly.

Hamilton yawned.

'I should let you rest,' continued his daughter, 'but I wanted to ask you if you can remember anything of what happened? If you can remember who attacked you?'

He looked at Edwina. The incident remained a blur.

'Because I think we know who did it and Davidson has seen to the person responsible so you don't have to worry about anything.'

Hamilton scowled, the skin puckering around the workable side of his face. The man wasn't even there, he wanted to tell her, and if *he* couldn't recall who confronted him how was it possible that Davidson could? 'Who?'

'It seems it was Mr Fernleigh.'

Hamilton's assumption had been correct, but what of Davidson's role in this, he wondered. Had the stockman warned him off his land, given him a belting? He hoped he had.

Edwina took his hand, patted it, as a mother would to placate a child. 'Can I get you anything?'

'Youth,' stuttered Hamilton.

'How about some of Han Lee's tea instead?' Her smile was warm.

'Run things,' Hamilton strained to get the words out, 'p-properly.'

'I am my father's daughter. How could I do anything else?' Edwina replied.

Hamilton watched the girl leave. There was pride, but in the pit of his stomach, something else, the beginnings of a knot.

❧ Chapter Thirty-nine ❧

Ten days later Edwina carried the mail into the study and closed the door. The newspaper was nearly a week old. She flipped through the pages, searching for any reports of untimely deaths. Page four made mention of Hamilton Baker's attack of the palsy. It was an insignificant article of a half dozen lines placed above the obituaries section as if queuing for inclusion. Next to it was a short piece on Mr Fernleigh. Edwina read the contents of the article quickly. Ridgeway Station's manager was still reported as missing, the journalist pondering on the man's fate and whether a body would ever be found.

The remaining mail consisted of two telegrams. Edwina lay both side by side. Compressed her lips and then opened the first.

It was from Luke Gordon. Her offer for Condo Station had been accepted. The paperwork was on its way to the solicitor's office in Wywanna, with Luke acting as guarantor for the sale. Luke's final sentence,

The deposit must be paid on signing. With a further six weeks before the full amount is due. Congratulations.

Edwina read and re-read the two sentences. It seemed to her that life was about to begin such was her excitement. The cable was a few days old. She'd not even inspected the property. Luke's word, his encouragement and support were enough.

Did she dare? Arriving home from Wywanna after meeting Luke, it had taken all of Edwina's strength not to conceal her shock at her father's improvement. To find him in the parlour, sitting upright, talking, limited though it was, had stunned her. The shame came immediately, her quickness to act, the searching of personal documents, the intent. Edwina came close to immediately returning to town, finding Luke and abandoning everything they'd discussed. But she didn't. Instead, Edwina waited.

One side of her father's body was sluggish and the drooping face remained, along with the slurred, imperfect speech and stumbling walk, and yet he appeared to be gaining strength. Well enough to resume lending money in the New Year? To take back the reins of a property on which they were slowly going broke? In her heart Edwina doubted it. And then there was Aiden and the problems she envisaged once he was in charge.

Edwina's fingers tapped the desktop. The thought of owning a large station out west gripped at her imagination like nothing else. To run such an entity. To be counted among the pastoralists of Queensland. To be assisted by none other than Luke Gordon. Who wouldn't say yes to such an opportunity? Edwina glanced at the door. Outside her father sat dozing in the parlour. How desperately she wanted to tell him the news. To explain what she was on the verge of accomplishing. Surely he would be proud. For wasn't this what he aspired to? Acceptance. Esteem. Success.

Did Edwina cross her fingers and go ahead? Justify her actions through her father's recent approval? And then tell him her great news when he was a little more recovered? There was only one thing needed: confirmation of the extent of the share portfolio.

Outside Aiden's voice was unnecessarily loud. 'I don't care what my sister told you. Today we're going to . . . Wait, where are you going? Come back here, Davidson. I said come back here. Damn and blast.'

How did you explain to someone that out here respect was earnt? Rising to lock the study door, Edwina hovered as the now familiar rap sounded.

'Edwina? Edwina, open the door. I said open this door right now. Davidson won't listen to anything I say anymore.'

'I'm busy, Aiden. Why don't you go and check the Ridgeway boundary?'

'And be shot by that hairy galoot? No thanks. Why don't you go out there instead?'

'I did,' said Edwina patiently through the timber, 'yesterday. And there was no sign of Fernleigh. There hasn't been since his disappearance and the paper says he is still missing.'

Having agreed to never mention Fernleigh's name again, the only thing they'd come to an understanding on, Aiden quieted. 'Fine. I'll go to the well and fill the barrels.'

A few minutes later her brother rode away.

Edwina tore the second wire open with shaking hands. It was from the Brisbane-based broker and her eyes widened at the detailed contents, a list of companies that matched those found in her father's saddlebag. Edwina gasped. They were beyond wealthy. They were rich. Eyes blurring, she set the cable on the desk and wept. To be living such an existence only to discover their lives needn't be so hard was almost too much.

A rainbow of glistening possibility presented itself and Edwina's imaginings took on an entirely different direction. Brisbane beckoned. A house on the river. Fine clothes. Domestics to deal with the drudgery. Such a future tempted and tantalised. The telegraph from Luke Gordon lay open on the desk. It wasn't too late to cancel the purchase of Condo Station.

Folding the cable, Edwina ran a finger along the crease.

Would a citified life suit? The land was all she knew and understood and if Edwina were honest it was not the manual labour that most bothered her. The lack of interest in her opinion was what hurt. The belief that, as a woman, she was less than a man. That wounded the greatest.

Edwina slipped the broker's cable inside its envelope. The shares belonged to her father. Pounds and shillings squirrelled away. Hidden from his children. Money he clearly didn't want them to know about. Let alone have. Hamilton Baker could keep it then. When combined with the stocks, the price of Condo Station didn't even amount to a sixth share. One day her brother would be a wealthy man and he'd undoubtedly lose what remained of their father's hoard. When that happened, Aiden would be pleased to have a sister he could come to.

It was decided then. She would choose the road less travelled.

'Hello?'

Recognising the voice, Edwina gathered the mail, sliding it into a drawer. Through the window Mason could be seen standing outside the front door.

Edwina's first thoughts were of the manager, Fernleigh. She wiped suddenly clammy hands on her skirt. 'Mason?'

Turning at his name, he walked the length of the verandah to the office. 'Do I have to come in there or will you come out?'

Edwina didn't have a chance to reply for Mason reached through the window where she'd been leaning and, gathering her in his arms, pulled Edwina through the opening before setting her on the ground.

'We do have doors,' she stated indignantly, pulling free of his grasp.

'Last time I used the door here it wasn't a good ending,' he replied with less enthusiasm than he'd arrived with.

'Whatever are you talking about?' Edwina was annoyed by his manhandling and equally worried by his visit.

'Nothing. I thought I'd find you looking pleased as Punch,' he said a little more brightly. 'A woman buying a station, and not just any woman either, a young single woman.'

Edwina shushed him. 'How did you find out?' she whispered.

'Luke Gordon,' replied Mason with a laugh at her secrecy. 'We've been doing some business together. And his half-brother, Angus, is my godfather. My mother thought it would be better to have someone closer to my own age.'

'Your godfather?' Mason knew everything then, including that Hamilton Baker was yet to learn of his daughter's activities. 'No-one is meant to know anything about it. Luke promised.'

'Luke and Angus have no secrets. With the size of their empire, they can't afford to. And I won't say anything. Walk with me.' He held out a hand, which Edwina ignored as they stepped onto the grass. 'When will you tell your father?'

'Nothing's been decided.' Chickens and turkeys scattered from their path as Edwina strode ahead, her blue skirt catching on the grass. Among the silvery gums a sleeping Jed lay curled at the base of a thick trunk.

'Luke thinks it's a done deal.' Mason leant against one of the trees. 'Have you got cold feet? I wouldn't blame you. It's a massive undertaking for a woman, if that's your intention to live up there and manage it yourself.'

'Did Luke send you over here to check on me?'

'Of course not,' answered Mason. 'I thought you'd be happy to share the news with someone. How is your father?'

'Getting better slowly.'

'I'd like to be a fly on the wall when you tell him about the property.'

So he'd come to hear about her plans, a proposal that was yet to be confirmed, which meant he suspected nothing regarding

330

Fernleigh. Edwina decided not to mention the manager's name. 'Can we talk about something else, Mason?'

'Sure.' He rubbed a hand over the bark of the gum tree. 'Whatever happens, will you be staying here then?'

Why was he asking her so many questions? 'Perhaps.'

'You're not giving much away, Edwina. Next you'll be telling me to mind my own business.'

'Yes,' admitted Edwina, 'something like that.'

'You'll find the timing a bit off, but this has nothing to do with your news, Edwina. I wanted to ask you something. I would have asked you the day you came to the station but you left so quickly.'

'I'm intrigued.' However, it was difficult not to be irritated. The land purchase was the biggest event of Edwina's life and it was already being discussed before papers were even signed.

Mason studied the distant wheat and then turned to face her. 'Will you walk out with me? Well, ride out I guess, considering where we live.' He gave a wry grin. 'Maybe we could go to Wywanna for the day. There's a café there. Admittedly, it's not very good . . . Or we could have a picnic by the creek. Anything you like. What do you think?'

It was a day for surprises. Edwina was lost for words. 'I don't know.'

'You probably thought me very forward the other week when you came to the station, behaving the way I did,' acknowledged Mason.

'A little, yes,' she confessed, remembering the kiss they shared.

'It's just when I put my mind to something I tend to act on it.' He knelt down and ruffled Jed's head; the dog yawned. 'I'd like to see more of you. Get to know you.'

Edwina was pleased Mason couldn't see her expression. 'Because of my buying the property?'

He faced her abruptly, concern in his eyes. 'You didn't listen to anything I just said. No, Edwina, because of you.'

'Oh.' This was unexpected. Edwina walked away through the trees. She couldn't deny that Mason had been in her thoughts, as had Will; however, between the two men it was Mason that fought for prominence. But both failed to win against the prospect of owning Condo Station and the planning required once it was in her hands. There was no doubting her liking of Mason. He was strong and confident and yet quiet and thoughtful and he appeared to appreciate her ability. The question was did she want to go out with him? Especially now when everything was about to change. Once Condo Station was legally hers, Edwina intended to go there and inspect the property with Luke. Perhaps even stay on for a few months to meet the new manager. It all depended on her father's reaction to the purchase, which could go either way.

'Edwina?' called Mason.

Retracing her steps, Edwina returned to the man waiting for an answer. Edwina wanted to say yes, but did she really want to get entangled in a friendship, a relationship? Walking out with someone invariably led to marriage and no matter how much she liked Mason, Edwina knew that she just couldn't go back to being at the beck and call of a man, nor was the role of wife something she felt she was suited to. There was a new world waiting for her, fresh opportunities. A chance to prove her ability. The timing was just horrid. 'I really don't know anything about you, Mason. I don't even know your surname.'

'I know, and I have some explaining to do. I need to tell you some things. Things about myself that I should have said before. I don't know why I didn't.' He held her gaze. 'The right moment never came up, I suppose, and ever since we met you seem to have had a bee in your bonnet about Charles Ridgeway.'

Edwina didn't understand. 'What's he got to do with anything?'

'Promise you'll listen to what I have to say.'

What was this secret causing the line on his forehead to deepen? 'Mason, things are changing every day for me. I don't even know if I'll be staying here.'

'That's not a definite no.' Mason took a step towards her. 'Are you telling me that a woman who buys a property doesn't know what she wants?'

Edwina knew that look in his eyes. 'I haven't bought it yet.' She took a step backwards. He another step forwards.

'Let's seal our agreement then,' he extended a hand, 'that you'll be neighbourly and allow me to at least get to know you a little better.'

There was no harm in that, decided Edwina as she reached out to shake his hand. Mason pulled her into his arms, holding her close. 'I don't do anything half-heartedly, Edwina. You should know that.'

She took a breath, her first impulse to struggle. In its place she met his demanding gaze, allowed the tightening of the embrace. 'Neither do I,' she countered. Mason lifted an eyebrow in response. Inexplicably Edwina tilted her head forwards, closing her eyes.

'What's going on here?'

They broke apart as her father shuffled along the verandah, a rifle in his grasp. At the kitchen window Constance ducked out of sight. Edwina felt Mason tense.

'Father, everything is alright,' she replied as they both approached the house. 'This is Mason. He's a friend of Charles Ridgeway,' she explained, knowing her father would be delighted at any interest shown in his daughter. 'My friend.'

'Mason? I know him as Charles. Charles Ridgeway. I'll ask you, boy, to step away from my daughter.' Although shaky, Hamilton lifted the rifle.

Edwina grew pale. 'What? No. That's impossible. You're Mason, Charles' friend.'

'Tell her, Ridgeway. If she knew who you really were she wouldn't set foot near you.'

'That's not true,' said Mason angrily. 'My friends call me Mason, Edwina. It's my middle name. That's what I wanted to tell you.'

'You're really Charles Ridgeway? But you let me think you were someone else?' Edwina moved from his side. Why had he done such a thing? Pretended to be Mason. Lied to her. 'Why didn't you tell me? You made me think you were someone else. I trusted you and you lied to me.'

'Thought he was someone else, did you, Edwina?' her father snorted, leaning on the verandah's wooden post for balance. 'He's a cunning one. Came here . . . asked to walk out with you . . . After what he did . . . Ruined everything.' He grew more breathless, his words choppy with effort. 'Probably set Fernleigh onto me that night. Did you sool your mongrel dog on me out of spite?' He grabbed at the post, steadying his balance, chest heaving.

Mason walked towards the verandah. 'Mr Baker, I don't know what you're talking about. However, as far as your daughter is concerned, I never meant to mislead her. I am known as Mason to my friends and that's how we were introduced. Wasn't it?' he asked Edwina.

'But why didn't you tell me the truth?'

'How difficult did you make that for me?' countered Mason. 'Always ranting on about Charles, thinking and expecting the worst of him. Think about it, Edwina. What would you have done if you'd been me?'

'Spoken up,' replied Edwina, 'considering the dealings going on between our two families and your slowness in repaying my father's loan. I can't understand how you could have led me to believe you were someone else.'

'And where would that have got me? Nowhere, considering your reaction. But let's not talk about deceptions, Edwina, not with the plans you have going on.'

Edwina looked from Mason to her father and back again. He had no right to be doing this, to be using her as a scapegoat for his dishonesty.

'Your good opinion was what mattered to me, Edwina, but I apologise for going about trying to obtain it the way I did.'

Hamilton straightened, cocked the rifle. 'Pretty fictions don't hold much here. Go.'

'Mr Baker, please,' said Mason, 'this is ridiculous.'

'Get off . . . my land.'

The rifle trembled as her father placed the stock of the gun hard to his shoulder. Mason continued walking forwards, telling him to put the rifle down before someone got hurt.

'Don't, Mason,' called Edwina. 'Stop.'

'I said leave, Ridgeway!'

'Father, please!' Edwina ran forwards as her father took aim and fired. The force of the weapon sent him reeling backwards, sprawling onto his back.

Mason was reaching for her, calling out her name, but Edwina couldn't answer.

A fiery pain blistered its way through her body and she halted instantly, shuddering back and forth, as if balancing on a wooden beam.

The sky overhead was far too bright. The clouds swirling uncontrollably as she collapsed to the ground.

❧ Chapter Forty ❧

He was still there. As the man was every morning. For hours he waited, day in, day out, hat in hand, thirty feet from the house. Unmoving, unmoveable. Grass crinkling with the dryness. Trees growing crepey from the sun. The birds so used to his presence that they happily hopped about his boots, one snappy little willy-wagtail perching on the dry leather. Even the collies were on his side. They too waited patiently. Condemning in their presence.

Hamilton itched cheek stubble, twisted his face in a grimace, backing away from the window.

Two weeks were behind them. Fourteen days of terrified waiting. Hours of heat-dredged days and listless nights. Minutes spent imagining the worst when the infection set in. Seconds of pounding blood in unhearing ears. The putrid stench of illness. He'd thought the delirium the wickedest of things. A creeping disease that took hold of his daughter. The mad ramblings. The thrashing of bedclothes. The terrible sweating.

And yet it was the resultant silence that skewered the heart.

At one point Hamilton decided to have a grave dug. To be ready for the inevitable. Two days were spent riding around the property in the buggy searching for the right spot. Not too lonely. Too hot or cold. With a view across the open grassland towards the rising sun. Away from the wheat and the dratted pear. In the end Hamilton couldn't do it. Couldn't embark on the beginning of the end. To Aiden he explained the unsuitability of every location, that there was no place good enough for his only daughter.

In truth Hamilton was simply incapable of beginning the long goodbye that would never end.

Outside, the man was leaving. Mounting the faithful horse. Not looking back. Ridgeway remained silent as he had since the beginning of his vigil. And with his arrival that first day Hamilton continued ignoring him, staring defiantly out the window at the man who waited for news. Never speaking, only lingering. Patient and hopeful. Steadfast. Stoic. Waiting for a few crumbs of knowledge that Hamilton refused to give. He wasn't welcome. The bastard would never be welcome. If not for him, none of this would have happened.

There was a new albatross. One to replace the prickly pear and his name was Charles Ridgeway. Hamilton snorted in disgust. Sat in the parlour and waited. As they all waited, the grandfather clock marking precious time.

'Well?' asked Hamilton when his son appeared.

'The same,' answered Aiden, 'still the same. Davidson's with her applying more maggots. I can't understand you allowing him to do that. It's disgusting.' The boy was white.

'The surgeons used it during the war, Aiden. The blackfellas, probably long before. They eat away the badness. It will help her.'

'If she lives.' Aiden's voice was barely audible.

Hamilton nodded. 'If she lives.'

'Edwina said Mason's name, Father. I thought you should know.'

'Well, now I know,' answered Hamilton. 'And it's Charles. Charles Mason Ridgeway. They are one and the same. Don't forget that.' Aiden left the room.

Hamilton clenched the passbook and telegrams found left in the study. They lived by his chair these days. The culmination of a lifetime's work. A reminder of the crimes committed over thirty years ago to amass the growing fortune. A few bits of paper, words smeared by recent sweat.

The record of a daughter's transgressions and, he supposed, his failings as a father.

Han Lee left tea for Hamilton and then carried through another of his concoctions to Edwina. The Chinaman was on permanent call, a position self-created. Like a nurse on night duty he tended to her sweats, forced bitter brews down her throat and watched over her while everyone else slept. This was not a man to be told otherwise. Han Lee was dedicated to Edwina's care and Hamilton could see no point worrying about the propriety of an oriental tending his daughter. Of a yellow-skinned gentlemen spending hours with her alone. Edwina was yet to wake. She might never awake, but she need not linger alone. So Hamilton let him stay with her. This was the tenth night in a row.

Hamilton dozed for a little, finally rising to limp about the homestead, opening doors and closing them. Stirring the air. Watching over those who cared for Edwina. He found Aiden sprawled face down and fully clothed on the bed. Constance asleep in a hammock outside the kitchen. Davidson among the gums, smoking and waiting. A trap was set in the trees. Aiden and Constance had seen glimpses of the skittish lion cub over the last few weeks. It seemed Edwina had told Davidson to capture the lion, and Davidson, having left meat for the animal regularly, was hopeful of ensnaring it now the cage was baited.

Inside, Hamilton hesitated at Caroline's room. They'd kept separate bedrooms following the births of their children, both preferring their private domains, but were equally willing lovers when desire struck. A day-dress still lay on the bed. The wardrobe was slightly ajar. The rug furled at one end as if his wife had just caught the edge of it with a toe. The lamplight shone on cobwebs clotted with dust and yet, somehow, the room wasn't empty.

On the rear verandah the corner of the house edged into darkness. Insects buzzed in the orchard. A dog whined. Old Jed lay nearby, waiting, as they all waited. Hamilton could almost feel the gentle suck of the night, the persistent tug of nothingness. It was not for him, he knew, but for Edwina. The blackness wanted the girl, his firstborn. It was hungry, but still Edwina fought on. On the threshold of her room Hamilton lingered, wanting to enter but feeling the push of remorse, of the binds that once joined them but were already unravelling. Within the dingy rays of candle-light Han Lee held Edwina in his arms. Their heads merging, the Chinaman cradled his child as he coaxed a little broth into her mouth, wiping the dribbling juice clean.

Han Lee looked up. 'The fever, Mr Baker, it is broken. Miss Edwina, she will be fine.'

'She will be fine?' repeated Hamilton.

'Yes, come see for yourself.' He pulled gently at the sweaty strands of hair sticking to her skin. 'She is with us again.'

Hamilton backed away slowly. 'Good,' he answered softly, 'I will let her rest.'

≈ Chapter Forty-one ≈

The obstinate neighbour was back the following morning. Hat in hand, waiting. Hamilton drew the curtains on the audacious fool. This was beyond ludicrous. Something needed to be done. Ridgeway didn't know, of course, that, no thanks to his interference, Edwina would survive and Hamilton didn't want to tell the man. He would prefer Ridgeway spent the rest of his life standing among the trees in the heat and the dust and the cold and the driving rain until he turned to stone.

'He didn't shoot her,' reminded Aiden from Edwina's bedside on his arrival.

'I know that.' Hamilton hovered in the doorway, maggots squished underfoot. If the black girl was going to sweep the floor why the blazes couldn't she do it properly?

'Considering how much you two dislike each other it's pretty brave of Ridgeway to keep coming back.'

'Brave be damned,' answered Hamilton in annoyance. 'In the beginning he probably thought that I'd give in, that he'd outwit me with his endurance. Ridgeway forgets. I'm older than he is.

I've been around. Yes, I've seen things. Besides it's all over and done with now. Edwina is on the mend.'

'Don't you think he should at least be told? That Edwina's alright. Or maybe even let him visit her. Just the once. Father, Ridgeway has been coming here for eighteen days straight.'

'You think I don't know that? I was the one who told him to get off my land.'

'Why do you dislike him so much?'

Hamilton leant on the doorframe. 'Just like your mother. Caroline was born with the superlative habit of niggling and niggling until she got her way.'

'I was just asking. He paid back the loan and he obviously cares about Edwina.' Aiden glanced at his sister. 'He's a potential suitor.'

'He is not. Have you forgotten his high-handed manner the day we first met him? And there are other things that have occurred. Things I'll tell you about another time.'

'I still think you should allow Ridgeway to see her. It's the right thing to do,' argued Aiden.

'Really? Considering your recent behaviour towards your sister that is a tremendous statement to make.'

Aiden turned the damp cloth on Edwina's brow. 'Things are different now.'

'Yes,' admitted Hamilton, 'they are.' The threshold of his daughter's bedroom was yet to be crossed. It was easier to see her from afar. The variegated light stippling the timber boards. The creeping shadows stilled by fledgling health revealing ashen features. 'Is she comfortable?'

'I think so.'

Around the room lay the accoutrements of injury and illness. Bandages, water, Davidson's daily gathering of pungent leaves and twigs that were burnt in the hearth every night and Han Lee's concoctions, the Wywanna town doctor having long since given up hope. Hamilton took a step away from death's trappings, his cane bashing the floor. There would be no feasting for the devil, as yet.

'Have you made a decision?' asked Aiden. 'About the property?'

'It's the shoulder that troubles me, son. What if she's a cripple?' he shared, having promised not to articulate the most terrible of thoughts. 'And she went behind my back. Took advantage. That's something not lightly forgiven.'

Aiden nodded thoughtfully. At least his boy understood. That was his son's greatest asset – he would never overstep the mark. 'Wake Edwina and bring her out here to sit in the sun.'

Aiden touched his sister's arm. 'And Ridgeway?'

'The man must be a fool to stand out in the heat the way he does. Anyway I really can't put up with him hanging about anymore. Every day, like some loitering swaggie hopeful for a scrap of food. The whole thing's untenable, preposterous. He should know better. Have some pride. But a good birth is no indication of sensibility. None at all.' Hamilton twisted the bottom of the walking stick into a wayward ant. 'If it takes one visit with Edwina for him to be on his way, then so be it.'

'So you'll let him see her?'

Hamilton dragged the wicker chair on the rear verandah into the sun and plumped the cushion. 'Wake her. Get your sister up.'

Never had the length of the homestead seemed so long a walk. But at least Hamilton could move with relative confidence, a boon when it came to confronting the enemy. In the parlour the rifle hung enticingly above the fireplace. Reluctantly he marched on, depositing the cane at the front door and stepping out into far too fine a day.

Once on the verandah they faced off. Mason squinting into the sun, towards the house; Hamilton fixing on a point above Ridgeway's right shoulder, lamenting on the chance of that bullet having strayed. The urge to go back inside and slam the door became almost unbearable, but Hamilton appeased his anger with one thought.

It had taken just shy of three weeks; however, very soon the boy would know his place. And he, Hamilton Baker, would have won.

Beyond the ever-present Ridgeway, the Chinese were working on the Sunshine Harvester. The horse-drawn wood-framed reaper with its sturdy metal wheels and five-foot comb was a cumbersome looking thing but it could gather and thresh the ripe heads, separate the grain from the chaff and deliver it for bagging. When it was operating. At the moment it was broken down and harvest was already in full swing.

'My daughter is recovering,' began Hamilton, drawing his attention from the plaited-haired men oiling his machine. 'You can see her, Ridgeway. Once only. And then you will go and never come back here. Are we understood? Never.' The boy's hesitation was obvious. 'I'll only make this offer once. Shake on it. You will never set foot on my land again.'

'If they're the terms,' Mason called across the grass, 'I accept.'

'Around the back of the house. You'll find her on the verandah.' Hamilton waited for Ridgeway to approach, their hands finally clasping firmly but briefly, their eyes reflecting mutual animosity. Hamilton liked it that way. He knew where he stood.

Once the loiterer was gone Hamilton sat at the porch table staring blankly ahead. From between the gum trees a tawny creature stuck its head out from behind the smooth-barked trunk. Hesitant in movement, the lion cub crept carefully across the ground, its gaze never leaving Hamilton as it suddenly broke into a run, diving under the house. It returned occasionally to chew the bones left behind by the dogs or play with old Jed. Canny with timing, no-one else was ever around.

One yell, and the animal's presence would be known. One command and its capture a certainty, Davidson's death-blow quick. Why were they bothering with the trap? The lion should be shot.

Hamilton didn't know why he let the creature alone. Perhaps it was simply because the baby lion had not done him any wrong.

⚔ Chapter Forty-two ⚔

Bed was the only place Edwina wanted to be. However, Aiden was insistent and he carried her out to the verandah, draping a blanket across her knees. Although she'd been sitting up in bed for the last two days, staring listlessly at the outside world, it was still a shock to be transplanted to the verandah with its hard-backed seat and too vivid sky. A myriad pains cascaded through her, ebbed and flowed in an unwelcome tide. Her brother began brushing her hair. Edwina told him to stop fussing, to leave her alone. This waking from torpor with the milling expectation from Aiden and Constance that she was almost whole again was wrong. Broken was how Edwina best described her condition, and some parts would never repair.

It was enough managing the small tasks of living. The breathing in of tepid air, the ache that sprang from a useless arm and the sickness that harboured in her stomach yet to be teased away. There were thoughts too. A swirl of memories good and bad to mingle with the pain. And the understanding that she nearly died. How was it she'd come to cheat death?

Beside her Jed yawned. 'Where are all the other dogs?' she asked.

'Tied up.' Aiden placed a shawl across her shoulders. 'Father says they are to be kept chained unless they're taken out on the property. It's because of the lion cub.'

'It's still alive?' said Edwina.

'Yes, but we'll capture it.' He adjusted the shawl.

It was too much — this bedside bustling — and she told her brother as much.

'What is the matter with you? Yesterday you slapped the bowl from Constance's hands.' Aiden threw the hairbrush into the bedroom. It clattered to the floor.

'I'll eat when I'm hungry. I'll not be forced.'

Aiden frowned. 'You'll eat when you're told.'

Edwina was still smarting from the indecency of the sponge bath the girl gave her. It seemed the hours were filled with Aiden and the aboriginal girl, but not her father; there was no sign of him since she'd woken and Edwina had not asked to see him. 'I'm tired, Aiden.'

'Father says you have to get stronger. Twice a day for an hour each you're to sit out here.'

'And if I don't want to?'

Aiden shrugged. 'Then you can walk back to bed by yourself.'

'It was Father who shot me?' Confirmation wasn't required. The sickbed imagining became reality with consciousness. And people wondered why she was ill at ease.

'Yes, it was. We wondered how much you remembered. It was an accident.' Aiden dragged a stool next to her, sitting a glass of water on it.

As far as Edwina could remember Aiden hadn't been there. 'Did Father tell you that?'

'Ridgeway said it was a mistake. That the rifle went off by itself,' explained Aiden. 'He carried you inside. I came home about an hour later and then went into town to fetch the doctor.'

'And then?' asked Edwina.

'Ridgeway left.'

Of course he would have. Why would Mason linger when he'd almost been killed? Edwina doubted their wealthy neighbour's return. There was a madness in this homestead and any right-minded person would do well to keep clear. Mason did what was required and then lied about the incident to Aiden, protecting all of her family. They didn't deserve such help. Edwina touched the bandaged shoulder. 'I dreamt there were maggots in my arm.'

'It was just a dream, Edwina, just a bad dream.' He patted her hand. 'Comfortable? Because you have company. I'll leave you two alone.'

The caller was unexpectedly standing before her.

'Mason?' said Edwina in surprise.

'How are you?' He moved to sit on the edge of the verandah at her feet.

It was so good to see him again. Edwina could feel his strength, the vitality running through his veins. She coveted that glowing good health, but more than that Edwina craved his company and comfort. 'Better,' she answered quietly, grateful now that her hair was brushed. It was difficult to form the right words. How did someone apologise for their father trying to kill him? You couldn't. 'I wanted to thank you for what you did, lying about the shooting.'

'It seemed the best thing,' replied Mason kindly. 'I was worried about you, Edwina. You've been sick for a long time. Eighteen days. How are you feeling?'

Was it really nearly three weeks since the accident? He was staring at the thick bandage on her shoulder. At the man's shirt she wore with the sleeve cut off. Edwina guessed how she appeared. Thin, pale and tired. And yet there was hope that they could still be friends, for he'd come back. 'I'm better, thank you. Have you seen my father?'

'Briefly,' replied Mason.

'I haven't, not since I woke.'

Around them the trees of the orchard dropped leaves that fell still to the earth.

'I'm sorry to hear that,' said Mason. 'It might take some time for him to come to terms with what he did.'

'It will take time for all of us.' Her father, guilty? Edwina never would have thought such an emotion possible.

'Luke sends his best wishes. He wanted me to tell you that the purchase of Condo Station is on hold until you are fully recovered.'

'I haven't thought of it, Mason, and truly I don't see how it could possibly go ahead now.'

'You will get better, Edwina,' said Mason firmly, 'and when you are ready you will sign those papers and become the owner of a fine piece of land.'

Only if her father agrees to it, she thought, for it was his money. The tiredness grew. Edwina struggled against it. 'Apparently my father is much recovered.' Which meant that Baker's Run was no longer hers to control.

'Yes, he seems to be.'

Mason gave nothing away. Had the two men argued? She expected as much, recalling her father's fury that day. It was remarkable that Mason was even allowed to set foot on the property. 'Then there will be no sale,' said Edwina. 'Please tell Luke –'

'I'll tell him nothing. It is your business and must be handled by you. All you need do is send for him. He will come with the papers when you're ready.'

'And if I'm not ready, ever?'

'Has your father taken so very much from you, Edwina, that even your spirit has gone?'

'Maybe we have taken from each other,' she admitted. 'Father and I both have our wounds.'

Mason rose. A hand forming a fist and then releasing, his anger controlled. 'I don't understand your family, Edwina. You bash at

347

each other like a raging wind and still you come back for more. I can't comprehend that type of loyalty. I really can't.'

Edwina felt he wanted to say more. There was a look about him. It may have been longing, but perhaps that was her wishing and, besides, she didn't know Mason well enough to know for sure. 'I'm sorry we argued that day.' She could forgive him his deception. It seemed such a small matter now.

'So am I. I must go. I promised not to stay long. Look after yourself. Be well.'

Edwina didn't want him to leave. She needed his quiet assurance, the sensible confidence. 'You will come back again?'

'To this property, this house?' Mason peered upwards into the orchard's canopy where streams of light sifted downwards. 'No, Edwina. I'll never set foot here again.'

She swallowed the sob in her throat. 'I'm very sorry to hear that.'

'What's done is done. Take care. Be well.' He leant down, kissing her softly on the cheek.

She listened as he walked away. That was it then. Considering her initial reluctance to walk out with Mason why would he persist now, even for friendship's sake? It had taken eighteen days for Mason to come and see her. To check on how she was. Edwina realised she was lucky that he'd come back at all.

❈ Chapter Forty-three ❈

A few days later Edwina was finally sitting at the dining-room table again. Hamilton hoped for something of a reunion with a roast leg of mutton, beans and potatoes served up by the smiling aboriginal girl.

'Good. We are all here. A family once again.' It was the first time he'd seen Edwina properly, up close. The first time since Ridgeway had scooped up his daughter, carrying her to the bedroom and then tending the wound. Ripping off the blouse and stemming the blood with his own hands. Tipping rum down her throat for the pain. Giving instructions. Hamilton understood that these ministrations went beyond concerned decency. Ridgeway cared for his daughter.

'Father,' said Edwina in acknowledgment as Aiden cut up her food.

'Edwina. To your good health.' There was no need for untidy words or platitudes. Simply a prayer of thanks for the food before them and her return to health. The subject need never be discussed again.

They ate quietly, the conversation stilted. Hamilton attempted once or twice to talk of happenings on the property: the work ethic of the Chinese, the tangible evidence of the pear dying – fledgling attempts that barely received a response. He watched as his daughter stabbed at the bloody meat with a fork, the liquids dripping, the injured left arm unmoving. Aiden glanced up from an already near-empty plate, eager to be gone. Yes, his family were indeed all back sitting at the table, on his property, this misery farm. Best to get things over with then.

Hamilton placed the folder before his daughter. Waited for the hurried explanation, the excuses, the plea for forgiveness. Edwina flipped open the file. Hamilton watched the pale, expressionless face studying the legal papers sent from Wywanna's solicitor.

'It's the legal documentation for Condo Station,' Aiden blurted.

Hamilton observed the slow pulse in Edwina's neck. A blue thread in diaphanous white.

He was against the purchase of the western Queensland property. Any man, any father in his position would be. Edwina was far too quick to act. It was as if she hoped for his death or at least an ailment that rendered him incapable of heading the household. Such duplicity would sour any relationship but for a child to attempt such a thing, Hamilton knew that this was a wounding that would take some time to recover from, if ever.

Across the table his daughter studied the document, holding her injured arm as she peered at the settlement details. This was an audacious act. Edwina's defiance was not over some small plot of land; instead the proposed transaction was enormous and the venture was brokered by Luke Gordon. Not him.

That fact stuck in Hamilton's craw and he didn't like it. Not one little bit. Discarded and overridden by a presumptuous daughter. His money parlayed by a rich outsider. And yet he was conscious of one overarching fact. Hamilton didn't have the gumption to embark on such a scheme. How could she, a mere slip of a girl, have the temerity to believe that she was capable of running such an enterprise? It made the mind boggle.

'As you can see, Edwina, I know about your little escapade,' said Hamilton. 'You were quick to see me kick the bucket.'

'The property is broke,' countered his daughter. 'The money-lending was our lifeline. I was trying to prevent a disaster.'

'Two days after my fall? Without even pausing to contemplate my recovery? I'd applaud the forethought if it wasn't a little too fast for my taste. Unconscionable behaviour.' The words bounced off the timber walls. Edwina stared at him. Aiden's mouth opened. Their faces said it all. They judged him, even his son. As if it were their right to weigh his faults and find their father wanting.

'Don't look at me like that,' he thundered. 'The shooting was an accident, while your actions were unforgivable. It is my money you were intent on using. Mine!'

'I know, but I acted with good reason, Father. You were severely injured and the property has not been making any money for a number of years. Every time I tried to offer a suggestion as to the running of the business you've ignored me.' She turned to her brother. 'Both of you have. What was I supposed to do? Wait and hope for you to recover only to be told that I had no idea what I was talking about? That I was only a woman and as such should stay out of men's affairs? I was trying to do something that would help this family. It is a good business decision.'

'It was a good decision for you, you mean.' Hamilton knew the dinner would digress to this. A messy finish.

'You intended to shoot an innocent man,' argued Edwina.

Hamilton shrugged. 'A trespasser on my land, Edwina. *My land.*' He settled in the chair as his children dropped their gazes. Hamilton was determined to ensure their lives returned to a semblance of normality. First, however, his own position as head of the household needed to be re-established. No-one was going to make a fool out of him, least of all his own daughter. 'Do you remember what I told you the day of the shooting? That Ridgeway came when you were away and asked permission to walk out with you.'

That's what he wanted, that look on Edwina's face, the obvious desire to know more. He was right then. Here was a singular opportunity to make his daughter understand once and for all the difference between right and wrong and that included staying away from people like their neighbour. 'And Charles Mason Ridgeway? Are you still enamoured with the man?'

'What sort of question is that?' queried Edwina.

So he'd stirred her from the lethargy. Two bright spots of colour dotted Edwina's cheeks. A far greater response than the one elicited by the thought of title deeds. They'd been together that morning. Embracing. Edwina's beatific face poised and waiting for a kiss. He was right then. The truth was out. Edwina was in love with the man and no doubt believed Ridgeway would come for her once she was well. It wasn't going to happen. There had to be a totalling of accounts.

Aiden was sworn against telling his sister of Ridgeway's daily vigilance. Promised never to reveal that a bargain was struck between Hamilton and Ridgeway. One visit only. Never to return.

'Charles Mason Ridgeway is no good. Well, you must know that yourself, my dear, considering you thought him another person altogether. He can't be trusted.' Hamilton dabbed at the corners of his mouth with a napkin. Constance was a far better cook than the old Scotswoman.

'And?' asked Edwina.

'You have proved ungrateful, but considering everything that has occurred I will make you an offer. You can have one of two things. Charles Ridgeway or Condo Station. Love or land. Your brother sits here as witness. What we agree on tonight will be adhered to.'

Edwina looked to Aiden. Clearly she doubted the proposition. Her brother bowed his head.

Patience was not a virtue Hamilton was endowed with, but he was quite prepared to bide his time. He knew women. Understood the muddled ticking of their hearts. His daughter may well be running her hand across the legal papers; however, her mind would be on that kiss. The thought of it. Of what it could bring. Escape and love. With the promise of money. And wasn't that what his daughter aspired to – a better life? Edwina would choose Charles Mason Ridgeway only to discover that the landed upstart was no longer interested. They had shaken hands on it and a gentlemen's agreement was never broken. So his daughter would choose him and lose Condo Station. Lose the two things she hankered for. No-one, least of all his daughter, was stealing his money, no matter how plucky the venture. Hamilton considered it a life lesson. He'd been through far worse.

'I choose the property,' came Edwina's slow reply. She rested her good arm on the edge of the dining table. 'Also I'll need money for livestock and staff, Father. But all that, including the purchase price, is in a budget already drawn up. One that's been checked by Luke Gordon. You would have seen it in the study.' She halted, wavering for the first time.

What had she said? The consumed mutton began to rise in Hamilton's throat. This wasn't at all what he'd planned. How could this be when Edwina was a woman with feminine failings? Why did she not choose Ridgeway?

'Father?'

Aiden was speaking, worrying about the overtiring of his sister.

That compressing of the lips, which Hamilton so often considered as petulance in his daughter was, he understood, something far more formidable: determination.

'Father?' prompted Aiden.

Saints preserve him. Outplayed by his daughter. Hamilton pushed back the chair, undoing the necktie that threatened to strangle him. The boy was witness. There was no reneging on his word and yet the thought of all that money. What could he do? There was no manoeuvre available in this simplest of options he'd devised and offered, a choice between two things.

'Was that not the answer you expected?' asked Edwina. There was no coy sweetness, only curiosity. 'Anyway, it is a small amount compared to your share portfolio.'

Hamilton reached for the water glass on the table. 'I never know what to expect these days, my girl,' he answered between gulps. 'It's up to you if you want to waste your life – and *my money* – on a block of dirt in the middle of nowhere. You thought it tough here. Wait till you move out west with the blacks and the flies and the dust. Then you'll wish for your old life back. Then you'll wonder why you ever complained while under my roof. And you will be moving out there as soon as you are well enough to travel. Sign the papers. I'll ensure the full purchase price is paid tomorrow.'

'Father,' interrupted Aiden, 'you can't send Edwina out there alone. It's not right.'

Reaching for the cane, leaning on the table, Hamilton rose. 'Your sister wanted the place and went behind my back to ensure she got it. Well now, Edwina will soon be the owner of Condo Station. And as the owner she must live there.' He turned to his daughter. 'There will be money for an overseer not a manager. That is your job, my dear.'

'But, Father,' Aiden stood, gestured to his sister, 'we don't even know if Edwina will be able to use her arm properly yet.'

'If she thought that were a possibility, Aiden, your sister wouldn't be taking on the responsibility. Would you, Edwina? Besides, she has Luke Gordon to assist her with any problems that may arise. She certainly doesn't need us. Do you, my dear?'

Edwina exhaled loudly.

'You see,' said Hamilton, 'she is relieved to be going out there alone. So now,' he rubbed his hands together, 'everyone is happy. You will have to get organised, my dear, to ensure you're there by Christmas.'

'Christmas – this is ridiculous,' complained Aiden.

'It's probably for the best, Aiden. Once I have left for the station Father will undoubtedly feel happier bringing the divorcee, Mrs Gloria Zane, home as his wife.'

A tightness erupted in Hamilton's chest. If not for the walking stick he may well have stumbled. What else did this little miss know? This daughter with her cunning ways. This girl-woman born of an inadequate wife. 'It's best you leave as soon as possible.'

'For once, Father,' answered Edwina, 'we are in agreement.'

≈ Chapter Forty-four ≈

Aiden collected the mail from Mrs Landry's Inn and, arriving home, set it on the table. With no-one venturing off the property since the shooting there was a pile of letters and papers to go through.

'Where is Edwina?' asked Aiden, removing his hat.

'Who knows,' answered Hamilton, tossing the unopened bills onto a table. 'Any news?'

Aiden sat down, crossing his legs. He smelt of horse sweat. 'Only that there's been a big crash in America on Wall Street.'

Hamilton looked at his son. 'What did you say?'

'Mrs Landry says it's in all the papers. There are businessmen committing suicide, companies have gone bust and some of the banks have closed.'

Hamilton rifled through the mail. There were a number of newspapers in the pile and he began scanning the headlines, his mind returning to Gloria and the collapse of the London market in September. 'This can't be happening. It isn't possible.'

'What isn't possible, Father?' asked Aiden. 'Whatever is the matter?'

The headline, when he finally found it, said it all. The American markets had lost thirty billion dollars in the space of two days. They were already in the first week of November. The crash had been and gone. The markets were still in turmoil. The paper fell to the floor. 'I'm ruined.'

'Father, are you going to tell me what's going on?' Aiden poured rum into a glass and handed it to him. 'Remember what Han Lee said. You're on the mend but you must try and not upset yourself.'

Hamilton swallowed the rum. It did nothing for him. The majority of his life savings were invested in shares. Among the letters was a telegram from his broker outlining the worst of his fears, but also offering some hope. There was still some money left. His advisor of fifteen years was savvy enough to sell the few Australian shares Hamilton held at the first whiff of what was happening abroad. His losses were major; however, there was some money left and it now sat in another of his personal bank accounts. An account safe from prying eyes, including those of his daughter.

'Father?'

'I don't want to talk about it, Aiden. Suffice to say that I too have suffered from this disaster.'

'Oh.'

If Edwina were here she would begin questioning him. Asking the size of his investments, the companies involved and the extent of his portfolio. What the possibility was of getting any of the money back. He could have done with the girl right now. Would have enjoyed venting his fury and shock at his enquiring daughter. But she wasn't here and there was no recouping what had been lost and he certainly wasn't giving Edwina the satisfaction of knowing of this setback. He looked to his son. 'Not a word to your sister.'

'But, Father, what about Condo Station. Shouldn't you reconsider her buying of it? I mean, if you've lost on the share market don't we need the money?'

'She wanted the blasted place so she can have it. Good riddance.'

'But, Father?'

'Not a word, Aiden. Not one word.' He held out his glass. 'More rum.'

⋘ Chapter Forty-five ⋙

A week later Edwina was in the parlour drawing up an inventory of station supplies and cross-checking it against one mailed to her by Luke Gordon. The requirements were considerable. Apart from the large quantities of flour, sugar, potatoes, vegetable seedlings and tobacco, there were bits and pieces needed, ranging from axes, nails and ammunition to saddlery items. Fortunately, as the station was government owned and being sold on a walk-in walk-out basis, everything from draught and stock horses to a number of drays and wagonettes, as well as a buggy, were included in the sale. Edwina glanced up from the exhaustive list as Aiden arrived back from Wywanna.

Constance set down the tray things. 'Anything else, miss?'

'An extra cup for Aiden please; he's just arrived home by the sounds of it.'

'Yes, miss. And the boss?' asked Constance.

'Not with me,' answered Aiden, entering the room and flopping down in the seat opposite Edwina.

Constance fetched a teacup from the sideboard in the drawing room and setting it on the tray left brother and sister alone.

Edwina smiled fondly at Aiden. The one thing buoying the thought of leaving her childhood home was the knowledge that Han Lee and his team would travel with her at the end of harvest. Her father was not pleased with this arrangement but as the Chinese were not contracted to do further work on Baker's Run, no agreements had been broken. The plots of land Han Lee now owned on the outskirts of Wywanna were to be run by other family members.

'Fernleigh's dead,' said Aiden. 'Found strung up on the other side of the dingo fence. He'd been mauled by dogs and pigs.'

Edwina gasped, setting her notes to one side. 'Who told you?'

'Everyone was talking about it at the Post Office.'

'He did it then?' Edwina didn't dare speak Davidson's name aloud.

'I suppose so. It's difficult to think otherwise. I always thought Fernleigh was involved. I mean who else could it have been? Father and Fernleigh do have history.'

'Do you think, is there any chance –'

'That Davidson will be connected to the murder?' interrupted Aiden. 'I doubt it.'

'I know there was little we could have done to stop it occurring, but it shouldn't have happened.'

'Lots of things shouldn't have,' replied Aiden.

The reproach stung. Her brother chose to remain quiet regarding the purchase of the property but she knew in her heart that Aiden didn't agree with her actions.

'Don't make of mess of things, will you, Edwina. I mean that's my inheritance you're playing with.'

'I'm entitled to a share, Aiden.'

'Husbands usually provide for their wives,' he countered.

'Well, I have no husband, do I? And anyway, there's still money. Father has it squirrelled away.'

'You better read this. I didn't say anything sooner because Father was adamant I didn't tell you.'

The newspaper Aiden passed her carried a headline speaking of a massive stock market crash in New York. Millions had been lost. There were stories of businessmen killing themselves. 'This is horrid.' Edwina met Aiden's concern. 'Father's shares?'

'I left him in town, Edwina. He's waiting to hear back from his broker about other investment opportunities. Father estimates he's lost at least sixty percent. The problem is that most of his shares were American. I thought you might reconsider your leaving now you know.'

If Hamilton Baker were in a bad mood before, Edwina mused, wait until he returned home having paid for a property he didn't want and now being faced with a financial crisis. She stared at the headline. Edwina knew that she should feel guilt-ridden. That a measure of accountability should compel her to sign over Condo Station to her father.

'I'm sorry, Aiden. I feel unhappy for Father's loss but I can't forgive the hardships we've been forced to endure when there has been money all along. More money than we could dream of.'

'Not anymore,' replied Aiden with a frown.

'When did he find out about this?' asked Edwina.

'A week ago.'

'Don't you see? Father could have told me about his stock losses or simply reneged on our agreement, but he didn't, Aiden. He wants me to leave.' Edwina folded the newspaper. She couldn't forgive any of it, their father's hiding of his true worth, the slap to her face and the cutting down of their mother's tree. The shooting was the final act. A curtain call. The property was her chance at a new life. 'There is still the farm and the remaining shares. You and Father will survive quite handsomely. If he chooses to share any of it with you.' It was enough. What was done could not be undone. 'There is another option. You should come with me, Aiden,' she offered. 'Start afresh.'

'I'm not like you, Edwina. I've never been very good with figures. Not the way you and Father are. And besides, if I went to Condo Station I'd be taking orders from you and we both know how long that would last before we eventually argued.' He folded his hands in his lap. 'I don't agree with your leaving or the way you went about things and I worry about you out there all alone when –'

'When I'm only a woman?' completed Edwina.

Her brother reddened. 'It's best I stay here with Father. He and I are chalk and cheese. I do what he says and I'm happy with that. And he needs someone around. No matter what he thinks. He needs family.'

He'd matured overnight, they all had. Well, there were different degrees of level-headedness. Edwina and her father were yet to speak or eat at the same table since the night she'd been given the ultimatum.

'Well, there'll be no stopping Mrs Gloria Zane now.' Edwina folded the newspaper. 'You best get ready for her imminent arrival after I'm gone.'

'Mrs Zane's left Wywanna, Edwina, and Father doesn't expect she'll be back.'

'What? When?'

Her brother shrugged. 'A few weeks ago I think. Father told me about her when we went to his rooms in town to drop off some things. Well, he had to. The place is so gaudy. Hardly Father's taste.'

Edwina pondered the divorcee's departure, speculating on which party instigated the end of the affair. It was a sorry mess and knowledge of it stung.

'No wonder he's been in a bad mood.' Aiden took the paper Edwina still held, turning to the third page. 'This is the other thing I wanted you to see.'

Woman buys Queensland Station

'That's you, Edwina,' Aiden tapped the paper, 'you're a headline. The paper is four days old but I saw Mrs Hilton in the Post Office and she'd heard from cousins down south that you made the papers in every state, including Tasmania. You know what she said to me? She said, "Aiden, you must be very proud and whoever would have thought that your father was so progressive."'

They sat in stunned silence before bursting out in laughter.

'I can't believe it,' said Edwina, wiping her eyes.

'Neither could I. Are you sure you want to do this, Edwina?'

Placing the *Wywanna Chronicle* aside, Edwina poured tea, her left arm in a sling. 'Even if I wanted to stay it wouldn't work. We both know that. Father and I are like a torn sheet of paper. He on one piece and I on the other. Too much has happened.'

'You say that, but sometimes when I see you two talking it's like a mirror image.' Aiden reached for his teacup. 'Do you hate Father now?'

'No,' she answered thoughtfully. 'I'm disappointed mostly. I feel like I hardly know him. Anyway,' she took a sip of the tea, 'I wouldn't have stayed here for much longer, even if the shooting hadn't happened. But it did. And you should know, Aiden, that Father missed his target. He was trying to shoot Mason that morning.'

The cup and saucer Aiden held rattled. 'He was what?'

'Hate is a very dangerous thing.'

Aiden ran fingers through his hair. 'I can't believe it. I knew he was furious that day at Ridgeway Station. Father and our neighbour definitely didn't get on. But shoot him?'

'It wasn't an accident, as Mason said. Father was shaking too much to aim straight and I ran forward at the wrong moment,' Edwina said ruefully. 'I keep asking myself what occurred to create such animosity,' she added thoughtfully. 'Not that we'll probably ever hear about it.'

'He blamed Ridgeway for the shooting. I know that much. It really makes the offer of the land or Ridgeway quite extraordinary.'

Edwina's brow furrowed. 'Why?'

Aiden rubbed at the fuzz that he was doing his best to coax into a moustache, much to their father's dismay. 'Ridgeway was here every day for eighteen days straight waiting for word of your recovery following the shooting.' He glanced at his sister. 'I'm sorry, I was sworn to secrecy. Anyway, Father ignored him. Even when things looked awfully grim he forbade anyone from speaking to him, but Ridgeway stood out there on the flat every morning for hours. Finally Father had enough. He said Ridgeway could visit you once only if he promised never to come here again. Then he gave you that choice. The land or Ridgeway.'

Edwina moved to the window, pulling aside the curtains drawn against the heat; outside, the country lay burnished brown. In the distance a cart held hessian bags of harvested wheat. One of the Chinamen was standing atop the dray, bending down to sew up the bags. Fourteen equally spaced stitches. It was the first year in Edwina's memory that the task of closing the sacks had not been hers. The wind lifted the wheat chaff, blowing the itchy fragments towards the house.

'It's difficult to believe Mason stood out there waiting for word of my recovery,' she finally replied. And yet he obviously had. He did care for her. Worried about her. Edwina drew the curtains closed and fronted her brother. 'So Father's intention was that I would lose both. I'd choose Mason, not knowing the bargain they'd struck. The problem is, Aiden, that when I last saw Mason he said he wouldn't be coming here ever again. So you see, I never thought there was a choice to be made.' She sat down, pouring more tea.

'So Father was fooled by his own trick.' Aiden leant forward in the horsehair chair. 'I'm sorry, I should have supported you. I should have told you sooner. But if you'd known that Mason cared about you, that he'd agreed to Father's condition just to see you one last time, would you have chosen differently?'

In the bottom of the cup the tea-leaves gradually settled. 'That's the problem, Aiden. I don't know.'

⊰ Chapter Forty-six ⊱

A month later

The brown wagons came into view escorted by Han Lee and Davidson. Edwina observed their approach, a hand shading her face as the wind blew the dust from their wheels towards the house in low, prickly sheets. The compact Clydesdales pulling the wagons walked with a smart gait, their feet lifting neatly from the ground and placed well forward in their stride. The draughthorses were known for being strong and long lasting, Edwina was depending on that. Three weeks of travel lay ahead once they left the property, a staggered journey with extra stops planned, their speed dependent on Edwina's health. Her body was slow to reach full recovery. A tiredness struck daily, demanding a midday sleep, and her appetite was limited. But leave they would in the morning, a useless left arm dangling painfully at her side, uncertainty a constant companion. On the verandah the shadow of her father disappeared through the front door with a slam.

Two of Han Lee's men were the drivers and they steadied the eight horses drawing each van in their oriental tongue, the two wagons creaking to a halt at the edge of the gum trees bounding the homestead. Han Lee rode at the front, Davidson at the rear ensuring protection, the two men never riding side by side. Edwina wet her lips, tasting dirt and beads of perspiration. If there was a choice to stay at least for a few more months . . . but there wasn't. It was time.

The distinctive wagons with their yellow undercarriages were fully loaded beneath arches of flapping canvas. Although she would make a show of inspecting the contents, with Han Lee in charge of the stores there was no better person to take delivery of the order. It took little conjuring to imagine the scene in Wywanna. The Chinaman and the aboriginal collecting the supplies ordered by the woman who'd purchased Condo Station. Edwina almost wished she'd been there.

Han Lee slid from his ride on her approach. Davidson watched them from a distance.

'It is all here?' asked Edwina.

'I checked everything. Twice.'

She knew Han Lee would. 'Good.' Edwina examined the contents of each wagonload, waiting as he undid the folded canvas, allowing her to peer inside the dark interior. 'Do you think we've forgotten anything?'

'No, Miss Edwina. Everything is here. But you? I worry about the travel.' He glanced at her arm, the waistband of the skirt hanging loose at the waist, clinched by a wide leather belt. 'It will be rough. No number of blankets and cushions will stop the jolting. I still think it would be better to wait. At least another month.'

'I know you mean well, Han Lee.'

'You are a very stubborn woman,' he commented.

She grinned in spite of the ordeal that lay ahead. 'I know.'

'There was a commotion in town. Once word got out that they were your supplies, a crowd gathered. Everyone wanted to see the woman who purchased the station. They were disappointed I think.'

Edwina would have shrugged were her shoulder capable of the movement. 'There is not much to see.'

'And your father,' continued the Chinaman, 'have you spoken with him yet? Have you made your peace with him?'

Edwina glanced towards the homestead. 'Our peace comes with no words, Han Lee. My father is a complicated person. Perhaps I am as well,' she added.

'He is a hard man, Miss Edwina, but he does his best. We will unhitch the horses and stable them for the night.' He gestured to the two drivers who began undoing the thick leather harnesses. 'Daylight then?'

'Yes, we leave at daylight.'

Davidson dismounted, observing the activity as if doubting the men's ability.

'I am to come with you, miss.' Constance appeared from the kitchen, shooing the chickens yet to be penned for the evening.

Edwina tilted her head. 'No, Constance, you have to stay here with my father and brother.'

'No, miss. Mr Baker said I'm to come with you. He don't want people thinking he sent you off with no-one to cook and clean and look after you. And she needs some looking-after she does,' said the girl with a definitive nod to Han Lee, 'she can't cook.'

'Is that what you want, Constance?' asked Edwina kindly, choosing to ignore the jibe.

The girl sought Davidson's approval. 'I got myself in trouble here, Miss Edwina. Best I go with you and keep my nose clean.'

'And what about you, Davidson?' asked Edwina. She didn't want Constance to have to defer to Davidson; however, they were married.

'He agrees, Miss Edwina,' the girl answered.

'Can you find someone else to take her place, Davidson?' Edwina would be grateful for the girl's company. The arrival at their destination would truly see her entering a man's world.

'I can send one of my men?' offered Han Lee.

367

'There'll be another girl here tonight,' replied Constance. The girl flicked an awkward glance at Davidson, plying dirt between her toes. The aboriginal glowered as normal before taking Constance back to the kitchen.

'The girl got in the family way with a white man, Miss Edwina,' explained Han Lee. 'Davidson was none too pleased and I think the person responsible paid a price.'

Edwina gasped. Could that man be Fernleigh or was her imagination running wild? 'How do you know that?'

'The notches on his forearm. We will see you in the morning, Miss Edwina.' Han Lee bowed, moving to oversee the men as the white-patched horses with their thick manes and hair-covered hooves were led away.

Edwina wondered if the death of Fernleigh was marked by scarring and if there was one fresh notch on Davidson's arm or two. If there was only one, she would know the truth of things – that Fernleigh had wronged her father as well as Davidson's young wife. The stockman was clearly the vengeful sort; however, knowing he carried his kills with pride didn't sit easily with her. Now, although shocked, Edwina could only be grateful that the stockman was on their side.

Alone, Edwina walked beyond the wagons, fixing on the gold-red horizon. Perspiration edged down her spine, stuck to the blouse, followed the curve of her thighs and legs. The nervousness was natural she supposed; nonetheless, the north-west track they were to take presented miles of unknown country stretching out towards the setting sun. Days of wearying travel would be interrupted by lonesome nights lying in a swag on the ground. And then at the end of the road, to greet her, a swatch of ground too large to comprehend. Hers to tend and make the most of. Edwina dearly hoped she was capable enough. For having dreamt a future into reality she'd stepped away from girlish fantasies and was about to embark on an expedition that was beyond adventure.

She would have liked to have seen Will one last time. To at least say goodbye. If he did return as promised he would find her long gone and wonder at her leaving. He'd wanted her to wait for him. No, expected her to was more correct. Like Mason, he'd been pushy, demanding, and yet Edwina had seriously considered his offer. It was a means to an end. An opportunity. She thought of him now, with his green eyes and broad smile. The way he'd stride through the orchard seeking her out, his cheekiness the morning she'd cut his hair and the kiss they'd shared. Her first. Had Will come back sooner, she may well have gone with him. But Will was yet to return, if ever, and she was leaving, so she would never know what may have happened between them.

Everything Edwina knew was here on this patch of earth. This irregular box bordered by water and pear and wire fences. A barely sustainable piece of dirt still carrying the voice of her mother, the scampering footsteps of her and Aiden as children and a father she loved but had never truly known. Edwina would never completely leave this land. She had risen from it, been moulded by its big sky and changeable seasons. The property had made her strong. Edwina knelt down, scraping at the baked dirt, cupping the hard-won soil before throwing it into the wind.

≪ Chapter Forty-seven ≫

It was done. Edwina was soon to leave. Outside sat the sturdy drover's wagons filled with stores for a new beginning. By this time tomorrow Caroline's daughter, his eldest, the little girl he'd once bounced on a knee would be gone. Hamilton poured rum into a tumbler, skolling the contents. On the study desk sat a plate of barely touched food, the kerosene lantern turning the meat and cabbage yellow in the half-light. It was not the night for eating. It was a night for drinking. The alcohol eased the aches that rippled down the left side of his body. Niggling twinges that came and went, a constant reminder of that dusty ride back from Wywanna and a brain that refused to reveal the faceless attacker. Would that he were young again, with the lean figure of youth and the intellect of remembering. Someone wished him ill-will but if it had been Fernleigh the man was gone now. Dead and buried.

The air was hot, draping the body with its heavy breath. Christmas would be upon them in a couple of weeks and still no rain. No summer storm to settle the dust or delay the morning's travel. The New Year could not come quickly enough for Hamilton. Months of losses lay in the dregs of this one: Gloria, his failure to do business with Peter Worth and the stock market crash. He'd considered doing himself in. A few were. Had the numbers of victims been greater the decision may have even been considered in fashion in view of the circumstances, but it was the Americans who appeared keen to step off the ledges of high-rises. Out here a fall from the homestead roof was useless.

Hamilton poured more rum, gumming the rim of the glass as he sucked up the dark fluid. There were positives. The heathen Fernleigh was dead, undoubtedly the past catching up with him, and there was still money left. A few shekels to keep the dingoes at bay. Enough for a monthly visit to Wywanna and an opportunity to make use of the rooms he rented. Aiden was old enough to accompany him on these outings now and with Gloria gone he'd be pleased for the company. Come April with the hope of cooler weather, the boy would be ripe for a bit of promenading down the main street. There'd be a bright, young thing wanting to catch his eye. A pretty, long-legged filly eager for that first kiss and the promise it would bring. A farmer's daughter, one of the smaller landowners, would have to suffice. Sensible and thrifty with just enough prettiness to capture a boy's interest.

Prior to the crash Hamilton's ambition was much higher. The money so carefully secreted away, most of that wealth, was to have been Aiden's. Not for his only son the shoddy beginnings he'd contended with. Shielding Aiden from the muck of life was one of Hamilton's great purposes in living. He knew what his boy was and wasn't capable of. Out of everyone in the family he was the least competent when it came to survival. It wasn't the lad's fault. The boy was a descendant of gentlemen. Of English estates and docile domestics. Of hunts and London mansions. There was blue blood in Aiden's veins, however much diluted over the generations, and it was natural once Hamilton breached God's gates, Aiden would need help. A manager to assist in running their holding, perhaps an accountant to check ledgers on a weekly basis, to ensure the

371

finances remained sound. Such things cost money, as did a wife. He needed the boy to survive and comfortably, for Aiden was his only son and he carried the Baker name, offering another chance of recapturing past glories.

Hamilton licked at the empty glass. Difficulties lay ahead, for the residue, the backstop, the monies from Ridgeway's debt that would have gone some way to cushioning the future were now spent on a piece of dirt. And there was nothing he could do about it. What had his mother said, his stubborn streak would be the death of him? Still, there was enough coin remaining to ensure a comfortable future.

Hamilton studied the map of Condo Station with its river frontage, massive paddocks and grassy plains. The middle of nowhere, that's where it was. He scratched at a stubbly cheek, deliberating once again the true worth of the enterprise. Common sense advised not to go near the place. Especially now with the papers talking of a depression. If cattle were bringing a pittance a month ago, they would be close to worthless now. Didn't the girl know that?

Edwina was not one to embark lightly on anything and there was a grit within her now that baulked at failure. It had been in her since childhood, along with that determined mouth. Trapped by a wily daughter, Hamilton took some time to swallow the cud of anger and view the matter coherently. Were Luke Gordon not championing her, Hamilton may well have gone back on his word, reckoning on Edwina quickly going bust, but with Gordon's involvement, how did a businessman ignore the possibilities that could come of such an association? And if Edwina succeeded, if she did well . . .

Hamilton pushed the decanter of rum aside. There'd been too much drink, too much wallowing. Finally clarity was restored. He'd been blind to the prospects of such a partnership. Much could be gained by the relationship. The eligible sons of the landed would be queuing for Edwina's hand now. For his girl offered what every pastoralist wanted of a daughter-in-law: land and beauty. Hamilton comprehended that despite his misgivings he couldn't have done things better if he'd planned this himself.

In a few months, six at least, for Edwina needed to be faced with the loneliness and difficulties associated with her decision, he and Aiden would visit Condo Station. It was, after all, important for a father to check on the welfare of his only daughter, offer assistance if required and ensure that those male of the species who were undoubtedly sniffing around were sorted through and dispatched as necessary. And the sheep? The proceeds from his small mob born of a nucleus of Ridgeway merino blood would be a fine wedding present. He would sell them in a month or so, as the rightful owner wasn't interested. Yes, it was going to be a very busy year.

Carrying the plate from the desk, Hamilton leant down awkwardly, depositing it on the rug. He'd put an end to Davidson's feeding of the animal a month ago and now enjoyed the fruits of having taken the task upon himself. Tapping the boards he sat back and waited. Sometimes it took hours, tonight minutes only. The cub jumped up on the windowsill. Perched there, the animal's ears pricked as if judging the safety of the room, then he sprang down to the floor, padding quietly across to the dish of food. The lion ate hungrily. The creature wasn't always fed such a plentiful dinner and he didn't necessarily return every night. Since that first day of convalescence when Hamilton dragged his body into the parlour, the animal was an infrequent visitor. The cub was canny, bypassing Davidson's attempts at capture, only appearing when Hamilton was alone, quick to depart at anyone's approach. Never to be seen if the dogs were unchained, but happy to roll about with old Jed on the parlour floor. Arriving to stalk back and forth when Hamilton quietly read, or preen itself on one of the chairs, the baby lion became something of a companion, the feeding of it a natural extension.

'So then, little one, you and I are rare creatures I think.'

The big cat, having finished the meal, sat back on its haunches. It was a lean animal now, having grown in the last few weeks. Hamilton noted the muscular thighs, the extent of the paws indicating future size. Visions of a fully grown lion sprawled on the dining-room floor next to his feet came to him and Hamilton chuckled at the whimsical thought. If Gloria were here she would laugh with delight at his eccentricity.

The lion yawned, stretching out on the rug. Hamilton approached the animal carefully. Kneeling on creaking knees, he reached out a hand, gently stroking the soft furry ears. He would miss his new friend. There was something about this exotic cat. The way it rubbed against his legs. Depended on him for food. Came and went silently as if knowing when its presence was required. But like all young things, maturity would be quick to come and Hamilton guessed the lion cub, like Edwina, could turn on him in the future.

The leather dog collar fitted the cub perfectly. The animal scratched at the choker, rolling around the room in an effort to dislodge it. Hamilton shut the window amid the animal's antics. All that was needed was a length of rope to secure the creature.

'I doubt my makings as a father.' Hamilton watched as the cub eventually tired and rubbed at its face with its paws. 'And as you are an orphan, my boy, I think it best that we find you a new home. And I have just the person to take on that responsibility.'

≪ Chapter Forty-eight ≫

Aiden and Davidson carried the trunk out of the room into the scant pre-dawn light. Edwina watched it go; enclosed within were all her belongings. The lantern emitted a dismal glow highlighting a mantelpiece empty of photographs, a bed stripped bare and the dressing table, already dusty. Even the netting above the bed was removed, folded and packed for the journey west. The bedroom that had been her sanctuary over many years now resembled a shell of ageing, cracked timber and an uneven floor. Still, it was hard to leave behind. To know not another morning could be spent gazing out through the orchard to a new day or that sleep would not be accompanied by a swathe of stars and the sprinkle of leaves on the roof. The choice was made but, at this very moment, Edwina found it hard to justify.

'Edwina?'

A figure stood in the doorway. She peered at the outline, lifting the lantern. 'Heavens, Will, is that you?'

He was a shadow in the gloom. 'Yes.' He moved towards the light.

'Will, I never expected to see you again. What are you doing here?' There was a strangeness about him; he swayed slightly, smelling of sweat.

'I said I'd come back, walked most of the night from Wywanna I did. Just to see you, to make sure it was true.' He turned on a heel, noting the empty spaces. 'It *is* true then. I see you chose not to wait.'

The tone of his voice was unsettling and he was clearly exhausted. 'Will, I don't know what to say. So much has changed since you left.'

'Obviously.'

Edwina walked towards him. 'Will,' she said softly. At another time she would have told him how good it was to see him, that he'd been missed, she may have even rushed to his embrace. 'Please don't be angry.' She touched his arm. 'I never expected you to return.'

'Really? But I said I would,' argued Will. 'It's not three months since I left.'

'I know, Will, but –'

'But nothing. You let me kiss you.'

'And you left me with a lion,' Edwina countered, unwilling to discuss their shared intimacy.

'So that's why you're doing this?' replied Will. 'Because of the cub?'

'Of course not, but it was wrong of you to leave it here.'

'Is it still safe?'

'Yes. We've been trying to trap it. It escaped.'

'And then what?' asked Will.

'Then it has to be returned to the circus. It's a danger to everybody.' Edwina sighed. 'What on earth did you think you were going to do with it?'

'I don't know. I thought we would have worked something out. Guess it doesn't matter much now.' He stared at her.

'Don't say that, Will, please. I didn't mean for any of this to happen.'

'From what I hear, you have it all planned out.'

'Then you know that I'm leaving this morning. Heading west to another property.' Outside the sky was brightening. She turned the knob on the lamp and it flickered out.

'Yes.' He stood in the middle of the doorway, rolling a cigarette. A slight beard gave him a rough appearance. 'It's all anyone's talking about in Wywanna. Oh yes, I have ears. They say you're a mighty lady now with thousands of acres and the Gordons themselves giving you a helping hand. So I know why you don't want me anymore. Better offer, eh?'

'No, Will, please don't say that.'

The cigarette flicked between his fingers, still unlit. 'It's the truth though, isn't it?'

'Will, this isn't just about you.'

'Explain to me then, Edwina, why you're doing this? Why you didn't wait?'

She walked across the bare room. Having bought Condo Station, a relationship with Will was now the very last thing on her mind. And there were good reasons why she was able to close the door on the short part of her life he'd shared, ones that went beyond the acquisition of property to the very heart of who she was as a person. It was only fair that she try to explain to Will the reasons why their relationship would never work. 'You told me that you would come back for me, you didn't ask.'

'What?' Will appeared bewildered.

'You didn't ask me, Will,' repeated Edwina. 'You never once questioned me about what I wanted to do, how I wanted to live my life. You just assumed that what you wanted was what I wanted.'

'Wasn't it?'

Edwina didn't answer; surely he understood what she was saying.

'You'd be with me,' said Will.

'Will, all of my life men have been telling me what to do. I can't live that way anymore. I need to be my own person.'

'We'd be together,' argued Will.

'And how did you think that was going to work?' asked Edwina.

'I'd have a job. So would you. I don't understand what you're talking about.'

'And how would we live? In a hut? With our days spent working for somebody else? And me cleaning and cooking in my little spare time?'

'We'd be together,' persisted Will more stubbornly.

'Will, how do I make you understand that it's not enough? It wouldn't be enough for me. I want more out of life.'

'You didn't before.'

'How do you know?' She lowered her voice. 'You never asked.'

Will lit the cigarette and took a deep puff. 'You're worried about money, but we'd make do. Plenty of folk –'

'Will, you're not listening to me. I don't want that life. It's not enough for me. Not now. Not after everything that's occurred.'

'And what has been going on? As I've walked all night to see you,' stated Will, 'you could at least tell me.'

'Okay. Things happened,' Edwina began slowly. 'Father was attacked on the road back from Wywanna, I was accidentally shot.'

'I heard that too. Heard you nearly died.' He drew heavily on the cigarette. 'You remember, don't you, what I said about your father? The papers said it was an accident. Was it an accident or did he mean to shoot you, Edwina? You can tell me. I'd understand.'

How could he understand? Even she didn't understand the complicated relationship with her father.

'There's bad people in the world and just because they're blood kin doesn't mean they can't do harm. I saw the way he treated you. Saw that mighty bruise on your face. And I was worried after I left that he'd hurt you; that's why I followed him that day.'

Edwina grew nervous. 'Followed him what day, Will?'

He drew on the cigarette. 'Coming back from Wywanna.' The exhaled smoke spiralled from his nose and mouth. 'Took an age he did to leave town: first he was at that place he kept for his lover, then at the Post Office. The old man was dead drunk. Could barely walk up the main street. Of course that was the day you made front page news for stealing the lion cub.'

'*You* stole the cub, Will, not me.'

Will ignored this. 'I'd planned on getting to him before he reached the bridge, but there were folks around. I was just going to talk to him, give him a piece of my mind and tell him to leave you alone. Then he caught up with some drovers and spent a time chatting to them. It turned into a long afternoon.'

Edwina took a step away from him. 'It was you who attacked Father?' How was this possible when Fernleigh was dead?

'Gave him what he gave you, I did. A punch to the face. It's against everything I believe in, but he'd hurt you and I wanted to hurt him back, Edwina. I'd done it once before, when my own father bashed my mother, when I was old enough. But I never expected your father to have a turn. No, I never wanted that to happen.'

'Oh, my God.' Edwina lifted a hand to her mouth.

'Your father never saw me coming. I was tired and hungry. I'd waited for hours and I rode straight up and clobbered him one. He fell hard. Like a sack of potatoes. I thought about staying to see if he was alright, but I was so angry at the way he'd treated you, Edwina. I did it for you.'

The bedsprings creaked as Edwina sat on the edge. 'Oh, Will.'

Will's boot crushed the cigarette on the floor. 'If you weren't so good at making yourself a headline I wouldn't have come till next week,' he continued, changing the subject. 'And then you would've been gone. Which would have made it easy for you, wouldn't it? You see, Edwina, I've a job now. It's not much of one, but I've been loading wheat on the trains, so I've money for rooms at a boarding house, I've . . . but it's not good enough now, is it? Not after what you've just told me. I'm not good enough.'

Edwina rose. 'I never said that, Will.'

'But that's what you think, otherwise you'd be asking me to go west to that property of yours.'

Edwina was stunned. 'Will, Aiden will be back any moment to find me. We're due to leave.'

'I thought you were better than that. I thought you loved me.'

'I never said that, Will. Never.' Edwina wrung her hands. 'You must go.' She was worried if her father recognised Will as the attacker, Davidson would kill him. 'Will, you must leave. It's not safe here for you. If my father –'

'You were like the moon to me, Edwina. Did you know that?'

He walked towards her. Gently touching her wounded arm, Will's fingers moved to linger on her neck. Edwina knew she should turn away, but when Will's lips met hers she couldn't. They stood there silently. His arm on her waist, their bodies barely touching. Kissing.

Distantly Jed's bark could be heard. When they broke apart, Edwina looked at Will, wondering what may have been if things were different, if she were different. She did care for him. She really did.

Aiden entered the bedroom. 'What on earth are you doing here? Get away from my sister.' He tugged at Will, yelling for help. Punches were thrown. However, Will was light on his feet; he pushed her brother and he tripped on the bed, falling to the floor.

The room filled with people as dawn broke in the east. Davidson halted Will's escape at the door as Han Lee extended a hand, pulling Aiden up from the timber boards.

The stockman twisted Will's arms behind his back.

'Are you alright, Edwina?' asked Han Lee.

'Yes, I'm fine. Let him go, Davidson. Will was visiting me before I left. He came to say goodbye. This has nothing to do with anyone else. He's done nothing wrong.'

'Except steal a lion cub?' queried Aiden. 'I never imagined my sister capable of such a thing.'

Her father was the last to arrive. He blinked in confusion, clearly wondering at the chaos. Then he saw Will. 'What the hell are you doing here?' The gradual expression of returning memory transformed into fury. 'It was *you*.' He pushed a finger into Will's chest. 'You were the one that punched me on the road that day.'

'It was Will?' Aiden clearly didn't believe it.

Will stopped struggling.

Edwina looked at her brother, then Davidson.

'It wasn't Fernleigh?' said Aiden.

'No,' answered Edwina, 'it wasn't.'

For once, Davidson's expression actually registered surprise.

'Take him away, Davidson.'

Edwina stretched out a hand. 'No, Father. Don't let Davidson take Will. One man has already died because of the attack on you that day.'

'For once in your life, Edwina, stay out of my business!' yelled her father.

Davidson dragged Will outside, binding his wrists with rope.

'Tie him up in the stables, Davidson,' instructed Hamilton. 'We'll see to him later.'

'Aiden, we have to do something,' whispered Edwina. 'If we leave Will to Davidson . . .' She was incapable of articulating what she thought. She rushed to the stockman. 'I know you cut yourself, made a pact to get the person who attacked Father, but please, don't take out your revenge on Will. He's my friend. I care for him.'

Aiden put an arm around her shoulder and began walking Edwina towards the waiting wagons. 'Forget about this. I'll speak to Father and Davidson and see what can be done to satisfy everyone's pride.'

'No.' Edwina ran back to where Davidson and her father were standing with Will. 'It wouldn't be right if anything happened to

Will. And if something does happen I'll inform the police, about everything that's been going on here. And I mean everything.'

Her father scowled. Han Lee stood nearby listening to the conversation and Edwina knew her father would be very aware of witnesses. 'March him up to the front porch, Davidson. Aiden and I will take him to Wywanna and leave him at the town limits.'

'And the lion cub?' asked Will.

'That animal is no concern of yours anymore,' replied her father. 'Consider yourself very lucky, boy, that I don't have you thrown in jail or worse.'

Edwina thanked her father. He grunted in response.

'You will make sure the cub is returned to the circus, Father?'

'Oh he'll have a good home with someone who deserves him,' he answered.

'Goodbye, Will.' Would she ever see him again? Edwina knew it would never have worked between them. For all of Will's concern and care, he needed a woman that would be content with the life he offered. He was better off without her by his side, but it hurt to look upon him knowing it would be for the last time, especially as he returned her gaze with sadness.

'Look after yourself, Edwina,' Will called, as she and Aiden headed back towards the wagons.

'I always knew you liked him,' admitted Aiden with a smile.

'Yes, I do. But he's a friend, Aiden. Just a friend. Nothing could ever have come of it.'

'You best get moving, Edwina.' Her father waved at her from the porch. Will was seated in one of the chairs, Davidson at his side. 'I'm sure you'll understand if an old man doesn't walk you out to your new life.'

What had she expected? A hug or a handshake from her father? They were doing well to be speaking to each other.

Aiden clasped her hand, kissing her on the cheek, wishing Edwina safe travels. 'You will write and tell me all about the trip and what the property is like and –'

Edwina shushed him. 'Yes, yes, I'll do all that. Be well, Aiden.' On the verandah their father waited. 'Look after him.'

'We'll be fine.' Aiden helped her up into the high wooden driver's seat where Han Lee waited to ensure she didn't fall. Lifting Jed, he sat the old dog at her feet. 'Have you enough cushions and blankets?'

'Yes.' Edwina bit her lip.

Another Chinaman took Han Lee's place in the driver's seat and the headman mounted up as the wagons jolted to movement. The teamsters twitched the reins and the vans turned steadily, the horses strong and confident, straightening onto the track that led away from the homestead. Ahead rode Han Lee, behind were their two supply wagons, the walking Chinese gathering together to eventually bring up the rear, two abreast with their hawker wagon the last vehicle in the convoy. The horses walked smartly, the dust pitting their faces in the morning breeze. Edwina grasped the seat with her good right hand, feeling every pothole and crack in the summer-dry ground.

'Are you comfortable, Miss Edwina?' called Han Lee. No longer dressed in a suit and necktie, he wore stockman's attire, the jacket coat-tails flapping on the horse's rump.

'Yes, thank you,' she replied. It was just as well the covered wagon prevented her from a last backwards glance. There were already tears in her eyes and the sight of her father and brother watching the procession, of Will staring after her, their figures dwindling in the distance, would have been far too much.

'You definitely the boss lady now.' Constance gave a wide grin as she ran from the kitchen to the second moving wagon, a bundle of belongings tied in a piece of material.

'Yes,' answered Edwina, 'I guess I am.'

❧ Chapter Forty-nine ❧

The wagons rolled down the road as if floating on waves of dust. There she was, Edwina Baker, travelling westwards to the station that was hers to run. Let's hope she didn't make a disaster of it, Hamilton prayed. For all their sakes, but especially hers. There was more than reputation riding on this. There was money. His. Hamilton thought he caught a glimpse of tawny fur inside the rear of the last dray. The lion cub would be discovered tonight and then it was up to his daughter to find a home for the creature she'd been a party to stealing. She could arrange for it to be returned to the circus. To explain to the authorities how the animal came to be in her possession. So, that was one win to him, at last.

It was done then. Edwina was gone. Dust from the departing wagon train stung his eyes. At least that's what he told himself as he wiped away a tear.

'Father,' interrupted Aiden, 'will we head straight into town?' He glanced to where Will sat guarded by the stockman.

Hamilton pinched the bridge of his nose. He was getting too old for such things. Maybe he should move into Wywanna for a couple of months. Leave his son to handle the farm during the week and then Aiden could join him on the weekends. The house wasn't the same. It hadn't been since the Chinese had cut down Caroline's tree. It was funny how he could pinpoint the exact moment of the change. As if in the woody plant's demise, the extinction of Caroline's frivolous memorial, the homestead had lost meaning for him. Caroline had returned once during Edwina's illness. Her presence had been there that night in her room, but now she was gone and Hamilton doubted his wife's return, even in his imaginings. Quite simply the house he'd built with his own hands didn't mean much anymore.

'Father, did you hear what I said?'

'Yes, yes. In a half-hour or so. Tie him to the chair until we're ready to leave. And I mean restrain him, Davidson. No taking matters into your own hands as I'm led to believe you've done before.' Hamilton met Will's gaze. 'We can't have any shenanigans going on here. There's been enough. We both know after Will's criminal behaviour that the idiot should have been put in a sack with a rock at birth and dumped in a creek, but we can't be taking the law into our own hands.' The stockman gave little away; however, an order had been given and Hamilton expected it to be obeyed. 'As we're on the subject of water, I should tell you that I saw Constance at the creek a couple of months back. She was the woman who drowned the half-caste child. She is your wife?'

This time Davidson nodded, holding up four fingers.

'Your fourth? Good God, man, do you have a death wish? Four wives?'

For the first time since his arrival on the property, Davidson smiled.

'And the child wasn't yours?' No answer was required. The fresh wound on the girl's face that day was evidence enough of her husband's wrath. 'I have one more job for you, Davidson. I want you to go out west with Edwina. Make sure she gets there safely. It's not right she's travelling with all those Chinese. Oh, I'm sure Han Lee is honourable, but how good is he in a fight if it comes to that? And the blacks out there? Well, who is to say how they'll take to a new owner. Talk to them. Placate them. Do whatever needs to be done if there are troublemakers.'

The stockman lifted the shirtsleeve, revealing the scars on his skin, the last relatively recent as if he was marking calendar days not counting lives.

'Yes, I know you can be relied upon to despatch anyone. No doubt you were admired on the Western Front. You didn't think I knew, did you? It was nearly a year after the war ended when you arrived and I noticed your actions immediately. The way you hold a rifle, handle a horse, almost stand to attention in my presence. The mark of an army man is hard to miss. You have my respect and a country's gratitude, even if Australia isn't capable of acknowledging you.'

Davidson observed him with cool detachment.

'See my girl safely out there, Davidson, and then come home. We'll be selling all the sheep in the New Year and Aiden will need as much help as you can give him. And, Davidson, take your people with you. Settle them out there. Yes, I had my suspicions. It may not save them from the missions or orphanages if they are discovered, but those who are of working age will at least find employment with Edwina and I think it will be better for them there than here.'

The stockman bowed slightly and left. Hamilton had always been more concerned with keeping the man in his employ than arguing about his reasons for silence. However, he would always speculate as to why Davidson chose to remain quiet. There was no scar near the man's neck and he'd have never been accepted into the army if he couldn't talk. Was his speechless existence due to the horrors of war? While he would always wonder, Hamilton appreciated that everyone had their own ways of navigating life. And strange though it was, for want of more evidence, he could only surmise that this was Davidson's way of existing in a white world.

❧ Chapter Fifty ❧

They passed Mrs Landry's Inn. Two horses were tethered to the railing outside, a stream of thick chimney smoke rising in the air. The owner of the inn looked up from where she was stooped over a copper, washing clothes. It was the first time in Edwina's memory that the woman waved in acknowledgment.

'Good for you, girly,' she cried in a crackly voice, 'good for you.'

Good for me. Edwina gave a weak smile. She felt anything but happy. Falling out with her father was no small thing. Having deceived herself into believing her decisions were based on concern, the truth was far more painful. Edwina stole from an ailing father under the guise of protecting her family, but in reality, she'd done it to protect herself. Now she was leaving home, alone, with a useless arm, which might never be fully recovered, to go to a strange place in the middle of nowhere. What on earth was she doing?

Two men appeared from inside the travellers' rest. One leant nonchalantly against a timber upright, the other, hands on hips; both observed the convoy.

The events of the last few months had made the reasons for her actions clearer now. Since the death of her mother, Edwina had been an outsider, sister to a father's favourite, working in a man's world and controlled by men. Edwina knew she couldn't live that life anymore. It was a simple decision forged through rashness, but it was now a choice she was already regretting. She'd not prayed since her mother's passing, saw little point in doing so now. However, Edwina recalled the comfort of calling on heaven and with a guilty sigh at the time past she closed her eyes. 'Dear Lord,' she whispered, 'I'm sorry. Sorry for what I've done. Help me.' There was no response. Only the whine of the wheels on the road, the stomp of hoofs and the squeak of leather and timber. What did she expect?

Edwina stared at the dirt track ahead as they passed the dwelling, the draught horses eager for the open road. It was not too late to turn back. There was nothing to stop her from acknowledging the enormity of her foolishness. Nothing except her pride.

'How are you travelling, Miss Edwina?' Han Lee called from up ahead.

'Fine. Very fine.' Her mouth stiffened into a smile. These were her people now. Her men. A rag-tag group from across the seas who trailed behind her because of one man. Somehow she'd gained Han Lee's loyalty and she did not want to lose it.

'Good. We will rest at noon.'

Perhaps it was the knowledge that it would be a long time, if ever, that she came this way again. However, as they continued along the road Edwina thought of Mrs Landry and the two bystanders watching the procession of wagons and men. A final goodbye of sorts from the district of Wywanna.

'Hello, Edwina.' Luke Gordon appeared next to her on horseback.

'Luke!' Edwina blurted out his name.

'I heard you were leaving today and thought it best I tag along for the ride, if that's alright with you. I thought you might need a chaperone, what with all these Chinese and him.' He dipped a chin towards the other side of the wagon, to where Mason rode alongside.

'Mason?'

'Do you mind, mate?' asked Mason. The Chinese driver was quickly dispatched, nimbly jumping off the slow-moving van. Sliding from his horse Mason tied the reins to the side of the wagon and then climbed up into the seat beside Edwina, assuming control of the team. 'Luke and I stopped at Mrs Landry's Inn and there you were in this great procession of wagons and men.' He clipped the reins, expertly steering the horses away from a deep hole in the road. 'I said to Luke that we could hardly leave you to go off on this adventure alone. So here we are.'

'But I thought . . .' stumbled Edwina. 'I mean, you said –'

'I waited days for word of your recovery, Edwina. You have no idea how worried I was so I came to an agreement with your father. I promised I wouldn't come onto his land again. In return he granted me that one visit. He didn't actually say not to see you ever again,' Mason continued sheepishly, 'although I understood that's what he meant.'

'But I don't understand, you made me think –'

Mason took her hand in his. 'I thought I could abide by the agreement. I shook on it. Gentlemen's contract and all that, but there are some decisions that can't be made in an instant and I regretted the bond the moment I rode away. Then Luke told me that you had bought the property and that you were travelling by yourself. So I waited for word of your departure date. It wasn't hard to find out. Everyone was talking of it.'

Edwina was stunned. 'So you're not angry?'

'About your father and the way he's treated you? Yes, I am, and I'll not forgive him for what he did.' He looked at her shoulder. 'You've done a brave thing buying Condo Station and starting life afresh.'

'I don't know. I went behind my father's back,' admitted Edwina. 'At the time I believed I was doing it for the right reasons.'

'If it was thought that you'd done the wrong thing, Edwina, you wouldn't have all these men supporting you.'

'Like bees to a honey pot, eh?' interrupted Luke.

'Are you still here?' replied Mason with a smile.

Luke pushed his hat further back on his head, and rode on to join Han Lee in the lead.

'The way you went about things was a little unorthodox, Edwina, but your father will survive. He's a tough man. I'd be very much surprised if secretly he wasn't quite proud.'

Ahead, Han Lee and Luke shook hands.

'They'll be firm friends,' noted Mason, 'and once Luke Gordon takes a liking to someone, well, they're a friend for life. So, Miss Edwina Baker, now you have a property and the loyalty of the Chinese and Luke Gordon to guide you. How does it feel?'

She held on to the wagon as they hit a bumpy patch in the road. 'I don't know.' Edwina certainly wasn't going to tell him how uncertain she felt about the future. 'It's strange to think so many people are willing to support me.'

Mason leant over and kissed her on the cheek. 'I'd like to do more than support you.'

'Mason, don't.'

'Can you please get over your aversion to my unexpected kisses?'

'I'm sorry, it's just that –'

'What, that you're not sure about me? About us? I'm coming with you to Condo Station, Edwina. Whether you like it or not. A few weeks on the road will have any knots between us sorted out, don't you think?'

There was pleasure in seeing Mason and equal concern at his expectations – particularly as he had just given her an ultimatum. He sounded exactly like Will. 'Would you like to come to Condo Station, Mason?'

'I, yes, I would.'

She'd off-balanced him. 'You must always ask first, Mason. Never assume.' Edwina certainly didn't want to lead him astray, nor could she make any promises, at least at the moment. Her head and heart were in two separate places, her body heading towards a new beginning. And yet here he was sitting beside her. Like Will, he'd come to claim her. And just like Will, his hopes would probably not align with her own.

'I'm not here to take possession of you, Edwina, or your property for that matter. We both have our own places, after all.'

Edwina held on to her arm as they hit another bump in the road.

'We could rig up a seat inside the wagon for you with a mattress,' suggested Mason. 'It'd be a bit hot but a darn sight more comfortable.'

'I'd rather be right here.'

Mason rolled his eyes. 'This isn't going to work if you don't do what I say.'

Edwina couldn't help but smile, remembering the last time he'd used that phrase on Ridgeway Station, the day of their first kiss. Then as now there was a cocky grin on his sun-browned face and she knew that he was in her life to stay.

'No, Mason. This won't work if you don't do what *I* say,' she told him. 'Understand, I still have a property to run,' she clarified.

'As do I,' he countered equally serious.

She nodded thoughtfully. 'If you have ideas of being with a docile woman content to obey you, best rethink this journey. I'll not be anyone's domestic, nor do I know if I even want to take on the role of wife. I will be station owner first and foremost and I will run my own affairs and my finances my way.'

'I think this is going to be a rather unconventional relationship,' muttered Mason.

'Are you prepared to be with me on those terms? That's if we can actually manage to get along for the next few weeks.' Would he agree? It was a lot to ask of a man and she knew that she probably came across as being extraordinarily inflexible; however, Edwina couldn't give up the chance of being in control of her own life.

Mason flicked the reins. 'I am and, to be honest, knowing the little of you that I do, Edwina Baker, I wouldn't have expected anything else.'

The relief was immediate. Here then was her equal. Mason understood.

Luke rode back towards them, drawing level with the wagon. 'Anyone else joining us that we should know about?'

Edwina swivelled on the hard wooden seat, clasping the frame; a blur of dust and men filled her vision. It was difficult to decipher what Luke pointed at for there were a further two wagons behind them as well as Han Lee's men. Then she caught sight of him, tall and erect in the saddle, gaining gradually on their steady progress. Behind him rode a number of other men. The women and children, she guessed, would be travelling under cover of the trees.

'It looks like you've been forgiven,' stated Mason.

'Yes, it does,' replied Edwina.

There he was, trailing them like the wraith he'd always been, her father's black factotum, the white-eyed crow.

❧ Author's Note ❧

An *Uncommon Woman* began with an idea based on an article in a 1930s Tasmanian newspaper. It reported that a woman had purchased a Queensland pastoral station. The fact that this buying of land warranted a headline in an island state far removed from the dusty interior of Australia signified the importance and the uniqueness of the event. The world had just staggered through the great stock market crash of 1929 and was in the grip of a devastating recession, and yet here was a woman laying claim to a remote rural property.

Great changes were occurring across the globe in the 1920s and 1930s. Automobiles were no longer the privilege of the few, hemlines were rising, and women were embracing the many opportunities that the modern age offered. The shifting times also challenged the golden age of the travelling circus, which reminded me of a story from my own family. While at the Ringling Brothers Circus in Moree in the 1950s, my father became enamoured with a lion cub. He offered the handler £50, all the cash he had with him at the time, and was refused. In later years, on retelling the story my father said he had a vision of the lion lying at his feet in the homestead dining room. In hindsight, probably not exactly appropriate for a sheep stud. And so another twist was added to *An Uncommon Woman*.

While researching this work, once again I had the privilege of listening to my father as he recounted the many stories passed down through the generations. I am fortunate that he shared so much. Thank you to my mother, Marita, for your encouragement and love, and to my beloved father, Ian, you will be forever missed.

To Penguin Random House – my publisher Beverley Cousins and managing editor Brandon VanOver – and my agent, Tara Wynne. Thank you for your friendship and guidance. Lastly, to the many booksellers, librarians and readers: thank you.

I am indebted to the following texts and recommend them for further reading:

Crops and Rocks: The Queensland Economy During the 1920s, Lecture on NQ History by D. May, 1984 (PDF online)

What Price Pastoral Leases? The Exploitation of QLD Aboriginal Labour by Pastoralists and Government, 1897–1968 by Loretta de Plevitz, 1998

Australia 1918–1950s by Mirams Southee

The Global 1920s by R. Carr and B. W. Hart

Journal of the Royal Historical Society of QLD, vol. xiii, no. 7, Aug 1988

State Pastoral Stations in QLD, 1916–30 by Kay Cohen

The Story of Australia's People: The Rise and Rise of a New Australia by Geoffrey Blainey

On the Sheep's Back: Past, Present and Future? by Ronald Anderson

Decades of Change by Itiel Bereson

Father's Right-hand Man: Women on Australia's Family Farms in the Age of Federation 1880s–1920s by K. Hunter

Wirth Bros Ltd Circus and Menagerie: Greatest Show on Earth, magazine, past review and program

Australia in the Nineteen Twenties by L. L. Robson

Nostalgia Australia: 1920s and 1930s by A. Sharpe

The Life of Philip Wirth: A Lifetime With an Australian Circus by Philip Wirth

Round the World With a Circus by George Wirth

Dreams of Jade and Gold: Chinese Families in Australia's History by P. Macgregor, Museum of Chinese-Australian History, CultureVictoria website. http://www.cv.vic.gov.au/stories/immigrants-and-emigrants/chinese-australian-families/dreams-ofA-jade-and-gold/

'Ringbarkers and Market Gardeners. A Comparison of the Rural Chinese of New South Wales and California', *Chinese America, History and Perspectives*, vol. 2006, by B. McGowan